"Those smell delicious…"

Lizzie placed one of the hot cookies on a napkin and set it in front of Paul. His eyes lit up in a look of sheer delight.

The smile on his face broadened as he said, "Ah, Lizzie, you do know the way to a hardworking man's heart."

She gasped and took a step back, and out of a long-practiced instinct her hand flew up to cover the scar on her face.

She wasn't trying to work her way into anyone's heart, least of all Paul's. He was her childhood friend.

"Lizzie." His tone softened. "I didn't mean to make you feel uncomfortable with my words. Please don't shy away from me."

Slowly, she lowered her hand.

"You don't need to hide your face from me, ever. I need you to understand that."

She gave him a slight nod, fighting the urge to cover her scar again.

And all the while she felt his gaze on her…

An Amazon top ten bestselling historical romance author, **Tracey J. Lyons** was a 2017 National Excellence in Romance Fiction Award finalist. She sold her first book on 9/9/99! A true Upstate New Yorker, Tracey believes you should write what you know. Tracey considers herself a small-town gal who writes small-town romances. Visit traceylyons.com to learn more about her.

After thirty-five years as a nurse, **Patricia Davids** hung up her stethoscope to become a full-time writer. She enjoys spending her free time visiting her grandchildren, doing some long-overdue yard work and traveling to research her story locations. She resides in Wichita, Kansas. Pat always enjoys hearing from her readers. You can visit her online at patriciadavids.com.

TRACEY J. LYONS

&

USA TODAY Bestselling Author

PATRICIA DAVIDS

Her Amish Legacy

2 Uplifting Stories

A Love for Lizzie and *The Farmer Next Door*

LOVE INSPIRED

INSPIRATIONAL ROMANCE

LOVE INSPIRED®
INSPIRATIONAL ROMANCE

Recycling programs for this product may not exist in your area.

ISBN-13: 978-1-335-74493-7

Her Amish Legacy

Copyright © 2022 by Harlequin Enterprises ULC

A Love for Lizzie
First published in 2019. This edition published in 2022.
Copyright © 2019 by Tracey J. Lyons

The Farmer Next Door
First published in 2011. This edition published in 2022.
Copyright © 2011 by Patricia MacDonald

For questions and comments about the quality of this book, please contact us at CustomerService@Harlequin.com.

Harlequin Enterprises ULC
22 Adelaide St. West, 41st Floor
Toronto, Ontario M5H 4E3, Canada
www.LoveInspired.com

Printed in U.S.A.

CONTENTS

A LOVE FOR LIZZIE

Tracey J. Lyons

From the time I put the first word on the page for this book, I knew without a doubt who it would be dedicated to. This book is dedicated to my friend and fellow author Amy Lamont, who has shown more strength and courage than anyone I know. You have inspired so many of us with your journey. Many, many blessings to you, my friend.

Acknowledgments

There are always so many people
who are part of the team it takes to make
the germ of an idea become a full-blown story.
First and foremost, I'd like to thank my agent,
Michelle Grajkowski, who puts up with all my angst,
and to all of my fellow Love Inspired authors,
you have opened up a whole new world of support
and friendship beyond what I could have ever
imagined. Thank you all so much. To my editor,
Melissa Endlich, thank you for making my dream
of becoming a Harlequin author come true.
To the fabulous team that Harlequin has put
together to get our work out there in the world,
you all deserve a hearty round of applause.
And finally, to my husband, TJ,
I couldn't do any of this without you by my side.

And be ye kind one to another, tenderhearted,
forgiving one another, even as God
for Christ's sake hath forgiven you.
—*Ephesians* 4:32

Chapter One

Miller's Crossing, Chautauqua County, New York

"Good morning, Lizzie."

Her long-time neighbor and friend, Paul Burkholder, greeted Elizabeth Miller, or "Lizzie" as everyone called her, from the other side of the screen door on the front porch. A tall man with mahogany-brown hair and dark brown eyes, his head barely cleared the top of the door. He was holding his flat-brimmed straw hat in one hand and a bag in the other. He wore a blue work shirt and black pants with thin leather suspenders, the ends buttoned inside the waist of his pants, the typical everyday clothing of a Miller's Crossing Amish man.

His face was clean-shaven, void of the full beard that marked the married men. She'd always thought him to be handsome. At twenty-three he remained single, while most of his friends were getting married, though she'd heard rumors at the last frolic that he wanted to change all of that. Paul might look like many of the other men in their church district, but Lizzie knew this man had a big heart. Maybe sometimes too big of a heart. He'd stuck by her through thick and thin.

Even all the times she'd pushed him away.

Lizzie knew over the past week she'd been pushing at him extra hard. This time of year was always a difficult one for her and her family. Her gaze slid to the hook on the wall next to the door. The place where her *bruder*'s black hat still hung. She swung her attention back to the man standing on the porch. Concentrating on the present kept Lizzie from thinking about that long-ago day. A day she tried hard to forget. Yes, some of her memories of that day remained foggy, stuck somewhere deep in her mind, like a splinter that she couldn't get out. Still, the end result could never be changed; no matter what she remembered, her brother, David, would still be gone and she would have this mark seared on her face.

Paul rolled his shoulders, the strong muscles flexing beneath the cotton fabric of his light blue shirt. Lizzie's hand moved to cover the scar on her face. Beneath her fingertips she felt the raised flesh. The jagged cut ran three inches long, from the edge of her eyebrow to just below her cheekbone. Vanity held no place in her life or in her community, but still some days it was hard to accept reality. She had a disfigurement that couldn't be overlooked. Over the years the members of her community had done just that, continuing to love her and accept her through the flaws.

The *Englischers*, though, they were different. Some of them would openly stare at her when they stopped by her roadside stand to buy their fresh eggs. They were one of the reasons Lizzie didn't stray from the farm very often. She couldn't bear it when people stared at her. Their looks left her feeling ugly and unworthy.

She felt Paul's gaze on her.

"Lizzie?"

She heard his concern and looked up at him, keeping her face turned ever so slightly.

"You seemed to have gone off there for a minute."

"Do you know what today is?" The second she blurted out the question, she was filled with regrets. It didn't do a person good to dwell on the past, to dwell on things that couldn't be changed, to question the path that God had set forth for them.

Paul looked through the screen door at her, his eyes darkening with emotion. His nod was barely perceptible when he replied. "I do. Ten years to the day of the accident that took your *bruder*'s life and left you injured." His voice softened as he continued, "Lizzie, like you, I miss David every day. And like you, I wish we could have changed the outcome."

She held up her hand. There was no need for him to continue. She knew he was referring to his part in the day. He'd come to the barn just as she'd tried to get David to stop jumping off the hay bales. But David, who had always been the daring sibling, had insisted he could make it from the top all the way down to the bottom in one jump. She had tried her best to grab hold of his arm, but he'd already begun moving through the air when she'd caught hold of him.

Her body had been carried along with his as they'd tumbled down the bales. That was the last thing she remembered before waking up in the hospital. Lizzie pushed the dark memory away as best she could. She looked at Paul. Moving off to the side of the door, Lizzie turned her head ever so slightly to the right, hiding the scar. From the safety of the shadows, she looked up at him, watching as a soft summer breeze ruffled through his dark hair.

Though the Amish did not commemorate the anniversaries of one's death like some of the *Englischers* did, she herself always paused for a moment on this day to remember David. He would have been close to twenty-three years old. Three years older than she was right now.

Pushing aside the sadness in her heart, she said, "I'm sorry. I should have begun our conversation with '*Gut* morning, Paul. What brings you around this fine day?'"

Holding the brown paper bag up, he replied in his deep, rich voice, "I have something for you."

"You know I can't accept a gift from you."

"You don't even know what is inside of here," he said, swinging the bag back and forth in front of her.

She had to admit he had piqued her curiosity. "Tell me what you brought."

"I brought you some brushes and watercolor paints."

Lizzie didn't like the idea that Paul had gone out of his way to spend his hard-earned money on something just for her. And considering that it wasn't useful to anyone else, she knew the paints and brushes would have to be kept out of sight.

Thinking how much trouble Paul's generosity could cause, Lizzie shook her head, saying, "*Nee*. You'll have to take these back to where you purchased them. I'm sure you can get your money back." Furrowing her brow, she gave him a stern look.

"I'll do no such thing. Besides, I found them at a yard sale, so there's no use in trying to return them. They only cost me a few dollars, Lizzie. And half of the paints have been used," he said. Then with a spark in his eyes, he added, "Think of this as my bringing you supplies for your art."

Lizzie had taken up artwork years ago. Sketching the surrounding landscapes had given her a bit of peace and helped to fill the void left behind after her brother's death. Since her *vader* would most certainly frown on using her time to dabble in something most Amish would consider frivolous, Lizzie managed to scrape together a few free hours each month to work on her craft. In her mind her drawings were no different from the beautiful quilts her friends made. Most sold them as a way to supplement their family's income. All of her drawings were carefully stored in a closet in her bedroom. As it was, Paul wouldn't even have known about her artwork except that he'd come upon her working on a new sketch at the edge of the back field last week.

The image she'd been drawing was of the freshly mowed hayfield. She'd been drawing the soft, round bales of hay, trying to capture the feel of the image before her, of the golden hues against the dark earth and the sky being bathed in the soft colors of dusk. The black-and-white sketch hadn't done the scene justice, but Lizzie didn't have any colors to use on the picture. She'd captured the image as best she could, with her pencil on the heavy white paper.

Resting her head against the doorjamb, she let her imagination wander. The idea that she could add color to her sketches and breathe life into them had her pushing the door open a crack. Seeing the opportunity, Paul shoved the bag into her hand.

"I know you can make good use of these. Your drawings are amazing, Lizzie."

She felt the skin on her cheeks warm with a blush.

Lizzie didn't get many compliments. *"Danke,"* she said, gripping the paper bag in her hand. "How is your family?"

Paul shrugged, answering, "They are fine. We've been busy at the shop."

Paul's family owned a cabinetmaking business. Even with him and his three *bruders* all working at the shop, they always seemed to be busy. All the more reason Lizzie appreciated the time he took to stop by to check on her family. There was only Lizzie left here to help on the farm. Her older sister, Mary, had married and moved away to her husband's church district last year. There were no other siblings left. Her *mudder* had been unable to have more children. Her *vader* worked from long before sunup to sundown, running their small dairy farm. Lizzie helped where she could, selling eggs, jams and baked goods at the roadside stand.

The farm life wasn't an easy one. Even so, she knew her *vader* wouldn't live his life any other way. She wished things were different. If she had a husband, he could help out. But Lizzie couldn't even imagine entering into a courtship. Absently she rubbed the side of her face. The scar was a constant reminder of the life she couldn't have. Most days she didn't even leave the farm. She felt safe and secure here, away from the prying eyes of those who wanted to see her face, those whose expressions carried all the questions of wanting to know what had happened to leave that mark on her.

Yet, Lizzie thought, she could be perfectly content to live out the rest of her life here, in quiet and safe solitude.

"What are your plans for today?" Paul asked.

Lizzie blinked, looking up at him, realizing the

screen door still separated them. She didn't want him to think she was being rude, so she asked, "Would you like to come in for some coffee and a muffin? I baked blueberry ones earlier this morning."

"*Nee. Danke* for the offer, though. I need to get back to work. I just wanted to give you the paints in case you were planning on drawing today." Paul set his straw hat back on his head.

"*Danke* again for your thoughtfulness," Lizzie said, looking past him.

Her gaze settled on the big red barn, where she knew her *vader* was finishing up with the morning milking. Her *mudder* had gone into the village of Clymer, a few miles from the house, to pick up some items from the Decker General Store. Cocking her head to one side, Lizzie looked through the dappled sunlight, beyond the shade of the big oak tree next to the house, and squinted her eyes, uncertain of what she was looking at.

"Paul, turn around and look down to the barn. Is that a cow I'm looking at?" she asked, pointing to a spot at the farleft corner of the barn, where the animal appeared to be munching on some grass outside of the fenced-off field.

Turning to look over his shoulder, Paul seemed to ponder her question and then said, "Lizzie, is your *vader* down at the barn?"

"*Ja*, he is supposed to be. Why do you ask?"

"Because there appears to be about half a dozen cows on this side of the fence."

"That is strange." She opened the door, stepping out to join Paul on the porch. "I think we should go see what's going on."

Tucking the bag into her apron pocket, she hurried

along with him down the graveled pathway, across the driveway and to the barn, where they both stopped in front of the open door. Lizzie could see at least a dozen cows wandering about the yard surrounding the building. She turned to look up at Paul, whose gaze followed in the same direction as hers.

"Something's wrong. "There's no way your *vader* would let the cows roam free."

A shiver raced along her spine as she stepped behind him, following him into the dark coolness of the same building where her brother had plunged to his death ten years ago today. Sucking in a deep breath, Lizzie tried to swallow the panic welling up inside her.

"*Vader!* Are you in here?" Lizzie called out.

They stopped in the center of the large expanse. Sunlight streamed in through the slats of wood on the outside walls. Off to one side were the feed bins. There was no sign of her *vader* here.

"I think we should check the milking parlor," Lizzie said, putting her hand on Paul's arm, guiding him forward.

Thick dust motes stirred through the air as they made their way to the back of the building, where the milking parlor was located. Lizzie rubbed the end of her nose. The hay dust always made her want to sneeze. She held her breath, waiting for the sensation to pass. When it did, she took in a soft breath. Paul held the door to the parlor open, then nodded, indicating she could enter first.

"*Ach! Nee!*" Lizzie covered her hands over her face, not wanting to believe that what she was seeing in front of her could be real. Quickly she dropped her hands to her side and ran to where her *vader* lay on the cement floor, silent and still.

* * *

Paul pushed his way into the room, not that far behind Lizzie. His heart thudded in his chest when he saw Joseph Miller lying on his back on the floor. Even from the distance of a few feet away, Paul could see the ashen color of the man's skin. He took in a breath and then gently but quickly moved Lizzie to one side so he could check on her *vader*'s condition. Kneeling beside Joseph, Paul placed his fingers alongside the man's neck, feeling the area where the carotid artery lay.

"Is he…?" Lizzie's voice was barely a whisper.

Paul held up his free hand, silencing her. He needed to concentrate. He moved his fingers up and down the side of the man's neck. At first he felt nothing, but then he felt a very faint throb. It wasn't much, but it was better than nothing.

"Lizzie, I need you to run up to the phone shack and call 911. Tell them you think your *vader* has suffered a heart attack." Even as Paul said the words, he couldn't be sure that was what had happened, but it would get the ambulance to arrive faster. "Tell them he is breathing, but it's very shallow."

He glanced up to find her still standing in the milking parlor, as if frozen in time. Tears rolled down her face, and her hands were knotted together in front of her apron. He could see her trembling. If her *vader* were to survive, Paul needed her help.

"Lizzie!" Hoping to jolt her into action, he shouted her name. "Lizzie! You need to go. Now!" Immediately Lizzie ran out the barn door.

The next few minutes were a blur. Joseph Miller lay on the hard floor of the barn, still as the air before a summer storm. Paul grew even more worried. He jostled the man's shoulder, calling out his name.

"Joseph! Can you hear me? Joseph!"

The man's eyelids fluttered and then stilled. Paul stayed beside the man, praying for his healing. The ambulance arrived, and after the paramedic did a quick assessment, he determined that Joseph needed to be transported immediately to the hospital in Jamestown, thirty miles away. Lizzie's mother, who'd been out running errands, came barreling toward the barn.

Pushing through the small circle of emergency responders, she cried out, "Paul! What's happening?"

He looked into eyes the same light blue color as Lizzie's. He saw Susan Miller's fear for her husband's health. Quietly he answered, "Mrs. Miller, I can't be sure. But the paramedic thinks it could be a heart attack."

The woman let out a sob and rushed alongside the gurney. Her midcalf-length black skirt flapped against her legs. "Joseph! Joseph!" she called out to her husband.

A younger medic caught up with her. "I can let you ride with your husband, but I need you to sit in the front. Do you think you can do that?" he asked.

Susan nodded, casting a glance around the tall man until her gaze found Lizzie. "Lizzie! I need you to come."

"I'm afraid we can only take one family member."

Lizzie's *mamm* looked as if she were about to burst into tears. Paul watched as she tucked her lower lip between her teeth, squared her shoulders and nodded at the man. Her hands trembled as she reached for the door.

Paul helped her into the front seat of the ambulance, making sure she had the seat belt firmly in place. "I'll see that she gets to the hospital."

"Run down to Helen Meyer's *haus*. Maybe she can help you get Lizzie to the hospital," Lizzie's *mamm* said.

"We need to get going," the driver said, putting the rig in gear.

Paul shut the door. Lizzie's mother smiled nervously from behind the window and nodded as they drove away.

Paul knew what had to be done. He would get Lizzie to the hospital. How could he not?

After the ambulance left, Paul realized he couldn't take the wagon into Jamestown. The trip would take a few hours by horse, and he couldn't be sure Lizzie's *vader* would survive. They needed to get there as quickly as possible. As Mrs. Miller suggested, he ended up running down to find their *Englisch* neighbor Helen Meyers, who was standing at the end of her driveway.

"I just saw the ambulance leave the Millers'. What's going on?"

"It looks like Joseph might have had a heart attack," Paul responded. Before he could even ask, she graciously offered to take them to the hospital.

"It was a blessing that I filled up my gas tank this morning."

Paul nodded politely. "I'll repay you for the gas."

"There's no need for that." She hastened to give him a smile. "We're neighbors and, *Englischer* or Plain, neighbors help each other out. Let's hurry—we don't want to keep Lizzie waiting."

He followed her to the back of the driveway and got into the passenger seat of the blue four-door sedan.

They found Lizzie standing along the edge of the road, near the Millers' mailbox. Paul got out and opened the back door, letting Lizzie slide across the seat first. He joined her, barely closing the door before Mrs. Meyers sped off.

Paul turned his head to look at Lizzie. He could see the tight lines around her mouth. She kept her eyes focused straight ahead.

He started to reach out his hand to cover hers but thought better of it. Even though years had passed since the tragedy that shook the Miller family, there were days when Lizzie still seemed so fragile to him. Today would have been a rough day even without her *vader*'s heart attack.

"Today is the day my *bruder* died, and my *vader* suffers from a heart attack. I don't understand the workings of God."

"It's not for us to question his motives, Lizzie."

"I know." She turned to look out the window.

They rode the rest of the way in silence. Before they knew it, Helen pulled her car in front of the hospital entrance.

"I'll let you off here so you can hurry to the emergency room. I'm going to park in the main lot."

"Please, Mrs. Meyers, you don't need to stay. I will find a way home," Lizzie said.

"She's right, there's no need for you to spend your day here. I'll make sure Lizzie gets home. We appreciate your help." He thanked her again as they left the car.

He cupped Lizzie's elbow and escorted her through the automatic sliding doors. They whooshed closed behind them. He felt her tense up as people stared at them as they walked over to the reception area. His heart squeezed as he watched Lizzie tip her head down and raise her hand to cover her scarred face. The strongest urge to protect her welled up inside of him. He took a deep breath before coming to a stop at the receptionist's counter, which was closed off with big sliding glass windows.

Paul tapped lightly on the window, getting the young woman's attention. She gave him a hard look. Paul attempted a smile. She slid one of the panels open.

"May I help you?"

"My friend, Miss Miller's father, was brought in by ambulance a short time ago. We were hoping you could direct us to where we can find him."

"Can I have the name of the patient, please?"

"Joseph Miller."

The woman typed his name into the computer sitting on her desk, then slid a clipboard across the narrow counter space that separated them, saying, "I'll need you to sign in here, please. And then have a seat in the waiting area. I'll call you when you can go down to the Emergency Room."

"How long do you think it will be?" Lizzie asked.

"I'm not sure."

Paul picked up the clipboard and handed it to Lizzie, along with a pen. He waited for Lizzie to add her name and then did the same. When they were finished, she exchanged the list for two visitor stickers, which they both stuck to the front of their shirts. He turned and spotted two dark green vinyl chairs set apart from the main waiting area.

"Come on—" he nodded in that direction "—let's go over there to wait."

Lizzie went ahead of him and sank down into the

first chair. He sat in the chair next to her. A long row of windows ran behind their backs. A low coffee table filled with dog-eared magazines separated them. His gaze settled on her. She sat on the edge of the cushioned seat, with her back hunched over and her hands clenched together on her lap. He felt so helpless and wanted to calm her nerves as best he could. He saw her take in a breath and then slowly exhale.

"Lizzie." He spoke her name in a low voice. "I'm sure your *vader* is in good hands. All will be well, I'm sure."

She pressed her lips together and nodded, keeping her eyes on the double doors at the far end of the room.

"I pray that he is. *Danke* for staying with me. I know you have other things you need to be doing," she said, keeping her voice low, as well.

Paul thought about how he'd originally planned to spend the day. For months now he'd had his mind set on breaking away from his family's furniture business. And he'd decided that this morning, after he'd gone to see Lizzie, would be the time he'd tell his *vader* about his plan to set up his own furniture shop. His *vader*'s furniture was very basic and serviceable. But Paul had always favored adding more detail to the pieces, while his *vader* liked to keep it plain and simple, a reflection of their way of life.

He'd been lucky to find a vacant storefront right next to the general store in the village of Clymer, a few miles south of their settlement. The rent on the space was good, too good to pass up. Not wanting to miss out, Paul had made a verbal agreement with the owner to lease the space. If everything went according to plan, he'd have the doors open as soon as possible. First he had to convince his *vader* to let him move forward. But deep down Paul knew he would risk the man's censure to follow his dream of owning his own business.

"I've heard rumors about you. About your plans for the future."

The sound of Lizzie's soft voice snapped him out of his reverie. "Who told you?"

"Though our land is vast, we live in a very close-knit community. Word gets out," Lizzie answered. She turned a thoughtful blue-eyed gaze to him. "Are you sure you want to break from your family business?"

He nodded. "I don't see it as breaking away. Maybe the move could be more of an expansion of the business. I've started to pick out the pieces I'm going to sell at the new store. It's been a dream of mine for a very long time. Sort of like you and your paintings." He grinned at her.

"I don't do my paintings for profit."

"No, you don't. But I—" His explanation was interrupted when he heard Lizzie's name being called.

"Come on, I think there's some news." Paul guided her over to the reception area. Once there, the woman instructed them on how to get to the emergency room.

He started through the doors and turned back when he realized Lizzie wasn't with him. She stood in the doorway to the long corridor, pale as a ghost. Her blue eyes were wide as she stared down the hallway.

Rushing over to her, he took her trembling hands in his. "Lizzie, your *vader* is going to be all right. I know it. Joseph is a strong man. As strong as the oxen he uses to plow the fields."

She shook her head. "That's not what I'm thinking about."

He furrowed his brow in confusion. And then it

dawned on him. On the day of the accident that had taken her *bruder*'s life and left her injured, the ambulance had brought her to this very hospital.

"Lizzie. I'll be by your side the whole time. I promise," Paul said.

"The last time I was in this building was all those years ago. I don't remember everything. Just…there was so much blood." She started to pull away.

She felt Paul place his hand under her elbow. For a brief moment Lizzie allowed herself to take comfort from his touch. It would be so easy to let him take the lead, but Lizzie wanted to be strong for her family. As they made their way down a long hallway, she tried hard to ignore the antiseptic smell. The acrid scent brought to mind what little she remembered about that long-ago day. She covered the scar on her face with a hand, feeling the soft ridge of skin, remembering the blood.

Lizzie jumped as the sound of Paul's voice jarred her back to the present.

"Here we are." He looked down at her and then nodded in the direction of the emergency room.

Lizzie appreciated the concern in his eyes, even though it did little to calm her nerves.

"Are you going to be okay?"

She dropped her hand against her side, nodding. Lizzie walked with him through another set of sliding glass doors and looked around the brightly lit area. It wasn't long before she saw her *mamm*'s plain black shoes poking out from beneath a curtained-off section of the large room. Heading that way, Lizzie slowly pulled back the white curtain and peeked in. Her *vader* lay on a narrow bed, with wires coming out from beneath a white blanket that covered him. His eyes were closed and his face looked very pale. Thankfully his chest rose and fell in a regular rhythm. Her gaze followed the cords to a monitor on a pole. She heard the beeping of his heart and saw a wavy line running across the flat screen.

"*Dochder*. You shouldn't be here." Her father's weak voice startled her.

Lizzie stepped into the tiny space, while her *mamm* stood to gather her in a hug. "It's going to be all right," she whispered against Lizzie's ear.

"I'm worried about you, *Vader*."

"I'm…" He paused, struggling to take a deep breath. "I'm going to be out of here in time for the next milking."

Her *mamm* gasped. "No, Joseph. That is *not* what the doctor said."

"What did they say, *mamm*?" Lizzie wanted to know.

"They could tell from the EKG that they ran in the ambulance that he's had a mild heart attack. He needs to stay here for a few more days while they run some more tests. They want to do a procedure called a catheterization to see if there is any damage to your *vader*'s heart."

"I won't be here for any of that," her *vader* grumbled. "I am in the middle of the first harvest. It's not like I have a strong son who can take over."

Lizzie stiffened at her father's harsh words. She knew better than he what the family had lost. Even though he'd never come out and accused her, she knew he blamed her for David's death. She felt her *mamm* give her hand a quick squeeze.

She released Lizzie, then walked across the polished

black-and-white floor tiles to her husband's bedside. She took his hand in hers and kissed the top of it.

Very quietly, but with a firmness in her tone, she said, "Joseph, you will do exactly as the doctors tell you."

"But who will take care of the cows and the crops?"

Paul and a tall man dressed in Plain clothes entered their room. Lizzie recognized Amos Yoder, one of the elders in their church district. He stood at the foot of her father's bed, wearing dark pants and a crisp white shirt tucked beneath his black suspenders. On his head he wore a dark brimmed hat with a black band.

"Joseph," he said, his deep voice resonating throughout the space. "You will not worry about your crops or your cows. The men and I can each spare a son to help out until you are well enough. The boys will rotate their days."

Her *vader* sighed. He avoided making eye contact with her. "See, this mess has already brought the two of you away from your work."

"It was nothing, Joseph. I was at the house, visiting already, and didn't mind coming with Lizzie to the hospital," Paul said.

Taking her *mamm* aside, Lizzie knew she and Paul had stayed past their time. And she didn't want to be the cause of any more stress for her *vader*.

"*Mamm*, I think I'll go home. I've kept Paul here long enough, and I have much to tend to back at the house."

"*Ja*, Lizzie, you go home. If there are men working at our fields and in our barns, they will eventually need to be fed. You must cook for them."

"*Ja*. Of course." Her *mamm* led her back to her *vader*'s bedside so she could say goodbye. "*Vader*, I don't want you to worry about the farm. I can help keep things running." Lizzie tried her best to put on a brave front. But the truth was she was worried.

"Ach!" Her *vader* half raised a hand off the bed, swishing it in the air as if swatting at a fly. "You go home and do your chores, *Dochder*. I'll be fine."

Though she wanted with all her heart to believe him, she couldn't be certain how much damage his heart had sustained. Lizzie bent to kiss him on the cheek, but he turned his head, avoiding her touch. Fighting back the tears, she simply patted him on the shoulder and left the emergency room. She walked back down the long corridor with Paul. The stale antiseptic smells receded with each step she took. Lizzie made it to the main waiting room and exhaled.

She turned to Paul and said, "Take me home, please."

They stepped out of the sterile air of the hospital into the fresh air and fading sunlight of another hot summer day. Lizzie stood looking at the golden light, thankful to God above that her *vader* had survived. While she waited, Paul found them a cab to take them home.

Lizzie settled into the back seat, relieved to be going home. Paul got in and sat next to her. The car was small, and their shoulders bumped. Lizzie could feel the warmth coming from Paul's body. He'd been so kind to her today. But she couldn't allow him to be away from his own work. They both needed to get back to Miller's Crossing. She couldn't bear to be away from home for too long; even the short time away today left her feeling uneasy. She worried about what she was going to find when she got back to the farm. There was livestock to be fed and cows to be milked. She had no idea where her *vader* had left the tractor or who was going to see to the remainder of the cutting in the field he'd been harvesting this morning.

Lizzie felt the uncertainty creeping in like fog on a cool morning. She tried with all her might to bolster her confidence, thinking she could do this for her father. She owed him all the help she could give him. She could run things while he was in the hospital, couldn't she? Lizzy breathed a sigh of relief as the cab turned onto the road that led to the Miller farm.

And then she gasped in surprise at the sight that greeted her.

Chapter Two

From across the field that separated the property from the road, Lizzie could see a row of buggies parked in front of the barn.

"Oh, my, Paul! Look at all of this!"

He tilted his head toward her and smiled, nodding toward the house. "I told you, as soon as they heard about your *vader*, everyone came to help."

As the taxi pulled into the driveway, Lizzie pressed her forehead against the passenger-side window to get a better view of the yard. She saw her best friend, Sadie Fischer, rushing toward them. Immediately Lizzie's heart swelled with emotion. She didn't know what she would do without her friend. Waiting for the cab to stop, Lizzie tore off her seat belt and opened the door, stepping straight into her friend's outstretched arms.

"Lizzie, I'm so sorry to hear about your *vader*."

"Danke," Lizzie mumbled against Sadie's shoulder.

After releasing her hold, Lizzie looked around, taking stock of the busy yard. Behind her she heard Paul paying the cab driver. She noted the crunch of the gravel as the car drove off. Paul came to stand near them.

"Is it true that your *vader* had a heart attack?" Sadie asked, her gaze darting from Paul to Lizzie.

"*Ja*. We think he's going to be fine, though," she answered, crossing her arms over her stomach as the full impact of her *vader*'s condition hit her.

With her sister, Mary, living in her husband's community in Montgomery County, a few hours from here, it was up to Lizzie to keep things running on the farm until her *mamm* or *vader* returned home.

Sadie quickly picked up on her unease. Her friend patted her on the arm, saying, "All will be well in time. Already we are all praying for his speedy recovery." Pointing toward the side yard, Sadie added, "See there? Those people are your friends and they care a great deal about your *vader*."

Lizzie looked past Sadie and saw a group of her neighbors and other community members standing in a circle, their heads bowed. The hems on the women's blue dresses flapped against their legs as a warm summer breeze blew across the yard. Some of the men had left their jobs to come and offer support. Even though she knew it was the way of the Amish to come and lend a helping hand to a neighbor in need, she still felt uneasy about having all these people at her home. It appeared, though, that Sadie and Paul were both correct: everyone was doing something to help.

Her lower lip trembled as she fought back her tears. "*Vader* sent me back. He said there was a lot that needed to be tended to. And it looks like he was right." Lizzie swiped a hand across her cheeks, starting to walk toward the house.

Paul fell into step beside them. "I see my *bruders*, Ben and Abram are here."

He nodded in the direction of the barn, where Lizzie could see fourteen-year-old Abram walking out of the barn with a wheelbarrow full of horse manure. Ben came out behind him, yelling that Abram had left a mess behind.

"So, three Burkholders have set aside their own chores for my family," Lizzie mumbled, nodding at them. They gave her a wave, and then she dipped her head to one side. "That was very kind of them to come by."

A monarch butterfly flitted in front of her face. Lizzie raised her hand, swishing it away, not in the mood to ponder the creature.

"I need to get to the kitchen. I understand there are men out in the field, working to bring in the rest of the hay that *Vader* was harvesting this morning. And then there are the cows to milk and feed. I'll need to cook something to feed everyone." She twisted her mouth into a thin line, making a mental list of the food they had on hand.

She knew there would be enough chicken for a stew, and there were several loaves of bread in the pantry, along with beans and potatoes. There were some zucchini squash, tomatoes, cucumbers and lettuce in the garden that could be picked.

Paul caught her gaze and smiled. "Listen to me. You have plenty of help everywhere, even in the kitchen. I suspect my *mamm* is here, too."

"What? I can't have your whole family at our house."

"Trust me, I have plenty of family to go around." He let out a chuckle. "With my five siblings, the lot of them would easily fill up your kitchen."

She managed to muster a smile.

He gently walked her and Sadie down the drive, up the porch steps and into the house, where a beehive of activity was going on. Excusing herself, Sadie rushed into the kitchen, making her way over to the long counter. Lizzie watched her laying out rows of sliced white bread. To her right another young woman was adding slices of cheese and turkey to one side of the sandwich. Paul had left her to go say hello to his *mamm*, who was dumping boiled potatoes from a large pot into a colander in the sink.

Lizzie realized she'd been standing in the doorway. Looking down at her apron, the same light blue color as her dress, Lizzie frowned. Despite her fatigue, with her *mamm* absent it was her duty to help run things in the kitchen. Pulling the apron she'd been wearing over her shoulders, she shrugged out of it. She hung it on one of the wall pegs near the front door. Her hand brushed against a boy's straw hat. The felt band looked brand-new. But Lizzie knew it was exactly ten years old.

Some days she wished her *mamm* would put the hat away. Seeing that hat reminded everyone of David. She put her house apron on and tied the sash around her waist. Having the hat here or not, Lizzie would never forget her *bruder*. Unlike in the homes of their *Englisch* neighbors, here there were no family photos, so they were left with only the memory of the images of their lives.

Lizzie closed her eyes, seeing David's face in her mind's eye. The eyes that matched hers in color, the dark hair that no matter how hard *Mamm* tried to brush it in place, always stuck out from beneath this hat. She imagined the dimples that appeared when he smiled. She heard his laughter. She shook her head to clear out those thoughts. Blinking away the emotions that seemed to come every time she thought of her *bruder*, Lizzie realized Sadie had stopped making sandwiches and was watching her with concern.

Crossing the room, she came over to her. "How about you let me get you a nice glass of the fresh lemonade that Mrs. Yoder brought over."

"That would be nice," Lizzie said as she took another apron from a peg and put it on. Tying the sash off, she followed Sadie into the kitchen.

Lizzie took the glass from her friend's hand, not realizing until this moment how thirsty she was. She took a gulp from the drink, letting the coolness slide down her parched throat. She set the half-empty glass on the counter, wondering where to begin. At the back of the kitchen, a door stood ajar. If not for her *vader*'s health, the laundry room would have been bustling with activity today.

Not only were the long summer days good for bringing in the hay, but they were also good for drying the wash. All through their community, backyard clotheslines would be filled with dark pants, white shirts and dresses. Monday was wash day. And the cars would come through in slow, long lines as the tourists tried to capture the image of their laundry on their fancy cameras or cell phones. Lizzie wanted to laugh because if they knew how much work was involved in getting a single load of wash done, maybe they'd see those images in a different way.

The dark pants, blue shirts, dresses and aprons would have to wait until tomorrow for their washing because right now there was a group of men waiting to be fed. Lizzie began helping the women carry out the bowls of potato salad and fruit salad, along with the platter of sandwiches and cutlery to a makeshift plywood-and-sawhorse table that had been set up underneath the shade of a large maple tree out in the backyard.

One of the women had gone to signal to the men that it was mealtime. She heard the clanking of the bell that hung outside the front door. In some homes a bell like this would be used to signal an emergency. Her father had installed a phone shanty on their property a few years ago. It was only used for business or for emergencies. Today she'd been beyond thankful for the convenience. Though it had seemed like an hour to her, the ambulance had arrived within minutes of her 911 call.

She knew in some Amish communities, the *Ordnung* forbade the use of any kind of phones, in which case a person had to travel to the nearest business to use one or depend on their *Englisch* neighbors to let them borrow theirs. Lizzie had even heard of some of the younger folks being allowed the use of cell phones. She shook her head at that thought. She couldn't imagine needing one of those.

Here in Miller's Crossing, New York, there were several Amish communities. The one where her family lived was allowed to have curtains on their windows and linoleum flooring in the houses. Lizzie felt pleased to have some of the more modern amenities. This brought her sister, Mary, to mind. As soon as the meal was over, she would get a message to her about their *vader*. Her sister had married Aaron Yoder last year and moved over an hour away. Mary and Aaron's church *Ordnung* didn't allow for such niceties in the homes. It had been a week or so since Mary's last letter. Lizzie knew her *schweschder* had had some trouble adjusting to her new life, but she loved her husband, so she was willing to try. The family was planning to be together the first Tuesday in October for their cousin Rachel's wedding.

Thoughts of Mary's new life and their cousin's wedding gave Lizzie pause. With her *vader*'s heart condition, she had no idea what tomorrow would hold, let alone if they could actually attend the wedding. As she spooned potato salad onto the plates, she thought about how all around her, family and friends were starting new lives, growing their own families. And here she was, still on the farm with her *mamm* and *vader* like a *bobbli*. Yes, she loved her life here, even if at times things did seem complicated. Even before his sudden illness, her *vader* had needed help on the farm. If she were to take a husband, things could be different.

As she so often found herself doing in times of stress, Lizzie ran her hand along the scar on her face. What man would want someone so disfigured? Out of the corner of her eye, she watched Paul acting kind with his *mamm*. Lizzie couldn't help but think of all the years of kindness he'd shown her. He was a good friend and neighbor. A fine man. Paul would make an excellent husband for one lucky woman.

But that woman would not be her.

Paul had spotted his *mamm* at the stove in the Millers' kitchen, getting ready to drain a large pot of green beans into a colander in the sink, and hurried over to take the heavy pot from her.

"Here, *Mamm*. Let me do this for you."

"*Ja*, my strong son to the rescue," she said, stepping aside to let him dump the pot. The hot steam wafted up between them as the string beans and water fell into the metal colander. Gently nudging him aside, she took the colander from him and shook the vegetables from side to side, helping the water drain out.

"I see you brought Lizzie home from the hospital. She looks tired and worried," his mother said in a soft voice.

"The doctors haven't told them much about her *vader*'s heart condition. From the sounds of it, he'll be in the hospital a few more days while they run some tests."

"*Danke Gott* you were there when it happened."

Leaning his hip against the counter, Paul wondered about the cause of Mr. Miller's heart attack. Then again, from what he'd heard, these health conditions generally did not manifest overnight. Still, he imagined the stress of trying to run this farm single-handedly hadn't helped. There had been rumors floating about in the community for a long time that the man had been working long hours, burning the candle at both ends, with not much help. Keeping that sort of pace for too long couldn't be good. Even though he generally worked long hours, Paul always left time in his week for time off to pray and reflect. As he recalled, Joseph Miller had been absent from the past few church meetings. A habit that was highly frowned upon by the church leaders.

"I'm not sure I did anything that mattered other than check to see if he was breathing."

His *mamm* patted him on the arm, saying, "You were there for Lizzie. And you made sure she got to and from the hospital. That's what's important, *sohn*. That's what she'll remember."

"I'm her friend—of course I was there for her."

He stopped thinking about Lizzie for a moment and then wondered what his *mamm* would do when she found out what his plans for the future were. Though he knew she wanted the best for him, he also didn't want to be the cause of conflict in the family.

"Paul…"

The sound of her quiet voice brought him out of his reverie. From the soft look on her face, he knew exactly what she was going to say about the relationship between him and Lizzie.

Paul cut her off with, "Please don't go there. To me, she's always been and will always be David's sister. Nothing more."

She gave him a thoughtful look, her brown eyes warm with love and bracketed with fine lines. She patted him on the arm, then said, "If that's how you want to see it. One more thing to consider, my *sohn*, that tragic day happened a long time ago. I know sometimes it's hard to understand *Gott*'s ways. But you and Lizzie, you need to make peace and put the past where it belongs. Your future could be bright."

"I'm friends with her. Nothing more," he insisted.

As she turned away from him to put the string beans in a large bowl, he heard her mumble, "For now."

Chapter Three

Taking the bowl from his *mudder*, he dropped a kiss on her cheek and then headed out to the backyard. He walked over to the food table and handed the bowl to Lizzie. She barely gave him any attention as she took the beans from him.

"I'll take that bowl off your hands," she said.

He tipped his hat to her and went to find a seat at the makeshift table.

While he dug into the midday meal, he became aware of Lizzy's gaze on him. He wondered what she was thinking. No doubt she was still feeling overwhelmed at finding herself in charge of the household for the moment. He gave her a smile, knowing that even if she didn't think so, she was more than capable of handling the situation.

He shuffled down a few spaces on the bench as his *bruder* Abram plunked his plate down and swung a leg over to sit beside him. Paul watched in awe as he emptied the plate of the large portion of potato salad in three forkfuls.

"You need to slow down, Abram, or one of these days you'll end up choking."

His brother smiled at him and shook his head, saying, "*Mamm*'s salad is still the best in these parts."

Paul nodded as he picked up the sandwich he'd added to his plate. Taking a generous bite, he realized he was hungry, too. He also realized he needed to get back home to do the chores there and help finish up the cabinet job he had been helping his *vader* with. Swallowing, he knew he had to talk to his *vader* soon. The man who owned the building Paul was interested in renting wanted to know how soon he could begin leasing it.

It was a good price and he didn't want to lose the opportunity to set up his own store there. It was a great location, only half a block up from the main intersection in the village. Paul knew the tourists would come into the store. They loved to buy Amish goods. He felt if he listed his furniture at a good but fair price that he would do well.

After finishing his meal, he took his plate over to the makeshift washing area that had been set up outside the kitchen. Leaving his plate there, he caught Lizzie's attention and waved at her. She gave him a half wave back. He walked around to the front of the Millers' house. As he made his way up the driveway, he looked off into the fields. He saw a wagon bringing in a load of hay bales. Near the barn, a line of cows with their udders full lumbered toward the milking parlor. All around him the air was filled with the earthy scents of the farm.

Ben met him halfway down the drive. As he came closer, Paul saw that he looked to be a bit concerned. Maybe there was a problem on the Millers' farm or he'd heard news about Lizzie's father. Either way he wasn't going to have to wait long to find out, because his *bruder* caught him by the arm and pulled him to the edge of the lawn.

"I was just up at our house and *Daed* is upset with some

news he heard from the owner of the general store. Is it true you've been looking into renting some shop space?"

A knot formed in the pit of his stomach as he met his brother's firm gaze. He'd hoped that word of his plans would not be spread around yet. But small towns being what they were, the thought that he'd be the one to deliver the news to his *vader* the way he saw fit had been ridiculous to begin with. Frowning at his brother, who'd grown so much over the past spring that he now stood eye to eye with him, Paul knew his *vader* had to be angry about this.

The Burkholders had been living in Miller's Crossing since their Amish community had been founded back in the 1950s by Lizzie's great-grandfather, Levi Miller. The group had traveled from Ohio in search of affordable farmland and had come upon this vast area of Chautauqua County. Over time, due to the changing economy, the farms had shrunk and the members of the community had taken to establishing lumberyards and other small but sustainable businesses.

Paul's father had served at one time as the head of their church. Now he was busy with the family furniture business. Though he knew his father would stay tied to their property, Paul wanted desperately to have his own business in the village. He was in his twenties now and wanted to be making his own way within Miller's Crossing.

"Paul, is it true?" Ben asked again.

"Yes," Paul answered as he looked at the deepening crease on his brother's forehead. Of all his siblings, Ben was the one who worried the most.

Continuing up the hill to the top of the driveway, Paul clasped his hand against his brother's back. "You let me deal with our *daed*."

"He doesn't want you to leave."

Paul shook his head. "I'm not leaving the family. I'm only going into town to sell my furniture."

"Plenty of *Englischers* stop by our shop," Ben said.

"They do. But we could be doing better."

"We are doing okay. There's always food on the table and warmth in the house." Ben's face turned red as he argued his point.

Paul didn't respond to his *bruder*, other than mentioning the fact that he wanted his own business. He enjoyed working with wood. Smelling the shavings from the floor in the saw room and working to build fine furniture brought him great joy. More importantly, he liked to work with his hands.

He wasn't moving out of their farmhouse; he was simply making his own way in the community, like any *youngie* who was old enough to do so.

"We should be getting home."

"Ja." Paul walked over to where his brother had parked the wagon, climbed up and sat alongside him on the bench.

Paul picked up the reins and slapped them against the horse's backside. The wagon jumped forward as the horse picked up its pace. On the short ride home, Paul thought about what he was going to say to his *vader*. Paul knew he wasn't going to be able to change his *vader*'s ways, but he also knew deep in his heart that he wouldn't be changing his mind, either. He nudged the horse to the right, making a wide turn with the wagon onto the dirt road that led to his family's ninety-acre parcel. Most of the land was covered in trees, which were eventually cut into lumber and used in their furniture business. As he drove past their family's large white farmhouse, he gave a tug on the leather straps of the reins, signaling for the horse to turn onto a narrow dirt roadway that allowed access to their barn. Up ahead stood the attached structure of the woodworking shop, where he and his *bruders* worked alongside their *vader*.

Knowing the path well, the horse came to a stop right in front of the open side door. Paul set the reins on the seat between him and Ben. He could feel his *bruder*'s gaze on him. The last thing on this earth that he would ever do would be to hurt his family. He prayed that his *vader* would see his reasons for wanting to open up his own shop.

He felt Ben's hand on his arm.

"I'll see to the horses. You go on inside," Ben said, still looking worried.

Paul jumped down from the wagon and ducked inside the doorway of the spacious workshop.

"Hallo! Is anybody here?" Paul strode through the large open area, where neat piles of lumber stood stacked shoulder height on top of a row of pallets.

"*Ja*. What's all this shouting?" His vader came out of the workshop, shaking the wood shavings off his leather apron.

Paul looked at the man who, if not for the slight hunch in his back, would be the exact same height as himself. "I've got things squared away over at the Miller house," he said, looking into eyes that were the same shade as his.

They also shared the same square jawline and cleft chin. Besides their age, their one big difference was the gray hair sprinkled throughout his *vader*'s beard.

"How is Joseph doing?"

"As far as I know, he's going to be in the hospital for a few more days while they run some tests."

His *vader* didn't say anything for a few minutes. Paul knew to wait for him to speak.

His *vader* nodded to the stack of wood slabs to the right of Paul, saying, "Help me bring two more of these inside."

Hoisting one end of the slab onto his shoulder, *vader* said, "Seems like there was a lot of excitement at the Miller house today. It will be some time before things return to normal."

"*Ja*, for sure and certain. But Lizzie had a lot of help today. And for many days to come, if her family needs it, no doubt."

"That's good."

Paul took the other end and followed him into the workroom. They set the wood on top of a large counter. On the wall at the back of the area was a large pegboard where all of the tools hung in neat rows. They worked in silence for a bit while they prepared for the project his *vader* had been working on. Paul knew better than to try to coax any conversation out of the man. So he waited.

When his *vader* stopped to wipe his forehead with a handkerchief, Paul knew the time had come.

"I've a thermos of iced tea over there on the table. Why don't you pour us some?"

Doing as his *vader* had asked, Paul came back to hand his father a full cup, saying, "It looks like you've got the Smiths' cabinet order almost finished."

"*Ja*. This was an easy project. They only needed a simple cupboard for their little girl's bedroom." His father said, then took a sip from the cup. He took his time drinking the cool liquid.

Paul found he wasn't all that thirsty.

"I heard from the owner of Becker's grocery that

you've been asking around about renting shop space in the village. Did he speak the truth?"

Paul met his *vader*'s hard stare. Even though he'd known this time had come, it didn't make standing here any easier. "*Ja*, he did."

"You're going to leave your family?" His face reddened.

"I am *not* leaving the family."

"That is what it sounds like to me, *sohn*."

"*Daed*. I've been looking at our sales numbers for the past few years and we could be doing better."

"We are doing well enough."

Paul sighed. "I want to put my furniture out where it will be seen by the tourists who are traveling through."

"We get plenty of them right now. Besides, I need you here to help with the farm chores."

Like most of the community, the Burkholders had both their farm and a business. Some families specialized in cheese production, others canned goods and bakery items. The Troyers had a very popular greenhouse business four miles from here. The Burkholders were cabinetmakers and furniture makers.

"I can still be doing my chores here and working on the family business." He knew he had to tread lightly, but in his heart, Paul also knew moving his side of the business was where his future lay. Expanding into the village would eventually bring the entire family more revenue. Paul wanted to make this work. "I would like to be able to do this with your blessing."

"You should be concentrating on finding a wife." *Vader* wagged his finger at him. "You get married, have children and then you can think about this business idea. Right now your place is here, helping me keep your *bruders* in line, seeing to the daily chores and working here—" he paused to spread his hands wide "—with your family."

Paul lowered his gaze to stare at the top of his boots. He wanted to give his *vader* time to think about the possibility of expanding, and yet if he didn't act soon, the shop would surely be rented out to someone else. He couldn't let that happen.

"You need time to think about this," Paul said in a quiet voice.

"*Nee*, I don't. Your place is here." His *vader*'s tone was dismissive. "Another order for a cabinet came in while you were over at the Millers'. I wrote the dimensions down. You can get started on that."

Paul loved and respected his *vader*, but he couldn't accept his decision. Not when Paul hadn't even shown him his plans for the new store, or explained to him how this would help the entire Burkholder family, not just himself. But his father had turned his back on him. The last time he'd wanted to go against his *vader*'s wishes had been the day David Miller had died.

Paul had wanted to go play with his friends in the barn, but it had been a particularly trying day at their house with the loss of one of their cows after a difficult birth. Paul remembered wanting to be allowed to play. That day he'd followed his father's wishes and stayed home. The outcome had left one friend dead and one scarred for life. To this day he'd felt that if he could have been there in that barn with his childhood friends, he could have prevented what had happened. Paul had never forgiven himself for what had happened.

Now, more than ever, he wanted to stand his ground. He wanted to see his dream of one day having his own store become a reality. He knew about the pride the Amish took in their families and their homes; after all he had the same pride. He'd taken his time when it'd been his turn to partake in *rumspringa*. Then Paul had thought about his life as an Amish man, the only life he'd ever known, and how he wanted to be a part of this church district. It had been seven years since he'd taken his vow and been baptized into the church.

He didn't see how taking the furniture business into town meant he wouldn't still be a part of his family's life here. His plan had always been to live here and work in the village. He had to find a way to make his father come around and give him his blessing. There would be plenty of time later to think about taking a wife and making his own home. He closed his eyes, and for the briefest moment pictured Lizzie standing by his side.

He knew that dream was further away from reality than owning his own business was.

Lizzie sat in her *vader*'s favorite chair, the one that had soft fabric covering plump cushions, and looked out the front window. It had been a very long day and she should have been sound asleep in her bed. But her mind wouldn't settle. There were too many thoughts and memories from this day swirling around in her head. Her *mamm* had sent a message saying she would be staying at the hospital with her *vader* overnight. Sadie had offered to stay over so Lizzie wasn't alone in the house, but Lizzie had sent her home. Lizzie didn't mind having some quiet time to herself.

Resting her elbows on the chair arms, she looked out the window and up into the night sky. There had to be a million stars shimmering against the inky blackness.

The moon was three-quarters full and cast a sharp glow over the landscape. She looked out over the yard, where the tree limbs swayed in the breeze, their shadows dancing over the dewy lawn. Behind her the clock on the mantel in the living room showed it was ten o'clock.

Lizzie curled her hand into a soft fist and tucked it beneath her chin. She sat for a few more moments, pondering the day. She thought about how kind Paul had been to her; from the moment he'd brought her the paints until the time he'd returned home, she'd felt his kindness. Lizzie wasn't sure she deserved it. For years she'd been pushing him away. Though she appreciated his friendship, there could never be anything more between them. Even the things they wanted in life were so different.

Paul wanted to open up a shop in the village. She didn't understand how he could walk away from his family business. He'd begun to tell her about it earlier today, but they were interrupted by the hospital receptionist. Lizzie was content to stay home with her parents and help run the household. He liked talking to strangers and making them beautiful furniture for their homes. She wasn't comfortable being around people she didn't know. Even on the days when she had to go to the village to shop for her *mamm*, she timed it so there would be hardly any crowds in the stores. Lizzie imagined she could be content to stay just as she was. And now, with her *vader*'s illness, she was needed here more than ever. And when she needed a break, she could go off with her sketch pad and draw.

Off in the distance she heard the sound of a cow mooing. Lizzie looked out toward the barn. She saw a tall figure holding a lantern high.

Her heart pounded inside her chest, and then the man

turned to look up at the house. *Paul.* Relief flooded through her as she stood up and went to open the front door. She stepped out onto the porch and waited for him to approach.

"Good evening, Lizzie."

"You gave me quite a fright, you know," Lizzie scolded him from the top of the porch step.

"I'm sorry. I wanted to make sure the cows were secure."

"That's very kind of you," she replied, putting her hand to her mouth to stifle a yawn. "Oh, my. I'm so sorry. I don't mean to be yawning at you." A nervous laugh escaped her.

Still holding the lantern out in one hand, he shoved the other into the side pocket of his dark pants. "Don't worry. I know you've had a very long day. Has there been any word on your *vader*?"

"*Nee.* My *mamm* is staying at the hospital with him tonight."

Through the darkness he studied her, as if trying to decide if it were safe for her to remain here alone.

Finally he said, "Promise me you will lock the doors."

"I will. *Danke* again for everything you've done."

"It was no trouble. I'll be back tomorrow to take a shift with the chores."

"Good night, Paul."

"Good night, Lizzie."

He turned and walked back down the pathway. She watched him until he was nothing more than a shadow in the fading moonlight. Long after Paul had gone, she stared at the barn doors. So many terrible memories of this day lingered inside that building.

She stepped back inside the house and shut the front

door, locking it behind her. Turning around she spotted the bag Paul had given her lying on the side table, where she'd left it this morning. She nibbled on her lower lip, contemplating what was inside. Colors. He'd told her she should add colors to her drawings. It was easy to imagine tufts of green grass and swaths of blue sky coming to life on the paper.

After going into her bedroom and opening the bottom drawer in the dresser, she took out her sketch pad and pencils. Then she came back into the living room, sat down, turned up the lamp and then flipped the pad open to the last drawing she'd been working on. The bare-bones image of the barn glared up at her. Her heart felt as if it were squeezing inside her chest as she looked at the plain lines she'd drawn a few weeks ago. Lizzie picked up the pencil and held it poised over the page. Maybe Paul was right. She needed to bring color to her work, and to her life, she thought. Perhaps only then could she erase the starkness of the memories that haunted her.

Sighing, she set the pencil down and closed her sketchbook. It had been a long, long day. Shaking her head, Lizzie mused. Nothing about the past could be changed. Nothing. She needed to stop dwelling on what might have been. Being here with her parents, staying within the close comfort of the farm, this was her life. There was nothing for her beyond the fences.

It was time she accepted that and put thoughts of love and family out of her mind. For good.

Chapter Four

The white sheets snapped in the warm breeze. Lizzie stood on tiptoe, attaching the last sheet to the line that ran from their back door clear up to the top of the old pine tree that stood in the middle of the yard. It had been a long week. Her father had finally come home from the hospital after a five-day stay. They had put something called a stent in to open up the damaged artery. Lizzie had been more than grateful for the community that had come out to support them.

Paul's *mudder* had stepped in to coordinate the kitchen help, making sure that there was plenty of food to feed the helpers. There had been a never-ending supply of Mrs. Burkholder's potato salad. The refrigerator still held some of those leftovers. As promised, each of the men had sent over *sohns* to help out with the feedings, in addition to finishing up the plowing and haying her *vader* had begun the day of his heart attack. As was the Amish way in times of need, her neighbors had been very generous with their time and resources. Lizzie hoped that one day she could repay them in kind.

As she hung the last sheet on the line, clamping the

wooden clothespin into place, Lizzie took a deep breath. Inhaling the sweet summer breeze, laced with the earthy scent of the freshly mowed alfalfa fields and the fully blooming pink rose bushes growing beside the back stoop, made her feel alive and grateful to live in such a beautiful place. Even with the steep and sometimes treacherous hills that surrounded Miller's Crossing, making it difficult to get around during the winter, Lizzie found comfort by simply being here, in this moment.

Since the return home of her father and seeing how wan he still looked, she knew it might be days before their life returned to normal. This morning he and her *mamm* had been driven to a follow-up doctor's appointment by their neighbor, Helen Meyers. Lizzie didn't know what they would have done without her. From the very beginning she'd been kind enough to offer up her services for any errands and appointments that her family needed a car for.

And right now there were a half-dozen men working out in the field and loading the hay wagons with freshly cut silage. The motor of the blower for the silo had been running for two days straight.

She paused on the porch step. Putting her hand above her forehead to shield the bright sunlight from her eyes, she looked out over the lawn to the closest field. She scanned the horizon, seeing a low wagon loaded with jugs of lemonade, water and red coolers. She turned her attention to the workers, not wanting to admit that she was searching for someone in particular. It wasn't long before she spotted Paul. He stood tall, his straw hat in one hand, while he wiped a white cloth over his face with the other. He had the sleeves of his blue chambray shirt rolled up above the elbows.

He turned then and saw her watching him. His mouth tilted up as he gave a slight nod. Embarrassed that she'd been caught gawking, Lizzie scurried into the coolness of the house. Today she was going to be baking up a batch of cookies for the men to enjoy on their afternoon break.

Once in the kitchen she turned on the oven, setting the temperature to preheat to 350 degrees. Then she began to gather the ingredients for her favorite cookies. She took the flour, white sugar, brown sugar and other dry ingredients from the pantry to the large farm table in the middle of the kitchen. The cookies she'd chosen to make today were called Double-Treat Cookies. The recipe called for peanut butter, salted peanuts and semisweet chocolate chips. She'd made them countless times over the years for gatherings. And never once had there been leftovers.

While searching for the butter, she realized that Paul had been here every day since her *vader*'s heart attack. It troubled her that he'd neglected his own work to be here. Blowing out a frustrated breath, she kept looking for those sticks of butter in the refrigerator that she knew were there somewhere. Turning around, she walked over to the stove and saw that the butter was sitting on the counter, right where she'd left it yesterday after baking buttermilk biscuits for their supper.

She picked it up and went back to the refrigerator, opened the door and took two eggs from the wire egg basket. Seeing the mound of eggs reminded her that she still needed to fill the cartons to take down to her roadside stand. She would tend to that after the cookies were baked. There simply weren't enough hours in the day to get everything done. She set to work sifting together the flour, baking soda and salt in a medium-sized bowl. Then, picking up the hand mixer, she combined the shortening, sugars, eggs and a generous teaspoon of vanilla in a large bowl until everything was light and fluffy. Looking around the table, she realized she'd forgotten to bring over the jar of peanut butter.

Lizzie had her head stuck in the pantry once again when she heard a knock on the front door. Quickly she grabbed the jar and hurried to see who was there. With the jar still in hand, she looked through the screen door to find Paul standing on the other side. His face was flushed from the heat. There were a few smudges of dirt on his otherwise neatly tucked-in shirt.

"Good morning, Lizzie." Paul tipped his hat to her.

She took a step back into the shadows, nodding at him. "Hello, Paul."

"May I come inside?" he asked with a gentle half smile.

She only now noticed he'd been holding an empty jug in his hands.

He stepped aside as she pushed the door open, allowing him to come into the house.

"I'm busy baking cookies."

He followed her into the kitchen. "I won't take up too much of your time—I promise. I came to get a refill of the lemonade."

"You can help yourself to the container in the refrigerator."

He set the jug down and washed his hands in the sink before he went to get the refill.

Lizzie set the peanut butter on the table and found that her hands were shaking as she unscrewed the lid, which seemed to be stuck.

"Here, let me help." He took the jar from her hands.

Paul's touch felt warm. Lizzie quickly removed her hands from the jar, clasping them in front of her. She watched him open the lid with one strong twist. Wasn't that always the way, she thought, a woman would work hard to get something unscrewed and then a man would come along and make it look easy as pie.

"You must've loosened the jar," he said as he winked at her, handing the jar back. "What are you making today?"

"My Double-Treat Cookies."

"You made them for the last frolic. They were good."

"Danke."

Silence descended on them. For a moment Lizzie thought Paul was going to take his lemonade and leave; instead he pulled up a stool from beneath the table and sat. He then folded his arms in front of him and rested them on the tabletop. Unsure of what to do, she offered him a glass of lemonade. Which seemed silly, considering he'd just filled up an entire jug with the sweet liquid. When he accepted, she busied herself with pouring him a glass.

Setting it before him, she said, "If you don't mind, I need to keep mixing the dough so I can have the cookies ready for the workers' next break." She thought he might leave then, but he only nodded, took a healthy gulp out of the glass, set it down and looked like he would be settling in for a bit.

Setting to work getting the dry ingredients mixed with the wet, Lizzie tried not to think about the fact that Paul was watching her every move. She knew he must have his own work to do and wondered why he was still here. She began to roll the dough into teaspoon-sized balls. Each one was rolled in a bowl of granulated sugar, and then after that was done, she spaced them apart on the cookie sheet.

She was flattening the dough balls with the bottom of a drinking glass when Paul said, "You're mighty good at baking, Lizzie."

"You haven't even tasted these yet, so how do you know how good they are?"

"I remember how they tasted the last time you made them. You haven't changed the recipe, have you?"

"Nee." Turning her back to him, she walked over to the oven and placed the first cookie sheet on the baking rack. Then she set the oven timer for seven minutes, even though the recipe called for eight minutes of cooking time. Sometimes the oven could be finicky. She didn't want the cookies to burn on the bottom.

When she turned back to the table, she found Paul looking a bit contemplative, staring off into space. His behavior was very unusual. Why was he here? she wondered again. Was he here to deliver her bad news? Shaking that thought away, she continued to load a second tray of cookies. The sound of his voice broke into her thoughts.

"Give me the glass and let me flatten them."

Her motion stilled as she looked across the table at him, meeting his gaze head-on. Her stomach jittered with butterfly nerves. "Why on earth would you want to help me bake? This is a woman's job. Shouldn't you be getting back home or back out in the field?"

He crooked an eyebrow. "Are you anxious to be rid of me so fast?"

"Nee," she mumbled.

Taking the glass from the table, he pulled the tray

closer to where he sat and began flattening the cookies with such intensity that Lizzie had to stop him.

"You don't need to hit them that hard, Paul. These are supposed to be plump cookies." She reached out to take the glass from him, except he held fast to it.

"I'm sorry. I'm having a bad day is all." Finally he handed the glass back to her. Frowning down at his hands, he shook his head. "I'm going to sign the lease papers for the shop in the village this week."

She pulled a stool out, sat opposite him and said, "This feels so sudden, and yet I know you've been thinking on this for a long time."

"Yes, I have. It's been consuming most of my thoughts. My *vader* is not happy about it. I've tried to speak with him, tried to get him to change his mind, but he won't budge. He thinks I'm going to somehow damage the family by doing this."

"I remember you started to tell me about this idea last week at the hospital. I'm sorry your *vader* feels this way."

He lifted his head and looked into her eyes. "I'm going to do this with or without his blessing."

Surprised by his determination, Lizzie didn't quite know what to say. "Paul, are you willing to put your family at risk for this choice?" She paused a moment, then went on. "I know how my own *vader* feels about keeping his family nearby. I imagine yours feels the same way about your staying on at the family business, keeping things the way they've been for years."

"Opening a second shop in the village will be good for everyone, Lizzie. More people will see the Burkholder name." He paused and then pointed out, "Your sister moved away and that changed your family."

"That was different. She moved away because her husband's family needed them more than we did." Lizzie realized it wasn't her place to tell Paul what to do.

Besides, who was she to give out advice? She kept to herself here at the house. Lizzie had little idea about what living or working away from the family farm would be like. She only knew that her place was with her *mamm* and *vader*. Now more than ever she needed to be here, selling her eggs and baked goods to help keep her family going. Just like Paul, Lizzie had responsibilities that couldn't be ignored.

"The thing is, Lizzie, as I've told you before, I've been dreaming about a place of my own for some time now. And I'm not leaving the family or the farm. I'm simply moving my furniture business into the town so more tourists will see what we do out here. You know many of those *Englischers* are afraid to drive around these parts. I think when they get a glimpse of the steep rolling hills out this way, they get scared off."

"Paul, you must do what your *vader* asks of you."

"I don't know about that. My plan will help the family earn more money. He's afraid my brothers will run wild if I'm not around as much."

"You could always bring the oldest ones with you," Lizzie suggested.

"*Nee*. They need to be around to do the chores and help with the wood deliveries. And *Daed* needs their help loading up the cabinets if we have to deliver them. It's not a problem with the bigger pieces because most times those are ordered by outsiders and picked up by a freight truck."

The timer dinged, and Lizzie left the table to go check on the first batch of cookies. She took a pot holder and pulled out what looked to be a perfect batch from the oven and then placed the pan on the stovetop. The house was soon filled with the scent of warm sugar and peanut butter.

From behind her, Paul said, "Wow! Those smell delicious."

Taking a napkin from the basket on the counter, Lizzie placed one of the hot cookies on it and brought it back to the table. She set it in front of Paul. His eyes lit up.

The smile on his face broadened as he said, "Ah, my Lizzie, you do know the way to a hardworking man's heart."

She let out a gasp and stepped back. Out of a long-practiced instinct, her hand flew up to cover the scar on her face. She wasn't trying to work her way into anyone's heart, least of all Paul's. He was her childhood friend—nothing more. She could see the confusion over her actions dawning on his face.

He reached his hand out toward her, and then placed it on the table. "Lizzie." His tone softened. "I didn't mean to make you feel uncomfortable with my words. They were a compliment to your fine baking skills. Please don't shy away from me."

Slowly she lowered her hand.

"You don't need to hide your face from me ever. I need you to understand that, Lizzie."

She nodded slightly, fighting the urge to cover her scar again. Instead she busied herself by putting the next batch of cookies into the oven. Then picking up a spatula, she removed the baked ones to a wire rack, where they could cool the rest of the way. Bringing the sheet pan back to the table, she repeated the steps, getting the next dozen ready to be baked. All the while she felt his gaze on her. Finally she stopped and looked at him, instinct telling her where his thoughts were.

"Paul, there are things that happen in our lives, things that shape us…shape our future. My future is here, in this house, with my family." Her voice dropped to a notch above a whisper. "And as much as you want me to, I can't speak of that day. I just can't."

"There are things you don't know…" His voice trailed off. He turned his head, looking over his shoulder.

Lizzie had never been so thankful to hear the sound of the car doors slamming closed. Wiping her hand on her apron, she walked to the front door to meet her parents. Paul followed closely behind her. Pushing the screen door open, she walked out onto the porch.

"*Mamm! Daed!* I'm glad you're home." Lizzie rushed down the steps, coming alongside her parents. She thought her *daed* looked tired. It must have been a trying day traveling an hour to the hospital and then, no doubt, sitting in the waiting area for a bit.

"Lizzie, run into the house and get your *daed* some iced tea and a sandwich."

"Yes, *Mamm*," she said, hurrying back up the steps.

Stepping off the porch, Paul met Mr. Miller on the steps, saying, "Mr. and Mrs. Miller. I just came by to check in and to get a refill on this jug of lemonade." He held the container up.

"That was right kind of you, Paul. And we appreciate your being here to help, along with the others." Mrs. Miller smiled up at him.

He extended a hand to her husband, offering his help. "Here, let me get you up these steps."

Mr. Miller batted at his hand. "No need for assistance. I can get up there on my own."

The man put a shaky hand on the railing and pulled himself up the first step. Then, taking a deep breath, he moved up the last three steps and plunked himself down in the nearest rocking chair on the front porch. "There. I told you I could do this. Those doctors wanted me to go for physical therapy. They want me to walk on a treadmill. I told them I could take my walks in the outdoors, right here on my own property."

Looking kindly at the man, Paul could see where Lizzie's stubbornness came from. Mrs. Miller followed her husband onto the porch. Smiling at Mrs. Miller, he could see the resemblance between Lizzie and her mother. Mother and daughter carried the same blue eyes and dark hair. Though Lizzie's hair was touched by some honey-colored streaks.

From the rocker, Mr. Miller looked up at him. His cheeks carrying only a tinge of color, and his mouth a bit drawn. It appeared that the exertion of the day was catching up with him. Paul knew little about the man's heart condition, but he imagined recovering from a heart attack and surgery could knock the wind out of a body. When the man nodded to the rocker next to him, Paul started to go over to sit.

"Wait, Paul, poke your head in the door and ask Lizzie to bring out an extra glass of iced tea."

Paul didn't have to, because at the same moment Lizzie came through the door, carrying two full glasses and a plate with a sandwich for her *vader*. He accepted them, thanking her. She went back inside. Paul handed the plate and a glass to her father and then sat down, taking a long sip from the other glass. The tea had a touch of sweetness added to it. He settled into the chair. Next to him he heard Joseph's chair squeaking against the wooden floor.

"I can fix that noise with a little wood glue if you like."

"*Nee.* I like the sound. I find it comforting."

They sat in silence, both looking out over the railing at the front yard, where a few of Lizzie's Rhode Island red hens pecked their way around the yard. Their russet-colored feathers looked even richer in the late-afternoon sunlight. The sound of a hay mower mingled with the clucking of the hens. Paul knew Joseph Miller took great pride in his farm. It must be hard for him to let others do his work and upkeep.

"You need to stop abandoning your own work to come here, Paul."

"I'm not abandoning my work. I was only taking my turn helping out in the fields. It was no trouble at all."

"I was hoping you came by to see Lizzie."

Sitting next to each other in the rocking chairs brought Joseph eye level with him. The man used that vantage point to make his point. Looking him square in the eye, Lizzie's father's gaze hardened a bit.

"You and Lizzie have known each other your entire lives. If not for the accident, things might be different for the two of you right now. I know that the Lord has plans for all of us. But having my oldest daughter living in another community, leaving one of my children dead and one scarred…well, that's a plan I haven't been able to figure out."

It shocked him to hear this man speak about that

day. Did Joseph truly know of the guilt that Paul carried with him? Still, his visits Lizzie were never about his guilt. They were friends, and right now she needed each and every one of her friends to help her and her family through this rough patch.

He knew he should set this man straight, but instead Paul said what came to mind first. "Mr. Miller... Joseph, it's not for us to question *Gott*'s motives."

"I'm left with little choice at the moment. This heart attack has left me with a lot of time to think. And I'm not one who likes to waste time doing that. I'd rather be out, working my land and tending to my cows. But this recovery has set me to thinking that I need to get my youngest daughter married off."

He'd known that this was where the conversation had been heading. After all, Amish men very rarely wasted time sitting about in the daylight hours. Still Paul found himself feeling uncomfortable at the idea of discussing marriage...particularly Lizzie's marriage.

"Without a son and with one married daughter living over an hour away in another district, I need to consider what's going to happen to my farm."

"I do understand, but I'm not a farmer. I'm a furniture maker."

"*Ja*. This I know. Perhaps I will find another man for her—one who likes to farm. Even considering her..." Struggling to find the words, he swallowed and then said, "Even considering her disfigurement, she would make a fine wife for any good Amish man."

In that very second something occurred to Paul; he'd never once considered Lizzie's scar as a disfigurement. He thought about her inner beauty and how she carried that over into her artwork. He wondered what Joseph would say if he knew of his daughter's talent? He heard some shuffling noise near the door. Turning his head, he looked past where Joseph sat. Narrowing his eyes, he tried to see through the shadows. Was there someone hiding behind the screen door? He couldn't tell.

Anger rolled through him, causing his shoulders to tense up as a knot formed in the pit of his stomach. Her life over the past decade had not been an easy one. Because of this he wanted Lizzie to be more than just someone's wife. She deserved to be loved and cared for. A surge of protectiveness welled up from inside of him. He clenched and unclenched his hands. Paul had been working hard to set up his own business; even if he wanted to do as Joseph suggested, he couldn't. Opening a new store always carried a risk of failure, and he wanted to be secure in his own right before he offered courtship to any woman.

The time wasn't right.

Looking at the man who so desperately wanted to keep his family and farm going, the only thing he could think to say was, "I'm sorry. I know this is a difficult time and you want to be sure Lizzie is safe."

"That isn't all I need. I need to have this farm carried into the next generation. Lizzie is the only hope I have left."

He nodded at Joseph. "I understand." Paul was only now beginning to understand the pressure Lizzie had been under. It was no wonder she'd turned to stealing time to work on her sketches.

Paul needed to find a way to give her some time to simply relax. Remembering the images he'd seen of the field she'd been working on, he thought maybe he could convince her to go there with him. He knew her art was a talent given to her by *Gott*. She should be able to use it freely. Maybe she'd be interested in a picnic. Out of the corner of his eye, he studied her *vader*, thinking how happy the man would be if Paul and Lizzie shared an afternoon together.

"Joseph, would it be okay with you if I took your daughter on a picnic?"

"That depends on what your intentions are."

"My intentions are to take your daughter on a picnic, as a friend."

Joseph leaned his back into the rocking chair, rubbing a hand down his gray beard. Paul could almost see the wheels turning inside the man's head. He knew Joseph wanted this to be the beginning of courtship.

"I suppose a picnic with you, as a friend, is better than nothing. You'll bring one of your *bruders* along." Turning his head toward the screen door, Joseph called out, "Elizabeth! Come out here, now!"

Lizzie practically flew through the screen door. "*Vader!* Are you all right?" Her face looked ashen with fear. Behind her, her *mamm*, who must have been thinking something was wrong, too, stood clutching the neckline of her dress.

"I'm fine." Turning to Paul, he waved a hand between them, demanding, "Ask her."

Left with little choice, Paul stood, walked toward Lizzie and asked, "Would you like to go on a picnic with me?"

Chapter Five

The midmorning light filled the far corner of Lizzie's bedroom. After finishing her morning chores, she'd come back in to be sure she had everything she needed before Paul came to pick her up. Even though it was a rare occurrence, other than on the Sabbath, for there to be a day off, Paul had managed to free up this particular Saturday afternoon. Walking around her bed, she went over to her dresser and gently slid the bottom drawer open. There, in a neat pile, lay all of the drawings she'd worked on over the last eight years. She took the top two pieces of drawing paper out and placed them next to her on the floor. Then she picked up the drawing pad, gathered the selected drawings and straightened up.

Lizzie took a canvas bag off the hook behind the bedroom door and put the artwork inside of it. She cast a glance toward the box on top of her nightstand, the place where she'd put the bag Paul had given her. She'd taken the paints out twice since the day he'd brought them over. She'd been surprised when she'd found three watercolor paintbrushes resting at the bottom of the bag. Lizzie had dabbled with the colors a few times. She was amazed at how the shades seemed to float across the paper. Seeing the colors bringing her work to life had made her heart soar.

Nibbling on her bottom lip, she waged a battle with temptation. Her parents would not be happy if they knew about this frivolous gift Paul had given her. Though Lizzie knew painting landscapes wasn't exactly forbidden, her *vader* would consider her art a waste of precious time. Today was supposed to be a day off for her. Surely she could use some of that time testing out some more of these paints. Finally she opened the lid on the box and took out the paints, tossing them into the canvas bag. Looping the straps over her shoulder, she walked out of the room.

Her *mamm* met her at the front door, holding a wicker picnic basket in her hands.

"Here, I fixed some extra food for you and Paul. There's water and soft drinks, along with a blanket. I think I remembered everything you put out last night."

"Danke," Lizzie said, taking the basket from her. She felt a strange fluttering in her stomach. It was as if there were something different about this day, something special. Even though Paul would be bringing one of his *bruders* along, Lizzie still felt like this could be more than just two friends going on a picnic. Smiling at her *mamm*, she stepped out onto the front porch.

Paul had just arrived. She spotted his younger *bruder* Abram sitting on the back of the buggy with his feet dangling over the edge.

He called out a hello and Lizzie waved back.

She waited on the top step while Paul stepped down from his family's buggy. He tipped his hat to her. She noticed he had on black pants and a white shirt. He'd even changed out his straw hat for his Sunday one. Lizzie thought Paul looked very handsome today.

"Good day, Lizzie." His glance slid to her *mamm* as he added, "Good day, Mrs. Miller."

"Good day to you, too, Paul. You've picked a fine one for a picnic."

"This day wasn't my doing—it's a gift from *Gott*." Paul beamed as he looked up at the crystal-clear blue sky.

"*Ja*. That it is," her *mamm* nodded in agreement. "I'm afraid Joseph is out for his morning walk. He'll be sorry to have missed you."

"I take it he's feeling better."

"So much better now that he's moving around more."

"That's good to hear." Paul swung his gaze back to Lizzie, saying, "Are you ready?"

"I am."

He took the basket from her as she climbed up into the buggy with the canvas bag. After she got settled, Paul went around to the other side and joined her, tucking her basket at their feet next to a smaller one. Lizzie suddenly felt like a bundle of nerves. She placed the bag on the seat between them. She fidgeted with her prayer *kapp*, then ran her hands along the front of her white apron, which covered her favorite pale blue skirt.

Paul glanced at the bag as he picked up the leather reins and urged the horse forward. "Are those your paint supplies?"

"*Ja*. I hope you don't mind that I brought them along."

"*Nee*. I'm anxious to see what you've accomplished since I gave them to you," he replied, concentrating on the roadway ahead.

"Not much, I'm afraid. I did take them out a few

times to try them. I love the way the colors move on the paper. Some of them look like bright gems. But others…" She paused to grimace at her mistakes. "If you're not careful when you mix them, they come out looking like mud."

Beside her, Paul chuckled. "Sounds like using watercolors can be a bit of trial and error. You must have a lot of drawings stored away. I mean, since you've been doing this for some time now."

She nodded. She'd never taken the time to count how many drawings she'd done over the years. She only knew that the bottom dresser drawer was filled to the top. And that didn't take into account the box of drawings she'd stashed away under her bed. Over time her eye had become keener for spotting things that would be good subjects. Like her recent drawing of the barn.

Looking off in the distance, she spotted a small herd of deer grazing near the edge of a tree line. Perhaps one of these days she would try her hand at sketching some animal figures.

"Still, today will be a fine day for picnicking *and* painting."

Out of the corner of her eye, Lizzie stole a glance at Paul. He seemed unusually interested in her artwork. The horse pulled the weight of the buggy along at a good clip. They rode by Sadie's house. Lizzie had seen her friend a few days ago and had decided not to mention her picnic with Paul. Sadie would have made a bigger deal out of this than it was. Today was nothing more than two friends spending an afternoon together. And yet Lizzie felt an energy coming from Paul that set her nerves on edge again.

Trying to alleviate some of her unease, she asked, "Where are we going to for this picnic?"

"A place I know you will love," Paul answered as he turned the horse to the left onto Angel Hill Road.

The mare trotted along the road that divided Miller's Crossing in half. Lizzie hadn't been out this way in a very long time. The horse began to slow as it climbed a steep incline. Lizzie felt bad for the animal and was glad when the land leveled out a bit. The wide vistas of Chautauqua County, New York, spread out before them. Rolling hills gave way to wooded areas. Off in the distance small lakes dotted the landscape.

"This is beautiful," she whispered, already imagining how this would look on paper. She would use greens and a touch of gold hues to bring out the early hint of fall color.

Lizzie's heart raced at the thought.

Beside her, Paul worked the reins with such confidence, Lizzie felt a bit in awe of his driving skills. The buggy slowed as it rolled down one steep hill, then crested up high on a rise where a beautiful church sat. The simple square structure had gray-colored siding and white trim surrounding it. A tall steeple rose from the center of the pitched roof. Two windows flanked the front door. A sign proclaimed this building to be the Clymer Hill Reformed Church.

Lizzie knew it to be a church used only by *Englischers*, and she realized how lucky those parishioners were to be able to worship here in the glory of God.

After parking the buggy in the shade of the building, Paul helped Lizzie down from the seat. Abram jumped down from the back and raced around to the front of the buggy. "I'll go find us a spot to sit," he called out, running away.

Lizzie laughed at his energy. She waited while Paul gathered the picnic baskets and her canvas bag. They walked side by side along the edge of the parking area, coming to where the pavement met the soft earth of a hayfield. Before them lay a vista powerful enough to take one's breath away. From up here they could see the farms and a patchwork of green-and-brown fields. Dust from a plow billowed up in the distance.

Paul extended his arm, pointing to their right, "That's your house, right over there."

"That little speck? Oh, my!"

In her excitement she gripped the side of his arm, her fingers flexing against a hard wall of muscle. "Wow! I wish I could come here more often. It's too far to walk, though. These steep hills are not easy on the legs. All these years I've been missing out."

With her gaze still on the horizon, Lizzie took in the beauty. Paul had discovered a lovely spot. She was glad he wanted to share this with her. Happiness welled up from inside of her. Lizzie let out a delighted laugh.

The sound of Lizzie's laughter was music to his ears.

"*Ja.* It would be a difficult walk. I only come up here in a buggy. It's a great spot to sit and think."

"Do you come here often?"

"I used to sneak up here when I was a young boy. And then after David's death… I came here a great deal." He'd watch the sky change colors in the evening light. He'd think about how horrible that day had been as he'd prayed for forgiveness. He still couldn't be sure if he'd been given that yet.

The beauty of this place was something to behold. Whoever the person was who'd picked this as a location for the church had done so knowing how these wonders could restore a person's faith. Even through all the pain and suffering that David's death had left behind, the one thing that had never wavered was his faith. The doubts he had were solely within himself.

"I can understand why you came here. There's a peace about this place. I think it's a wonderful spot to sit in reflection."

He looked down at her, taking in her honey-colored hair and her perfectly placed prayer *kapp*. He looked at her face, seeing a wistful smile appear and maybe hope reflected in her eyes.

Taking another chance, he spoke in soft tones, saying, "And I think it might be a wonderful place to paint."

With her gaze still fixed on the horizon, she nodded.

Paul wasted little time in joining Abram at the spot that he'd picked out for them on top of a rise. From here they could see out over the fields. Spreading the blanket out, he was anxious to see what Lizzie had brought in her bag. But first he had to deal with his *bruder*, who was running circles around them.

"Abram. You need to slow down," Paul gently warned him. "The last thing I need is for you to fall and get hurt."

"I'm not going to get hurt. Can I take my sandwich and go over there?" Abram asked Paul, pointing to a stone wall at the edge of the field.

"*Ja*. But stay where I can see you," Paul told him, handing Abram a bag with an egg salad sandwich.

Then he turned his attention back to Lizzie, watching as she took out a sketch pad, the paints and supplies.

His breath caught when she pulled out two larger sheets of paper. The images were stunning.

Reaching across the blanket, he asked, "Might I take a closer look at these?"

"I'm afraid they're not very good."

"Lizzie, how can you say such a thing? These are beautiful." *Like you*, he almost added. But instead he turned his attention to the image of a field that he recognized.

As he continued to look at her art, she arranged her paints and brushes on the blanket. She asked him if there might be a plastic lid she could use in the picnic basket. Setting the artwork down, he opened the top of the wicker hamper her mother has sent and found a round container of macaroni salad. He took the lid off and handed it to her.

"Will this do?"

"Hand me that bottle of water, please." She pointed to one of two lying side by side next to the sandwiches.

He did. She unscrewed the cap and dumped a few drops of water on it, cleaning it off.

Paul wondered what she was going to do with the lid and water.

"I'm going to put the paints on this. And the water will help thin out the colors," she explained.

"Ah. I should have known."

"I went to the library last week and looked up some books on watercolor painting. It seems the author of this one book is a very famous watercolorist. That's what they're called, you know. I couldn't spend too much time there, as I was supposed to be picking up some items for *Mamm* at the general store. But I did have time to learn how to blend colors. That's what I've been working on."

While Lizzie worked in her sketch pad, Paul set up their lunch. Sandwiches, salad, drinks and chocolate whoopie pies for desserts. It appeared their *mamms* hadn't left a thing out of those baskets. He knew both sets of parents were hoping for a good outcome from today. He rolled his shoulders, preparing himself for the conversation. And he had something else he needed to discuss with her, an idea that could help her family.

But first things first. He was starving.

"Which sandwich do you want, egg salad or tuna salad?" he asked.

"Why don't we split them?"

"Good idea." He found paper plates and napkins at the bottom of the basket his *mamm* had packed. After carefully unwrapping the sandwiches, he arranged the halves on two plates.

After giving her one of the plates, he took the plunge. "You know, I've been talking with your *vader* about us."

She'd been working on the top of her painting. Her brush strokes of blue tones spreading across the paper. He realized it was the same color as the sky above them. She paused midstroke, looking up at him, seeming to ponder his words. Lizzie set the artwork aside and put the brush on the lid. Then she picked up the half of the tuna salad sandwich and started nibbling at the edges of the bread.

Clearing his throat, Paul made a great effort out of studying the egg salad sandwich he'd been holding. He took a healthy bite, and then in four more, the sandwich was gone. Beside him, Lizzie continued to nibble away at hers. Not saying a word.

In a fit of frustration, he said, "Don't you want to know what we've been discussing?"

Calmly she placed her half-eaten portion back onto the plate. She picked up the water bottle, twisted off the cap and took a sip. Then she set the bottle back in the exact spot where she'd picked it up.

She avoided looking at him. "A few weeks ago, I overheard the two of you talking about our courtship."

His heart sank. Had she heard everything? Her *vader*'s words had sounded harsh to Paul. He could only imagine how Lizzie had been affected. He took her hand in his, feeling her fingers tremble. Rubbing his thumb across her knuckles, he wondered at all she had endured. Lizzie deserved so much better. She deserved happiness. She deserved to do her artwork out in the open. The world needed to see her talent. But first he needed to talk about their relationship.

She beat him to the punch by saying, "Paul, I know a courtship between us would make our families happy. But…" She stopped, pulling her hand from his. She rubbed it along her scar. "My *vader*, he needs to be sure his farm will last into the next generation. We've talked about this before, you and I. You are not a farmer. Besides, this—" she indicated the side of her face "—is going to make it difficult for me to find a husband."

Shaking her head, she looked down at the painting she'd been working on. Lowering her voice, she added, "I'm just not ready for any kind of a relationship."

Anger surged through him, causing him to question the reasons for things he couldn't change. He wanted to fight for her. But most important he wanted her to fight for her own confidence. He wanted to see Lizzie happy and at peace. And he cared for her enough to know that if she couldn't see a way to make a life with him, then he prayed she would find happiness with someone else.

As he sat there looking at her, willing her to change her mind, Paul realized he didn't want Lizzie to have a life with anyone else.

"Lizzie. I don't believe this to be true. You are warm and caring. You love to cook. I think you need to give yourself time to think about a courtship."

"*Nee*. I will find another way to help my family."

By now he'd learned to recognize the stubborn set to her jaw and knew she was finished with that conversation. But Paul saw the opportunity to discuss his next idea and took it.

"There is a way for you to do just that."

She looked back at him. "What are you talking about?"

He shifted his weight on the blanket, leaned back and rested his weight on his elbows, stretching out his legs and then crossing them at the ankles. When he was sure he had her attention, Paul nodded in the direction of her watercolors.

Lizzie pursed her mouth into a tight line. She shook her head. "Paul Burkholder, I want you to get whatever thought you have about my art out of your head this instant."

"You haven't even heard me out. At least let me tell you my idea."

She folded her arms across her chest. Her eyelashes dipped, and he could see her waging a silent battle. Paul waited. And waited. And waited.

Just when he thought she would never respond, finally she said, "All right. Let's hear it."

Chapter Six

Pushing off his elbows, Paul sat up tall on the picnic blanket. "I want to sell your paintings at my store. They are stunning and I know that the *Englischers* would love them as much as I do. I can make all of the frames for them. And Lizzie, all the money you make from these could help your family."

"Nee!" Suddenly she stood up. With her hand on her hips and her back rigid, she stared him down.

Her eyes were filled with a sharp determination, but he also saw something else around the edges. Her expression softened. She stepped over the paintings she'd created, then walked off the blanket. Paul started to go after her. Lizzie wandered a few feet away from their picnic spot. He wanted to give her time to think about his offer, but there wasn't a lot of time to be had. Over the past couple of weeks, he'd been working day and night, getting his shop ready to open. He'd done what they call a soft opening this past Friday and it had gone quite well.

Paul walked up beside her, placing his hand on her shoulder. He had to convince her to do this. "Lizzie, I need you to think seriously about my offer. You need to trust me when I tell you this will work." Pausing to let his words sink in, he repeated, "Selling your paintings can help you and your family."

"You need to understand, no one knows I do this. No one except you, Paul. And I trusted you not to tell anyone."

Taking her by the shoulder, he spun her around to face him. "I haven't told a soul about your work."

He watched as she took in a deep breath and then exhaled. It hadn't been until after he'd come to help with the Millers' chores that the full extent of the their hardship had hit him. On the surface the farm looked like it was running well, but up close, Paul could see where the barns were run-down, in need of paint. And some of the equipment was in need of repair. This plan had to work. Lizzie selling her art could be the only way to help her family make ends meet. And like it or not, she was the only sibling left who could do anything to help her family. He had to make her see this.

She continued to shake her head. "I'm not like you. I'm not strong enough to go against my *vader*'s wishes."

Her words stung him. Did she think his decision hadn't been hard? "You are wrong about that. I thought long and hard before deciding on what would be best for myself and my family. You and I talked about this. You know how I felt."

"I didn't mean to insult you. I'm upset that my life can't be what everyone thinks it should be. But I don't want sympathy, either," she explained, stepping away from him.

Dropping his arms to his sides, he realized something Lizzie didn't see: she was far stronger than she or anyone in her family thought. He knew she could make this choice, but he didn't want to push her so hard that she would retreat back to the safety of her home. Paul knew she rarely left the farm. He knew how she planned her trips to the village on days that weren't busy ones. Just the other day he'd seen her waiting in the shadows outside of the general store, making sure the place was nearly empty before going inside.

He needed to tread lightly. So he tried a different tactic.

"Fair enough. How about this? We don't tell anyone who the artist is. The intrigue of your anonymity would certainly add a certain mystery to the work." He gave a shrug. "I think you might find that you do very well in my store."

She remained silent, though he knew she'd been listening to him. Paul turned, walking back to the blanket. He heard a gasp and looked over to make sure Lizzie was okay. But then he saw what had caused her reaction. Toward the horizon, where the earth met the sky, was a row of soft, billowy white clouds. Brilliant rays of golden sunlight streamed toward the earth, folding them in a warm glow.

Hope surged through him, filling him with *Gott*'s love and peace.

Lizzie faced him. "I'll think about what you've asked. Let me pray on this. Can you allow me that one thing?"

Feeling as if the weight of the issue had lightened a bit, Paul nodded. "Okay. But—"

She put her hand up. "No buts, Paul. You need to let me figure this out. My way."

"I can do that," he agreed, picking up the empty paper plates and packing them back in the picnic basket.

"Let me help with that," Lizzie said, coming over to join him.

She grabbed the water bottles and tossed them into the nearest recycling bin. Their hands collided when they both reached for the salad container. Paul felt her jolt of surprise, yet still he allowed his touch to linger on her hand for a few seconds longer than was proper. She tilted her head, looking into his eyes. A hint of a blush appeared high on her cheekbones. He captured her gaze with his. He saw her doubts and fears mingling with something else…hope.

"This is all going to work out." Lowering the tone of his voice, he whispered, "I promise, Lizzie."

She moved away from him, busying herself with putting her paints and watercolors away. "We need to be getting back."

"*Ja.* I don't want your parents to worry," he agreed, and then added, "Before you make up your mind, will you at least come by and visit Burkholder Amish Furniture Store?"

They worked together to fold the blanket. Then Lizzie took the blanket from him, saying, "*Ja*, I can do that."

There was a bit of morning drizzle the next day, followed by a severe thunderstorm. Lizzie stood at the only window in her bedroom, watching as the remnants of the dark clouds blew across the sky. The willow tree in the side yard bent in the wind, its light, feathery branches dancing along the rain-soaked earth. Tiny rivers of water flowed in front of the barn, trailing along the driveway. She knew the neighbors who still came by to help her *vader* on the farm were waiting out the storm. Since everyone would be getting a late start, she decided to take the extra time in prayer.

Kneeling beside her bed, she folded her hands and

closed her eyes, and she said a silent prayer. "*Gott*, thank You for the rains to keep our crops growing. Thank You for watching over my *vader*. Give him the strength he needs to continue to heal. Bless my friends and family. Watch over my friend…" She paused, thinking of the hard choice Paul had made to take his furniture business into the village. She worried about this idea of marriage that both of the men had. Lizzie didn't know how to pray about that. Then she thought about the path Paul wanted her to take, with her artwork in his shop.

Lizzie so wanted to do the right thing. Framing her thoughts, she continued with her prayers. "Please watch over my friend, Paul Burkholder, and guide him in the way You see fit. And please show me the path You want me to take. Amen."

Pushing her hands against the mattress, which was covered in a simple yellow bedspread, she rose, brushing her hands down the front of her dress. A sliver of sunlight spilled through the windows, bringing light into the room. The storm had finally passed. Going downstairs, she went into the kitchen and began to gather the ingredients for the loaves of bread that needed to be baked. Because of the two risings needed to get the loaves just right, the process would take most of the day. Lizzie planned on having the dough set for its first rise before the next round of workers arrived.

Before she knew it, a few hours had passed. She was in the middle of making honey butter when there came a light tapping on the front door. After grabbing a dampened towel from the edge of the sink, she wiped her hands on it as she made her way to the door. A smile popped onto her face when she saw not only her cousin,

Rachel Miller, but her friend Sadie standing on the other side of the screen door.

"Come in! Come in!" Stepping aside, Lizzie beckoned them to enter. She saw right away that the women hadn't come empty-handed. Sadie carried in a wicker basket full of fresh vegetables, while Rachel brought in big clear jugs of what looked to be iced tea.

"I wasn't expecting anyone to stop by this soon. I've just put today's bread loaves into pans for their last rising."

Lizzie looked at Rachel, who seemed to be beaming with joy. Her light blond hair was swept up in a bun, with her prayer *kapp* resting neatly on top of it. With her wedding only a few weeks away, she imagined Rachel must be getting excited.

She patted Rachel on the arm. Looking into her pretty hazel eyes, she said, "I'm so pleased you came by."

Sadie, in her usual spirited way, pushed past them, bustling into the kitchen. "We've come to lend you a hand. I imagine it isn't easy cooking for all those hungry men."

"There's only about half the crew we had the first week after my *vader*'s illness. He's starting to do simple chores again, *Gott* be praised," Lizzie told them as she took the basket of vegetables from Sadie and set them on the countertop near the sink. Then she took the iced tea from her cousin, thinking about her happiness at finding someone she loved to spend the rest of her life with.

"The day is drawing near for your wedding, *ja*? You must be getting excited."

"I am. Jacob and I are going on a train trip for part

of our honeymoon." Rachel's eyes lit up with excitement. "It's going to be my first time on a train. But we just found out that my *aenti*, Rebecca, is unable to come to the wedding. She fell and broke her hip last week. She's the one I was most nervous about Jacob meeting. I know we're not supposed to have favorites, but she's my most beloved *aenti*."

Hearing the lilt in Rachel's voice and seeing the joy on her face gave Lizzie a pang in her chest. Her cousin had been most fortunate to marry for love. Arranged marriages were not all that uncommon within their communities. Arranged or not, Lizzie knew her chances of having a wedding of her own were slim to none. Not wanting to think about that anymore, she busied herself by preparing to get the loaves of bread into the oven.

She took off the damp cloth from the tops of the bread pans and set them aside. The air immediately filled with the pungent yeasty scent. Though she was tempted to poke a finger into the spongy dough, she knew better. In about an hour they would come out of the oven a delicious golden color, ready to be eaten. Behind her, Sadie and Rachel chattered away about weddings and the latest gossip. Lizzie had been so busy with her *daed* over the past weeks that she'd little idea what had been happening in their community outside their farm.

"And then I heard that Paul's brother, Abram, is considering *rumspringa*."

This declaration came from Sadie. "Did Paul mention this to you, Lizzie?"

Lizzie spun around, nearly toppling over a sheet pan that her *mamm* had left on the stove top. Reaching out, she managed to catch it before it fell.

"I haven't heard this." Slowly she turned to find both

women staring at her. "What? You both think that Paul and I have been gossiping together?"

"Maybe there have been other things going on, like the beginning of a courtship." Rachel wiggled her pale eyebrows at Lizzie. "He has been spending a lot of time here."

Lizzie's hands trembled, as she was reminded of Paul's conversation with her while they were on their picnic. She hadn't spoken to anyone about her feelings on the matter of a courtship, other than Paul.

She made a half-hearted attempt to shrug off Rachel's suggestion. "He's been putting in his fair share of time helping on the farm and he's been busy working on his new furniture shop in town."

Having been her closest friend since they were small children, Sadie noticed her discomfort first. Her brow furrowed in worry, she put her hand on Lizzie's forearm. Guiding her across the linoleum floor, she urged her to sit down in one of the wooden chairs that surrounded the plank table.

"*Es dutt mir leed.* I'm sorry if our chatter has upset you."

"*Nee,*" she assured them, mustering up a tiny smile.

While Sadie gathered two more chairs to bring them into a little semicircle, Rachel took three glasses from the cupboard and filled them with the iced tea she'd brought. Lizzie took a deep breath, fighting the urge to break down and have a good cry.

"Look, Sadie, you of all people should know that there can never be anything more than friendship between Paul and myself. I can't be with him in any other way."

"I think you're wrong. This is a tight-knit community and no one would ever want to see you get hurt again."

Lizzie picked at her apron, and Sadie placed her hand on top of hers. "You need to think about getting married, Lizzie."

Tears sprang to her eyes as remnants of her recent conversations with Paul swirled through her head. "Who would want me? Who would want to wake up every morning and look at this?" Lizzie gave Sadie and Rachel a full view of the scarred side of her face.

"Lizzie!" Sadie's voice rose a notch. "No one cares about your scar."

"Listen to what Sadie is saying." Rachel tried to calm Lizzie with a soothing tone of voice.

"I am listening. And don't either of you dare give me the '*Gott* wouldn't give you more than you can handle' speech." The words came out in a choked whisper.

Sadie frowned as she said, "Lizzie, we're just trying to be helpful."

She hated the hurt she saw on their faces. Her stomach felt as if it were twisting into tight knots. Sadie and Rachel sat in patient silence, waiting on Lizzie. But she remained silent.

Finally Sadie spoke. Her soft, melodic voice quoted one of their community's favorite sayings. "Life is too short to stay mad for very long."

"I feel like I've been in limbo for a very long time," Lizzie admitted.

She'd been thinking about Paul's offer to her. He was giving her a way out; she only had to find the courage to take it.

"Maybe it's time to think about making some changes."

Once Rachel and Sadie were situated, and they'd all taken a sip of their tea, she looked at her friends.

"Lizzie, we know it's been rough at your house. How is your *daed* doing?" Rachel asked.

"Much better, *danke* for asking."

Sadie leaned in a bit to scrutinize Lizzie. She shook a finger in front of her face. "*Nee, nee.* This is not about your *daed.* I know you've got the strength of an ox when it comes to this sort of thing. This sadness is about something else. Am I right?"

Lizzie blew out a soft breath, finally answering, "*Ja,* you are *recht.*"

"Rachel and I will keep your confidence. No matter what. You can trust us," Sadie added. Both of the women nodded at her.

Lizzie realized she wasn't ready to tell them about her artwork and Paul's shop yet. She needed time to think about everything. If the plan to sell the paintings didn't work out, then no one else would be the wiser. Still, Sadie and Rachel both sat forward on the edge of their seats, as if waiting for some big revelation.

"Paul and I went on a picnic."

"You and Paul went on a picnic!" Rachel let out a squeal as she clapped her hands together.

Sadie echoed her sentiment. "A picnic—you and Paul! Well, it's about time."

"It's not what either of you are thinking."

"Oh, yes, it is. *This* is the beginning of your courtship," Sadie quipped.

She wrung her hands together, feeling the tension set in her shoulders. "No." She shook her head with such vehemence that she nearly knocked her prayer *kapp* off.

"Then tell us what happened, Lizzie," Sadie said.

"Paul and I discussed the courtship idea everyone is so set on, and I told him the same thing I've been telling everyone else. It's not going to happen. We are good friends, that's all."

"I don't think that is all," Rachel chimed in.

Lizzie knew she could count on these women for anything, but on this subject, she would remain steadfast. There could be no future for her and Paul.

"I'm fine with our decisions. I'm fine with being an *alt maedel*."

"I'm so sorry," Rachel offered, shaking her head.

"Don't be sorry for me. You are going on an adventure with your new husband. I don't want you to worry about me." Lizzie's heart swelled with happiness for her cousin.

"While we're gone, I'm going to write to you every chance I get, and you will let me know how things are going with you and Paul."

"There will never be a 'me and Paul.'"

Silence descended on the trio of women. Lizzie bowed her head. Sadie continued to pat her hand. The clock on the living room wall struck three times at the same time the buzzer on the oven signaled the bread needed to be checked. Lizzie stood to shut the timer off and, using a pot holder, pulled the rack with the bread out of the oven. Normally seeing the golden color gave her such delight. But today not even the sight of the perfect freshly baked loaves could lighten her mood.

Behind her, Rachel said, "I have to be going. I promised Jacob I would stop off at his grandmother's house to pick up a wedding gift she has for us."

After Rachel left, Sadie and Lizzie stood alone in the room. Shrugging her shoulders, Lizzie said, "I need to keep my hands busy. I think I'm going to bake up some cream puffs as a special treat for the workers. Can you keep me company while I do that?"

"I'd like nothing better."

When she went to the pantry to take out the ingredients, she realized there wasn't enough baking soda for the dough.

"*Ach!* I've got to get better at making sure I stock up on my ingredients."

"I have to go into the village for a few things myself. We could walk together," Sadie suggested. "Besides, some fresh air might give you a different perspective on what we were talking about."

"I'm not so sure it will change anything. But a walk into town would be nice. Besides, I told Paul I'd stop by his new shop. Let me find my parents to let them know we'll be going. I think they are out in the garden."

She let Sadie go out the back door ahead of her. And after following the pathway around the side of the house, she found her parents outside, tending to the vegetables.

"Sadie and I have to go to the village. I need some baking soda. Do either of you need anything while I'm there?"

Her mother gave a quick shake of her head. "*Nee. Danke* for coming to ask."

"We shouldn't be too long."

She felt Sadie's hand brush along her arm. "We need to get going."

Saying their goodbyes, they headed off. At the end of the driveway, Sadie tugged on her arm, pulling her to a stop. "Now that we're alone, do you want to tell me what's *really* going on?"

Chapter Seven

Paul opened the door to the Burkholder Amish Furniture Store, stirring up a thin cloud of dust motes that danced along the sunbeam coming through the front window. He'd have to see to sweeping and dusting again. Already he'd found out that running a business took a lot of energy. But he had more than enough to spare when it came to seeing his dream come true.

Beneath his foot, the floorboards creaked as he walked into the large room. A long counter stood in the middle of the floor. The walls were covered with wallpaper that featured pink roses against a cream-colored background. A few years back this had been a ladies' clothing store. Three years ago the shop had closed when the owner had died and the family hadn't wanted to continue with the business. Until Paul had signed the lease papers, the single-story building had been vacant.

He set the take-out coffee he'd bought at Decker General Store on his way here, down on the windowsill just inside the front door. Putting his hands on his hips, Paul looked around, seeing all the work that still needed to be done. It wasn't difficult to imagine more of his furniture scattered about the room and the walls full of Lizzie's artwork hanging above his designs.

Paul took a small notepad and pen out of his vest pocket and began making a list of what still needed to be done. Though he'd been working around it, that ugly wallpaper needed to come down. Next up would be another thorough cleaning, and then seeing if the heavy counter could be moved over to one side of the room. He'd decided after the recent soft opening that the counter would work better if it was located off to the side.

Walking around the massive counter, he looked under the lip of the thickly planked top, checking to see if the structure was sound or if it was secured to the floor. It appeared that it was in good shape and was not attached to the floor. With a little brute strength, he felt sure that he and his *bruders* would be able to move it to another location. That would open up the space so he'd be able to showcase some of the larger pieces of furniture. He'd also been working on making simple wooden toys out of the scrap lumber from their shop. For some reason those items always grabbed the attention of shoppers. If he could get them in the door to look at those, chances were customers would be interested in seeing his handmade wooden tables, cabinets and chairs.

He continued to walk around, jotting down ideas as he went. He picked up his coffee and took a slow sip of the strongest black brew in the village. He took in the view from the window.

Across the street he saw a Plain woman walking with two children in tow. The stoplight in the center of Main Street turned red. A few cars and a blue pickup truck waited for the light to change. He saw two more

Amish women walking into the general store next door. One of them turned and he realized it was Lizzie. He recognized her friend Sadie walking next to her. Paul started to wave to them, then realized they weren't looking in his direction.

He leaned against the edge of the doorway, thinking about his recent conversation with Lizzie. He knew that, for the moment, they both wanted different things, but in the end they wanted what was best for their families. Lizzie was so intent on doing right by her parents, he hoped she didn't lose sight of what she stood to gain. Paul still couldn't fathom the pain the Miller family had suffered over the years. He knew that he, himself, missed David every day. The loss had to be so much more for them. And Lizzie. He'd tried to be there as often as possible in the beginning, but over time they'd both grown older. Now he was entering his midtwenties, and his family was expecting him to settle down, choose a wife and have many children.

Of course he wanted all of those things, too. But he wanted them on his own terms. Well aware that if both *vaders* put their heads together, they could make a union between Paul and Lizzie happen, Paul still believed he should be the only one deciding his future. Most days Paul grappled with the fact that his father still didn't approve of his new business venture.

While Paul mulled things over, he waited for Lizzie to come out of the general store.

Fifteen minutes later the two women walked out of Becker's, and Paul didn't waste any time going out onto the stoop to beckon them over.

"Paul Burkholder! Look how you've transformed Davidson's Dress Shop! It's amazing!" Sadie said, bouncing up onto the steps, her excitement contagious.

"Come inside and I'll show you around." He tipped his hat to the women as they came to join him.

Lizzie cast a sidelong glance at Sadie, making him feel as if they'd been talking about him behind his back. Deep in his heart, he'd secretly hoped she'd come to town to tell him that she was going to take him up on his offer to sell her artwork in his shop. Paul offered a hand to help Lizzie up the steps. Shaking her head, she tucked a small bag into her apron pocket, freeing her hands. She put one hand on the old iron rail and stumbled on the step.

"Oh!" She let out a gasp as she clutched the rail to keep herself from falling.

Paul quickly caught her by the elbow. "Lizzie." He kept his voice low. "I've got you."

He looked at her pretty blue eyes and saw something he couldn't quite put his finger on. Trepidation? Wariness? Maybe a touch of excitement? He hoped she was bringing him good news.

Shaking off his touch, she said, "I'm fine. Now show us what you've got going on in here."

Stepping aside, he gave a slight bow and allowed both women to enter the shop ahead of him. Pride welled up inside him. This was the first time he'd shown this store to the people who mattered the most. He wondered if Lizzie and Sadie would think his idea as farfetched as his *vader* did. He found what he wanted more than Lizzie's consent to place her art on his walls was her agreement that he'd made the right choice.

"Welcome to the Burkholder Amish Furniture Store."

Lizzie tilted her head to look up at him. She opened

her mouth as if to say something, then didn't. Her face softened as she spun about, taking in the store and all the furniture that was within. When she turned back to him, she tucked her lower lip between her teeth, pondering. He thought he saw just a tiny bit of approval reflected in her eyes.

"It's like I've been telling you—I've had this idea about bringing my furniture closer to the public for a very long time. And if the soft opening I had last week is any indication—" he paused to wipe his brow "—I think my shop is going to be quite successful."

Lizzie finally spoke, asking, "Your *vader*, he's finally come around to your way of thinking?"

"Not exactly." Paul walked over to the counter area.

Coming to stand next to the counter, she commented, "You're risking a lot going against him."

"*Ja*, but this feels right to me. It's like *Gott* has led me to this." He saw the realization dawning on her face and knew then that Lizzie understood why he was doing this.

He needed to find his own way. Apart from his family. He was also doing this for his family, even if his father didn't quite see it that way. Like Lizzie made sure to take care of her parents, Paul was doing his best to take care of his, while at the same time finding a way to secure his own future. He'd prayed long and hard about it, looking to *Gott* for guidance, finally knowing this would be the right choice.

Pointing to the counter, he said, "I'm thinking this needs to be moved out of the way. The people who came in the other day had to walk around it in order to see the other stuff. I'd like to display some of the larger pieces in the middle of the room, with the chairs closer to the front. And I think putting baskets filled with wooden toys for *kinder* in the window might bring the customers in."

"I think you should put one of your chairs in the window. You make lovely chairs, Paul," he heard Lizzie say.

He gave her a quick smile. Her compliment meant a lot to him.

"Danke."

Sadie rubbed her hand along the smooth top of the counter. "Do you worry about your furniture being counterfeited? I've heard of this becoming more and more of a problem."

Well aware of this practice among *Englischers* to claim they were selling Amish furniture, he'd already found a way for someone to tell that they were getting an original Paul Burkholder piece. Paul had created a very small brand with the initials *PB* that he burned into the bottom of each piece of furniture he made. But he knew that little could be done to stop the counterfeiting. He wanted to focus on selling his pieces to customers who would appreciate owning a sturdy chair that would last for years. Right now he had no plans to sell his things anywhere but his own store.

"Nee. I have a mark that I put on all of my pieces."

Sadie nodded. "That's a very smart idea. Don't you agree, Lizzie?" Sadie cast her friend a look that Paul couldn't read. Something was amiss between the two of them.

Lizzie frowned.

Sadie gave an almost imperceptible nod of her head, her gaze swinging from Lizzie to him. Even though he had three sisters, Paul would be the last one to say he understood women.

He stuffed his hands into his pockets. It appeared the two of them were at some sort of a silent impasse. He worried that maybe Lizzie had come here to decline his offer.

"I think the rent for the place is affordable," he said to break the silence.

"*Ja*. That's *gut*. You don't want to get in over your head in the beginning. How much furniture do you have ready?"

She was obviously stalling. He could wait her out.

Paul answered her question. "I have a lot of the *kinder*'s toys, chairs—which seem to be quite popular—cabinets, some smaller end tables and three dining room sets." He nodded to the spot where he'd placed them in the middle of the store. "I put those on display and have already taken some orders."

"I like that idea." She looked around again, adding, "But this wallpaper has to go."

He chuckled. "What, you don't think the roses will look good next to my chairs?"

She wrinkled her nose. "Blooming on a bush, they would look lovely. On the walls of a furniture store, they are too frilly. You could take it down and then paint the walls a nice pale yellow. That would brighten the area. Maybe you could add some wicker baskets to the window display. The toys would look attractive stacked inside those."

"I'd like to add a big oval braided rug to the center of the room. One of the dining sets would go there. I can hang a few chairs up on the walls. Or I can save that space for your..." He stopped talking, realizing that he had no idea if Sadie knew about her friend's talent.

"You need to keep room for Lizzie's paintings," Sadie called out from the other side of the counter.

"I told her," Lizzie let him know.

Sadie gave them a mischievous smile. "I made her tell me." Strolling toward them, she added, "And if you want her to sell her paintings here, then my guess is she's very good at her art."

Paul blew out a relieved breath.

"I'm still not sure, Sadie."

"*Ja*. You are. What did we talk about on our walk all the way here, Lizzie?"

"You told me that what I do is no different than the Yoders' quilt making. That while their tapestry is cloth, mine is my watercolor on canvas."

"That's the truth. They make a decent amount of money selling their quilts to the *Englisch* tourists," Sadie said, coming up alongside her friend. "I could tell from the look on your face when you were discussing it with me just how happy your painting makes you. I haven't seen you so excited in a long time. Come on, Lizzie. Take Paul up on the offer."

She bowed her head, fingering the pocket on the front of her apron. Her voice quiet as she said, "There's still so much to work out."

He rested an elbow on the countertop, reminding himself that no matter how much he wanted this, he needed to tread carefully where Lizzie was concerned. He didn't want to scare her away, not when she was so close to finding a solution for her family. Not when she was so close to finding her own way.

"No, there's not," he commented. "You and I and, I'm assuming, Sadie—" he nodded in her direction "—are all in agreement that your work won't carry your name.

No one outside of these walls will ever know who the artist is. I promise."

He cocked one eyebrow, looking directly at Lizzie. "So, are we in agreement?"

All of the time she'd spent in prayer, plus seeing Paul and Sadie standing there with hopeful expressions on their faces, made Lizzie finally realize that perhaps this was *Gott*'s answer. If they thought she had such talent, surely others might, too.

She looked at Paul, standing here in his shop, the Burkholder Amish Furniture Store. A feeling of pride welled up inside of her. To her, he was the bravest man she knew and not just because of this. Because he never backed down and he never turned away from her. Not once. She wanted so much for some of his bravery to rub off on her.

The thought brought a smile to her face. And before she knew it, she was agreeing to their partnership.

"Okay. I'll do it."

Sadie grabbed for Lizzie, hauling her into her arms and squeezing her so hard, some of the breath swooshed from her lungs.

"Sadie! Let me go." Laughter bubbled up from inside of her, as Sadie's excitement was contagious.

Sadie finally released her hold. Stepping back to look at Lizzie, she said, "I'm so happy for you. This is going to be *gut* for you and your *mamm* and *vader*. Just you wait and see."

"Let's hope you're right. I'm still worried what will happen if my *vader* finds out."

"He won't," Sadie assured her.

Lizzie was simply going to have to go on faith. After

all, Sadie and Paul could be trusted. Since she planned on doing her artwork in private, she wouldn't be forced to deal with any of the customers. She could continue to keep to herself, and that suited her fine. Turning around in a circle, she looked at all of the space, paying particular attention to the walls. It was difficult for her to imagine the paintings she'd done hanging there. Blinking, she found herself looking right at Paul. The corner of his mouth quirked up as he met her gaze.

Extending one hand, he offered, "Shall we shake on our deal?"

Chapter Eight

She nervously gave him a nod, then placed her hand inside of his. His large hand swallowed hers. She felt the rough callouses of his hard work etched along the pads of his fingers. Paul gently gripped her hand. In his hand she could feel his strength. When she looked into his dark eyes, Lizzie saw his deep and abiding affection for her. Lizzie knew he wanted more than just friendship, but she just couldn't give him what she didn't feel. Not right now. After a moment she pulled her hand out of his grasp. Putting her hand in the pocket of her apron, she found herself wanting to hold on to his warmth for as long as she could. But that was not proper for an unmarried Amish woman.

Sadie cleared her throat, reminding them both they were not alone in the room.

Paul rubbed his hand down his neck.

Lizzie fumbled with the bag in her pocket.

Sadie reminded her, "We should be getting back. We don't want to worry your parents."

Paul's gaze finally slid away from her. He picked up his notepad and pen, and then he walked them to the door. "I'm going back your way—why don't you let me give you a ride?"

"That would be nice," Sadie responded.

Snapping out of her thoughts, Lizzie added, "*Ja.* I need to get back to the house if I'm to get the cream puffs made up in time for supper."

"You're making cream puffs?"

She nodded.

"I don't think our neighbors realize how lucky they are to be helping out at your father's farm."

His compliment brought another smile to her face and a blush to her cheeks. She loved cooking and never saw it as an added chore. Lizzie did her best thinking while mixing and kneading dough of all sorts. And now she could spend some of that time thinking about her next watercolor project.

Closing the shop door behind them, Paul took a key out of his pocket and locked it. He brought the buggy from around the back of the building, and then helped Lizzie and Sadie up to their seats.

Even though Paul stayed off the main route that ran through Miller's Crossing, the traffic was heavy today. He kept the wagon partway on the shoulder of the road, giving the cars and trucks as much room as possible. Still, some of the cars whizzed by them, while others slowed to a crawl. A red SUV pulled to a stop in front of them. The passenger window rolled down, and a woman stuck her head out the window. She pointed her cell phone at them and started taking pictures.

Both Sadie and Lizzie dropped their heads to their chins, averting their faces from the lens of the camera. Lizzie covered her face with both hands, wishing she were riding in her parents' buggy. At least then she'd have the sidewall to hide against. Paul turned his back to the right, doing his best to conceal her with his body. He gave the reins a gentle slap against the horse's hind-quarter, urging the animal along as he ignored the tourist. The wagon jostled over a pothole. Lizzie's shoulder bumped against Paul's. She slid away from him so their bodies weren't touching. Eventually the car pulled away, but she knew it would be only a matter of time before another one came along.

Paul couldn't protect her forever.

Even though wintertime was not her favorite season, on summer days like this she longed for the quiet solitude that came with the snow-covered ground. The tourists stayed away from their community during the winter, and Lizzie did her best baking during those months. Not only did the house fill with wonderful scents, but the heat from the oven filled the kitchen with much-needed warmth. Now that she'd agreed to show her artwork at Paul's store, she could also use her time to do more watercolors. Her mind began to swirl with the images she'd like to put on paper. She wanted to continue to work on the one she started while she and Paul were on their picnic.

They went up and down one of the longer rolling hills. Lizzie lifted her face to the sky, feeling the warm breeze wash over her skin. A hawk circled above them. Down in the valley she could see fields of freshly mowed hay. The cuttings were in neat rows, waiting to be picked and formed into square bales by the baler. The road passed a fenced-in field where some cattle lazily grazed.

She cast Paul a sidelong glance, observing how deftly he handled the horse and buggy. The leather reins were looped loosely through his strong fingers. With a simple tug on those straps, he led the horse around a pothole. Today they'd made a big decision. She hoped with all her heart that it would be the right one.

"Do you think I was pressuring you?" His deep voice carried to her over the breeze.

She looked up at him in surprise, wondering how he'd known her thoughts. "*Nee*. I am doing this for all the right reasons. My only hope is that if my *vader* ever finds out where the extra money is coming from that he'll be able to forgive me."

"There won't be anything to forgive, Lizzie. You are only doing what needs to be done to save your family."

Lizzie wanted to believe him. But as they continued home, the self-doubts continued to swirl around her.

Beside her, Sadie fidgeted. *"Was iss letz?"* Lizzie asked. "What's wrong, Sadie?" When she continued to move around on the seat, Lizzie warned, "If you don't hold yourself steady, you'll end up dumping us both out on the road."

Leaning in close, Sadie whispered into her ear. "I'll tell you when we're alone."

She would just have to be satisfied with that answer. They rode in silence for the remainder of the trip home. Lizzie had Paul let them out at the end of the driveway.

Once they were standing alongside the buggy, Paul said, "Lizzie, I need you to bring me a half dozen of your watercolors. If you get them to me in the next few days, I can get them framed properly and hung on the walls."

Lizzie started to tell him that she'd changed her mind when he said, "You've got to trust me on this, Lizzie. All will be well. I'm sure of it."

Looking up at him sitting tall and oh so sure of himself on that buggy seat, it wasn't lost on her how handsome a man he was. Lizzie's heart skipped a beat. She didn't comment on what he'd said, only giving him a nod as they said their goodbyes.

Paul had barely pulled away before Sadie started talking to Lizzie. Her hands moved about, the motions punctuating each word. She was talking so fast that Lizzie could hardly keep up with what she was saying.

"There *is* something going on between you and Paul. And I think it's high time you both admitted it!"

She stared at her friend, frustration rolling through her. "We've had this conversation before. I told you we are just *gut* friends."

Sadie's eyes narrowed, and her mouth puckered. Folding her arms in front of her, she appeared to be taking a stance. For the life of her, Lizzie didn't know why Sadie had decided now was the time to discuss this matter.

"I've seen the way he looks at you, Lizzie. His eyes get this serious look in them. And you might not realize this, but you also get a look on your face."

"I do not!"

Sadie's head bobbed up and down. "*Ja.* You do."

Curious, Lizzie asked, "How do I look?"

"For one thing, you seem to blush *a lot* when you're with Paul."

Lizzie looked away from Sadie, embarrassed that she couldn't hide her feelings when she needed to the most.

Continuing with her assessment, Sadie added, "Plus think about all the things he's been doing for you that go above and beyond what all the other neighbors have done over the past few weeks." Lowering her voice, she said, "And Paul is selling your art to help your family because he cares a great deal for you. It's more than just friendship. And I'm thinking I might stand right here at the end of your driveway until you admit that what I'm saying is true."

Lizzie loved Sadie with all her heart, but right now she didn't want to discuss this. There was still so much that needed to be done before the day ended. She stepped around her friend. She started down the drive, but then she paused to look over her shoulder at her dear Sadie, who stood there trying to look formidable and failing miserably.

Lizzie gave her a lopsided smile, saying, "You can't stay there. Besides, it's time to start supper. Your *mamm* will be worried about you if you don't return soon. And I have to get my cream puffs made."

With that she hurried off, but not before she heard Sadie grumbling about how right she was and how wrong Lizzie was. She felt sorry she couldn't make her understand her feelings on this matter. Everyone knew that Paul Burkholder would make a fine husband. But not for Lizzie.

If he decided on a courtship with another woman, she would lose the special friendship she'd always had with him. A lump formed in the back of her throat. What would she do then?

As if to rid herself of this thought, she gave a quick shake of her head. She needed to concentrate on the here and now, and not think about what might lie in the future. Lizzie slowed her steps as she approached the front porch of her home. She heard the creak of the rocker. Pausing with one foot on the bottom step, she looked up to see her *vader* seated in his favorite spot.

"Lizzie. What kept you so long? Your *mamm* and I were beginning to worry about you." Her *vader* sat with his head resting against the back of the chair.

"I'm sorry for being late. After we were finished at the grocery store, Sadie and I ran into Paul. He gave us a tour of his new store."

"This store of Paul's, it is a big one?"

"He took over the space that used to be a dress shop. The building is the one across the street from Decker's store."

"*Ja.* I know which one you're talking about." He sat up taller in the rocker. "I understand Paul's *vader* isn't pleased with his son's choice to open this store."

"Paul and his *vader* are working through this."

Her *vader* grunted his displeasure, saying, "Paul should abide by his *vader*'s wishes."

Shifting her weight from one foot to the other, she avoided his gaze, instead concentrating on the way the breeze carried the sweet scent of honeysuckle through the air. Knowing better than to say anything further on the subject, Lizzie asked, "Is *Mamm* inside?"

"*Ja.* She's working in the kitchen. Lizzie, would you do me a favor and bring me out my Bible?"

She pushed open the screen door, seeing her mother standing at the sink with a teakettle in one hand. She was looking out the window, her mouth tilted with a smile. Even on those hard days, her *mamm* always seemed to find something to smile about. She wondered what the cause of it was today.

"I've been watching the wrens working on their nests out in the birdhouses." She glanced at Lizzie and then, looking back out the window, quoted, "'By them shall the fowls of the heaven have their habitation, which sing among the branches.' Psalms 104:12. Come join me for a minute at the window."

"I have to fetch *vader*'s Bible."

"Do that and then come back."

Lizzie found the Bible on the stand next to her *vader*'s favorite living room chair. She grabbed it, took it out to him and then rejoined her *mamm* at the sink. Standing shoulder to shoulder with her, she saw the tiny lines surrounding her eyes and noticed the gray streaks running through her hair.

"Look at that one!" Her *mamm* let out a laugh. "The little bird has been pecking and poking at the others the whole time I've been watching them."

Lizzie saw the bird dip down and seemingly shove the other bird off the ledge of the birdhouse. The white house had three stories to it and was attached to a high pole, so it stood well off the ground. The birds worked at a frantic pace, emptying the space of the old nest. Soon a new one would replace it. Then the birds would move in, the mother bird would lay her eggs and in a few months' time a new family would hatch. The tiny fledglings would then take flight, leaving the nest forever.

She couldn't imagine ever leaving her family behind.

Her *mamm* turned to her and smiled. "Have you been having a *gut* day so far?"

"Ja."

"I heard from your sister Mary today. She and Aaron will be here in time for Rachel's wedding. She wanted to come sooner to visit, but two trips would be too much for them to make."

"They must be busy."

"Ja, Aaron is helping his family begin their harvest.

It would be selfish to insist they come here now to visit your *vader* and then again for Rachel's wedding."

"I understand," Lizzie said, taking the baking powder out of her pocket. "I was going to make cream puffs for the workers, but I fear the day has gotten too late to start another baking project."

"You did all those loaves of bread. They'll be happy with that, for sure and certain."

Lizzie went to the counter, where she'd left out the ingredients earlier, and put them back on their shelves in the pantry. Then she and her *mamm* began to make the evening meal. From the porch came the sound of the rocker creaking. She heard the soft turn of a Bible page, then the muffled sound of her *vader*'s voice in prayer.

"*Gott*, I ask you for patience. Patience with my recovery from this illness that has taken over my body, patience for the harvest and patience for my daughter Elizabeth. Help her to see your way and the way that is best for this family. Amen."

Her *mamm* must have heard his words, too, because she turned to face Lizzie. She let out a long sigh.

"Do you remember the nerves that Mary had right before her wedding?"

Lizzie nodded.

"But then she discovered how much she loved Aaron and how good her life with him could be. Lizzie, your *daed*, he only wants what's best for you."

"His prayer said it all, *Mamm*. He wants what's best for his family. I'm not sure he cares what my feelings on the matter of marriage are. I know that I'm supposed to follow his wishes, but…" She let out a frustrated sigh, thinking about how, with Paul's urging, she'd committed to doing something to help her family. She just couldn't discuss this with them yet.

Absently she ran her fingertips over her scar. Thinking how her *mamm* had been the one to nurse her back to health. She'd been the one to sing softly to her at night as she had cried herself to sleep. Her *mamm* had been the one to clean her wounds, the one to hold her close and whisper comforting prayers. She'd understood Lizzie's anguish then, just as she understood Lizzie's uncertainty now. She realized now that she wanted to unburden herself. And she would have done so, but Lizzie knew it wasn't right to expect her *mamm* to keep her plan from the rest of the family. Especially her *vader*.

Lizzie vowed right then that if this venture became a financial success, she would tell them about it. But until that time, she knew it was better not to get anyone's hopes up.

Dropping her hands to her side, Lizzie said, "I have nothing to offer a *mann*."

Her mother reached out to her, tapping a finger lightly against Lizzie's chest, over the spot where her heart lay.

"You have everything a good *mann* would want, right here inside of you."

Perhaps it was the excitement of the day catching up with her, but suddenly Lizzie found herself wiping away tears. Taking her *mamm*'s hand in hers, she gave it a gentle squeeze, whispering, *"Danke."*

As they turned their attention to preparing and serving the evening meal, the day wound down and Lizzie was finally able to make an escape to her bedroom. Once there she shut the door and leaned her back against it, relishing the silence. Reaching down, she unlaced her black leather shoes, setting the pair right in front of her nightstand like she did every night. Then she slid off her dark stockings, enjoying the feel of the coolness of the evening air on her bare legs, and draped them across the bottom of her bed.

Padding across the bare floor, she made her way to the dresser, knelt down and opened the bottom drawer. She pulled out the first five drawings and spread them around her, trying to decide if any of them were worthy to sell. She twisted her mouth, trying not to grimace at how bad these looked. After pushing them aside, she hauled out the entire drawer and placed it onto the floor. Swishing her hand through the mess of paper, she gazed at the array of colors and sketches. Why did this choice have to be so hard? she wondered.

Finally she settled on six of her more recent works of the fields surrounding the Miller farm. The images were in various stages of the seasons. Her particular favorite was one of the field behind the barn. She remembered working on this during the early spring. The newly formed buds on the trees and the fresh green grass poking through the earth so recently ravaged by the winter's cold had captured her attention. Looking at this watercolor, she found her spirit being filled with hope and warmth.

The remaining watercolors depicted the field transforming from spring to summer, eventually ending with a winter scene. Lizzie remembered how hard this one had been to work on. She'd only used a few colors from her palette. Adding grays and deep blues to the white paper, creating a very chilly looking winter scene. She hoped Paul's handiwork with the framing would add a touch of warmth to the starkness of this image.

Gathering the watercolors, she stood up and walked back to the bed, where she laid them out. She took the canvas bag she'd taken on the picnic off the coat rack on the wall and then very carefully, so as not to wrinkle the paper, slid them one by one into the bag. A tingling feeling of excitement wound its way along her spine. Lizzie had no idea what kind of money she could get for these, but she knew even the tiniest bit could help. The sale of her eggs, baked and canned goods at her roadside stand did help, but this, well, this could be far greater than anything she could imagine. She could help her family by taking some of the financial burden off them. Maybe her *vader* would eventually understand that Lizzie didn't need to take a husband in order to help run the farm the farm.

"Ach!" She was getting ahead of herself. Bowing her head, she asked the Lord once again for guidance.

"Dear *Gott*, thank You for giving me this talent. Help me to use it for good. Remind me that wealth in this world that has nothing to do with money. Thank You for looking over my family. Amen."

She raised her eyes to see the muted glow of the last of the setting sun reflected on the wall. She walked to the window and pulled aside the curtain so she could take in the full view of the final vestiges of the day fading to dusk. Her mind raced to memorize what lay before her. The colors in the sky meeting the horizon, melding together in beautiful reds and pinks. The barn in the foreground and the fencing surrounding the pasture all bathed in this stunning, soft, heavenly light. She heard the soft mooing of one of the cows and the rustle

of hooves as the herd wandered over the pathway leading to the edge of the pasture.

She knew then that she was using her talent in the
way that *Gott* had intended. If only she felt confident that
her parents would be as happy about her artistic talents
as Paul was. Pushing those thoughts aside, Lizzie hurried to get her sketch pad. Once she had it in her hands,
she raced back to the window, where she spent the next
hour sketching the glory as dusk became twilight. The
more she sketched, the deeper her inner peace became.
Gone were her self-doubts, and in its place came the
knowledge that she could create beautiful images that
captured the farm life that she'd grown up with.

The clock in the living room struck nine times. Lizzie
looked up from the paper, surprised that so much time
had passed. She started to flip the top of the sketch pad
closed when her eyes caught sight of the barn and then
the watercolor she'd started working on when she'd been
with Paul. These two works had been giving her fits and
starts since she'd first drawn them. The barn painting
carried with it a lot of memories and pain, while the
other reminded her of things she might never have in
her life. Maybe one day soon she'd find the time to get
back to finishing them.

Putting her supplies away, she got ready for bed.
There was another busy day ahead tomorrow. But long
after she'd made herself comfortable under the blanket,
her mind was still wandering, full of thoughts of the
future. She knew one thing for sure and certain. Tomorrow she would go to Paul's shop and leave him the
watercolors she'd selected. No matter her doubts, Lizzie
knew this was the only way she could help her family.

Chapter Nine

Paul stood inside the Burkholder Amish Furniture Store, watching the rain dripping from the awning hanging over the front window onto the sidewalk outside. What a dreary day, he thought, but a good day to putter around his shop. He'd finished making the small rocking chairs here and the larger pieces of furniture he was still making back at his *vader*'s shop. His *bruders* had come by late Friday to help him move the large wooden counter from the center of the room over to the side. He'd decided to use it as the cashier area. Not anticipating a lot of store traffic today, he'd decided to organize that space, in addition to rearranging the furniture displays.

He'd been reading up on what attracted buyers. Even though, he suspected, most of them came inside simply because they saw the word *Amish* on the store sign, Paul wanted to continue to keep things fresh inside the store. Looking around, he felt such pride in all that he'd accomplished in the short time he'd been open. He turned his attention to the stack of mail next to the cash register and was thumbing through it when a car pulled up in front of the store.

Recognizing the sedan, he went to the front door. He saw Helen Myers sitting behind the wheel of the car, and next to her in the passenger seat sat Lizzie. Helen leaned across the seat as Lizzie got out, giving him a big wave.

"Hey, Paul. Congratulations on your new store. I'll stop by when I'm not busy running errands."

Ducking under the overhang, he called out, "*Danke*, Helen."

Lizzie pushed the door closed and hurried to join him. The rain had turned to a spotty drizzle. He noticed the drops on her gray raincoat and in her honey-colored hair. She looked up at him and gave him a nervous smile.

"I hope you're not busy," she said in a soft voice.

He let out a laugh. "No! This rain is keeping everyone at home." Paul stood there looking at her, so happy she'd come by today.

"Can I come inside?"

"Oh. Yeah. Sorry about that. Here, let me get the door for you." It was then that he noticed she was hugging a canvas bag. When she entered the store ahead of him, he asked, "Are you in town to do some shopping?"

"*Nee.* I came to bring you these."

Before she even made it to the counter to set her bag down, Paul was hoping she'd finally brought him some of her watercolors.

"I was going to come yesterday, but we were so busy at the farm and my *vader* was feeling strong enough to do light work. So *Mamm* needed me to keep an eye on him." She let out a laugh. "He thinks he can do what the rest of the men do, but he's not ready for a full day just yet."

She set the bag up on the counter. Patting the dampened fabric, she turned to look at him. He could see the uncertainty clouding her eyes.

"Lizzie, this is very exciting!"

"Now, don't be getting ahead of yourself. I'm not even sure you'll like the ones I've chosen."

Stepping close to her, he caught the faint scent of lemons and noticed the tiny freckles on her nose. Softening his voice, he replied, "I know I'll love whatever you decide on."

"So, now you're going to be my number-one fan?" she teased.

"*Ja.* And I can guarantee I can sell whatever you bring here."

She dipped her eyelids and nibbled her lower lip, her hand still resting on the top of the canvas bag. He could see the edge of the watercolors peeking out. Paul knew it had cost her a lot to come here. He'd been so busy these last few days that he hadn't even seen her. But Lizzie had never been far from his thoughts. And now here she was, putting her talent and her courage on the line. He knew enough to handle the situation with great care. Lizzie could be as stubborn as the day was long. But this was a matter of trust, and the last thing he wanted was to frighten her away and send her running back home.

She reached into the bag to slide out the sheaf of papers. Paul raised his eyebrows. He shook his head in disbelief. Where had she been hiding these? he wondered. He'd only seen a few of the pieces she'd been working on. But one look at these images and he immediately recognized the hard corner of the barn, the white clapboard fencing, and the rolling green pastures dotted with new spring grass to be the field outside the barn where the Miller cows grazed. He helped her lay the artwork out on the counter.

"Lizzie. You've outdone yourself. These are lovely." Paul gazed from the artwork to her.

There was a sparkle in her blue eyes he'd never seen before. A light pinkish blush rose on her cheekbones. Her face took on a glow at his praise.

"I thought I could part with these the easiest. And I think they are what you're looking to put in your shop."

He ran his fingertips over the papers, nodding. "These landscapes will most certainly complement my work. Wow! Lizzie, I had no idea you had these."

"Oh, there are a lot more where these came from. But I must admit that my earlier work is pretty primitive. Art is like so many things in life—you need to keep practicing until you get it right."

Gathering her hand in his, Paul gave it a gentle squeeze. "You're right," he said, wanting to tease her, but instead his voice came out in a strained whisper.

She started to tug her hand out of his reach, but he held fast. Lizzie held his gaze and he could see the struggle brewing inside of her. A bit of the sparkle left her. Her mouth tightened into a thin line. Paul didn't know how else to convince her that this was the *right* thing— that *they* could be right together. Somehow his thoughts were no longer just about Lizzie selling her art here.

Finally she said, "*Nee*, I'm far from right. Just think about what we're doing here today. I went behind my family's back. Even if the end justifies the means, I wish I didn't feel so bad about it."

He gave her a quick wink. "You want to know something?"

She cocked her head to one side, waiting for him to answer his own question.

"I'd be very worried about you if you didn't feel that

way about coming here. Family is important to both of us. After all, they are the reason we are both here. Come on—I'm going to show you where all the framing will be done. We can take these to the back room and pick out the ones you think will be the best fit."

"How difficult can that be?" Lizzie asked.

He let out a laugh, thinking Lizzie had a lot to learn about the different types of wood that could go into making a frame. The right choice made all the difference.

Picking up the watercolors, he directed her to the back room. "I'll get you started."

As they entered the work area, he said, "You can hang your coat on the hook over there." He pointed to a spot on the wall near the back door.

Once she'd done that, Paul showed her to the place where he'd set up the framing area. Corners of frames hung on a pegboard behind the counter. "You can pick out anything you want. I have the wood set aside for your frames."

Lizzie studied the choices. "I like the darker colors for the fall picture."

"That's a good choice." He took the corner piece from the pegboard and lined it up along the edge of the paper. *"Ja."* He agreed after seeing the match.

They couldn't have been there for more than ten minutes when Paul heard the front door open. "I've got to go see who came in. You keep working on this." He excused himself.

Walking through the doorway, back out into the front of the shop, Paul saw an Amish man bent over, looking down at one of the small children's rocking chairs he'd created last week. As the man stood and turned around, Paul recognized him. Squaring his shoulders, he walked across the floor to greet him.

"*Vader*. What brings you into the village on this rainy day?"

The man scrunched up his eyes, narrowing his gaze to look at his son. "I've come to see for myself this folly my son has entered into."

Paul called on every bit of strength and patience he had. His *vader* had no business coming here and insulting him. But his *vader* deserved his respect, no matter how hard it was to give at the moment.

"I don't see this as a folly. This is where my future lies."

The man scoffed. "That remains to be seen." Waving a hand around, he continued, "You've been working on some new pieces, I see."

"*Ja*, I have." Paul wondered if this meant he might be softening toward the idea of this store.

"I've a lot of work orders that need filling."

Since Paul had been talking with his *bruders*, he knew that wasn't exactly the truth. Their cabinet shop had been slow these past few weeks. Right before Paul had opened, he'd been working on finishing up the one big order they'd had all summer. All the more reason for his *vader* to realize that having a place here in the village was needed.

Shoving his hands in his pockets, he studied the man standing before him. Age was slowly making its way over his face, leaving behind wrinkles that fanned out around the corners of his dark eyes. His hair and beard were almost all gray. And now Paul noticed a slight hunch to his *vader*'s shoulders. He knew his vader was getting on in years, but he also knew the man's life as a cabinetmaker was nowhere near over.

"Paul, I'm going to get right to the point of my visit. I want you to close up this shop and come back to our business. I can't have you splitting us up."

"I don't think I'm doing that."

"*Ja.* You are. I know that Ben and Abram have been helping you here. Taking time away from their projects at the cabinet shop."

"They offered to come over after their day was completed. And you know I would never pull them from you," Paul said, feeling the anger and frustration at his *vader*'s narrow-mindedness creeping over him.

Aware that Lizzie could overhear what was being said, he tried again. "I want to do this. And I'm doing this for all the right reasons."

"What? You think coming here to be closer to the *Englischers* is our way? We need to stick together to keep our community growing. And here you are wandering off like you're having a *rumspringa!*" His *vader*'s voice rose.

Paul shook his head. Keeping his voice low, he said, "It's nothing like that, and you know it. I've told you again and again that I'm doing this to not only secure my future but to secure a future for the entire family."

His *vader*'s face reddened. "And what of *your* future? Have you plans for a courtship yet?"

Paul looked over his shoulder, trying to figure out how much of this Lizzie was overhearing. He didn't want to be having this exchange with the man. His *vader* came closer to him. Paul stood his ground.

"You know how to respect your elders."

"I do respect you."

Vader shook his head. "At the moment I'm not sure."

"Give me time to make this work."

"And what of your courtship?" *Vader*'s expression softened a bit as some of the anger left him.

Paul looked over his shoulder once more. Lizzie was being awfully quiet back there. He wanted to answer the question, but he didn't want her to overhear his response.

"Paul, answer my question."

He frowned, replying, "I'm working on that, too."

"Listen to me, *sohn*. I know your life has had its share of ups and downs. And the Miller boy's death has stayed with you a long time."

Paul raised his eyebrows in surprise. He'd never discussed David with his *vader*. He wasn't sure how to respond, so he waited for him to finish his thought.

"You've always had a soft spot in your heart for Joseph's youngest daughter. Perhaps we should consider speaking to him…"

Holding up his hand, Paul interrupted his *vader*, stopping him from going any further. "*Nee*. Now is not the time to discuss that."

His *vader* sighed in exasperation. Some of the earlier anger seemed to have returned, because his voice rose again as he spoke. "I'm telling you, Paul, time is not going to stand still while you make up your mind about your future! If I need to intercede on both of these matters on your behalf, I will."

"Please, *Vader*, like I said before, give me time."

"You don't have long."

He escorted him to the door. Holding it open, Paul waited while he stepped out into the overcast day. The rain had stopped and the clouds were breaking up. Tiny patches of blue sky poked through the darkness of the sky. The lighter sky did little to clear the darkness from Paul's day. He waited as his *vader* got into the buggy and drove away. Turning, he went back inside to find Lizzie standing at the counter.

As he approached her, he attempted a smile, but failed miserably. "I'm guessing you overheard all of that?"

"*Ja*, I did," Lizzie answered.

She'd heard every word and her heart was breaking for him. Lizzie leaned toward him. She could see the confusion reflected in his eyes. She wanted more than ever to take some of that pain away, but she didn't know how. She put her hand on his arm. She felt his strong pulse thrumming under the pads of her fingertips. She felt the strength in the hard sinew of his forearm. Lizzie's heart melted just a bit. She didn't quite know what to do with this new feeling. She only knew that she wanted this sensation, whatever it was, to last.

For as long as she could remember, Paul had been there for her. And like his *vader* had stated, he'd been there as a constant friend and shoulder to lean on since the day David had died. She and Paul never really spoke about that day. Now she found herself wondering how he'd managed to cope over the years. She knew he'd a great faith in *Gott*, just as she did. Perhaps he drew his strength from Him. Maybe one day soon they would be able to speak about David and what a great loss his death had been for both of them.

For Lizzie's family it had also meant the end of the future for the farm. Without David there was no son left to carry on. She'd heard Mr. Burkholder telling Paul he wanted to go to her *vader* to perhaps discuss a courtship. She and Paul had already discussed the reasons why that would never work. Paul was never going to become a farmer. He was a woodworker, a furniture maker. It was his life's calling. And her family couldn't afford to hire farm help. The only way to help her family continue to make ends meet was for her to sell her artwork. As she tried to hold fast to those arguments, Lizzie could no longer deny her growing feelings for Paul. But for right now, she wanted to make him feel better about today. About his encounter with his *vader*.

Squeezing the top of his wrist with her fingers, she said, "I'm sorry about the things your *vader* said to you."

"*Danke*. I wish he'd listen to what I'm saying. Truly listen. Doesn't he know that the last thing I would ever want is to make trouble for our family?"

"I'm sure he knows. But the old ways are hard to let go of, Paul." She took her hand away from his arm.

He frowned, creating lines on his forehead. She could almost see his mind racing with thoughts. This had to be so hard for him. But Lizzie could tell his talents lay here, in the beautiful furniture he made. She turned to look around the store. Her gaze found the twin set of children's rocking chairs. They were so adorable and would make a fine addition to someone's home. She pictured a small child rocking away, perhaps with a book or doll in their tiny hands. The thought gave her pause. She'd never thought about having children of her own and now here she was, standing next to Paul, looking at his creations and thinking such thoughts.

"Lizzie?"

The sound of Paul's voice interrupted her daydream. "Hmm?"

"What's got you smiling?"

"I..." She hesitated, blinking as her thoughts collided

with the present. "I was just admiring your furniture. You do such fine work, Paul. You should be proud."

"I am. Now, if only my *vader* felt the same way you do."

"He'll come around."

"We are two peas in pod, you and I." His gaze softened as he looked down at her.

Lizzie's breath caught in her throat. She wasn't sure how to respond to his comment; instead she asked, "I decided on the frames. Would you like to come see what I've picked out?"

"Of course," Paul answered as he let her go ahead of him to the back room.

Lizzie couldn't contain her excitement. She wanted him to be as pleased as she was with her selections.

"Look at this barn wood." She had the sample piece of wood covering about half an inch of the painting. The weatherworn wood held a subtle gray patina. "I think I want that for all the frames. The look is fitting with the fields and that portion of the barn that's showing on the side."

He nodded. "I agree. This choice is much better than the darker frame you first looked at."

She set the artwork down, clapping her hands together. Lizzie couldn't remember the last time she'd felt this happy. She wanted to hold tight to the sensation. Paul must have felt her excitement, because he put his hand on her shoulder.

"I'm glad you're coming around to this idea."

"Me, too. *Danke* for pushing me to do this."

With a gentle nudge, he turned her to face him. "I'm so proud of you, Lizzie."

The look she saw in his eyes held more than pride.

Lizzie's heart began to race as her stomach did the strangest little flip-flop.

She whispered his name. "Paul."

He gazed deep into her eyes, and she knew his feelings for her were more than just friendship. Lizzie pulled away from him. Even though she felt the shift in their relationship, she couldn't help thinking she wasn't ready for this.

Then Paul spoke so softly that Lizzie had to lean in to hear him. "One day soon, Lizzie Miller, you will know that you can trust what is going on between us with your whole heart."

Then Paul turned his attention back to the frame. Running his hand over the wood, he told her, "I'll get these made up tonight."

"All right." Gathering the canvas bag, she realized that she needed to be hurrying back home. "I have to go." She was almost to the door when she turned around and said to him, "I'm working on Rachel's wedding gift. Would you be able to make me up a small recipe box?"

"Of course. Are you going to be giving away all your special recipes?" he asked, grinning at her.

She laughed at him. "Not all of them. Just a few of my jam recipes."

"I'm sure Rachel and Jacob will love your gift," he added.

"I hope so." Lizzie paused in the doorway. She looked up at Paul as her stomach gave her that little flip-flop sensation again. She didn't like feeling confused about Paul. Gripping the straps on the canvas bag, she said, "I'll see you in a few days."

He gave her a nod and gently closed the door behind her.

Chapter Ten

The next few days flew by as Lizzie found herself rushing to complete her wedding gift. She'd already made up the blueberry and the blackberry jams. Today she planned on finishing up with a batch of apple butter. She loved making this recipe because it was a perfect way to use up extra apples. However, for her cousin's wedding present, she'd used only the finest Cortland apples. The entire kitchen smelled like warm apples and cinnamon. As she took the canning jars out of the hot water bath, she couldn't help but ponder her last meeting with Paul.

Lizzie had felt that their relationship was changing. For a long time now, she'd known his feelings were more than that of just a friend. Once again her long-held insecurities reared their ugly heads. She was having trouble imagining herself as a wife. As far as she was concerned, Paul deserved someone far better than her. And yet he stuck by her through the good and bad days. In her heart of hearts, she knew there weren't many men like him.

And in her heart of hearts, she also knew she no longer saw him as just a friend.

She picked up the stainless steel ladle and began scooping the apple butter into the sterilized canning jars. The warm, spicy steam wafted up out of the jar. She filled a half-dozen jars. Then she screwed the metal lids in place. When that was done, she lined them up alongside the other filled jars, admiring her handiwork. After the jams and butter were cooled, she planned on packing them up in a basket. Lizzie also had the recipe cards in a neat pile on the counter, waiting for the recipe box Paul had said he would make for her.

These three recipes were the ones that were the most popular at her roadside shed. She let out a contented sigh. These were the best choice for the gift.

She heard boots stomping on the porch and knew her *vader* had come up for his morning tea. Anticipating this, she'd set a teakettle over low heat half an hour ago. Taking it from the stove top, she set about making his favorite cup of tea. Simple black tea with two teaspoons of sugar and a dollop of cream.

"Hello, *Daed*," she called out as he came into the *haus*.

"*Dochder*. I see you've got my tea brewing. *Danke*." Sitting down at his usual spot at the table, he said, "I'll have you know it's a fine late summer's day out there. The last cutting is going to be this week. Just in time for your cousin Rachel's wedding."

Lizzie was looking forward to Rachel and Jacob's big day. Her sister, Mary, and her husband would be arriving soon. Her *mamm* had been cleaning out the spare bedroom all week. This very minute the freshly laundered sheets were hanging to dry out on the clothesline, flapping in the breeze.

"You look to be having a great day, *Daed*."

"I am at that, Lizzie. This morning I woke up before the light of dawn and for the first time did not feel the effects of my illness. The doctors were right. Three months later, I'm as fit as a fiddle again."

After setting the pitcher of milk in the refrigerator, Lizzie took him his tea.

"I think your sister will be here today."

Lizzie raised an eyebrow, curious as to how he would know that.

"I can't keep the surprise from you, not on a day as fine as this. Her letter last week let us know when she was arriving. That's why your *mamm* has been so busy getting that room ready."

It had been almost a year since Lizzie had seen Mary. They had so much to catch up on. With Rachel's wedding and their *vader*'s illness, no doubt their chatter would fill an entire afternoon. But Lizzie couldn't wait to get her sister alone to talk about Paul.

No sooner did those thoughts leave her head than the sound of a ruckus came from out in the yard. After wiping her hands on a dish towel, Lizzie followed her *daed* outside, where they found Paul helping her sister and Aaron down from the wagon.

Lizzie took off at a run, meeting her sister halfway down the walkway. "Mary! I'm so excited that you're finally home." Lizzie let out a squeal of delight as she ran into her arms.

Their *mamm* came out from around back, running so hard, she was out of breath by the time she got there. "It's wonderful to have my *dochdern* together!"

Stepping back, she cocked her head to one side, giving Mary the once-over, observing, "Mary, you are glowing. This can only mean one thing!" their mother exclaimed, her eyes tearing up. "You're going to have a *bobbli*!"

Rubbing a hand over her stomach, Mary took hold of Aaron's arm, pulling him in close. "*Bopplin.* We're having twins."

Mamm's hand flew to her chest. "Twins! This is wonderful news."

"If it's all right, I'd like to get Mary into the house. It was a long trip and she needs to put her feet up," Aaron advised, putting a protective arm around Mary's shoulders.

Mary swatted her *mann*'s arm. "Aaron, I've told you before, I am not an invalid."

"Come along anyway," her *mamm* said, taking Mary's hand and escorting her up the steps.

Lizzie watched as her family moved to the house, leaving her alone beside Paul. Fussing with the front of her apron, she found herself happy to see him. She'd missed him. Lizzie wondered if he felt the same way about her.

"That was nice of you to bring my sister and her *mann* here."

"I had to pick up a furniture order from the workroom at my *vader*'s. There are a few cabinets that I'd finished up before I opened my shop, and the customer is ready to receive them," he explained. "The trip out here was no trouble. That's *gut* news about your sister."

"*Ja.* It is. I'm going to be an *aenti*."

"You're going to make a fine one, at that, *Aenti* Lizzie."

"Oh, my, when you say call me that, it makes the news seem that much more real."

"I have the recipe box you wanted for Rachel and

Jacob's wedding gift." He reached around to get the small box from underneath the wagon's seat.

The box looked so tiny in Paul's strong hands. He handed it to her. Lizzie stared down in awe. The cherrywood box had tiny hearts carved into all four sides. On the top were the words *Made with love.* Running her thumb over the smooth wood, Lizzie knew Rachel would get much use out of this.

Raising her eyes, she met Paul's clear gaze. "This is lovely."

"Danke." Nodding at her, he said, "Go ahead and open it."

Carefully she lifted the lid and peered inside to find a white envelope that had been folded in half. "What's this?"

"It's for you," he answered, rocking back on his heels.

Lizzie had never seen him so excited. She didn't know what to expect, but whatever was inside had Paul beaming. "I can't imagine what this could be."

"Lizzie, just open it up already."

"Okay, okay." Lizzie reached in and removed the envelope.

As she unfolded the paper, she realized it was thicker than it looked. *What on earth?* She broke the seal open and was shocked to find cash inside.

"Paul, what is this? What have you done?"

"Oh, I didn't do anything, Lizzie. It was you. This is from the sale of your first piece of art."

"This can't be. The watercolors have been there for less than a week." She stared at the money in disbelief. Quickly, she thumbed her fingers across the bills. "There must be a hundred dollars in here."

A broad smile stretched across his face. "One hundred and seventy-five dollars, to be exact."

In her excitement over seeing what he'd brought her, Lizzie pushed convention aside and flung herself into his arms. Her entire being vibrated with emotions. This money would help her family at a time when they needed it the most.

"Oh, Paul!" Her voice hitched. "Thank you." She squeezed him tightly.

The air around them seemed to grow still. Lizzie felt Paul's arms wrapped around her. She laid her head against his chest and heard the strong beating of his heart. She couldn't hold back a grin, because hers felt as if it were going to burst from her chest. For this one brief moment she allowed herself to feel safe and loved.

Lizzie pulled back a bit and stared up at him. She saw his powerful love reflected in those beautiful dark eyes. If she'd ever doubted his feelings before, now, in this very instant, Lizzie saw and felt the things he'd been trying for so long to tell her.

"Lizzie... I—"

She yearned to hear him say the words that would change her life. But the only sound she heard was that of a loud tractor engine shattering their moment. Paul dropped his arms at the same time Lizzie stepped out of his reach. Blinking up at him, she wanted to tell him to leave before her *vader* caught them in a compromising situation. But Paul just stood there watching her. She could tell he wasn't going to be moving anytime soon from where he stood.

Worry began to nibble at her conscience. Would he stay there until her *vader* came out of the house to check on them? Would Paul continue to honor their agreement now that she'd made the first sale of her art at his shop? But the biggest question she couldn't get out of her mind was how could she ever have a future with this furniture maker when her family needed a farmer?

Paul's arms felt empty without Lizzie standing in them. He knew that her feelings for him were deepening. She didn't know it, but he'd been watching her grow and change over these past months. He'd been holding out hope that she would come around to selling her art and, after that proved successful, grow to trust him…to love him. Now that those things had happened, she hadn't said that she loved him. But he could see the change in the way she felt about him from the look on her face. She wasn't looking away from him. And he hadn't seen her pull away or turn her face to hide her scar in weeks.

These were all good things and an answer to his many prayers.

Paul could be patient a bit longer. The rest would come. And one day soon he and Lizzie would declare their love for one another.

He heard the sound of Mary's laughter and Aaron joining in.

Then Joseph called out, "Lizzie! Where have you gone off to? Come join the rest of the family to welcome your sister home."

The screen door slapped closed behind the man as Joseph came out onto the porch. "There you are."

He saw them together, and Paul watched the man's eyes narrow in disapproval.

"Come. Come inside," he said, motioning to Lizzie. "Paul, you're welcome to have some pie with us to celebrate Mary's return."

"*Danke* for the offer, Joseph. But I have to get this order delivered." Paul nodded to the cabinets still needed to be unloaded. "I need to be getting on. I'm glad your family is all under one roof again."

"*Ja*. It's a happy day, indeed." The man made a big show of adjusting the straps on his suspenders.

Paul took the hint. He waved to Joseph, then turned to face Lizzie. "I'll look for you at Rachel and Jacob's wedding reception."

"I'd like that. And, Paul?"

"Yes?"

She patted the pocket she'd put the money in. "This is still just between us."

"You can count on it."

"*Gut*. I'll see you at the wedding."

Chapter Eleven

The day of Rachel and Jacob's wedding dawned gray with a cool drizzle. Soon the roads and fields surrounding the Miller farm would be covered with buggies. This was a big day in Miller's Crossing. Rachel and Jacob had a lot of family members who'd be attending, besides their friends and neighbors in the surrounding communities. From what Lizzie had heard, they were expecting almost five hundred people to show up. She'd heard about weddings where over one thousand people came to join in the celebration, so she supposed this wedding might be considered small compared to that.

She imagined if she were to have a wedding of her own, it wouldn't be anywhere near that size. The image of Paul standing tall and handsome flitted through her mind. Lizzie realized she had a long way to go as far as her feelings for him were concerned. These feelings of love were so new and fresh. A part of her wanted to embrace the sensation, while another part of her was so scared by the notion, she didn't know what to do. He'd been so kind to her over these past weeks. She looked at the spot where she'd put the money he'd brought her.

The small basket sitting on top of her dresser held the future of her family. She needed to bring him more of her artwork. She decided after the wedding was done that she'd make plans to go into town to his shop.

Aware that it was getting late, Lizzie ran her hands along the front of her best Sunday dress, making sure there wasn't a wrinkle to be seen. She ran a brush through her hair and then took great care to wind it up into a bun at the back of her head. After that she carefully pinned her prayer *kapp* on her head. The rich smell of freshly brewed coffee wafted upstairs. She headed down to join her family for their morning meal.

Her *vader* sat at the head of the kitchen table and looked up as she came into the room. His bushy eyebrows came together. "Getting a late start, aren't you, Lizzie?"

"I'm sorry," she said, heading to the stove to replace his second cup of coffee with some herbal tea.

His last doctor's visit had gone quite well. But he'd been warned about his caffeine. He needed to cut back.

Vader eyed the teapot. "Lizzie, I hope that's not for me."

Turning her head, she looked over her shoulder at him. "And what if it is? You heard what the doctor told you."

"*Ja.* But I will make do with less coffee before I ever switch to *that.*"

Resigned that she couldn't change his mind, she set the teapot off to one side on the counter. Mary and Aaron came in to join them. She thought her sister looked a bit pale, so she opened the narrow cabinet next to the stove and pulled out a box of ginger tea bags.

After grabbing the teapot, she placed a bag inside and then poured hot water from the kettle over it.

While the tea brewed, she said to her sister, "Come. Sit, Mary. I'm steeping some ginger tea I think might do you some good."

Letting Aaron hold the chair out for her, Mary sat. "*Danke.* These babies are already making their presence known. Can you get me some dry toast? Sometimes that helps with this morning sickness, too."

Mamm walked behind Lizzie, carrying a slice of toast on a white plate. "This should do the trick."

Grabbing a cup of tea for herself, Lizzie joined the family at the table. Her *vader* bowed his head and began the morning prayer.

"Lord, *danke* for this day. *Danke* for the food on our table. We are grateful for the bounty You've bestowed upon us, not only in our food, but in our growing family. May You bring blessings upon Rachel and Jacob on what I know will turn out to be a fine day. Continue to guide us all in the way You see fit."

"Amen," Lizzie whispered.

Paul stood with a group of his friends, watching the buggies roll into the yard. For over an hour he'd been waiting, looking for the right one. The problem was the buggies for the most part looked the same and, in a crowd as large as this one, it was going to be hard for him to pick out Joseph Miller's. The drizzle from this morning had given way to a sunshine-filled afternoon. The dark clouds had dissipated, leaving behind a sky as blue as the ocean.

From his vantage point Paul took in the large food tent placed in front of the barn. Alongside that was a rented food trailer. The smell of the wedding *roascht* filled the air. The roasted chicken and vegetables would continue to cook until it was time to serve the throng of people. Then the tables would be laden with the chickens, potatoes, carrots, celery and wedding cakes and pies.

Ben jostled his arm, bringing Paul's attention back to the line of buggies along the roadway.

"I think that's the one you've been waiting for." He nodded toward the Millers' vehicle.

Paul caught a glimpse of Lizzie through the window of the back seat of the buggy top and gave a wave. Paul watched as Joseph followed the direction of one the neighbor boys, driving almost all the way down to the end of the second row before finding an opening to park in. Joseph helped his wife and then Mary down from the buggy. Lizzie came next. The family came toward him, and he saw the women carrying their wedding gifts. Paul felt a bit of pride well up inside knowing that Lizzie was carrying the recipe box he'd made.

"Good afternoon, Paul," Lizzie's *vader* said, stepping out in front of his family to greet him. "We've a fine day for this celebration."

"*Ja.* That we do, sir." Paul's gaze met Lizzie's. He couldn't help but notice how pretty she looked today. She wore a dress he'd seen her wear to church services. The light blue color matched her eyes. Her honey-colored hair was up in a neat bun, underneath her prayer *kapp*.

"There's a lot of people here," Lizzie commented. "And even a few *Englischers*."

Paul saw the shadows of wariness in her eyes. She stepped back. His instincts made him want to reach out to her, to tell her not to worry, that he'd protect her from whatever she was afraid of. She ran her hand up along the right side of her face, her fingers skimming the scarred area. She didn't need to hide herself from others. He wanted to take her in his arms and comfort her. He needed to assure her that he'd always protect her, no matter what.

Except, if he were to be honest with himself, he knew he couldn't always be there to protect her. The one day she'd needed him the most, he'd been too late. Too late to save his friend David and too late to keep Lizzie from harm's way. Paul vowed he would continue to do his best to give Lizzie the life she so deserved.

Out of the corner of his eye, he caught Lizzie's *vader* watching them. Paul gave Joseph a nod and then started to walk toward the festivities. He continued to say hello to those he knew, but his attention never wavered from Lizzie. He wanted to grab hold of her hand. But he knew it wouldn't be proper to display his affections in public. His thoughts filled with the memory of their time together up on Clymer Hill. The day had been perfect for a picnic, and watching her paint, he'd been amazed at the talent she possessed.

They entered the wedding tent, where Paul joined his family. Lizzie's family sat on the benches in the row across from them. They all settled in for the three-hour ceremony.

The congregation began to sing the opening hymns as Rachel and Jacob were led off to a room with the bishop and ministers for their time of *Abroth*, admonition and encouragement. After they returned, the bishop preached a sermon about love and faith. When it came time for the Bible reading, Paul quieted, preparing his mind and heart to hear the words.

After Rachel and Jacob came forward and answered their vow questions, there came the closing prayer and then they were pronounced *Frau* and *Mann*. After the service Paul ran to catch up with Lizzie but saw her being swept away by Sadie and a few other women. She laughed at something Sadie said. It warmed his heart to see her so happy.

He joined his *bruders* under the branches of a large oak tree. Jebediah Troyer, one of the church elders, came up to him.

"How is your business faring, Paul?"

"The shop is doing better than I anticipated," Paul answered, fighting the urge to rub his hand across the back of his neck. He knew the elders had been watching the situation between him and his *vader*.

"I'm glad to hear that. You keep up the good work. I know your family will come around to your way of thinking eventually. We are praying for that."

Paul was surprised that the elders felt this way. Normally they sided with the head of the family in situations like this.

"But if it doesn't work out that way, you will return to your *vader*'s shop."

He knew better than to speak openly at a wedding about his thoughts on the Burkholder Furniture Store. Paul thanked the elder and turned as Jacob and Rachel caught his attention. The bride, wearing a new white *kapp*, and the groom, with his wide-brimmed hat—signaling that they were now a married couple—wandered around the masses of people. They tapped the single young men and women on the shoulder, pairing them off for the meal. When they came to him, Paul shook his head. The only woman he wanted to share his meal with was Lizzie. He wouldn't feel right turning down their pairing, but hoped he wouldn't have to be put in the position of declining.

Rachel bubbled with happiness. "Paul, Jacob and I want you to come with us."

Taking hold of his arm, she tugged him along to the grassy clearing, where another dining tent had been erected. "I can't…"

"You don't even know who we've picked for you," Jacob said, slapping him on the back.

He ducked his head and entered the tent. Lanterns hung from the sides of the tent and lining the tables cast a warm glow, lighting the way. The air smelled of the wedding *roascht* and wildflowers. There were Queen Anne's lace, lavender and fern fronds filling the dozens of canning jars. Outside the tent, the *kinder* chased the fireflies, hoping to catch a few to put in their empty jars. His gaze swung back into the tent filled with young couples. Some looking happier than others about their handpicked tablemates.

Then he saw her. Standing on the other side. She had her hands folded together in front of her. Her head was a bit downcast. At this very moment Paul wanted to do away with this silly tradition of walk-a-mile among the *youngies*. Unfortunately this wasn't his wedding.

"Come." Rachel beamed up at him.

She led him right to Lizzie.

"Paul!"

He heard the relief in her voice and watched as some of the tension fell from her face. He cocked his head to one side, saying, "Lizzie. It looks like we've been paired off."

"Ja."

Taking her by the elbow, Paul led her to an open spot at the long row of tables. Leaning down, he said in a soft voice, "I've been wondering where you got off to."

"Sadie and I went inside the *haus* to leave our wedding gifts. I was hoping to avoid this."

He chuckled. "Me, too. At least they put us together. I would have been angry if you'd been put with another man."

"I wouldn't have accepted," she assured him.

"I'm glad we'll be together."

"I've played at this game plenty of times before, Paul. And mostly I've been alone or left to eat with my parents." She gave a shrug, adding, "It's no big deal, but I like this go-round much better."

Paul felt a tightening in his chest. He hadn't meant his words to be hurtful. In all the years he'd stood by and watched Lizzie grow from a young girl into a young woman, it hadn't occurred to him the pain she'd been enduring. In a society that valued marriages and family, it was difficult to be single.

"I'm sorry if I sounded insensitive."

"You weren't being insensitive. You were being honest. I like honesty."

The tent filled with more couples. Pretty soon the seats across from them and on either side of them became occupied. Some of the people he recognized, and others he'd never seen before, as they came from neighboring church districts. He watched as, one after the other, their tablemates averted their eyes from Lizzie.

He felt her stiffen when a particular young man outright made a sour face in her direction.

Seeing firsthand what she'd been enduring for years sickened him. He thought he might have to ask the stranger to leave the table. Lizzie must have been sensing his thoughts, because she gave him a warning look and a quick shake of her head.

"I could ask him to leave."

"*Nee*. Don't bother. I'm fine, really."

Still he saw the hurt in her eyes and watched as she started to shield her face with one hand. He wasn't having any of this. This was a festive and joyous day, and she deserved to enjoy herself. Grabbing hold of her hand, he pulled her off the seat.

"Come on."

Leaving her napkin behind, she left the tent with him. He found them a quiet spot at the edge of the yard, away from prying eyes.

Tugging her hand out of his grip, she stood still. He suddenly realized his abrupt actions might not have helped matters.

"Paul, it's all right. I'm used to that sort of thing."

"You shouldn't have to be used to it." He scuffed the toe of his boot along the ground in front of him. "I never understood until today."

"Few people do. But I don't want people to like me or want to be with me because they feel sorry for me, either." Folding her arms across her chest, she meandered around to the other side of the pine tree they'd stopped at. "Don't ever feel sorry for me."

He heard the hurt and a bit of determination in her voice and felt like the worst kind of the worst.

Laying his hand against the rough bark, he dragged

it along as he joined her on the other side. Up until this point it had been a beautiful day. He didn't want to ruin it with the silly notion that he was sure Lizzie was thinking, that somehow he was spending time with her out of pity. He stopped moving when he came to her. She had her face turned downward, her eyes half-closed. Paul could see the scar on her cheek, except to him it was no longer a scar.

It was a part of the woman he loved.

"Elizabeth Miller, I don't feel sorry for you. You are one of the bravest, most courageous people I know. I had no idea, all these years, what you must have suffered at the hands of strangers, at the hands of those who know you," he added, thinking about the words her *vader* had said to him that day, months ago, on their front porch.

Joseph had been wrong to assume that Lizzie couldn't find love on her own. Saying that his daughter's appearance would keep her from finding a husband had been downright wrong.

Oh, Paul knew the man had said those things out of desperation, but still Lizzie deserved so much better than that. From the distance came the sound of singing. He gazed down at Lizzie, rubbing his thumb over her chin.

"Do you want to try again for something to eat?"

"*Nee.* I'm not hungry."

He tipped his head to the side, "Lizzie, don't let them keep you away."

"I'm not. I had a snack when Sadie and I dropped our gifts off, before the ceremony started."

"You're not just telling me that to make me feel better?"

"And what if I am?" she admitted.

"Well, I'd be sad that we didn't get to share Rachel and Jacob's wedding feast together." Pushing away from the tree, he offered, "Let's go see if there's any food left."

At that very moment Paul's *vader* approached them with two men flanking him. Paul recognized Silas Yoder, and from the looks of the other man, who was dressed in a white collared shirt and tan pants, Paul knew him to be an *Englischer*.

"Here you are! I want you to meet someone." His *vader* took hold of his arm, taking him away from Lizzie.

"This is Kurt Reynolds, a friend of Jacob's *vader*. He went by your shop today."

The man pushed a pair of sunglasses on top of his head, saying, "Yes, I stopped by on my way out here for the wedding. I didn't realize you'd be closed on a Thursday."

"*Ja.* We close our businesses on wedding days," Paul explained.

He didn't want to talk business. He wanted to spend time with Lizzie. She'd stepped off to the side to let him carry on this conversation.

"I've been hearing great things about your furniture. I also heard that you have a limited selection of watercolors."

Lizzie gasped.

Paul covered her reaction by taking the gentleman by the arm and leading him farther away from her. He didn't miss his *vader*'s raised eyebrows. Clearly he was surprised to hear Paul was selling art in addition to his furniture. Perhaps if the man gave Paul's venture more attention, he wouldn't have to be hearing about this. Paul tried his best to keep his frustration out of this conversation. Besides, this day was supposed to be about happiness and love, not business. He wanted to be with Lizzie.

He wanted to tell her he loved her. Today would have been a perfect day to broach the idea of a real court-ship between them. First, though, he wanted to tell her everything about the day David died. Because deep in his heart Paul knew they couldn't begin any sort of a life together until the past was laid to rest.

Suddenly he noticed that she was pulling away from him. He saw her walking off to meet Sadie Fischer. Paul started to call to her, but she turned to him, tilted her head ever so slightly and smiled.

He smiled back. The moment was interrupted by the sound of the *Englischer*'s voice.

"Would it be all right if I stopped by your furniture shop tomorrow?" he asked.

Paul snapped his head around to give the future cus-tomer his attention. "*Ja, ja.* You can come by tomorrow. That would be *gut.*"

"Good. I'll see you then."

The man held his hand out, and Paul shook it. Over the top of the man's head, he watched Lizzie join Sadie, say something in her ear and then walk off with her.

What could they possibly be talking about?

Chapter Twelve

"Lizzie! I've been looking all over for you. Do you want to come join in the singing with me?" Sadie came bounding across the lawn to meet up with her.

Her friend's bright personality always made her feel better. At some weddings, hymns would be sung after the ceremony while the presents were being opened or as an activity late into the night. And normally she enjoyed singing the hymns, but not tonight. Paul had invited her to go with him and they'd been interrupted. She found that she didn't want to go with anyone else.

"Would you mind taking a walk with me to the cake tables instead?" she asked Sadie.

"I've been seeing some delicious slices of cake being passed around. I hope there is at least some left."

Leaving the men to talk business, Lizzie fell into step alongside her friend.

"I feel like it's been days and days since we've seen each other."

Nodding her head, Lizzie agreed. "*Ja.* I've been busy feeding a lot of workers who are helping with the harvest on the farm, and working on my watercolors.

And my sister came home with news that she's having twins."

"Congratulations. You're going to be an *aenti*. I'm so happy for you and your family," Sadie said, giving her a warm hug. Then, taking a step back, she added, "I've heard some other news."

"What might that be?"

"That you have been spending a lot of time with Paul lately."

Lizzie nibbled her lower lip. Of course it would be silly to think that in a town this size anything could be kept quiet.

"Tell me this means the two of you are in a courtship." Sadie clapped her hands together.

"We are not. But…"

"Oh, but what, Lizzie? There should be no buts allowed when it comes to you and Paul being together." In her exuberance Sadie spun around. "You deserve to be happy."

Lizzie couldn't agree more. Laughing at Sadie, she commented, "I wish I had even half of your confidence."

Sadie stilled. "Do not be fooled, my friend. There are things that continue to elude me."

"Like what?"

"Like why you insist on taking so long to get to the cake tent."

Sadie linked her arm through Lizzie's. They laughed and chattered the rest of the way across the yard, finally entering the area where tables covered with white tablecloths were laden with platters of cakes and cookies. After picking up a slice of cake with blue frosting, she followed Sadie back outside. They found an empty space at one of the tables.

They dug into their cakes. When they were finished eating, Sadie asked, "Do you think your *vader* would allow you to be courted by Paul?"

Lizzie shrugged. "I'm not sure. These feelings are still so new to me. And I haven't told Paul how I feel yet."

"You need to do this. Soon. Paul is a fine man and he could be snatched up by someone else," Sadie warned, waving her fork in front of her face. "Maybe Paul will get his letter to prove his good standing in the church from the bishop and then he can ask for your *daed*'s blessing."

She knew Paul had been baptized and that getting the *Zeugnis* was merely a formality. "I don't know. I think you're getting ahead of yourself." Lizzie tried not to panic over the idea of Sadie even suggesting that Paul might find another woman.

"I've known for a long time that Paul is the right one for you." Poking the end of her fork at her, Sadie, added, "Trust what is in your heart."

Lizzie thought that might be easier said than done. Sadie wanted to wander around the wedding, visiting with friends and family, but Lizzie didn't feel up to it.

"Go ahead, Sadie. I'll wait for Paul."

"If you're sure."

Lizzie gave her a nod. "I am. Now run along."

Sadie had always been the more social one between the two of them. Even as young schoolgirls, once they'd gone out to the playground, Sadie had been the one to round everyone up for games, while Lizzie had lingered on the edge of the circle. She didn't mind that her friend went off to socialize. Lizzie enjoyed sitting here, watching everyone around her. Knowing that Paul wasn't far away. He'd be coming back to find her soon.

And if her guess were right, he'd be bringing news of a big sale with him.

Lizzie had a feeling that the *Englischer* wanted to purchase some of Paul's furniture. She didn't mind waiting, though after a while she did tire of sitting alone and decided to walk about the grounds, stopping to say hello to her brother-in-law Aaron's mother, Sara Yoder, who was busy talking to some friends. Lizzie paused to listen to their conversation. They were discussing how large the gathering was and how happy they were for Rachel and Jacob.

Though Sara Yoder wouldn't be discussing Lizzie's sister Mary's impending birth, Lizzie knew the news was a joyous time for both of their families.

As Sara Yoder and the other women went on about the wedding, Lizzie believed in her heart that this is what the Amish community was best at, welcoming new family members into the fold. Lizzie knew that, no matter what, she would never want to live anywhere other than right here. No matter what happened between her and Paul, her home would always be in Miller's Crossing.

Leaving the women's circle, she walked up a small rise, turning around at the top. Below her lay the wedding. Buggies lined the back field in rows, three deep. The canvas walls of the tents had been rolled down to help keep the bugs out. Through the plastic window cutouts, she could see the lovely lanterns all lit up. It looked so pretty. She tried to imagine what it would be like to have a grand wedding day such as this for herself. Lizzie knew it would all be too much for her.

She wouldn't mind a simple wedding ceremony with her family and close friends attending. As the singing continued and the *kinders* ran in circles on the lawn,

Lizzie allowed herself to dream about her wedding day. Of course the *mann* she'd pick would be Paul Burkholder. Not only was he a *gut* friend, but he was kind and caring. Now that she thought about it, he'd always been a part of her life. And she couldn't imagine her life without him.

She wandered down near the barn, with the fireflies buzzing around her. Lizzie let out a sigh. There must be a million stars shining in the sky tonight. She had to find Paul to show him this glory. Suddenly she was startled by a sound coming from the bushes.

Paul walked toward her out of the darkness.

"Oh, it's you, Paul. Did you have a *gut* meeting?"

"I did." He came closer and put his hands on her shoulders.

She felt his strength and warmth emanate through his hands, and she felt his…love. They stayed like that for a few minutes, until Paul let go. She gave him a questioning look, wondering what this was all about.

"The man, Mr. Reynolds, he wants to come by the shop tomorrow. He's interested in the dining room set. You know, the one I've had on display since I opened?"

She nodded.

"And, as you know, he's heard about your art. As it turns out he knows the person who bought the first piece. I guess they've been raving about you."

"Me?" Lizzie felt panic rising. No one could know she was the artist. No one.

Paul immediately grabbed her hands, holding them in his. "I promise no one except for myself and Sadie know you're the artist. What I should have said is they are raving about the anonymous artist."

She breathed a sigh of relief. "That's better. Well, I'm pleased this day has turned out well for you and for me."

"The day has been better than okay, Lizzie. With the sale of the dining set and your artwork, some of the burdens are being lifted from us and our families. I've been thinking this could be a good time to reconsider our relationship."

The expression on his face made her laugh.

"You're joking!"

"Actually I'm quite serious about this. I'd give you more time to think about this, but I think you've had enough time already."

"Not even courting me yet, and here you are, bossing me around."

"I would never." He picked up her hands, brought them to his lips and kissed the top of each one. "I've waited a long time for us to court and I need everything to be just right."

Her eyes widened. Was he going to kiss her on the lips? Tonight she'd be perfectly content with the affection he'd been showing her. But the thought of his mouth on hers made her feel like nothing else on earth. Not even the joy she took from her paintings and watching the sunset could compare. He came closer, his arms grazing hers. She looked up into his eyes and once again felt overwhelmed by the love she saw there.

She so wanted to have the courage to pour her heart out to him, to say the words he most wanted to hear. But she didn't want to give her heart to him only to have her *vader* take all of this away if he didn't approve of a courtship between them.

Then he said, "I'd like to come by your house tomorrow. I have something I need to tell you."

"*Ja*. I'd like that," she answered as a tiny bit of doubt managed to creep back in.

Lizzie did her best to fight off any uncertainty about their relationship, deciding that loving someone could be a hard and sometimes unpredictable part of life.

"The night is getting on. Let me get you back to your parents."

Lizzie let him hold her hand as they walked back to the cake tent. She tipped her head back one last time, wanting to memorize the beauty of the night sky. The stars sparkling way up in the heavens gave her hope. A star shot across the inky sky.

"Paul! Did you see that?"

"I did."

She squeezed his hand, looking forward to what tomorrow might bring.

Sitting on the edge of his bed, Paul bowed his head in morning prayer. Afterward he rose, took his hat from the peg behind his bedroom door and walked downstairs to the kitchen. His *mamm* stood at the stove, stirring a pot of what smelled like bread and butter pickles. The tangy odor tickled his nose.

Looking up at him, she said, "Good morning, Paul. Do you have another busy day planned?"

"I do." He didn't explain further.

After pouring himself a cup of coffee, he leaned a hip against the counter while he sipped the dark brew.

"Your *vader* tells me that your shop is doing well. He said an *Englischer* is buying one of your dining room sets."

"*Ja*, he is."

Setting the stainless steel spoon on the spoon rest, his *mamm* turned to give him her full attention.

"This rift between you and your *vader*... It's going to end soon."

He couldn't tell if that were her wishful thinking or a command to make it happen. Either way he planned on dealing with his *vader* later today. When it came to stubbornness, the two of them were evenly matched. Knowing this estrangement had not been easy on his *mamm* made him realize he needed to fix the situation. Soon.

But first things first.

His *mamm* ended the silence. "Let me make you some eggs before you head out."

Putting his coffee cup in the sink, he declined his *mamm*'s offer to cook him breakfast. "*Danke, Mamm*, but I've got a lot going on this morning."

She put her hands on her hips, giving him a stern look. "You're going to skip breakfast? You'll be starving by noontime."

He dropped a kiss on her forehead and he said, "I'll be fine, *Mamm*."

Putting his hat on, Paul headed out the door. He went into the barn, and after hitching the mare to the buggy, climbed up into the seat and started out to the Miller house. Though he'd rehearsed in his head what he wanted to say to her a hundred times, to actually tell her the things in his heart and on his mind made him very nervous.

He'd never felt this way before; the sensation that his stomach was all tied up in knots had him shifting on the seat. He prayed one more time, this time asking *Gott* for strength. Taking a deep breath, he blew it out as he made the final turn into the Millers' drive. He spotted Lizzie on the front porch, sitting next to her sister.

Lizzie had been so happy when she'd told him that her sister would be having twins. One day he wanted to have a family of his own.

He wanted to have a family with Lizzie.

Stepping down from the buggy, he looped the leather reins over the hitching post next to the house. Squaring his shoulder, he climbed the steps to greet Lizzie and Mary.

"Paul Burkholder, did you know my sister has a talent as an artist?"

He looked at Lizzie, who shook her head.

"I may have heard a rumor. Good morning, ladies."

He noticed a slight blush creeping over Lizzie's delicate cheekbones as she acknowledged him. "Good morning, Paul."

Dropping her brush into a canning jar filled with water that looked as if it had been clouded with several colors, she turned to look up at him, saying, "Aaron is out in the fields with *Vader*, and *Mamm* went into the village with our neighbor Mrs. Meyer to pick up some prenatal vitamins for Mary. I decided to put some more work in on the picture I started a few weeks ago."

He walked in front of Mary and stood behind Lizzie, looking over her shoulder. His heart clenched when he saw the image of the barn. The fine lines of the building set against the backdrop of the summer field tugged at him. The barn doors were cracked open just enough to see the darkness inside the building. He noticed that Lizzie had added in a lilac bush on the right side. Glancing over his shoulder, he noticed there wasn't one there. It struck him then. She'd painted this scene as she'd remembered the setting from that long-ago day. With each stroke of her brush, Lizzie managed to pull a peaceful beauty out of a day marred with tragedy.

He was in awe of her talent.

"Hey. Can you take a break?" Paul inquired.

"Mary, will you be okay if Paul and I take a walk?" Lizzie asked.

"Actually, if it's all right with both of you, I'd like to take Lizzie for a ride back up to Clymer Hill."

His mention of their picnic spot brought a sudden smile to Lizzie's lips.

"Let me put these things back in my room," Lizzie said, gathering the painting and her art supplies.

As soon as Lizzie went inside, Mary said to Paul, "I need you to be careful where Lizzie is concerned. She's been through a lot in her short life. I don't want to see her hurt again, Paul."

"I would never hurt her."

"I understand. But since there is no official courtship between you, you must know how fragile she can be." Mary shifted her weight in the rocking chair.

"Do you need me to get anything for you?" he offered.

"I'm fine, *danke*. One more thing. My sister has led a very sheltered life. Even in the short time that I've been home, I've seen the changes in her. Changes for the *gut*. Please don't do anything to ruin that."

Paul would never do anything to intentionally hurt Lizzie. He knew that Mary meant well, still it bothered him that she would think that he was the sort of man who would lead a woman on and then walk away. If Paul had his way, he would never leave Lizzie. Ever.

Chapter Thirteen

As Paul drove them to their special place at Clymer Hill, he thought about what Mary had said to him. He, too, had seen the change in Lizzie. While part of it might be due to their changing relationship, he wanted to believe the happiness and confidence starting to grow in Lizzie had come from within her. He parked the buggy, raising his eyebrows in worry. He hoped bringing her here would be the right thing.

Helping her down from the buggy, Paul didn't think he had the strength to talk about David's death. In order to give her the love he had, Paul needed to tell her everything. Digging deep in his soul, he called upon his faith in *Gott* to help as he walked hand in hand with the woman he loved. They made their way over to sit on the bench situated on a grassy knoll overlooking Miller's Crossing.

She tipped her head to the sky, letting the sunlight bathe her in warmth. Paul smiled as he gazed at her. He knew she'd no idea of how pretty she was. They were taught at a very young age that thinking of one's appearance, other than cleanliness, was considered shallow and not serving the Lord. Lizzie was as far from shallow as a person could get. He rubbed his thumb across the top of her hand. She turned to give him a small smile.

"Lizzie, I…" He stopped himself from saying the last two words: *love you*. With all his being, he loved her. But before he could say those words, he needed to confess his sin.

Nervously he looked out over the vista, watching a hawk circling above the field, searching for its next prey. The bird flapped its wings once and then let the breeze carry it over the field. The bird soared higher and higher, until it was just a speck in the sky.

Keeping his eyes focused on the horizon, he said, "Lizzie, I want to talk about the day David died."

She said nothing, and Paul let the silence hang between them. Why did life have to be filled with such pain? he wondered. When still she didn't respond, he faced her so he could see all of her. The happiness he'd seen in her eyes a short time ago was gone. Her skin looked ashen, and her mouth was downturned, but it was the look in her eyes that shattered his soul.

The light blue color had turned a dark and stormy shade. Tears glistened at their corners. Lizzie pulled away from him. Her body stiffening as her hand slid out of his grasp. Paul's hand felt cold and empty without hers in it. Memories from that day flooded his mind. He closed his eyes, seeing those images again…

It was as if time had stood still and he was that thirteen-year-old boy again, on the cusp of becoming a man. At the time of the accident, he'd been helping his daed *finish up a cabinet when they'd heard the sound of the bell tolling. Three rings sounded in quick succession, followed by a short pause and then three more.*

He rushed to the doorway, calling out, "Daed! There's trouble!"

"Ja! *Clancy Yoder stopped by here a few minutes ago. There's been an accident over at Joseph Miller's farm.*"

Paul's stomach clenched. He was supposed to be out playing with his friends David and Lizzie Miller, but at the last minute he'd been asked to help finish up a furniture order for the Englisch *family down the road. Catching up to his* vader, *who was already in their buggy, Paul hitched himself up on the seat beside him. The buggy sped onto the roadway, where they joined a dozen other worried neighbors who'd heard the alarm.*

When they reached the Miller farm, a line of black buggies were already crowding both sides of the driveway. Jumping from the seat, he and his daed *hurried along with everyone else, heading toward the barn.*

Running as fast as he could, he pumped his arms and legs harder and harder until his lungs burned. Neighbors shouted as he bumped into them. He didn't care; he had to get to the barn. He elbowed his way through the group of men blocking the large double-hung white doors. Once inside he paused and bent over at the waist, trying to catch his breath. Gulping in the dust-filled air, he coughed. He raised his head, wiped his hand over his mouth and hurried toward the men who stood huddled around a small body.

A brown-booted foot poking out from beneath a loose pile of hay. David. No! Paul's chest tightened. The rest of his friend's body was twisted at an odd angle at the bottom of a stack of tall hay bales. As he moved closer, he heard sobbing. A pool of blood lay beneath David Miller's head. He fisted his hand against his mouth to keep from crying out...

Paul swiped his hand over his eyes, feeling the prick of the tears well up behind his eyelids. The memory still made him choke up. He swallowed hard, feeling the same panic.

Finally he said, "Lizzie, on that day, after I saw David and I couldn't find you, I thought you might be..."

He couldn't bring himself to finish the sentence. He pulled in a deep breath. His heart was racing, and his stomach muscles were clenching at the memories flooding his mind. Memories he tried so hard to forget. He felt her hand on his, and some of the warmth returned.

"I had searched for you, but it was so hard to see through the groups of neighbors who had come to help. I remember a tall man stopping me. Blocking my path. 'This is no place for a young boy,' the man said."

Paul blinked again. "I remember trying to push past him. I called out to you."

"I don't remember much from that day, Paul. I am so very sorry."

"Ethel Yoder told me to go outside and wait with the others." He could still feel the coolness of the woman's hand where she'd touched his arm.

"I asked her where you were. She kept telling me to leave. And then I finally saw you..."

He remembered sidestepping around the woman. He wasn't leaving until he found Lizzie. Time stood still as the crowd parted. There, a few feet away from her brother, lay Lizzie, her head propped up against the sharp edge of a plow blade, her white prayer kapp *lopsided on her head. Light brown hair hung down on her shoulders, matted together with moisture. Paul wrung his hands together.*

There was a large gash that covered her face, and someone was applying a cloth to stop the bleeding.

Blinking hard, Paul banished the image. He turned to looked at Lizzie. Right here, right now, right this very minute. She didn't even come close to resembling that little girl. She sat here, next to him, with her tear-streaked face, and he thought she looked beautiful. He felt her anguish and wanted to take it all away.

Lizzie's heart felt as if it were breaking into a million pieces. The hurt and pain welled up from somewhere deep inside.

"Why are you doing this now? Why are you ruining this beautiful moment?" she pleaded.

Fresh pain tore through her heart, searing her soul like an open wound. Her head throbbed. She touched the scar on her face, feeling the pain all over again. "Why, Paul?"

"I know how hard this is to hear. But we've been going round and round all these years, avoiding talking about your brother. Talking about our part in the day. We need to go through this pain in order to come out on the other side, healed."

He clutched her hands, his eyes darkening. "I need to be healed, and I know you want that, too."

She sobbed, wanting to run away. The tears rolled down her face. Even though she felt the warmth from the sun on her skin, shivers raced down her spine. He put his hand on her back, covering the exact spot, giving her strength and hope.

"I wasn't supposed to be out in the barn at all. I don't remember much about that time, but I do remember waking up in the hospital and my *daed* being angry with me. He said he'd told me not to go out there to play. I don't understand why I went against his wishes. If I'd listened to him, David might still be alive."

"Lizzie. I was supposed to be there, too. I told David I'd come over. We were going to climb the hay bales. This is as much my fault as it is yours."

Lizzie didn't know what to make of all of this. She knew that *Gott* would never give them more than they could handle. She laid her head against Paul's shoulder, feeling his strength.

"Maybe the fault doesn't lie with either of us. Maybe it was nothing more than an accident that no one could have prevented." She remembered now how impulsive David had always been. He'd been the one to swing from the rope in the tree in the backyard. He'd been the one to ride his bike as fast as he could down the long hills, while she and Mary had looked on.

Even at that young age, David had been a risk-taker, while Lizzie had always been the one to stand there watching him.

Finally she said, "We don't know how things would have turned out if you'd been there. No one knows. All the times you came by my parents' *haus*, all those years and all those visits—was it because you felt guilty?"

She didn't think she could take it if he said yes, because that could mean only one thing: that this relationship was his way of making things up to her for David's death.

"At first I came because I was so worried about you. And then, *ja*. I guess I had a lot of guilt. I felt terrible that your *vader* was left without a son."

Lizzie swallowed.

"Then I knew we shared something more." Cupping her face between his hands, he tipped her head back, his gaze capturing hers.

Lizzie's breathing picked up. The look in his eyes began to change, going from hurt and pain to hope.

She felt the calluses on the pads of his thumbs as he stroked her jaw.

"I want to kiss you, Lizzie," he whispered. "Would that be all right?"

She nodded.

He lowered his head and gently touched his lips to hers.

He raised his head, resting his forehead against hers. "I'm sorry. That was too bold of me."

"*Nee.* The time was right for our first kiss."

He looked at her with an intensity she'd never seen before. It might be too soon to express his feelings to her, but Paul couldn't hold them back any longer.

"I love you, Lizzie. With all my heart and soul, I love you."

Tears sprang to her eyes again. "Paul." Her voice hitched with emotion, knowing that once she said the words, she couldn't take them back. Her heart blossomed as she spoke. "I love you, too."

His smile stretched from ear to ear. "I can't believe I'm hearing you say those words. Lizzie, you mean so very much to me. And I know there's still so much to be done to make our courtship work."

"Like getting my *vader*'s permission. He still wants a son-in-law to take over the farm." She reached out to touch his face, smiling when she felt the light stubble beneath her fingertips.

This was the first time she'd touched his face. He felt like warmth and light and love.

As he covered her hand with his, she felt the corners of his mouth turn up.

Then he replied to her comment about her *vader*. "Maybe once Joseph sees how well your paintings are doing and the fact that I can support a family with my furniture store, he'll come around."

Lizzie wanted to believe him. She knew that her *vader* could be very stubborn when it came to what he wanted in his family and for his farm. She also wanted to believe that he would like to see his daughter happy.

Happy. She let the feeling sink in. For the first time in as long as she could remember, Lizzie felt not just happy, but happiness.

Gathering her in his arms, Paul pulled her close. "Oh, Lizzie, I love you so much. But I think we need to be getting back. I don't want to worry your parents."

"That wouldn't be a good thing to do," she agreed.

When he started to help her up off the bench, she put her hand over his chest, stilling his movement. Beneath her fingers, his heart beat at a strong, steady rate. She closed her eyes, imagining their life together. Maybe they could have one of the smaller farms off in the distance. Perhaps there would be children. Lizzie knew if they were blessed with a son, she would name him after her brother and pray that he wasn't as impulsive.

"Elizabeth Miller. When we return to your home, I'm going to ask your *vader* if I may court you. It's time to make this official."

Lizzie's heart swelled.

He kissed her forehead. "Let's get you home."

Lizzie wanted the ride home to last forever. She wanted to savor the moment when Paul had told her he loved her for as long as she could. But as soon as he turned the buggy into the driveway, she knew trouble had come their way.

Chapter Fourteen

She saw an unfamiliar car parked in front of the house. The blue SUV looked out of place next to the buggy. There was a man standing in front of the driver's-side door. Her *vader* was standing in front of the stranger who towered a good foot over his height. His face was red as a beet and he was pointing at the man, then pointing toward the road. Lizzie had never seen her *vader* this angry.

Lizzie grabbed hold of Paul's arm. "Hurry!"

"Oh, no," he muttered.

"Do you recognize the man?"

"*Ja.* He's the one who stopped by the wedding to ask about buying some of my furniture. I can't imagine what he's doing at your house."

The buggy jerked as Paul pulled the mare to a sudden stop. He jumped down, leaving Lizzie to catch up to him.

"Joseph! What's going on here?" Paul asked, stepping between the two men.

"This man—" her *vader* pointed a finger at the man "—he came out here asking about some art. I told him

more than once we don't have any art here. I don't know
what he's carrying on about."

Lizzie's heart sank like a rock. This couldn't be happening. How did this man find out who she was or
where she lived? She cast a questioning glance toward
Paul, who only shook his head in confusion.

"I went by your shop today, Paul. Your brother was
there. After I bought the dining room set, I took a look
at the watercolors. My wife loves to collect Amish artwork. The ones you have would be perfect for her collection. Ben, he told me the art was limited editions,
and there were no artist markings. But then he looked
at the one I was interested in and said he recognized
the scene. He pointed me in this direction. I'm so sorry.
I didn't mean to cause any trouble."

"I don't know what this man is talking about. He's
been describing our fields perfectly. I don't understand."
Her *vader*'s voice quieted as he looked to Paul for answers.

She caught the *Englischer* staring at her, seeing the
scar on her face. His glance collided with hers, and
Lizzie saw him grimace. Quickly he looked away from
her. The old insecurities came rushing back in like an
out-of-control tidal wave, leaving her emotions shaking.

She never should have left the farm.

Doing her best to hide the scar, she lowered her head,
taking a step forward. Knowing it would be wrong to
keep the truth from her *vader*. She had never wanted
him to find out, but the truth always had a way of coming out. She glanced over at Paul, thinking, *How could
this have happened?* He was supposed to protect her.
He'd promised her no one would find out. And now
Lizzie had to face her family. She had to face the one

person who had doubted her for the past decade. The man who would never forgive her for David's death. She bit back a sob, unable to think clearly.

"I have something to tell you, *Vader*," she said, her voice barely above a whisper.

All her hopes and dreams for a future with Paul came crashing down. But she couldn't bear to keep this from her *vader*, even if she'd done it for all the right reasons; he deserved to know what she'd been doing.

"You need to tell us what, *Dochder*?" *Vader* asked, as his face turned even redder.

"*I'm* the one who paints the watercolors Paul sells."

Silence descended on the group. Tension snapped in the air like lightning. Lizzie kept her eyes downcast. She couldn't look at her *vader*. And she didn't want to see Paul. All the things they'd just confessed to each other…all the love they'd declared…it meant nothing now. If Paul couldn't protect her, then no one could. Just like the day of the accident. The cold reality hit her with such a jolt, she almost fell to the ground. Summoning what little strength she had left, she raised her eyes to meet her *vader*'s gaze. She felt foolish thinking that selling her art to help out the family would work. Shame at her deception shook her to her soul.

It broke her heart to see his disappointment in her.

"Go to the house. Now."

Gulping back the sobs, she turned, doing as she was told. Entering the house, she heard the car door slam shut and then the stranger driving off. She heard her *vader* order Paul off the property.

But not before she heard Paul's voice defending her. "She did this to help your family, sir."

The screen door banged shut behind her as she fell into her *mamm*'s arms, sobbing uncontrollably.

"There, there, *Dochder*. It's going to be all right. I promise." Her *mamm* led her upstairs to her bedroom, where she helped Lizzie lie down on the bed.

Mary came in with a cool, wet washcloth and gently placed it over Lizzie's eyes.

"My dear, sweet Lizzie. Like *mamm* said, this is all going to be all right. *Daed* will come around. You'll see."

Breathing deeply, Lizzie worked at calming herself. Turning onto her side, she hugged her knees to her chest. The cold compress fell away from her eyes. When her sobs finally quieted, she said, "I sold the art-work to help you and *Daed*, *Mamm*."

"Lizzie, when did you start doing this?" her *mamm* asked.

"I started painting soon after David died. After *Daed*'s heart attack, Paul and I came up with this plan to sell my art at his shop. It was the only way I could think of to help bring money into the family. My road-side stand certainly wasn't going to be enough, and there was no man in my life to marry and bring here to live to help on the farm…" She paused for a mo-ment, gathering her thoughts. Her lower lip quivered as she whispered. "Because of the way I look, there will never be a husband for me to bring home to take David's place."

She felt the mattress dip as her sister sat next to her. "Oh, Lizzie! Don't say such a thing! Those thoughts are not the truth."

For a long time Lizzie thought her future as an *alt maedel* was set, and then she'd fallen in love with Paul.

Her heart ached. She placed her hand over the spot in her chest where it lay beating. For the briefest of moments she'd felt happiness bursting from inside, and now all hope was once again lost.

"I saw you painting earlier today. I guess I assumed *Mamm* and *Daed* knew you did this."

Lizzie shook her head against the pillow. "*Nee*. I was afraid that they would see my drawings and watercolors as a frivolous pastime. There's always so much work to be done on the farm and I only drew when I had free time. In the beginning I used the drawings to cope with the accident."

Pushing herself up off the bed, she pointed to her dresser. "Go open the bottom drawer, *Mamm*." While her *mamm* did that, Lizzie bent over, and reaching underneath her bed, she pulled out a box.

She put the box on the bed between her and Mary, flipping the lid open to reveal dozens of drawings and paintings.

"Oh! *Dochder!* Your work is so beautiful!" her *mamm* exclaimed from across the room.

"Look at what you've done," she said, spreading the artwork out in front of her. "I can see why that man wants to buy your work."

"*Mamm*, do you see that box on top of the dresser?"

Mamm nodded.

"Open it up."

Standing, *Mamm* reached for the box. Carefully lifting the lid, she peered inside. "Lizzie! There's over one hundred dollars in here!"

"That is from the sale of my first watercolor. Paul..." Fresh tears sprang to her eyes. Swiping her hand across her face, she took in a determined breath. "He sold one of my pieces last week."

Hanging her head, she added, "I was going to put it with the money from the sale of my jams. I now know thinking I could convince you that I was doing so well with my jams and baked goods was a silly notion. I'm so sorry."

Mamm came across the room to join Lizzie and Mary on the bed. Putting her arms around both of them, she said, "I love both of you so much. And Lizzie, *ja*, you were wrong to keep your paintings from us. You shouldn't have gone against your *vader*'s wishes. We will have to pray to ask for forgiveness."

"Yes, *Mamm*." Even as she agreed to pray, Lizzie found she couldn't get the look on her *vader*'s face out of her head.

She had disappointed and hurt him yet again. Lizzie couldn't bear the thought that she'd brought more pain and, worst of all, shame to her *vader*'s home. The man had been through so much over these past years. From now on she would be a good *dochder*, doing as he asked of her. And if that meant finding a farmer to marry instead of a furniture maker, then so be it.

They all heard the screen door open and snap shut. *Mamm* quietly left the room. That left Lizzie and Mary alone. Poor Mary looked so tired. She didn't need to stay to comfort her.

"Mary, you look exhausted. Go lie down. I'll be fine." Though she used her best confident-sounding tone, Lizzie knew she'd failed in convincing her sister, because they both knew she was anything but fine.

Gripping her hand, Mary said, "You will get through this. We've survived far worse, you know."

"I do know. But this pain—" Lizzie thumped her chest "—that I'm feeling inside here… I've never felt this before."

"It will get better. I promise." Mary pulled her into a quick hug and then pushed her growing figure up from the bed. "I'm going to go put my feet up."

She watched her sister walk slowly from the room, thinking at least one of them had done the right thing. The sound of her parents' voices floated up the staircase. She tiptoed to her bedroom door and opened it a crack to hear what they were saying.

"She went against my wishes. Not only that, she outright deceived us. I'm not ready to forgive Lizzie yet. I need time to think about what she's done."

"Joseph. We both know that Lizzie's heart was in the right place."

"I need time to think and to pray on it."

Closing the door, Lizzie shut out their voices. Leaning her back against the hard wood, she knew what had to be done.

She picked up the paintings, the very ones her *mamm* had been looking at, off the floor, and placed them back in the bottom drawer. Pushing the drawer closed, she straightened up, catching sight of the watercolor of the barn. The one she'd been working on just a few short hours ago. She touched one corner, rubbing her thumb over the image of the lilac bush. It had been in full bloom the day of the accident. The bush had been cut down a few years ago. It had lived out its life.

Her hands began to tremble. Lizzie pressed them together, willing the motion to stop. Her fingers felt so cold. Lizzie shivered. She had more work to do. Ignoring the gnawing inside her stomach, she left the painting on the dresser, turning her attention to the paints and brushes. She kept her mouth firm, quelling the urge to cry again. She picked up the tubes of watercolor paints, bringing them over to the box on the bed. Looking down at the pieces of paper with all those images— some sketched out and some with colors added—she saw her dreams fading away. She let the tubes of paint tumble from her hands to join the tattered drawings. Numbly she crossed back over to the dresser, picked up the brushes and placed them in the box.

She stood there, looking down at the gift of color that Paul had given her. The side of her face underneath the scar started to ache. She brought her hand up, lightly rubbing the area where the skin puckered. She hadn't felt pain in the area in a very long time. Not since the day Paul had brought her these gifts. She had no use for any of this. She folded the cardboard flaps together, then shoved the box as far as her arms could reach, underneath the bed.

If Lizzie had learned one thing from all of this mess, it was that she should have followed her instinct and never left her family's farm. The life she thought she could have with Paul was nothing more than the dream of an innocent heart. Her life, for now, and as it always had been, was right here.

Chapter Fifteen

Paul stood on the Millers' front porch with a bouquet
of wildflowers in his hands. The late summer daisies
and the lavender he'd found alongside the road fluttered
in the breeze. He hadn't seen Lizzie in two very long
days. He'd wanted to come earlier but knew she and her
family needed time. For him, though, time was running out. Over these past months he'd grown to know
Lizzie so well. He knew what made her smile and what
made her pull away. It was the pulling away part that
had him worried.

She'd given him her heart the other day. And then,
just like that, it had been taken away. He stood there
on the porch with the bees buzzing in the bushes next
to it. A pot clanged in the kitchen. He heard female
voices. He leaned in, listening for the sound of her voice.
Shuffling his feet, he raised his hand and knocked on
the door.

Lizzie's *mamm* answered the door. "Good afternoon,
Paul."

"Mrs. Miller, I'm not going to waste any time with
pleasantries. I need to see your *dochder*."

"If it's Lizzie you're coming to see, I'm afraid she's refusing to take any visitors at this time."

Expecting this to happen, he said, "I understand. I brought these flowers for her." Extending his hand, he waited for her to receive them.

She took them from him, pausing to smell the fragrant scent. Raising her eyes, she said, "*Danke.* I'll be sure to give these to her."

"Please tell your *dochder* that I still love her." Paul walked away, leaving a bit of his heart behind.

Paul returned two days later, determined to see Lizzie. This time he was met at the door by Mary, who informed him that Lizzie had gone for a walk. He was about to climb up into the buggy when he caught sight of her walking around the far side of the barn. She didn't see him, and Paul used that to his advantage. In a few long strides he stood before her. She came to an abrupt halt in front of him.

Lizzie drew her mouth into a thin line and he thought all might be lost. Then he looked into her eyes and saw her profound sadness. The way he figured it, she wouldn't be looking that way if she didn't still love him.

Not wasting any time, he got right to the point of this visit. "Lizzie, I know you're angry with me. I've come to apologize for what happened the other day. I had no idea that man would come here. I'm sorry he did."

Lizzie sidestepped around him. He spun around, wasting no time in catching up with her brisk pace.

"Come on, Lizzie. Talk to me."

Ignoring him, she kept right on moving, trying to outpace him, which of course was a ridiculous thing to try and do, considering she had to take two steps to his one.

"Lizzie. Please."

Finally she stopped moving. With her back to him, she spoke. "You need to leave."

He shook his head. "I'm not leaving."

"You can't stay where you're not wanted."

"I'm not leaving until you listen to what I came here to say."

He reached out a hand and touched her upper arm, gently turning her to face him. "Lizzie, I love you. And you told me you loved me. I believe, here—" he fisted his free hand, thumping it against his chest, his voice breaking as he continued "—in my heart, that you still do."

Tears rolled down her cheeks. Her mouth tried to get the words out. Finally she managed to say, "I can't love you anymore."

"Lizzie, you can't mean those words," he implored her.

"I should never have let you convince me to continue with my watercolors. By doing so, I've brought nothing but pain and shame into my parents' home." Shaking her head, she said, "I've put my paintings away."

"*Nee*, Lizzie." Over and over he shook his head. "*Nee*. The Lord gave you that talent for a reason."

Raising her hand, she held it out in front of her as if to push his words away. "*Nee*. The Lord would never bring this pain on me. No matter how much I loved you, I can't bear the thought that I broke my parents' hearts yet again. Please don't sell any more of my watercolors. I don't care what you do with them, but don't sell any more."

Then Lizzie ran up the walkway, raced across the porch and hid inside the shelter of the Miller home. Paul could hear her sobs coming from inside the house. Choking back tears, he hung his head. This wasn't how he wanted things between them to end. Without Lizzie in his life, he had nothing. He wasn't about to let her go without putting up a fight. Because he knew *Gott* intended for them to be together. But how could he convince her?

Another three days passed. Three days in which he closed himself off from the world. Standing in the middle of the Burkholder Amish Furniture Store, with his hands on his hips, Paul surveyed his handiwork. Though the spot where the dining room set stood was now empty, his plans were to replace it with a brand-new one. But without Lizzie, the joy he took in working with his hands had dimmed. Without her by his side, he felt as if nothing mattered. He looked at the walls where her watercolors hung.

Fighting back the pain, he walked over to the painting she'd done of the field where they'd had their first picnic. He remembered how excited she'd been seeing the view from the hillside. Paul could still see the way her hand had moved over the page. Brushstroke after brushstroke, she'd created this stunning image with seemingly little effort.

He'd fallen in love with her even more that day.

She'd come so far since then. He'd watched her confidence blossom as she'd been brave enough to trust in her talent and to trust in them. He couldn't let her escape back into seclusion. Lizzie didn't belong on the farm. She belonged out in the world, where she could share her artwork. She belonged with him.

Looking at the yellows and greens, he still felt the awe of her talent.

Her *Gott*-given talent.

He couldn't let her throw this all away. She'd been

given that talent for a reason. Just like others in the community created beautiful quilts, Lizzie's hands created lovely watercolors. Her heart and soul were in these watercolors. He knew she'd never be able to forgive herself if she stopped creating art and left all of this behind. Lizzie wasn't meant to be a farmer's wife. She was an artist.

Reaching up, he took the framed watercolor off the wall. He carried it to the back room, wrapped it in brown packing paper, cut a length of string from the spool that hung on the pegboard and then tied a neat string bow on the top. Carrying the painting under his arm, Paul walked out of the shop.

The trip out to the Miller farm didn't take more than twenty minutes, but to Paul it felt as if hours had passed. His insides were telling him he needed to get to Lizzie. When he finally made it to their property, he stopped the buggy next to the barn. His horse pawed at the soft earth. Paul's senses picked up. As he jumped down from the buggy seat, he heard the sounds of crying coming from inside the barn. Quickly he went to the building, peering inside the tall sliding doors. Dust motes danced around his shadow. A woman stood in the middle of the large room. He could see her arms wrapped around her middle. The prayer *kapp* covered her honey-colored hair.

Lizzie.

She gave no indication that she'd seen him. Paul stepped into the dimness, heading straight for her. In long, easy strides he met up with her in the middle of the barn and gathered her in his arms. She nestled her head underneath his chin as he held her close, feeling her shaking. Rubbing his hands along her back, Paul tried to ease her pain.

"Oh, my dear, sweet Lizzie. Please don't cry."

"I've ruined everything," she sobbed into his chest.

"No, no. You haven't ruined anything."

He let her cry some more, holding her as tightly as he could, willing his strength to flow to her. Praying for his own strength. Remembering that horrible day so long ago. The very day that had set their future in motion.

Paul knew that David wouldn't want to see his sister in so much pain. He knew that David would want her to forgive herself.

"Lizzie," he said, taking a chance that he was sharing the things her *bruder* would want her to hear. "It's time for you to forgive yourself. You need to let go of the past...let go of things we can't change."

She continued to cry, shaking her head against his chest.

"Lizzie. You need to forgive yourself. Please forgive me. We've come so far. I can't let you go now. Please don't make me let you go."

"I... I'm so filled with pain. I don't know what to do with any of these feelings."

"Give them up to the Lord. He will protect you and heal you. Lizzie, I know together we can bring the light back."

She stepped away from him. Scrubbing her hand across her face, she looked down at the floorboards. It was then he noticed the crumpled paper. He bent down and picked it up.

"What's this?"

"The picture of the barn I've been working on. The image has been stuck in my mind for so long, I finally put it down on paper. You've seen this..." she said, hiccupping.

Paul worked to smooth out the wrinkled edges, seeing that it was indeed the watercolor of the barn. He focused on the lilac bush.

Tapping the spot with a finger, he said, "This isn't here any longer."

"The bush was there the day David died," she explained. Sweeping her hand out in front of her, she whispered, "I can't do this anymore."

"Wait here—I'll be right back." Taking the picture of the barn with him, Paul hurried out to the buggy, where he exchanged it for the one he'd brought from the shop.

He came back inside and handed it to her. "Here, open this."

Her fingers trembled as she pulled the string loose, releasing the brown paper.

"Look at this picture." He tapped the glass. "This is the watercolor you painted the day we went on our picnic. I know you remember this day, Lizzie."

She shoved the painting back at him, turning her face away from him. Cupping her face in his hand, Paul had her facing him again. Though he could see her turmoil, he knew he had to convince her that they needed to be together.

"Every painting you do shows your beauty and your strength. The day we went to this field for our picnic, that was the day I fell in love with you. No matter what happens, Lizzie, I will always love you. And nothing you can say or do will ever change how I feel."

"I won't let you love me!" Lizzie shouted as she ran past him, out of the barn.

Clutching the painting in one hand, Paul went after her.

"Paul!" Joseph Miller's voice boomed behind him.

He stopped in his tracks, watching Lizzie moving away from him one more time. He turned to find her *vader* standing in front of the barn doors. He wondered how long the man had been outside.

"*Ja*. I heard what you said to my *dochder*."

"Then you know I love her."

"I do. But I also know you need to give her a little more time."

"I'm not sure I can do that."

The man's bushy eyebrows pulled together as his stare bore down on Paul. He waited.

"I've looked at Lizzie's paintings. I understand why she does them. You are right—she has been given a great talent. I know she's been doing nothing but using it for the good of our family. Perhaps I've been hard on her. These years have not been easy ones, Paul."

"I know, sir."

"I needed her to marry a farmer. Instead she has fallen in love with a furniture maker. One who, I might add, convinced her to keep secrets from her family."

Joseph wagged a finger at him, "Your *vader* and I were very close to going to the bishop over your actions. In the end, though, we've decided your decisions, while misguided, had been made for the right reasons."

Frowning, Paul didn't know if he should apologize or defend his actions and feelings for the man's *dochder*. In the end Joseph was the one to concede.

"Like it or not, my Lizzie loves you. If you can convince her to come back to you, you have my blessing to be married."

Chapter Sixteen

The floor felt cool beneath her bare feet, reminding Lizzie that cold fall air would be settling in before she knew it. Putting on her black stockings and black shoes, she finished getting dressed. Her entire body ached. Not from illness, though. She ached with the familiar pain of loss. Letting Paul go was going to be harder than she'd imagined. Lizzie knew he'd been hurting. They were both hurting. Sighing, she wished loving someone were easier.

From the kitchen she heard the sound of the teakettle's whistle. She went downstairs and found only Mary in the kitchen, padding around with bare feet.

"Mary! You should put on your stockings at least."

"My feet are so swollen. And they feel hot. I'm letting them cool for a bit," Mary explained, turning around to look at Lizzie. "You look tired."

"I'm afraid I haven't been sleeping well."

After walking back to the stove, Mary took two mugs out of the cabinet above it. "Come, join me for some tea. I'll make us up a pot of Earl Grey. I know it's your favorite."

"*Danke*. I'd like that. Are there any muffins left?" she asked, knowing there were some left in the basket when she'd gone to bed last night.

"I think only corn ones. *Daed* took the blueberry ones with him when he left for the fields this morning. Aaron went along to help him with the harvest."

Lizzie accepted the mug her sister handed her. Bringing it under her nose, she inhaled the sweet fragrance of the bergamot oil the tea was known for.

"Come on, let's go sit out on the porch."

"What about your feet? Won't they get cold out here?"

"I'll be fine," Mary replied, laughing.

She joined her sister on the swing. Lizzie looked down at her sister's stomach, noticing the soft rounding of her belly. It gave her a comforting feeling to know that two little lives lay safely in Mary's womb.

"You must be excited about the babies."

Mary's eyes lit up. "We are. Aaron is hoping for boys, but I'd like one of each." She gave her head a slight shake. "*Nee*, that isn't true. I don't care if they are girls or boys as long as they are healthy."

Lizzie rested her head on Mary's shoulder, feeling safe and secure and loved.

"Tell me, *liebschen*, how are you holding up?"

"I'm taking things one day at a time." Lizzie felt guilty at having to admit that.

There was something to be said for life staying on course. Ever since this change between her and Paul, she could hardly keep up with all of the emotions.

"I understand Paul has come by several times since the incident." Mary pushed her toes against the porch, putting the swing into motion.

"We're calling that day an *incident*?" Lizzie cocked an eyebrow, meeting Mary's gaze.

Mary let out a soft, very unladylike snort. "I don't know what else to call it. Lizzie, do you love Paul?"

Her heart ached so much, she wanted to weep from the pain of it.

In a soft voice she answered her sister, "*Ja*. With all my heart, I love Paul Burkholder."

"Then you need to work this problem out."

"I'm not sure we can."

"Was *Vader* finding out about your artwork really so bad?" Mary wanted to know.

Lizzie shrugged. "On that day, *ja*. It was bad. That man came here, looking for me. The look on his face when he noticed my scar was too much for me to bear. I'm better off here at home. Not out in the world. Besides, Paul is not a farmer."

Mary put her foot flat on the porch floor, stopping the motion of the swing. "You need to stop thinking that way."

"*Vader* needs help on the farm. We can't afford to hire anyone. The money from the art sales would have helped things."

"*Ja*. Maybe so." Mary looked thoughtful for a moment and then she said, "Aaron and I have decided to stay."

"Stay here? For how long?"

"Hopefully for the rest of our lives. We want to raise the twins here, in Miller's Crossing. *Daed* needs the help on the farm, and Aaron is a farmer, after all."

"And Paul is a furniture maker."

"Maybe now you can forgive him, Lizzie. Forgive yourself."

"I'm trying to, Mary. My mind has been a jumble of thoughts and feelings that I've never felt before… I just don't know what to do with it all."

"Lizzie, this is all natural."

"Yes, but is love always this hard? Just when I thought my life was sure to be that of an *alt maedel*, Paul Burkholder, a boy I watched grow into a fine man, comes along and takes my heart."

Mary put her arm around her shoulders, pulling her closely. "Ah, my dear Lizzie. This is a *gut* thing for you. Love is a wonderful part of life. There are so many of us in this community who marry because it's the right thing to do for the family. But we have both been blessed with men who love and cherish us. You need to remember that and thank *Gott* for it."

They sat for a few minutes longer, watching the birds pick at the feeder.

"You need to let your heart open back up and trust what is inside."

"When did you get to be so wise?" Lizzie poked her in the arm.

"I've noticed that being with child has made my senses keener."

Together, they laughed.

"I've missed you, Mary."

"And I you." Resting her forehead against Lizzie's, Mary added, "Now go find Paul and settle this issue between you once and for all so we can get on with planning the next wedding."

Lizzie left her sister on the porch, deciding to walk into the village. She needed the time to think, and the few miles of walking alone would help her clear her mind. As she made her way up the driveway, she noticed that all around her the land seemed to be changing. The fields had turned from green to gold. Here and there on the side of the road were dried leaves. Raising her eyes, Lizzie caught sight of tinges of golds and reds on the leaves, evidence that the seasons were changing.

Spotting a maple tree just beginning to turn red, she imagined how the colors would look on her art paper. She continued walking, trying to put the words Mary had spoken into perspective, realizing how much she had truly missed Paul. The place where her heart was in her chest began to ache. Lizzie rubbed her hand over the spot, wishing she'd never fallen in love. Then she wouldn't know this heartache.

In the next instant she realized how much she missed him. She missed his smile. She missed his touch. She missed seeing the excitement on his face every time he talked about the Burkholder Furniture Store. Even if the Burkholders didn't agree with their *sohn*'s choice, Paul deserved to be a successful businessman. As mad as she was at him, she would not begrudge him that. Lizzie thought he deserved to find happiness, too, just not with her.

She felt a wetness on her face and realized she'd been crying. Swiping a hand across her eyes, she fought back a sob. She couldn't imagine Paul with anyone else, and yet she couldn't imagine him with her. She'd known all along that she wasn't worthy of love. She'd told Paul that many times over. Why hadn't he listened? Why had she given in?

Lizzie stopped moving, spent from feeling sad and lonely and angry. Off in the distance she saw the top of the church spire on Clymer Hill Road. The sunlight poured out of the heavens, making it appear as if it were made out of silver. That place meant so much to her and Paul. Lizzie couldn't explain the feeling washing over her. She had to go find Paul.

The sound of the sander broke through the morning silence. Paul had been out in the shop at their homestead since well before dawn. He'd been busy working off his frustration by finishing a tabletop. The showroom floor looked empty without the dining room that he'd sold to the *Englischer*. Though he'd known when he'd picked this slab out he'd had only one person in mind.

Lizzie.

His plan had been to surprise her with a lovely table as a wedding gift after she agreed to marry him. Now as he stood here amid the sawdust, some of the last words she'd spoken to him rang in his ears.

I won't let you love me, she'd said.

Pressing hard, he slid the sander over the wood, trying to erase their last moments together. The hurt he'd seen in her eyes still brought him pain. The thing was, he couldn't imagine loving anyone else. And now that he'd had time to think about them, he realized he'd always loved her. All those times he'd told himself they were just friends had been nothing more than his denying his true feelings.

"Paul. *Sohn. Sohn!*"

He turned when he felt a tap on his shoulder. *"Daed!"* He pulled the orange foam earplugs out of his ears and shut the sander down.

"I've been calling to you. Guess you couldn't hear me above all the noise."

"Sorry. I've been trying to get this tabletop finished." Cocking an eyebrow, *Daed* asked, "A special order?"

"*Ja*. What's on your mind?" Paul asked.

"I know things have been strained between us since Rachel and Jacob's wedding."

"*Ja*." Paul wiped a hand across his brow.

If he'd learned nothing else being Amish, it was the power of forgiveness. He'd been just as guilty as his *daed* in their dealings with the shop, and in the end with the hurt they'd caused each other.

As soon as he'd finished sanding, he planned on heading over to the Miller house. He'd been there three times already, and each time Lizzie had turned away. Maybe today would be different.

After pulling out a stool, *Vader* sat, resting his forearms in front of him on the workbench. "I'm not getting any younger, you know. And life is too short to stay mad at each other."

Paul nodded. "Agreed."

"Do you think we can work our way through this?"

"I do." Reaching out, he captured his *daed*'s hand with his, wondering when it had become hardened with arthritis and roughed with time.

"I understand your need for independence. Maybe I've been a little hard on you these past years. But that's only because I love you. And maybe a little bit because I need you here in the shop. While they're helpful, your *bruders* don't seem to have the passion that you do when it comes to woodworking."

"Ben and Abram don't mind helping out."

"I know. But you have more ambition."

Paul let go of his *vader*'s hand. He blew the sawdust off the tabletop and ran his hand over the smooth cherrywood. "I only want what is best for the family, *Daed*. I would never leave here."

"I know. Perhaps I was afraid you'd be snatched up by some *Englischer*'s company. They pay well from what I hear."

"I'm doing fine with my own furniture."

"I've been hearing talk of your shop. I was at the general store the other day and Mr. Becker told me your shop is getting a lot of foot traffic."

"I've been keeping busy."

"The long and short of it is, I'm fine with you having the furniture shop in the village. And I'm fine if you want to have a courtship with Lizzie Miller. Not that it's my blessing you'll be needing."

Paul grinned. "Joseph already gave me his."

Slapping his hand on the workbench, *Vader* stood, declaring, "Break time's over!"

Paul untied his heavy canvas work apron, took it off and hung it on a hook near the entrance. "I've got to be heading out for a bit."

He had one thing on his mind and that was to find his Lizzie and convince her that they belonged together. No matter what the obstacles, together they could overcome anything. Paul didn't want to waste any more time without her.

Chapter Seventeen

He saw her coming over the rise, her pale blue skirt flapping against her legs. Lizzie was moving at a pretty good clip. Pulling the reins toward him, he rolled the wagon to her, bringing it to a stop along the edge of the road.

"Paul." She ran up to the wagon, out of breath. "I was coming to find you."

"On foot?" He jumped from the wagon and reached for her hand.

"*Ja.* I was going for a walk to think about things...to think about us. And then I saw the Clymer Hill Road church spire. It's so beautiful today."

Looking over her head, he saw the church off in the distance. It surely was one of the prettiest places in the area. "Would you like me to take you up there?"

"If you have time."

He started to say, for her he'd always have time, but Paul was still trying to gauge her mood. Something had changed—that was for sure. When he took her hand to help her up on the wagon bench, she didn't shy away like he expected her to.

Moving to the middle of the seat, Lizzie smiled at him as he settled in next to her.

"It's a lovely day for a ride, don't you think?"

Paul didn't know what to make of any of this. He knew whatever was going on had to be serious. "Lizzie. I'm not sure what's going on here."

"I've something to tell you and I need to say it at our special place."

He led the horse and wagon up the long hill to the church. The wheels rattled over the oil-and-stone roadway. In less than ten minutes they reached the spot. Paul sat in the wagon, staring out at the view, thinking that this was all he'd ever wanted out of his life. His *Gott*, this bountiful earth's beauty and Lizzie.

"Do you want to get down?" she asked.

He saw a shadow of worry in her blue eyes. Putting his hand over hers, he said, "Let's go sit on our bench."

Together, they sat, looking out over the fields and valley, looking toward the horizon. Their fingers were intertwined. They sat that way for a long time, until their breaths came in unison.

Lizzie broke the silence by saying, "I've been very stubborn these past days."

"I hadn't noticed," he teased.

"*Ja*. I think you did. I had a talk with Mary today. She told me some things I hadn't considered before."

"Like?"

"Like the fact that love isn't easy to come by. But when you find it, you should never let it go."

Paul stayed quiet while he thought about how to go about thanking Mary.

Keeping her eyes averted, Lizzie continued. "My life has been a struggle. But a lot of that I put on myself.

After David died and I woke up in the hospital knowing my face, my life, would never be the same… I found it easier to keep to myself. To keep all my feelings inside. To let very few people get to know me. The one constant I've had in my life, other than my family, has been you, Paul. And I almost did the unforgivable. I almost let you go. There's one more thing I need to tell you."

Lizzie reached out to take his hand in hers. "Paul. I remember. I remember that last day with David. I don't think any of what happened was our fault. I was going to the barn to get him. I told him we weren't supposed to be there. I remember climbing high up those bales of hay. We were almost touching the rafters. And David, he was talking about flying through the air. I saw him jumping from bale to bale, his little body leaping high between each one. I tried to find a foothold on the next bale. And then we were tumbling. I lost sight of David. Then the next thing I remember was waking up in the hospital."

Paul tried his best to blink back tears.

"I never once thought you were to blame."

"I know, but for years I blamed myself."

Gripping his hands, she gazed up at him. Paul saw her hurt, fear and guilt slip away.

She blinked and then gave him a small smile, saying, "I'm ready to let the past go and look to the future."

He couldn't imagine his life without her in it. But to hear those words coming from his Lizzie…his heart filled with love.

"Lizzie, never once has my love for you wavered."

Paul stood, pulling Lizzie up off the bench. They faced each other as a cool breeze swirled around them. He brought her hands to his mouth and kissed them.

Then, releasing them, he cupped her beautiful face in his hands. He ran his thumb along the scar. And then lowering his head, he kissed the roughened skin. She tried to pull away, but he held her in his loving hands.

"I love every part of you. From your head to your toes, Elizabeth Miller. I love you."

"I love you with all my heart and all my soul. With all that I am, Paul Burkholder."

He kissed her, feeling her love and strength. Releasing her, he turned them to face the horizon.

"I think David would be very happy if he could see us together."

He held fast to her hand. "I know he would be."

Gathering her in his arms, he held her tightly. She smelled like sunshine and lemons and love. "Why don't we go give our families the good news about our courtship."

Tipping her head back, she looked up at him, and laughter bubbled out of her. "Are we courting?"

He nodded. "Your *vader* has already given his blessing for our marriage."

Tears sprang to her eyes. "Oh, my. Then I guess our future has already been decided." And they couldn't have been happier.

Epilogue

"Let me see!" Laughter bubbled up out of Lizzie as Paul led her through the door of their new *haus*.

Shortly after Paul had declared his intentions and acquired his *Zeugnis* from the church, with Joseph's blessing, he and Lizzie had gotten married. Lizzie had insisted she only wanted family and close friends at the wedding—not the entire community—which had been fine with Paul. He thought they'd waited long enough.

Paul had finished the dining room table shortly after their wedding. And today he'd be showing his handiwork off to his new wife, who at the moment stood squirming in his arms. Chuckling, he said, "Lizzie, patience is a virtue."

"Hmm." She laughed again. "If I stand perfectly still, can I open my eyes?"

"Yes."

Making sure she was standing in the right spot, at the head of the table, Paul said, "Okay. Open your eyes."

She let out a gasp, her eyes widening. "Paul! It's *wunderbar*!"

Moving around the table, she took in every inch of

his work. The cherrywood top had been a splurge, even though he'd known that pine would be simple and plain, lasting years. Paul had wanted to give his Lizzie something that would last a lifetime. He wanted something that could be passed from generation to generation, long after they were gone to be with *Gott*.

Lizzie began tipping her head this way and that, and then bent to look underneath the table. He couldn't imagine what she could be searching for.

"Lizzie?" he questioned her. "Is something wrong?"

"*Nee*. I'm looking for your mark."

He walked around the table and joined her at the side. Taking her hand in his, he guided her fingers under the table, until they touched the spot where the small circle lay. Rubbing their fingers over the grooves of the brand, he felt the letters *PB*.

They sat down on one of the benches that had been a wedding gift from his family. Other than their bed, the dining set was the only furniture in their two-bedroom home.

"I have a gift for you, too." Lizzie stood and then disappeared into the bedroom. She returned with a flat package.

"Open it."

Paul tipped his head, giving her a curious look. He tore the tape off the wrapping, lifted the paper away and then gasped when he saw the watercolor.

"I know you loved that barn painting, and I destroyed it. Lucky for both of us, I remembered all the details."

Running his fingers along the edges of the barnwood frame, he felt at a loss for words.

"Ben did the frame for me," Lizzie admitted. "I

thought we could hang this above the mantel in the living room."

"I think that would be a fine place. I'm sorry the room is so empty."

"Paul, I'm not worried about the furniture," Lizzie assured him as she returned to her place next to him on the bench.

"If I'd had more time before our wedding, I could have made you some more furniture."

Lizzie pulled him toward her and kissed him soundly on the mouth.

Lifting her head, she said, "It wouldn't matter to me if our *haus* were empty, because as long as we are together, these walls will be filled with love."

* * * * *

Double Treat Cookies

This recipe makes 8 dozen cookies.

Ingredients

2 cups all-purpose flour
2 teaspoons baking soda
¼ teaspoon salt
1 cup butter (2 sticks) softened
1 cup of granulated sugar,
plus ¼ to ½ cup reserved for shaping
1 cup packed light brown sugar
2 large eggs
1 teaspoon vanilla extract
1 cup creamy peanut butter (or for extra crunch you
can use 1 cup chunky peanut butter)
1 cup chopped salted peanuts
1 6 ounce package semisweet chocolate chips

Preheat your oven to 350 degrees F.

1. In a medium bowl, sift together the flour, baking soda and salt.

2. In a large mixing bowl, beat together the butter, sugars, eggs and vanilla until fluffy. Then blend in the peanut butter.

3. Add the dry ingredients to the butter and sugar mixture.

4. Stir in the chocolate chips and the peanuts.

5. Shape dough into small balls about 1½ inch in diameter, then place them 3 inches apart on ungreased baking sheets.

6. Using a glass, dip the bottom in the reserved granulated sugar and flatten each cookie.

7. Bake until brown, about 8 minutes. Transfer cookies to wire rack for cooling.

These cookies can be stored in a container and will stay fresh for up to five days. You can also use butterscotch chips in place of the semisweet.

THE FARMER NEXT DOOR

Patricia Davids

This book is dedicated with deep love and affection
to my mother, Joan, a true wise-hearted woman.

And all the women that were wise hearted did spin with their hands, and brought that which they had spun, both of blue, and of purple, and of scarlet, and of fine linen.
—*Exodus* 35:25

Chapter One

If the Amish farmer standing outside her screen door would smile, he'd be a nice-looking fellow—but he certainly wasn't smiling at the moment. His fierce scowl was a sharp reminder of all her life had been before—tense, fearful, pain-filled.

Faith Martin thrust aside her somber memories. She would not allow the past to follow her here. She had nothing to fear in this new community.

Still, the man at her door made an imposing figure blocking out much of the late afternoon sunlight streaming in behind him. His flat-topped straw hat sat squarely above his furrowed brow. That frown put a deep crease between his intelligent hazel eyes.

Above his reddish-brown beard, his full lips barely moved when he spoke. "*Goot* day, *Frau*. I am Adrian Lapp. I own the farm to the south."

His beard told her he was married. Amish men were clean-shaven until after they took a wife. He had his pale blue shirtsleeves rolled up exposing brawny, darkly tanned forearms folded tightly across his gray vest. A familiar, nauseous odor emanated from his clothes.

Faith's heart sank. It was clear he'd had a run-in with one of her herd. What had he been doing with her animals?

She managed a polite nod. Common courtesy dictated she welcome him to her home. "I'm pleased to meet you, neighbor. I am Faith Martin. Do come in."

He made no move to enter. "Is your husband about?"

It seemed the farmer next door wasn't exactly the friendly sort. That was too bad. She had prayed it would be different here. "My husband passed away two years ago. It's just me. How may I help you?"

Her widowed status seemed to surprise him. "You're living here alone?"

"Ja." She brushed at the dust and cobwebs on her apron and tried to look like a woman who managed well by herself instead of one who'd bitten off far more than she could chew.

His scowl deepened. "Your creatures are loose in my fields. They are eating my beans."

Faith cringed inwardly. This was not the first impression she wanted to make in her new community. "I'm so sorry. I don't know how they could have gotten out."

"I tried to catch one of them by its halter, but it spat on me and ran off with the others into the cornfield."

She saw the green, speckled stain across the front shoulder of his shirt and vest. Alpaca spit, a combination of grass and digestive juices, was unpleasant but not harmful. What a shame this had to be her new neighbor's first introduction to her alpacas. They were normally docile, friendly animals.

Faith never tired of seeing their bright, inquisitive faces waiting for her each morning. Their sweet, gentle natures had helped her heal in both body and spirit over the past two years.

"The one wearing a halter is Myrtle. She's the expectant mother in the herd. You must have frightened her. They are leery of strangers."

"So I noticed," he answered drily.

"Spitting is their least endearing habit, but it will brush off when it dries." Faith's encouraging tone didn't lighten his scowl. Perhaps now wasn't the time to mention the smell would linger for a few days.

"What did you call them?"

"Alpacas. They're like llamas but they have very soft fleece, softer than any sheep. Originally, they come from South America. How many did you say were in your field?"

"I counted ten."

"Oh, no!" Fear blotted out any concern for her neighbor's shirt. If all of her animals were loose in unfamiliar country, it would be difficult, even impossible, to round them up before dark.

Her defenseless alpacas couldn't spend the night out in the open. Stray dogs or coyotes could easily bring down one of her half-grown crias, or they might wander onto the highway and be hit by a passing car. She couldn't afford the loss of even one animal. She had everything invested in this venture and much more than money riding on her success.

Please, Lord, let me recover them all safe and sound.

As much as she hated to be seen using her crutch, Faith grabbed it from behind the door. It was wrong to be vain about her handicap, but she couldn't help it. It was a personal battle she had yet to win.

The pickup truck that had crashed into their buggy

two years ago had killed her husband and left her with a badly mangled leg. Doctors told her it would be a miracle if she ever walked again, but God had shown her mercy. After a long, difficult recovery she was able to get around with only her leg brace most of the time. But chasing down a herd of frisky alpacas required exertion and speed. Things she couldn't manage without added support.

She pushed open the screen door, forcing Adrian Lapp to take a step back. She didn't miss the way his eyes widened at the sight of her infirmity.

Let him stare. It wasn't something she could keep secret. She knew her crippled leg made her ugly and awkward, a person to be pitied, but she wouldn't let it be her weakness. Right now, the safety of her animals was the important thing, not her new neighbor's opinion of her. "Where did you see them last?"

"Disappearing into the cornfield beyond the orchard at the back of your property."

"I will need to get their halters and lead ropes from the barn." She left him standing on the porch as she made her way down the steps.

Adrian quickly caught up with her. "I'm sorry, I didn't know... I will take care of the animals for you. There is no need for you to go traipsing after them."

His offer was grudgingly given, but she sensed he meant well.

"I'm perfectly capable of catching them." She didn't want pity, and she wasn't about to leave her valuable livestock in the hands of a man who didn't even know what kind of animal they were.

Hobbling ahead of him across the weedy yard, she

spoke over her shoulder. "Once I catch them, can you help me lead them home?"

"Of course."

Faith headed toward the small, dilapidated barn nestled between overgrown cedars some fifty yards from the house. In the harsh August sunlight it was easy to see the peeling paint, missing shingles and broken windowpanes on the building. The Amish were known for their neat and well-tended farmsteads. She had a lot of work ahead of her to get this place in shape.

She didn't know why her husband had never mentioned owning this property in Ohio or why he had chosen to leave it sitting vacant all these years, but finding out a month ago that she owned it couldn't have come at a better time.

She pulled open the barn door. Copper, her mare, whinnied a greeting. Faith spoke a few soft words to her as she gathered together the halters and lead ropes that were hanging on pegs inside the doorway.

Adrian took them from her without a word and slipped them over his shoulder. She was grateful for his help but wished he wasn't so dour about it. Why couldn't her alpacas have chosen to eat the beans of a cheerful neighbor? Maybe she didn't have any.

She led the way around the side of the barn to the pens at the rear. The gate panel that should have been wired closed had been pushed over, offering the curious alpacas an easy way out. Why hadn't she paid more attention when her hired help set up the portable pen and unloaded the animals? Now look what her carelessness had wrought.

Adrian removed the thin wire that had proven to be

an ineffective deterrent. "Do you have a heavier gauge wire than this or some strong rope?"

"I'm sure there's something in the barn that will work."

"Then I should find it." He turned back toward the barn door.

Faith called after him. "Shouldn't we find my animals first and then worry about how to keep them in? It's getting late."

He didn't even glance in her direction. "It won't do any good to bring them back if they can just get out again."

She pressed her lips closed on a retort. She had learned the hard way not to argue with a man. Her husband had made sure she understood her opinions were not valued.

Leaving her new neighbor to rummage in the barn, Faith headed toward the rows of trees that stretched for a quarter of a mile to the back edge of her property, knowing he could easily overtake her. It was slow going through the thick grass, but at least she knew her alpacas would be well-fed through the summer and fall once she had her fences in place.

It didn't take long for Adrian to catch up with her. As she expected, his long legs made short work of the distance she had struggled to cover. A twinge of resentment rippled through her before she firmly reminded herself it didn't matter if someone could walk faster than she could. All that mattered was that she walk upon the path the Lord had chosen for her without complaint.

Adrian wasn't sure what to make of the woman charging ahead of him through the tangled grass of the old orchard. Her handicap clearly didn't slow her down much. He'd been curious about his new neighbors as soon as he'd spotted the moving van and large horse trailer inching up the rutted lane yesterday.

The farmstead had been deserted since he'd been a lad. It hurt his soul to see the good farm ground lying fallow and the peach orchard's fruit going to waste year after year. He could do so much with it if only he had the chance.

Even though he'd seen he had new neighbors, he hadn't gone to introduce himself. He didn't like meeting people or answering questions about his life. He liked being alone. He preferred to stay on his farm and work until he was bone-tired and weary enough to fall asleep as soon as his head hit the pillow at night.

Too tired even for dreams...or for nightmares.

He wouldn't be here today if Faith Martin had kept her animals penned up properly. This was costing him an afternoon of work that couldn't wait.

He glanced sideways at her. She was a tiny slip of a woman. She didn't look as if she could wrest this land and buildings back into shape by herself. A stiff wind could blow her away. Why, the top of her head barely reached his chin whiskers.

A white prayer *kapp* covering her chestnut-brown hair proclaimed her to be a member of the Plain faith, but he didn't recognize the pattern. Where had she come from?

She wore a long blue dress with a black apron and the same type of dark stockings and sturdy shoes that all the women in his family wore. As she walked beside him, the breeze fluttered the long ribbons of her *kapp* about her heart-shaped face, drawing his attention to the slope of her jaw and the slender curve of her neck.

She was a pretty little thing with eyes bright blue as a robin's egg. She had long eyelashes and full pink lips.

Lips made for a man to kiss.

He tore his gaze away as heat rushed to his face. He had no business thinking such thoughts about a woman he barely knew. What was wrong with him? He'd not taken this much notice of a woman since his teenage years.

He used to look at Lovina that way, used to imagine what it would be like to kiss her. When they wed he discovered her kisses were even sweeter than he'd dreamed. After her death, he'd buried his heart with her and raised their son alone until...

So what was it about Faith Martin that stirred this sudden interest? He studied her covertly. She pressed her lips into a tight line as she concentrated on her footing. Did walking cause her pain?

Her eyes darted to his face, but she quickly looked away as if she were uncomfortable in his presence. Her glance held a wary edge that surprised him. Was she frightened of him?

He hadn't meant to scare her. He quickly grew ashamed for having done so. He wasn't used to interacting with new people. Everyone in his family and the community knew of his desire to live alone. He truly had no reason to be surly with this woman. Her alpacas hadn't actually damaged his crop.

He glanced at her again. How could he set this right? How could he bring back her smile?

Adrian abruptly refocused his attention to the task at hand. He had a corncrib to finish and more work waiting for him at home. He didn't have time to worry about making a stranger smile. He would help her gather her animals and then get back to his labors. A few moments later they reached the end of the orchard.

The fence that separated her land from his had fallen down long ago. Only a few rotting uprights remained to mark the boundary. Beyond it, his cornfield stood in tall, straight rows. There was no sign of her odd creatures. They could be anywhere by now.

Faith cupped her hands around her mouth and called out, "Myrtle, Candy, Baby Face. Supper time."

He listened for any sound in return but heard only the rustle of the wind moving through the cornstalks. What did an alpaca sound like? Did they moo or bleat?

She took a step farther into the field. "Come, Socks. Come, Bandit."

Suddenly, a wooly white face appeared at the end of the row a few yards away. He heard Faith's sigh of relief.

"There's my good girl. Come, Socks." The animal emerged from the corn and began walking toward her with its head held high, alert but wary. It was butternut-brown in color with a white face and four white legs. Its head was covered with a thick pelt of fleece, but the long neck and body had been recently shorn, leaving the animal with an oddly naked appearance. It approached to within ten feet, but wouldn't come closer.

Faith glanced at Adrian. "Give me one of the halters and a lead rope and wait here."

He had no intention of venturing closer. Although the animal looked harmless, he still reeked of Myrtle's earlier disapproval.

Faith walked toward Socks with her hand out. The animal made a low humming sound, then ambled up to her and wrapped its long neck around her in a hug.

"Were you lost and scared? It's okay now. I know the

way home." She crooned to it like a child as she slipped the halter on, then scratched behind the alpaca's ear.

A second animal stepped out of the corn. It already wore a halter. Adrian recognized it as the one that had spit on him. As soon as she caught sight of him, she turned back into the cornfield.

Faith led Socks to Adrian and handed him the lead rope. "Try not to scare her. If one gives an alarm cry, they may all scatter."

Faith took several halters and ropes from him and disappeared into his cornfield without another word. Adrian found himself alone with the strangest animal he'd ever beheld.

He studied the creature's face. It was calmly studying him in return with large, liquid black eyes fringed with long black lashes. Besides doe-like eyes, Socks had a delicate muzzle with two protruding lower teeth. Her narrow, perked ears reminded him of a rabbit. Her round body was similar to a sheep, but she had long legs like a deer. Looking down, he saw two large, hooked toenails on each front foot that could have belonged to a giant bird.

When Socks tried to nibble his beard, he drew back abruptly, uncertain of her intentions. "I have orders not to scare you."

Socks hummed softly and didn't spit.

So far, so good.

Reaching out, Adrian scratched behind her ear as he'd seen Faith do. Socks closed her eyes and nuzzled into his hand. Her thick wool was as soft as anything he'd ever touched. He smiled at the sound of her hum. They might be odd-looking creatures, but they had a certain appeal. When they weren't spitting.

He ran a hand down her camel-like neck. She stood, patient and unconcerned. With his confidence in her temperament restored, he gave free rein to his curiosity. He wanted a closer look at her strange feet.

As soon as he grasped her leg, Socks lifted her foot as any well-trained horse would do. To his surprise, the bottoms of her feet were soft pads much like a dog's foot, not a hoof at all.

Straightening, he stroked her nose and chuckled. "It appears the Lord assembled you from leftover animal parts."

Socks looked past him and called softly. He turned and saw another alpaca, this one black as night, emerge and look in his direction. Should he call out to Faith or would that scare the animal?

It looked more curious than frightened. He gave a gentle tug on the lead rope and walked with Socks toward her friend. He made a soft humming sound, hoping to soothe the animal and not frighten it into running away. Was he going to help Faith, or was he about to make things worse?

Tired, hot and discouraged, Faith emerged from the forest of corn thirty minutes later with only two of her alpacas in tow. The sun was touching the horizon. It would be dark within the hour. How would she find the others then? She would need dozens of people to comb this acreage properly in the dark.

It seemed she was destined to meet more of her neighbors tonight and not under the best of circumstances.

She had no doubt they would come to help. That was the Amish way. She would not be prideful. She would ask Adrian Lapp to gather a group to help in her search.

To her surprise, Adrian wasn't where she had left him. She glanced around, wondering if she had come out of the corn in the wrong place. No, this was the spot. Had he gone back to his own work? What kind of neighbor was he, anyway?

"I shouldn't be judgmental. Perhaps his work is as pressing as mine." As usual, Myrtle proved to be a good listener and followed obediently behind Faith.

"All I have to do is round up my missing animals, start a business and ready a dilapidated house to pass inspection in a week's time so I may become the guardian of my brother's child. I'm sure Mr. Lapp is equally as busy."

Tears pricked the backs of Faith's eyes as she struggled through the long grass. The past two years had been incredibly hard. First, there had been the terrible crash and her husband's death. She'd spent weeks in the hospital afterward. Her small savings had covered only a fraction of her medical bills. Thankfully, the congregation at her church had taken up a collection to pay the rest, but it left her little to live on. It had taken her more than a year to get back on solid financial ground.

Then, three months ago came word that her brother and his wife had been killed in a flash flood, leaving their five-year-old son an orphan. As the boy's only relative, she was willing and eager to take Kyle in. She'd been halfway through the maze of paperwork and home studies needed to approve his adoption when her landlord had informed her he had to sell the farm she'd been renting.

Her adoption plans fell apart. She couldn't take in a child when she was about to lose the roof over her head.

But in the midst of her despair, the Lord had delivered what seemed like a miracle. A delinquent property tax statement had arrived in the mail addressed to her husband. It was then that she'd learned she owned a house and farm in Ohio. She'd spent every penny she could scrape together to pay the bill and move.

She hadn't expected to find the place in such deplorable condition.

Was this God's way of telling her Kyle didn't belong with her? Did He want Isaac's child raised in the English world her brother had chosen instead of in her Amish faith?

Why would God see fit to give Isaac's child into her care when He had denied her children of her own?

She had no answers to the questions and doubts that plagued her. It would be all too easy to sit down and bawl like a baby, but what would that fix? She sniffed back her tears and blinked hard, refusing to let them fall.

Tears hadn't made her husband a kind man. They wouldn't bring back her brother or undo any of the pain she had endured. They certainly wouldn't build fences for her alpacas, clean her house or make it a home for a lonely little boy.

She stopped to rest her aching leg and looked heavenward. "I know You never give us more than we can bear, but I could use Your strength right now. Help me, Lord. I beseech You."

As always, she felt the comfort of God's presence in her life whenever she turned to Him. She must not let her despair or her fears gain the upper hand. God was watching over her.

Had not the letter come in her hour of need telling her she owned this land? So what if it was going to take hard work to make it livable? She knew how to work. God would provide. She had faith in His mercy. Here in Ohio she had started Kyle's adoption process again. Now she had to prove to a new agency worker that she had a safe home and a stable income.

Which was exactly what she didn't have yet.

Drawing a deep breath, she started forward again. The time for tears was past. This was the new path the Lord had chosen for her. She had to believe it would be better than the life she'd left behind.

Chapter Two

When Faith emerged from the trees, she stopped short in surprise. Adrian Lapp stood beside her barn with all eight of her missing alpacas clustered around him in their pen. It seemed her prayers had been answered, and apparently her grumpy neighbor had a way with animals.

Not two minutes ago she had been piling unkind thoughts on his head.

Forgive me, Lord. I judged this man unfairly. I won't do it again.

Walking up to Adrian, she said, "I can't believe it. You found them."

"It was more like they found me."

Bandit stood close beside him, sniffing at his beard. He gently pushed the inquisitive black alpaca away and opened the gate so Faith could add her two to the herd. Adrian said, "I fixed the pen. They shouldn't get out again."

"Thank you. I was so worried I wouldn't be able to find them before dark. This move has been hard on all of them."

"And on you?"

Her gaze locked with his. Did she look like such a mess? She must. Embarrassment sent heat flooding to her face. Socks chose that moment to nibble at the rim of Adrian's straw hat. He pushed the alpaca gently aside. Faith concentrated on removing the halters from her pair.

"Where have you come from, Faith Martin? Surely not South America like your animals."

His interest seemed genuine. Some of her discomfort faded. "Originally, I'm from Indiana, but on this move I came from Missouri."

"That's a lot of miles."

It was, and many more than he knew. Her husband had been affected with a wanderlust that had taken them to twelve different communities in the ten years they'd been married. Faith was determined that this farm would be her final home. She wanted to put down roots, to become a true member of a community, things she'd never been able to do during her marriage.

Besides, she had to make a home for Kyle. A place where her brother's child could recover from the tragedy of losing his parents and grow into manhood. This was her last move. If it was God's will, she didn't plan to leave Hope Springs, Ohio, until He called her home.

"I'm grateful for your help, neighbor. I have fresh lemonade in the house. Can I offer you a glass?"

He opened the gate and slipped out, securing the panels with a quick twist of heavy wire, then double checking it to make sure it would hold. "*Nee.* I must get back to my work."

With her overture of friendship soundly rejected, she nodded and started toward the house.

He hesitated, then fell into step beside her. "What are your plans for this place?"

Oddly pleased by his interest, she said, "I want to enclose the orchard area with new fence. In the future I will divide it into separate pens so I can rotate where the alpacas graze. In spite of their behavior today, the fencing is really to keep predators out. My babies won't try to wander once they become accustomed to their new home. After that, I need to fix up the barn well enough to store winter hay for them." She walked slowly, more tired than she cared to admit.

"So my beans will be safe in the future?"

He hadn't really been interested in her plans, only in making sure his crops wouldn't be destroyed.

"*Ja,* as soon as I have the fences up. Of course, I will pay for any damages my animals caused."

"That won't be necessary. Do you plan to do all this work yourself?"

Faith paused and drew herself to her full height of five-foot-one. "I'm stronger than I look. I'm not afraid of hard work. With God's help I shall manage."

His eyes grew troubled. "I was going to offer the names of some young men who could use the work. That is why I asked. I did not mean to offend."

He had a gruff manner, but he was clearly sorry to have upset her.

Her defiance drained away, leaving her embarrassed. "I don't have the money to pay a hired man. Once I sell the yarns I am spinning, I will consider hiring someone."

"A light purse is nothing to be ashamed of."

"You're right, but I don't want people here to think I will be a burden on them."

"We would not think such a thing, Faith Martin. It would be un-Christian." There was a hint of rebuke in his words.

Amish families and communities supported all Amish widows and orphans. It was everyone's responsibility to care for them, but Faith needed to be able to take care of herself.

At her age and with her disability, she had no hope of marrying again. Even if such an offer came her way, she would never place her fate in the hands of another man. No, never again. The thought of doing so sent cold chills down her spine.

She looked up to see Adrian studying her intently. His frown had returned, but she wasn't frightened by it now. It was more bluff than substance.

He said, "If you find this farm is more than you can handle, I'll be happy to take it off your hands. For a fair price."

"I'm not interested in selling. I plan on staying here a long, long time."

"Then I pray you fare well among us, but do not forget my offer."

Faith watched as he strode away with long, easy strides. She saw a man at ease in his surroundings and at home on his own well-tended land. Not overly friendly, but not unfriendly. She found him…interesting. If his spouse was pleasant, they might prove to be good neighbors. She liked the idea of having someone close by to count on in an emergency.

She had turned down his offer to buy the place, but she sensed he didn't believe she could make a go of it on her own.

Why shouldn't he doubt her? She doubted herself.

For years Mose had hammered into her head what a failure she was as a wife. She couldn't give him children. It was her fault all his business enterprises failed because she didn't work hard enough.

In her heart she knew he was wrong, but after a while it ceased to matter. She had simply accepted the unkind things he'd said and kept quiet.

But Mose was gone now, and she had to believe in herself again. This was the time and place to start.

Watching Adrian cross the field toward his farm, she wondered what it would be like to have a strong, handsome man like Adrian Lapp for a husband? She shook her head at her foolish musing.

A woman could not tell if a man would be a good husband by his looks. Mose had been a handsome fellow, but his good-looking face had hidden a mean nature at odds with the teachings of their Amish faith.

She forgave Mose for the good of her own soul. He was standing now before a just God, answering for his sins while she was free to live a quiet and humble life. It would be enough.

She wondered if other Amish wives suffered silently as she had done. She prayed it wasn't true. In her heart she wanted to believe in the gentle nature of men who professed submission to God in every aspect of their lives—but there was no way to be certain. Only God could see into the hearts of men.

Pushing aside the host of unhappy memories gathered during her marriage, Faith entered her new home determined to finish sweeping away years of debris and clutter, from the house and from her heart. She was ready for her new beginning.

"I heard someone has moved into the old Delker

place. Do you know anything about it?" Ben Lapp handed the next set of boards up to Adrian who was perched on the top of the new corncrib.

Adrian knew there would be no end to his brother's curiosity. He might as well tell him everything he knew. "*Ja,* I met her yesterday. Her name is Faith Martin. She is Amish and a widow."

"I don't suppose she has a pretty daughter or two?" Ben asked hopefully. At seventeen, Adrian's youngest brother was in the first year of his *rumspringa,* his running around time, and always on the lookout for new girls to impress.

Adrian hated to dash his hopes. "Sorry, but she said she was alone."

"Too bad. A pretty new face would be welcome in this area."

Adrian recalled Faith's soft blue eyes and the sweet curve of her lips. "She is pretty enough."

"Really?"

Adrian caught the sudden interest in Ben's tone and grinned. "Pretty enough for a woman in her thirties."

Ben's face fell. "She's an old woman, then."

"Do you consider me old? I'm but thirty-two."

Adrian tried not to smile as he watched the struggle taking place behind his baby brother's eyes. Finally, Ben said, "You're not so old."

"Not *so* old. That's good to know for I was thinking of getting a cane when I went to market."

The thought of a cane brought a sudden vision of Faith struggling through the long grass with her crutch. How was she doing today? And why was he thinking about her again?

Ben grinned. "Tell me more about the widow. What's she like?"

Determined, pretty, kind to her animals, wary, worried. A number of ways to describe his new neighbor darted through Adrian's mind, but they all sounded personal, as if he'd taken an interest in her. "She raises alpacas."

"Alpacas? Why?"

"She spins their fleece into yarn for sale."

"I remember grandmother Lapp sitting at her spinning wheel. It was fascinating to watch her nimble fingers at work even when she was very old."

"I remember that, too."

"I never understood how chunks of wool became strands of yarn. Whatever became of her spinning wheel?"

"I suppose it's in *Mamm*'s attic if one of our sisters doesn't have it."

"It's sad to think someone is living at the Delker farm now."

"Why do you say that?" Adrian hammered the last board in place.

"Because we could eat all the peaches we wanted from those trees. No one cared. Now, we'll have to get permission. Is the house still in decent shape?"

"From the outside it doesn't look too bad. I'm not sure about the inside." Maybe he should stop in again and see if there was something Faith needed done around the place. That would be neighborly.

Not that he was looking for an excuse to see her again. He wasn't. He grew annoyed that she kept intruding into his carefully ordered world.

Ben backed down the ladder. "Do you even remember the people who lived there before?"

Adrian followed him. "I remember an old *Englisch* woman yelling at our cousin Sarah and I when we were helping ourselves to some low-hanging fruit. I must have been ten. She scared the daylights out of us. I think she went to a nursing home not long after that. When she passed away, the place stayed vacant."

"Is the new owner a relative?"

"That I don't know."

"Didn't you try to buy the place a few years ago?"

"More than once. I got a name and address from the County Recorder's office and sent several letters over the years, but no one ever answered me. I even tried to buy it from her yesterday, but she wasn't interested in selling." He could still hear the determination in her voice when she turned him down.

Determination was one thing. A strong back was another. She'd need both to get that place in working order.

"It's odd that she'd show up after all this time. I wonder why?" Ben mused.

Gathering together his tools, Adrian started toward the house. He'd spent more than enough time thinking about Faith Martin. "It's none of our business."

"Not our business? Ha! Tell that to *Mamm.* She'll be wanting every little detail, and she'll have it by Sunday next or I'll eat my hat." Ben fell into step beside Adrian.

It irked Adrian that he couldn't get Faith off his mind. What was she doing? Were her alpacas safe? Was she having trouble putting up fences for them? It would be a big job for one woman alone.

Ben wrinkled his nose in disgust. "What's that smell?"

Adrian swiped at the shoulder of his vest. The dried juice had brushed off, but not the aroma. "Alpaca spit."

"That's nasty. I didn't know they spit."

"Only if you scare them."

"I'll avoid doing that."

"Me, too, from now on."

"Before I forget, *Mamm* wanted me to remind you to come to supper tomorrow night."

Alerted by the sudden uncomfortable tone in Ben's voice, Adrian stopped. "Why would I need reminding? I come to supper every Wednesday evening with the family."

"That's what I told her."

Adrian closed his eyes and sighed deeply. "Who is it this time?"

"Who is what?" Ben looked the picture of innocence. Adrian wasn't fooled.

Leveling a no-nonsense, tell-me-the-truth look at his brother, Adrian repeated himself. "Who is it this time?"

"Edna Hershberger," Ben admitted and flinched.

"Edna? She's at least fifteen years older than I am."

"Her cousin is visiting from Apple Creek. Her younger female cousin. I hear she's nice-looking."

"Why does Mother keep doing this?" Adrian started walking again. He wasn't interested in meeting marriageable women. He would never marry again. He had sworn that over his young wife's grave when he'd laid their son to rest beside her.

"Mother wants to see you happy."

"I am happy." The moment he said the words he knew they were a lie.

"No, you're not. You haven't been happy since Lovina and Gideon died."

The mention of his wife and son sent a sharp stab of pain through Adrian's chest. He bore wounds that would not heal. No one understood that. "I'd rather not talk about them."

"It's been three years since Gideon died, Adrian. It's been eight years since Lovina passed away."

"For me, it was yesterday."

God had taken away the people he loved, leaving Adrian an empty shell of a man. An empty shell could not love anyone, certainly not God, for He had stripped away the most important parts of Adrian's life.

Adrian went through the motions of his faith, but each day it became harder to repeat the platitudes that no longer held meaning for him. Disowning his Amish faith would only lead to being separated from his remaining family. For their sakes he kept his opinions about God to himself.

Ben laid a hand on Adrian's shoulder. "You can't blame *Mamm* for worrying about you."

Adrian met his brother's gaze. "Mother needs to accept that I won't marry again. You can tell her I've made other plans for tomorrow evening."

"What plans?" Ben called after him.

Adrian didn't answer him. Instead, he walked to the end of his lane and up the road for a quarter of a mile to where a small field of tombstones lay enclosed by a white wooden fence. A fence he painted each year to keep it looking nice.

He opened the gate and crossed the field to where an old cedar tree had been cut down. The stump made a perfect seat for him to sit and visit with his wife and son.

The breeze blew softly across the open field. Beyond the fence he saw fat black-and-white cattle grazing in a neighbor's pasture. Overhead the blue sky held a few white clouds that changed shape as they traveled on the wind. He took off his hat and looked down at the small tombstones that bore the names of his wife and child.

"It's another pretty day, isn't it, Lovina? I remember how much you enjoyed the summer evenings when the days stretch out so long. I miss sitting with you on the porch and watching the sun go down. I miss everything about both of you."

Tears filled his eyes as emotions clogged his throat. It took a minute before he could go on.

Clearing his throat, he said, "We've got a new neighbor. Her name is Faith Martin. I think you'd like her. You should see the strange animals she has. They spit. I think I like sheep better and you know how much I dislike them."

Clasping his hands together, he leaned forward with his elbows propped on his knees. "*Mamm* is at it again. She's trying to fix me up with a cousin of Edna Hershberger. I wish she would learn to leave well enough alone. I don't want anyone else. You will be my only wife in this life and in the next. If Gideon had lived, it might have been different."

The tears came back, forcing him to lift his head. "A boy needs a mother, but he's with you now. I know that makes you happy because it gives me comfort, too."

He sniffed once and wiped his eyes with the heels of his hands. "I'm not going over to *Mamm*'s for supper tomorrow. I'm sorry if that disappoints you. I've decided to go over to Faith Martin's. That place needs too much work for a woman alone to do it all. I can spare an hour or two in the morning and again at night. The days are long now," he added with a wry smile.

The memory of Faith declaring she wasn't afraid of work slipped into his mind. "She reminds me of you a little bit in the way her chin comes up when she's riled. She said an odd thing yesterday. She said she didn't want people here to think she would be a burden. It makes me wonder who made her feel that way in her last community."

Having said what he needed to say, he rose to his feet. "Enough about our neighbor. Give Gideon a kiss for me. I miss you, Lovey."

So much so it was hard to put into words. "Sometimes, I wake at night and I still reach for you. But you aren't there and it hurts all over again."

As he walked away, he wondered if Faith Martin woke in the night and reached for the husband who was gone.

Chapter Three

Faith woke to the sound of a persistent clanking coming from outside her house. Squinting, she could just make out the hands of the clock on her dresser. Six thirty-five.

Her eyes popped open wide. Six thirty-five! Panic sent her heart racing. Mose would be so angry when he discovered she'd slept late.

Throwing back the sheet, she sat up and stopped as every muscle in her body protested the quick movement. Had he beaten her again? What had she done wrong this time? She couldn't remember.

Swinging her feet off the mattress, she reached for her clothes. They weren't on a chair beside the bed. Looking around the strange room, she saw them hanging from a peg on the wall. Her panic dropped away like a stone from her chest. She drew a deep breath.

Mose might be gone, but his imprint remained in her life. In moments of mindless panic like this one. In nightmares that left her weak and shaking in the night.

Faith began to recite her morning prayers, letting

the grace of God's presence wash away her fears and restore her peace.

Dear Lord, I give You thanks for this new day, for my new home and for the strength to face whatever may come my way. I know You are with me, always. Watch over Kyle and keep him safe. If it is Your will, Lord, let him join me here, soon. Amen.

A few years ago her morning prayers had been much simpler. *Please don't let me make Mose angry today.* Sometimes, she wondered if she would ever be truly free of him.

She stood and crossed to the open window. The sound of hammering started up again. It was coming from her orchard, but she couldn't see anyone. What was going on?

She dressed and set to work quickly brushing out her hip-length hair. When it was smooth, she parted it straight down the middle and began to make a tight roll of it along her hairline pulling all of it together and finally twisting the remainder into a tight bun, which she pinned at the back of her head. With her hair secure, she donned her *kapp* and pinned it in place. Outside, the clanking continued.

Sitting on the edge of the bed, she buckled on her leg brace, wincing as the padded bands came into contact with her chafed skin. She was paying for all the time she'd spent working and sweating the past few days. She needed to apply more salve to the reddened areas, but that would have to wait. Her priority was finding out what was going on outside.

After leaving the house, she limped to the barn to check on her animals. Copper dozed in her stall. The alpacas, all ten of them, as Faith quickly counted, stood or lay in their pen outside. Relieved, but with mounting curiosity, Faith made her way into the orchard.

A few yards from where she had stopped building the fence the evening before, Adrian Lapp was pounding a steel fence post into the ground. He'd already added several stakes along the string she had laid out to mark the boundary of her pen.

What was he doing here? She hadn't asked for his help. As quickly as her objections surfaced, she swallowed them. Humility was the cornerstone of her Amish faith. Being humble also meant accepting help when help was offered.

Adrian hadn't seen her yet. She watched as he effortlessly drove in the stakes with a metal sleeve that fit over the top of each post. Compared to the heavy maul she had used to painstakingly pound each post into the ground, his tool made the job much easier. And he didn't even have to stand on the wooden box she had used just to reach the top of the six-foot-tall t-posts.

All right, he was strong and tall. It was a great combination when building fences, but that didn't mean she needed to stand here staring. She had half a mind to go back to the house and let him finish the row, but her conscience wouldn't let her. This was her property now. She was the one who needed to take care of it.

"Guder mariye," she called out in her native Pennsylvania Dutch, the German dialect spoken by the Amish. "You've done a lot of work while I was lazing abed. *Danki.*"

He stopped pounding, wiped the sweat from his brow with his shirtsleeve, and nodded in her direction. "Good morning to you, too. You have accomplished quite a bit here yourself."

His gaze swept across the posts that she'd put in yesterday, the yard she had mown into order with an old scythe and the fresh laundry waving on the clothesline she'd strung between two trees beside the house.

"I could have done more if I'd had a fence post driver such as you have there." She walked toward him to look at the tool.

"They aren't expensive. You can pick them up pretty cheap at farm auctions."

"I will keep that in mind."

It seemed to Faith that he wanted to say more, but instead, he returned to pounding the post he was working on until he'd sunk it another two feet into the ground.

"I appreciate your help, Mr. Lapp, but I can manage on my own. I'm sure you have plenty of work to attend to."

"Call me Adrian. I've got a few free hours today. Do you have a wire stretcher? I can put up the fencing after I get these posts in if you do."

"It's in the barn along with the rolls of woven fence wire I want to use. Are you sure you have time to do this? I hate to impose."

"I'll do the posts this morning and come back this evening to finish putting up the wire. Unless you object?" He grabbed another stake, measured off the distance with a few quick steps and began hammering the post into the ground.

"That will be fine." Other than taking care of her animals, she would have the whole day free to work on the house. Adrian's help was a blessing she hadn't anticipated.

Still, she had plenty to do to get the house ready for the social worker's arrival next Wednesday. Would

God understand if she did a little extra work on Sunday? Sundays were days of rest and prayer and a time for visiting with friends and family even if there wasn't a service.

Since Amish church services were held every other Sunday, she would have another week before she had to face the entire congregation. Would they all be as kind and helpful as her new neighbor? He had a gruff way about him, but his actions spoke loudly of a kind heart.

After watching Adrian work for a few more minutes, Faith realized there was nothing she could do to help him and she was wasting time. She left him to his work and returned to the house giving thanks to God for her neighbor's timely intervention.

Inside the house she applied salve to her chafed leg, then set about making breakfast and a pot of strong coffee. An hour later, just as she was pulling a pair of cinnamon coffee cakes from the oven, Adrian came to the screen door.

She fought back a smile. With the windows wide-open to the morning breeze, she had been sure the smell of her baking would reach him.

He said, "I finished the row of posts you had laid out."

She set the second hot pan on the stovetop. "Already? You've saved me a lot of work. *Danki*. Would you like some coffee?"

He hesitated, then said, "I would."

When he came inside, her kitchen instantly felt small and crowded. Unease skittered over her skin. She moved away to make more room between them.

He looked for a peg to hang his hat on, but there wasn't one. He settled for tossing it on the sideboard and took a seat at her table. When he wasn't looming over her, Faith could breathe better.

He motioned toward the wallpaper with its faded yellow flowers. "You will have a lot to do to make this a plain house."

"*Ja.* It will be a big task. Every room is wallpapered." She tapped the floor with her foot. "This black-and-white linoleum will be fine but there is pink-and-white linoleum in the bathroom."

The colorful flooring and wallpaper would all have to be taken out. The Amish lived in simplicity, as they believed was God's will. They avoided loud colors and worldly things such as electricity in order to live separate from the world. Hopefully, the bishop in her new community would give her plenty of time to make over the house from English to Amish.

She would have the option of painting her walls blue, green or gray. The brightly patterned linoleum on the bathroom floor would have to go. She could leave the planks underneath bare or replace the linoleum with a simpler, more modest color. It was all on her list of things to be done. A list she was whittling down much too slowly.

She cut two pieces of coffee cake and carried one of them along with a cup of coffee to the table. Adrian accepted her offering with a nod of thanks. "The county will take down the electric lines leading to the house, but you will have to take down the ones leading to the barn."

"I know. At least the gas stove still works and I was able to have the propane tank filled before I arrived."

Fetching a cup of coffee and a piece of cake for herself, she said, "I've cooked on a wood-burning stove, but I'm not a good hand at it."

Adrian's look of sympathy said it all. She sat down at the table with a heavy sigh. "I take it the *Ordnung* of this church district doesn't allow propane cook stoves?"

"*Nee,* we do not. The stove must be wood-burning or coal-burning. But you may have a propane-powered refrigerator and washing machine."

The thought of chopping wood or hauling coal on top of her other chores was enough to dampen her spirits. She glanced sadly at the stove. It was old, but it worked well. She would hate to see it go.

It was always this way when she moved to a new community. Each Amish church district had their own rules about what they allowed and what they didn't. Each bishop in charge of a district often interpreted those rules differently.

She had lived in several communities that used tractors in the fields instead of horses. When they'd lived in Mifflin County, Pennsylvania, their church district permitted members to drive only yellow buggies, another place only gray ones. Here in Hope Springs the buggies were black.

She would have to make all new *kapps* for herself, too. The women of each district wore distinctive patterns. She would get around to that if, and only if, she met with the approval of this community and they voted to accept her as a new church member.

If they didn't accept her, she would have to look for another nearby district who would or live as an outsider. "I must meet with your bishop soon."

"Bishop Zook is a good man. He will help you learn your way among us."

"Is he a good preacher?" she asked, half in jest. Church services often lasted three or more hours.

"I've only fallen asleep twice during his sermons." Adrian didn't crack a smile, but she saw the twinkle of humor in his eyes. It surprised and delighted her.

"Then he must be *wunderbarr*. I'm looking forward to my first church Sunday already."

Adrian changed the subject. "Are you a relative of Mrs. Delker, the woman who used to own this place?"

"No, but Mose, my husband, was a grandchild of hers. I inherited this farm after he passed away. It's odd really, because he never once mentioned owning a farm in Ohio."

"I tried to buy it from him about five years ago."

"Did you? That must have been when we were raising chickens in Nebraska. Why did he say he wouldn't sell?"

They had certainly needed the money. The chicken houses had been another of her husband's failed business ventures. They'd left Nebraska owing money to everyone from the feed store to their landlord. Only Mose's last venture, buying her first four alpacas, had actually turned out well.

She never understood how her husband talked people into loaning him money for his wild ideas or how he could just pick up and walk away without looking back or even feeling badly for those who'd lost money because of him. Every time they moved, they left hard feelings behind.

Would this new community receive her into the church if they knew her husband had left debts unpaid all across the Midwest? She was sorry now that she had mentioned Nebraska to Adrian.

"Your husband didn't give a reason why he wouldn't sell. He never answered my letters."

She wanted to tell Adrian how lucky he was *not* to have done business with her husband, but she wouldn't speak ill of the dead. She rose and took her cup to the sink. "We moved around a lot. Perhaps your letters missed him."

"Perhaps. Do you find it hard to talk about him?" he asked quietly.

"Yes." She kept her back to Adrian. It was hard to talk about Mose because there was so little she could say about him that was good.

"I understand."

The odd quality in his tone made her look at him closely. The pain in his eyes touched her heart. Why was he so sad?

He rose abruptly and crossed the room to pick up his hat. "I must be going."

"Wait a moment." She quickly wrapped the remaining coffee cake in a length of cheesecloth and added a small package wrapped in brown paper and string to the top. She held it out to him. He stared at her as if he didn't understand.

"It's a small token of my appreciation for all your hard work. A pair of socks made from my alpaca yarn. Please tell your wife that she is welcome to visit anytime. I'm sure she and your children will enjoy meeting my animals."

Adrian blinked back the sudden sting of tears. Gideon would have loved to have seen Faith's animals and Lovina would have liked this new neighbor with her determined ways. It was so unfair that their lives had been cut short. So unfair that he had to go on living without them.

"Is something wrong?" Faith inquired softly.

He took the packages from her. "My wife and son passed away."

"I'm so sorry. You must miss them very much."

Adrian met Faith's sympathetic gaze. Oddly, he found he wanted to talk about Lovina and Gideon. Somehow, he knew Faith would understand.

"I miss them every day. My son would have liked your alpacas. He had a way with animals, that boy did. He was always finding lost and hurt creatures and bringing them home for me to make well."

"Little boys believe their fathers can do anything."

"Too bad it isn't true."

He hadn't been able to save his wife or his son. That bitter truth haunted him day and night.

He blinked hard to clear his vision. Faith's face swam into view. She understood. He saw it in her eyes. It was more than sympathy and compassion. She had been in the same dark place that surrounded him.

"How old was your son when he died?" she asked.

"Four."

"You mustn't think me cruel, but four years is a gift. I wish I might have had four years, even four days, with my daughters."

"You've lost children, too?"

"Twin daughters who were stillborn. I always wondered if that was why Mose was never able to settle in one place. If we'd had a family, maybe things would have been different. Only God knows."

"I wanted at least six children. Lovina wanted a dozen or more. Gideon was the first and he was perfect."

Adrian couldn't believe he was talking to this woman about his family. He hadn't been able to talk to anyone about them since Gideon's death. Maybe it was because she'd known the same kind of tragedy that he felt she understood what he was going through. Maybe it was because Ben had brought the subject up yesterday.

Whatever the reason, Adrian suddenly decided not to bare more of his soul. Remembering was too painful.

He said, "The coffee cake is appreciated. I'll be back tonight to help finish your fence. I need my bean crop kept safe from your overgrown rabbits."

"Your help has been most welcome, neighbor."

He settled his hat on his head and walked outside into the summer sunshine. At the foot of her steps, he stopped and looked back. She stood framed in the doorway, her arms crossed, a faraway expression in her eyes. He wondered what she was thinking about.

Was she thinking about the children and husband she had lost or the work that needed to be done? Did she find it hard to go forward with her life? Somehow, he didn't think so.

Faith Martin was a remarkable woman.

The moment the thought occurred to him, he began walking, putting as much distance as he could between himself and his disturbing neighbor.

He'd come to Faith's home today to do his Christian duty by helping a neighbor, but he'd also been interested in seeing exactly what shape the place was in. The more he saw, the less he expected she would be able to manage it alone.

He might yet be able to buy the land. If he made some improvements for her, well, that would mean less work for him later.

Having a fence around the orchard was a good idea. Letting the alpacas graze down the overgrown grass would make it easier to mow later, or he could put sheep in to do the same job.

At the edge of his hay meadow, he stopped and glanced toward Faith's house once more. Helping her might turn out to be a good idea—from a business point of view. Not because he wanted to spend time in her company.

His wife might be gone, but he wouldn't be untrue to her. Lovina had been the one love of his life. He had no business thinking about spending time with another woman.

He had come to Faith's place to lend a hand. He hadn't been looking for sympathy or a shoulder to cry on. He hadn't planned on finding someone who could understand the pain he lived with. Yet, that was exactly what he'd found with Faith Martin.

Was that why he found her so attractive? His feelings toward her troubled and confused him.

He had already promised to help her. He wouldn't go back on his word. As promised, he would help her get her home in order as a good neighbor should, but he wouldn't spend any more time alone with her.

Chapter Four

It was shortly before noon on Saturday when Faith heard the sound of a horse and buggy approaching the house. She dropped the sponge she'd been using to wash grimy windows into her pail, dried her hands on her apron and waited to see who had come calling.

The buggy stopped in front of her gate, and three Amish women stepped out. They all carried large baskets over their arms.

"*Guder mariye,*" called the oldest woman. She wore a bright, beaming smile of welcome. Behind her came a young woman with black hair and dark eyes followed by another woman with blond hair.

"*Guder mariye,*" Faith replied. A faint flicker of happiness sparked inside of her. She was free to make new friends here—if they would have her. She wouldn't have to hide her bruised face or bear pitying looks from those who suspected her husband's cruelty.

The leader of the group stopped at the bottom of Faith's steps, adjusted her round wire spectacles on the bridge of her nose and switched her heavy basket to her other arm. "Welcome to Hope Springs. I am Nettie Sutter."

She indicated the dark-haired girl standing behind her. "This is my daughter-in-law, Katie."

"And I am Sarah Wyse," the blonde added. "My cousin is your neighbor to the south."

"Adrian?"

Sarah nodded. "When I heard he'd met you, I thought it best to rush over and assure you the rest of Hope Springs is more hospitable than Adrian is."

"He has been most kind and welcoming."

"He has?" Sarah exchanged astonished glances with her companions.

Faith swept a hand toward the front door. "Do come in, but please excuse the condition of the house."

"None of us can keep our houses free of dust in the summertime. With all the windows open to catch any breeze, the dust piles up before you know it."

Faith had more than a sprinkling of dust to contend with. She had twenty years worth of accumulation to haul out. She was thankful that she had made a coffee cake for herself while making one for Adrian that morning. At least she had something to offer her guests.

The women gathered around the kitchen table, each one setting her basket on it. Sarah opened the lid of the one she carried and began to pull out its contents. "We brought a few things to help you settle in and get this old house in order."

Out of her basket, Sarah brought cleaning supplies, plastic pails, pine cleaner, rags, sponges and brushes. "Where shall we start?"

Faith was speechless. She hadn't expected help from the community so soon.

Nettie picked up the pail and carried it to the sink. "I will finish these windows for you. Sarah, why don't you take a broom to the front porch and steps? Elam, Eli and his boys will be here to paint this evening."

"I'll get this food put away." Katie opened her basket and brought out two loaves of bread and a rhubarb pie with a gorgeous lattice crust just begging to be eaten. A second later she began unpacking mason jars filled with canned fruits and vegetables.

Faith was overwhelmed by their kindness. "*Danki.* This is far too much."

"No thanks are needed," Nettie assured her.

Perhaps not needed but gratefully given. Faith asked, "Who are Elam and Eli?"

Nettie smiled broadly. "Elam is my son and Katie's husband. Eli and his sons live down the road a piece. Our farm is a little ways beyond that toward Hope Springs."

"Where do you need me to start?" Katie asked, looking over the kitchen.

Faith took a second to gather her thoughts. "I've cleaned out one bedroom upstairs, but the others haven't been touched in years. If you want to start in one of them, that would be great. Sarah, perhaps you could help me drag the mattresses outside so I can beat the dust out of them."

Sarah held out her hand. "Lead the way."

The house quickly became a beehive of activity. Old bedding was taken out, walls and floors were scrubbed free of grime and rubbish was hauled out to the burn barrel. Everywhere inside the house, the crisp scent of pine cleaner filled the air. In one afternoon the women managed to do more inside the house than Faith had accomplished in four days on her own.

Her heirloom clock was striking five when the women gathered in the kitchen once more. Faith wiped her forehead with the back of her sleeve. "I don't know about you, but I've worked up an appetite. I believe I will sample this pie. Would anyone else care for a piece?"

Nettie smiled brightly. "I thought you'd never ask."

"Where are your plates?" Sarah was already moving toward the cabinets.

"To the left of the sink." Chuckling, Faith turned to Katie. "Would you like some?"

"Yes! I could eat the whole thing."

Nettie grinned. "That's because you are eating for two."

Faith endured a sharp stab of wistfulness but quickly recovered. "Congratulations. When is your baby due?"

"The last week of November."

"Is this your first?" Faith gathered forks for everyone and brought them to the table.

Katie shook her head. "It will be my second. We already have a little girl, so we're hoping for a boy."

Nettie sliced into the pie and slipped a piece onto the plate Sarah supplied. "Either will be fine with me as long as it is a healthy grandbaby."

Faith decided it was the perfect opening to share something about herself. "I am expecting a little boy soon."

Everyone's glances fell to her trim waist. She chuckled as she appeased their unspoken curiosity. "I'm hoping my nephew can come to live with me soon. That's why I have to get this house in some kind of order."

"Is he visiting for the summer?" Sarah asked. The women all took a seat at the table.

Sadness put a catch in Faith's voice. "*Nee,* he is not coming for a visit. I hope he will live with me until he is old enough to marry and have a family of his own. My English brother and his wife were killed recently in a flash flood in Texas when their car was swept off the road. Fortunately, Kyle, their son, wasn't with them at the time. I'm all the family he has now."

Sarah reached across the table and laid a hand over Faith's. "I'm sorry for your loss. I lost my sister not long ago, so I understand your grief."

"*Danki.* I had not seen my brother for many years. He fell in love with an English girl and left our faith. I've never met his son. I'm trying to adopt him, but the process is painfully slow."

Nettie finished dishing out the pie and handed the plate to Faith. "It will be a hard change for him coming from an *Englisch* life to live in an Amish home."

"I am worried about that. What if he says he doesn't want to live here?"

Sarah gave Faith an incredulous look. "What little boy wouldn't love to live on a farm?"

"One who is used to television and video games." Faith was giving voice to one of her biggest fears. That Kyle would hate living with her.

"To worry about such things is to borrow trouble," Nettie chided. "God is bringing this child into your life. He knows what is best for all of us."

"You're right. I will put my trust in Him." Faith took a bite of her pie and savored the sweet tart flavor and tender, flaky crust. Nettie Sutter really knew how to make good pie.

"Tell us about yourself," Katie prompted. "I hear you have some unusual animals."

"I have ten alpacas. I raise them for their fleece. I spin it into yarns. Once I get this house in order, I will start looking for a place to sell my work."

Sarah brightened. "I work at a fabric store and we sell many types of yarn. The store owner's name is Janet Mallory. You should speak to her."

"In Hope Springs?" Could it possibly be this easy to find a market for her work? Faith dared not get her hopes up.

"Yes, we are on Main Street, downtown. You can't miss it. It's called Needles and Pins. Janet is always looking for things made by the local Amish people to sell in her store. We get a fair amount of tourists in Hope Springs. Amish handmade items sell very well, although most of our yarn is bought by local Amish women for use at home."

Faith said, "I'm grateful for your suggestion. I will come in once I have my house in order."

Sarah leaned forward. "Is it true that your animal spit on Adrian? His brother Ben said he smelled as bad as a skunk."

Faith felt the heat rush to her cheeks. "Myrtle did spit on Adrian. I don't blame him for being upset."

Sarah laughed, a sweet light sound that made Faith smile, too. "I would have given anything to see Adrian lose his composure. What did he say?"

Faith crossed her arms over her chest and mimicked his deep stern voice. "Your creatures are eating my beans."

"*Ja,* that is just the way he talks." Sarah giggled again, then took another bite of her pie.

Faith couldn't let them think Adrian had been unkind. "He was upset, but he helped me catch them. Except for Myrtle, the others seem to like him. He's also been helping me build fences to keep them in."

Sarah sobered. "Adrian is coming over to help you build fences? That's interesting. He has stayed mainly to himself these past few years."

Faith's curiosity was piqued. Wanting to learn more about her stoic neighbor, she asked, "Why is that?"

Sarah glanced at the other women, then back to Faith. "Adrian's wife died shortly after their son was born. He raised the boy by himself. His son was his whole world. One afternoon, Adrian was walking home from his field that lies across the highway from his house. His son saw him coming and raced out to greet him. He ran right into the path of a car and was killed in front of Adrian."

Faith's heart twisted with pity knowing the pain he must have felt. "No parent should have to bury a child."

Nettie sighed heavily. "There is no greater sorrow. That is how we know God loves us. For He allowed His only son to die for our sins so that we may rejoice with Him in heaven for eternity."

From the tone of her voice and the sadness in her eyes, Faith knew that Nettie was speaking from firsthand experience. She said, "It is our solace to know they are waiting to greet us in heaven."

"Indeed it is," Nettie agreed.

Katie was the one to break the ensuing silence. "I have never seen an alpaca up close. May I take a look at yours?"

"Of course." Faith took pity on the expectant mother having to listen to such a somber conversation. Rising to her feet, she motioned for Katie to follow her. Nettie and Sarah deposited the dirty plates in the sink and quickly joined them.

Outside, they crossed the yard in a tight group. Nettie eyed the sad state of the barn. "You will need to find a strong husband to get this farm in shape. We have several bachelors in our church district who would make a good husband to you and a father to your nephew."

Quickly, Faith said, "I have no plans to marry again."

"Not even if the right fellow happens along?" Katie teased.

"I'm too old to remarry," Faith added firmly.

Nettie started laughing. "No, you aren't. I'm getting married in a few weeks. If I found someone at my age, you can, too. It is all up to God."

Katie asked Nettie a question about preparations for the upcoming nuptials, and the two women began an animated discussion.

Faith slowed her pace and hoped that would be the end of her part in the conversation, but Sarah shortened her stride and dropped back beside her. "Nettie is right. It's up to God."

"It is up to me, too. I see no need to marry again."

She felt Sarah's keen eyes studying her intently. Finally, Sarah said, "Your marriage wasn't a happy one? I understand. We won't speak of it again."

Faith could only wonder if Sarah's experience in marriage was the same.

As they rounded the barn, Faith saw her alpacas were all grazing except for Myrtle. She stood alone near the barn door. Faith called out to them. "Come here, babies. I have people who want to meet you."

They all raised their heads to look at her, but only Socks ventured close.

"Will they spit at us?" Katie asked.

"They only spit if they are startled. Sometimes they will spit at each other if they are annoyed, but for the most part they all get along."

"They are so cute," Katie gushed.

Faith had had the same reaction the first time she'd seen one. "They are wonderful animals. They are docile and they are quite smart."

"Which one spit on my cousin?" Sarah leaned her arms on the top of the gate.

Faith pointed. "That was Myrtle. She's the gray one standing by the barn door. She is expecting in a few weeks."

Katie started laughing. "I know just how she feels. Being pregnant makes me moody, too. Some days I feel like spitting at my husband. Poor Elam knows to stay out of my way when I get in a temper."

Nettie and Sarah joined in Katie's laughter. Myrtle moved as far away from the noise as she could get. She huddled by the corner of the barn and watched them all with a wary expression.

Faith felt a glimmer of hope begin to grow in her heart. She would enjoy having these women for friends. It seemed things were beginning to look up for her in this new place.

"Here you all are!"

Faith looked past Myrtle as a woman walked into view from around the corner of the barn. Myrtle took quick exception to the stranger coming so close. She spat and galloped to the far side of the pen, giving an alarm call that sent the entire herd milling in panic.

The middle-aged woman stood frozen with a shocked expression on her face as alpaca spit dripped from her chin.

Katie clasped her hands over her mouth. "Oh, no, not her."

"Who is it?" Faith asked, knowing full well she didn't want to hear the answer.

"The bishop's wife," Katie whispered.

"You should have seen the look on Esther Zook's face." Sarah started giggling again. "I'm sorry, I can't help it. It was the funniest thing. Poor Faith, I've never seen anyone so contrite."

Adrian, sitting in the corner of his living room, continued his pretense of reading the newspaper while he listened to his cousin regale his mother with her story. Sarah was a frequent visitor in his home. They had been close since they were children.

"What did you think of her?" his mother asked.

"Adrian's new neighbor or the bishop's wife?" Sarah began giggling again.

Glancing over top of the paper, Adrian saw his mother frown at Sarah's levity. "I meant Faith Martin."

Sarah shrugged. "She seems nice enough. She is certainly a hard worker."

His mother transferred her gaze to him. "It's a pity she is handicapped for there are several bachelors around who are on the lookout for a new wife."

Compelled to defend Faith, he said, "She walks with a barely noticeable limp. It isn't a handicap."

"I'm sure there is someone who is willing to overlook such a minor imperfection." She gave him a pointed stare.

He turned the page and ignored her broad hint. He wasn't on the lookout for a wife. His mother would eventually learn to accept that.

Sarah, a widow herself, rolled her eyes. "*Aenti* Linda,

if you mean Toby Yoder and Ivan Stultz, I don't think they would mind a wife who walks with a limp. Not as long as she can cook and clean, mend clothes, run a farm and milk twenty cows twice a day while they spend their time gossiping at the feed store. Why, they would both be thrilled to have such a woman."

"You might be right," his mother admitted.

Adrian couldn't stay silent any longer. "Maybe she doesn't want to marry again. Did you think of that?"

"What woman doesn't want a husband and children of her own?" his mother countered.

"The love between a husband or wife doesn't die because one of them is with God. It lives on." He didn't care if she knew he was talking about himself.

Her gaze softened. "Of course not, but we can love more than one person."

I know. I loved a wife and a child and God took them both.

"Sarah hasn't remarried," he pointed out, keeping his painful thoughts to himself. His cousin ducked her head. Her smile vanished. He was sorry he'd brought the subject up. Sarah's husband had passed away from cancer over three years ago.

Glancing from Sarah back to Adrian, his mother gave him a fierce scowl. "Sarah has not closed her heart to love. It will find her again when God wills it. Hopefully, before she is too old to bear children."

He went back to his paper, knowing his mother would always have the last word.

Sarah said, "Faith doesn't have to worry about that. She already has a child on the way."

"What?" Adrian and his mother demanded together in shocked surprise.

Sarah couldn't keep a straight face. "She is adopting her brother's child."

"Well, that changes things a little," his mother mused. "Not all men want a wife and a child at the same time."

Sarah propped her elbows on the table. "Faith insists she won't marry again, and I believe she means it."

Linda waved aside her comment. "Nonsense. Once she has had the chance to meet a few of our fellows she'll change her mind. Let me think. Micah Beachy might be just the one. He's got a nice little farm over by Sugarcreek and he's never been married. I'll have to invite him over for a visit next month."

Intrigued by Sarah's comments, Adrian asked, "She specifically said she won't remarry? Does she intend to raise a child alone?"

Sarah turned in her seat to face Adrian. "*Ja.* What did you think of Faith when you met her?"

"I think she is going to have a hard time making a go of that farm. She doesn't have the money to hire help."

He understood Faith's reluctance to marry again. Suffering the pain of losing a spouse and child was more than anyone should have to bear. Loving someone meant risking that pain again. He wasn't willing to take that chance.

"The peaches in her orchard should be nearly ripe. If she sells her fruit, she'll be able to make some money, won't she?" Sarah asked.

Adrian shook his head. "The place is so overgrown, she'll have a hard time even getting to the fruit. Those trees haven't been pruned in twenty years. Most of them are so old they may not even bear fruit anymore. The peaches she does have will be small because no one thinned out the fruit when it was setting on."

"I told her to bring some of her yarns into Needles and Pins. I'm sure Janet will allow her to sell them there."

He turned the page of his paper. "It will take a lot of yarn to fix up that farm."

His mother left off cleaning the kitchen counter and began wiping down the table. "What kind of shape is the house in?"

Sarah brightened. "It's not too bad. I didn't see any water damage inside, so the roof must still be sound. But it was so grimy. It took us hours to get the walls and floors clean. Elam Sutter, Eli Imhoff and his two sons managed to get the outside of the house painted but not the barn. I'm afraid it's in need of a few repairs first."

"More than a few," Adrian added, unable to stay out of the conversation.

His mother folded her arms over her ample bosom. "Then everyone will have their work cut out for them. It is clear our sister is in need. We cannot turn our backs on her."

Folding his paper and laying it aside for good, Adrian said, "Do you really think everyone will feel the same way? She isn't even a member of our church. Clearly, she didn't make a good impression on the bishop's wife."

His mother waved aside his objection. "Esther Zook will get over being made a laughingstock. She won't hold our new neighbor to blame for the actions of her animals. Esther knows her Christian duty, and when she forgets it, her husband will remind her."

Adrian exchanged glances with Sarah. She obviously wasn't in total agreement with his mother. She knew Esther Zook's opinion could sway many of the women in the community if she chose to rebuff Faith.

He rose to his feet. Grabbing his straw hat from the peg beside the front door, he slapped it on his head.

"Where are you going?" his mother asked.

"To see a woman about some peaches."

He left the house and headed for the hay meadow that separated his property from Faith's farm as fast as his feet could carry him. With him out of the way, his mother could finish fussing in his kitchen and talk about him freely. Not that his presence ever stopped her.

She meant well, he knew that. He appreciated that she came by to cook and clean for him each week even though he didn't need her help. What he didn't like was her interference.

Twice he'd found Lovina's and Gideon's clothes had been packed away in a trunk in the attic. He never said a word to his mother. He simply put the clothes back into the bureau beside his own. He wasn't ready to let go.

Adrian's rapid steps slowed as he approached Faith's house. He wasn't sure exactly what he wanted to say to her. He wasn't even sure why he'd come. As he neared the front of her house, he saw she had moved her spinning wheel onto the front porch, probably to take advantage of the cooler evening breezes.

Her head was bent over the wheel as she concentrated on her task. With deft fingers, she pulled fleece from a bundle into long slender strands. Her feet pumped the pedals and made the wheel fly, spinning the fleece rapidly into yarn that wound around a pair of spindles.

It wasn't so much the art of her work that caught his attention. It was the look on her face. The worry and pain he'd seen before were gone, replaced by an expression of serenity. A sweet, soft smile curved her lips. He caught snatches of a song she was humming. So this was how Faith Martin looked when she was happy.

He couldn't bring himself to interrupt. Instead, he leaned on her rickety gate and simply enjoyed watching her work.

He had once wished to see her smile. He had no idea the sight could steal his breath away.

As much as he wished to let her work in peace, he had come here for a reason.

Chapter Five

"You make that look easy."

Faith jerked upright, searching for the source of the voice that startled her. She relaxed when she caught sight of Adrian leaning against her front gate. What was he doing here this late in the day? Her fence was finished.

How long had he been watching her?

Did he disapprove of the song she'd been humming? Mose had always hated it when she'd sung or hummed.

Faith slowed her spinning wheel to a stop. It wasn't fair of her to compare Adrian to Mose. They were two very different men. Even from the small amount of time she'd spent with Adrian, she could see that. She had to learn to let go of the past.

She said, "It is easy when you find the right rhythm. What can I do for you this evening?"

"I have come with another proposition for you."

Disappointment stabbed her. He'd come to make another offer on her land. Was she foolhardy to hang on to her dream of a place of her own?

She gathered up her loose fleece and placed it back

in a blue plastic laundry basket. "I am still not interested in selling my land."

"What about your peaches?" He opened the gate and walked to the foot of her steps.

She shifted her basket to her good hip. "You want to buy peaches from me?"

"Not exactly. I'm willing to harvest your fruit and sell it for shares."

Faith pondered his surprising offer. She already had more work to do than she could possibly get done before Kyle arrived. That was, if the adoption when through. Selling peaches hadn't entered her mind. She had thought only of canning some for herself.

The extra income would be most welcome if Adrian was willing to do the work. "What share would you be asking?"

"I was thinking of a seventy/thirty split."

That was generous. "Seventy for me, thirty for you?"

He cracked a smile as he shook his head. "*Nee.* I would be doing the majority of the work."

Maybe so, but she wasn't going to *give* her produce away. "The fruit is all mine. If you will do fifty/fifty, I'll consider it."

"The crop will go to waste if I don't pick it for you. In that case, you'll get nothing."

He spoke the truth and she knew it. "Very well, sixty/forty and we have a deal."

Nodding once, he said, "*Goot.* We have a deal."

She expected him to leave, but he didn't. The heat of the day had waned. A cool breeze slipped past her cheeks and rustled through the leaves of the trees beside the house. For her, evenings were the best time of the day. She said, "I have some sweet tea made. Would you care for a glass?"

He hesitated. She thought he would refuse, but to her surprise, he said, "*Ja.* That would be nice."

"Let me put my fleece away and I'll be right back with some."

She hurried inside the house, feeling strangely light-hearted. When she came out again, he was sitting on the bottom step. After handing him the glass of tea, she awkwardly sank down on the step beside him. His hand shot toward her. She flinched away before she could stop herself.

He withdrew his hand slowly. The frown she was beginning to know so well settled on his face. He regarded her with a quizzical look in his eyes.

Faith stretched her bad leg out in front of her and tried to pretend nothing had happened. "I hope the tea is sweet enough."

"Does it hurt much?" he asked softly.

She rubbed her thigh and swallowed hard, uncomfortable with his sympathy. "Not as much as it used to."

"How did it happen? If you don't mind my asking?"

She didn't mind talking about the accident. It was talking about her marriage that she shied away from. "A pickup struck our buggy when we were on our way home from church."

Adrian took a sip of his tea, then stared out across the yard. "Is that how your husband died?"

"Mose was killed instantly." Faith stared into her glass as she relived those painful days.

"My son was struck and killed by a car. The English, they go so fast in their big machines. What in their lives makes them rush so?"

"It seems to me they are afraid they will miss something important."

"What was more important than my son's life?"

"Nothing." She wanted so much to reach out and comfort him. What would he think if she did? She tightened her grip on her glass.

After a moment of silence, Adrian shook off his somber mood. "I understand Myrtle met the bishop's wife today."

Faith pressed a hand to her cheek. "Please don't remind me. It was horrible."

"Sarah thought it was quite funny."

Faith cast him a sideways glance. "That was the worst part. Everyone was trying so hard not to laugh while I was stuttering my apologies."

"I'm sure you told her alpaca spit will brush off when it dries."

"Of course I did."

"Did you also mention how long the smell lingers?"

"I suggested she wash her clothes with baking soda to cut the odor as soon as she got home."

"I don't recall you giving me that information."

She tried to look innocent. "Didn't I?"

"*Nee.* I will assume you were too worried about your animals to pass along that important piece of advice."

"*Ja,* don't think for a minute it was because you were scowling so fiercely that the words flew out of my head."

"Did I frighten you that day?"

She shrugged. "A little."

"Are you frightened of me now?"

She knew he was referring to the way she had flinched from him a few moments ago. She stared down at the glass in her hand, avoiding his gaze. "You have been most helpful to me. I could not ask for a better neighbor."

It wasn't an answer to his question, but it was the best she could do. He said nothing more. The sounds of cicadas rose and fell as they started their noisy evening songs. As abruptly as it started, their song stopped, and the silence stretched on for another awkward minute.

Faith racked her mind for something to say, but Adrian beat her to it. "I will go through your orchard on Wednesday and see if the fruit is ripe enough for picking."

"It's a mess. There are downed branches and dead trees all through it."

"We had a bad ice storm a few years back. I imagine most of the damage is from that. However, many of the trees are getting old. Peach trees only live about twenty years and these were planted at least that long ago."

"Do you know if they are freestone or clingstone peaches?"

A hint of a grin tugged at the corner of his lips. "The ones I snitched as a *kinder* were all freestone and extra sweet."

She smiled at his confession. It was easy to imagine him as a mischievous child. "*Goot.* Those are the best kind for selling at market."

Faith smoothed her skirt with one hand. It should have felt strange to be sitting beside Adrian and discussing the work that needed to be done on the farm, but it didn't. It felt comfortable. It was only when the conversation turned personal that she grew uncomfortable.

The shadows had grown long, and the cicadas resumed their evening serenade. Adrian finished his drink and rose to his feet. "It's getting late. I should go home."

Faith tried to stand but didn't quite make it. Embarrassed, she gathered herself to try again. Adrian stepped close and held out his hand to aid her.

Faith's heart began hammering so hard she was sure he could hear it. Fear made her mouth dry. Adrian wasn't Mose. She didn't have to be afraid anymore. They were brave words but hard to live by. She ignored his hand and pulled herself upright using the railing.

Adrian saw the change that came over Faith when he offered his hand. Was it pride that made her struggle to her feet alone? He didn't think so.

He saw the flash of fear in her eyes, although she hid it quickly. What reason would Faith Martin have to fear him?

He let his hand fall back against his side. If his presence was unwelcome, he would not force it upon her. "I will see you Wednesday, then."

She twisted her hands together as she avoided looking at him. "I may not be here. I'm taking my yarns into town. Your cousin Sarah was kind enough to invite me to bring my work into her shop. After that, I will be here, but I'm expecting the social worker from the adoption agency. I'm trying to adopt my brother's child."

Was that why she seemed so worried? Was she afraid her adoption wouldn't go through? He tried to picture her with a babe in her arms. She would make a good mother.

He said, "You don't need to be here while I survey your orchard. We can discuss what I find another time. I promise I won't eat up your profits."

She smiled halfheartedly at his humor. He wanted

more. He wanted a real smile from her. "How are your beasts adjusting to their new home?"

"They seem quite happy in the pen you built for them. Thank you for your help with that. They are growing fat on the thick grass in the orchard."

"Will I disturb them working in there?"

"I do not think so. They may disturb you for they are quite curious. You're likely to find them underfoot and investigating everything you do."

He nodded toward the barn. "Has your expectant mother had her calf?"

"A baby alpaca is called a cria, not a calf." She relaxed as she talked about her animals. The haunted look faded from her eyes.

"Cria." He rolled the unfamiliar word on his tongue. "Has Myrtle had her cria?"

"Not yet. I think it will be few more weeks before she becomes a mother again."

"This is not her first babe?"

"Bandit and Baby Face are both her offspring."

"You have chosen unusual names for your unusual creatures."

"My husband and I rented a farm from an English family when we lived in Missouri. I let their daughter name all the new babies."

"You will be able to name this one yourself."

She glanced shyly in his direction. "Perhaps I will give you the honor."

He stroked his beard as he considered her offer. "I could name it for its mother. *Shmakkich.*"

"Smelly? I will not call my new baby Smelly."

"Then you must find a better name yourself for that is my only suggestion." He handed her his empty glass.

She took it without hesitation. Her eyes crinkled with humor. "I did not think you would shirk from a difficult task."

"A challenge, is it? Very well, I shall name it Stinky."

"Nee." She shook her head.

"Foul Breath."

Faith giggled. *"Nee.* I will not call any creature Foul Breath. If that's the best you can do, it will remain nameless."

Her smile was back and Adrian was content. "I shall give it some more consideration. Good night, Faith Martin."

"Guten nacht, Adrian."

He started toward home but stopped a few yards away. Turning around, he called out, "What about Skunk?"

"Nee! That's the worst name ever."

"But what if it's black with a white stripe down its back?"

"Not even then. Be off with you, foolish fellow." She shooed him away with one hand, but she was smiling.

It wasn't until he was nearly home that he realized he was still smiling, too.

Faith guided Copper onto the highway and headed toward Hope Springs. The horse kept to a brisk trot, but it wasn't long before several cars were backed up behind Faith's buggy waiting to pass her on the next open stretch of road. The driver of the first car that went around her gave her a friendly wave. The second car drew alongside but didn't pass. When Faith glanced their way, she saw the passenger had the window rolled down and was aiming the camera in her direction.

Faith quickly turned her face away. No matter which

Amish community she lived in, it was always the same. There were always a few tourists who just had to snap a photograph of an Amish person. They never seemed to realize it was rude.

The second car sped away, and Faith was free to enjoy the green rolling countryside. It was easy to see how fertile the land was as she passed farm after farm with tall cornfields and fat cattle grazing near the roadside.

The outskirts of Hope Springs came into view after several miles. Faith had no trouble finding her way to the fabric store. She pulled Copper to a stop in the parking lot beside three other buggies.

As soon as she pushed open the front door of Needles and Pins, she was greeted with the scent of a floral and vanilla potpourri and the sound of chimes. The store was small, but it was crammed from floor to ceiling with bolts of fabric in every color. At the rear of the store a white-haired woman stood behind the counter. She looked up from her work and smiled in greeting.

"Welcome to Needles and Pins. Is there something I can help you with?"

Faith worked to quell the nervousness making her stomach queasy. She needed to find a market for her work as soon as possible. One of the things Kyle's social worker would be looking at was her financial situation. Faith needed proof that she earned enough to care for a child. Sending up a quick prayer, she said, "I'm looking for Janet."

"Then look no further. I'm she."

Faith approached the counter. After introducing herself, she opened her bag and pulled out a sample of her yarn. "Would you be interested in purchasing some hand-spun baby alpaca yarn?"

"I might be." Janet took the skein to examine closely.

"The black color is natural. It's from one of my crias."

Janet looked up in surprise. "You raise your own alpacas?"

"*Ja,* I have ten animals. Some are white, I have one black, several grays and two that are butternut-brown. I can die the wool for you if you have customers that want a particular color. It's very soft yarn and very strong." Faith forced herself to stop babbling.

Running her hand over the skein, Janet said, "I can see this is quality work, Mrs. Martin. I would be interested in buying all you have in black and dark gray. I'm not sure about the other colors. Perhaps I will take a few of them and see how they sell."

Faith struggled to hide her excitement. She had prayed to make a big sale today, and her prayers were being answered.

Janet continued, "If you are interested, I could post your yarn for sale on my website. I get a fair number of internet orders."

"That would be *goot, danki.*" This was better yet.

Faith sorted her yarns for Janet and pocketed the money with a happy heart. She was preparing to leave when Sarah came out from the back room. Smiling, Sarah came forward carrying several large bolts of powder-blue material. "Faith, how are you? Have you brought in your yarn?"

"*Ja.* Janet was kind enough to purchase several dozen skeins. If they sell well, she will buy more."

Sarah leaned close. "I will do my best to steer our customers toward them."

"I appreciate that."

"I have been instructed by Nettie Sutter to invite you to our widow's meeting on Friday night."

Such meetings were common in Amish communities where widows sought to remain active and productive members of the community even into old age. Faith had been a member of such a group in her last church district.

As much as she wanted to say yes, Faith didn't have time to devote to social visits. "Perhaps I can join you when I've settled in."

"Fair enough. We are finishing two quilts that will be auctioned off next month. We help support an orphanage in Haiti with the money we raise and we give to the church to help our members who have medical bills and such. Several times a year we hold a large auction. Some of the women in our church have started a co-op to help members market and sell their work."

"I'm not much of a hand at quilting," Faith admitted.

"Don't worry, we will find something for you to do. We meet at the home of Naomi Wadler. Her daughter and son-in-law run the Wadler Inn and Shoofly Pie Café. You passed by it on your way in town. Naomi's home is behind the inn."

Faith remembered the Swiss-chalet-style inn at the edge of town. "What time are the meetings held?"

"Five o'clock."

"I look forward to the day I can meet with you."

"Wonderful. Have you decided to join our church?"

"I plan to ask the bishop about it soon."

"I must warn you that once you are accepted, you

will be fair game as far as Adrian's mother is concerned."

Perplexed, Faith asked, "Why do I need a warning about his mother?"

"*Aenti* Linda fancies herself a matchmaker. Adrian and I are her only current failures. I admit she does have a knack for putting the right people together. You will provide her a new challenge. Hopefully, I can get a break from chance meetings and uncomfortable suppers at her house where I feel like a prize hen on display."

Faith shook her head. "She may matchmake all she wants. I have no intention of marrying again."

"That is exactly what Adrian says."

Faith began to rearrange the yarns left in her basket. "It is a shame he feels that way. He would make a good husband."

"He's a handsome fellow, I'll give him that."

"He's much more than that. He's kind and generous, strong and hardworking. He's everything a woman could desire in a mate."

As soon as she realized she was rambling, Faith looked up in embarrassment. Sarah stared back with a look of compassion on her face.

Faith wanted to sink through the floor. She hadn't realized how much she had come to admire Adrian or how much she wanted to be admired by him.

Sarah reached out and laid a hand on Faith's arm. "Adrian still grieves deeply for his wife and son. He says the love he holds in his heart for his first wife doesn't leave room for another. He speaks with conviction when he says he will never love again. A woman who sets her heart on my cousin is likely to find heartache instead."

* * *

Adrian started his assessment of Faith's orchard under the close supervision of her alpacas. The herd followed him everywhere, observing his activity with wide curious eyes. Their heads bobbed back and forth on their long necks as they tried to figure out what he was up to.

Before long, the group grew tired of simply watching him. They began a new game, bounding away, then racing back at him, dodging aside at the last second to avoid a collision. Soon, several mock battles broke out between the youngsters. They chased each other around the trees, kicking and knocking their long necks into one another. Socks and Baby Face reared up and began a boxing match as they hopped about on their rear legs.

Adrian chuckled at their antics. It was like being surrounded by five-foot-tall puppies. He began to understand Faith's attraction to them. They were adorable. Like their owner.

Only Myrtle refused to join the fun. She spit at those brave or foolish enough to encroach on her space. Adrian had no trouble staying away from her.

He finished his task and was letting himself out the gate to the orchard when he saw Faith returning. His spirits lifted instantly. She was sure to smile when he recounted her animals' antics.

She drew her horse to a stop beside the barn door. He held the mare's headstall as Faith descended from the buggy. "Did you sell all your yarn?" he asked.

She pulled a large hamper from the backseat. "Not all of it but a large portion. I hope you have some good news about my orchard."

"You have very curious animals prowling out there."

Her face filled with concern. "Did they give you trouble?"

"I was able to dodge their charges and most of the spit."

"I will wash your shirt if need be."

"*Nee,* I'm only teasing. You have about ten trees that should be cut down. They are too old and diseased to bear fruit. They can be cut up and stacked for firewood. They should dry out enough through the fall to burn well this winter."

Faith set her basket on the ground. "Should I replant more peach trees in their place?"

"If I were you, I'd diversify with some plum and apple trees. Since they flower at different times, you will be less likely to lose the entire crop if we get a late freeze in the spring.

Her eyebrows shot up. "So you think I will be here in the spring? Have you decided I can make a go of this place?"

"You have made a good start," he admitted.

"Only because you've done the majority of the outside work. Your help has been a godsend."

Adrian grew uncomfortable with her gratitude. He hadn't started out to help her earn a living. He'd had his own selfish reasons for doing the work needed. He had hoped she would sell her farm to him.

Did he still want her to leave?

No…and yes.

He hadn't once thought of Lovina all through this day. He'd thought only of what Faith would say, what would make her smile. Faith made him forget his pain.

He didn't want to feel this sense of wonder when she

was near, but he did. Seeing her smile shouldn't make him happy, but it did.

Adrian turned away and started to unhitch the horse. Faith made him feel things he didn't want to feel. Things that had died in him when Lovina died.

Faith said, "I can manage. I'm sure you have your own work to see to."

"I've wasted the best part of the day here. I might as well stable your horse. It won't take that much longer." His voice sounded unnaturally harsh even to his own ears.

Faith took a step back and ducked her head. "I should get these things up to the house. The social worker will be here soon."

As she hurried away, Adrian could've kicked himself for stripping the happiness from her eyes. Had he been wrapped up in his own grief so long that he'd forgotten how to be kind?

Chapter Six

Faith put her yarns and baskets away and worked up the courage to return to the barn. She had upset Adrian, but she didn't know how. Was it something she said? He'd done too much for her to let him go away angry.

She paused at the kitchen door, remembering Adrian as he had first appeared to her, dark and scowling. In spite of his fierce appearance, he'd been nothing but kind to her. She had come to care for him, to see him as a friend, yet she had scurried away from his displeasure like a sheep running from the wolf. Why was it still so hard to stand up for herself?

Because I'm afraid.

Was Adrian's kindness only an act or did her old fear make her suspect evil where it didn't exist? If she couldn't be sure, how could she do business with him, accept his help, allow him into her life?

Learning to trust again was harder than relearning to walk had been. Perhaps that was the reason God had brought her to this place. Because she had to begin somewhere. If this was her first test, she had failed miserably.

No, that wasn't true because she wanted to trust

Adrian. The real problem was that she no longer trusted her own judgment.

Dear Father in heaven, give me strength and wisdom. Let me not judge others lest I be judged in return. Help me to see the good in men and not suspect evil.

Bolstered by her prayer, Faith left the house, crossed the yard and pulled open the barn door. Adrian was busy forking hay into Copper's stall. He hadn't seen her return.

Unobserved, Faith took a moment to admire the way he made the work look easy. His strong arms and shoulders drove the fork deep into the hay and lifted a bundle with ease. Beneath the sweat-dampened shirt he wore, she could see the muscles tightening and rippling across his back. Her breath quickened as she realized she wasn't seeing him as a friend should. Embarrassed, she looked away.

He was a strong, handsome man, and he was proving himself to be a good friend and neighbor. That was all. She wouldn't let it be anything else.

He caught sight of her. "I'll be done in a minute."

He didn't seem angry now. She took a step closer. "I'm sorry I upset you earlier."

His eyes widened in surprise. "You did nothing to upset me. I'm the one who should be sorry. I let my ill humor ruin your day. That was wrong. The help I gave you was for selfish reasons. Please forgive me."

"You are forgiven. For what selfish reason have you worked here day in and day out?"

He hesitated, then sighed. "I thought if you couldn't make a go of this farm, I could buy it from you. The work that I've done here would have had to be done anyway when I took over."

"I see. Thank you for telling me this."

"I no longer think you will fail, Faith Martin. You

have the will to succeed, and as you once told me, you aren't afraid of hard work."

A sound outside drew her attention. Faith's heart leaped into her throat when she saw the automobile pulling to a stop in front of her house. In the front seat she could see a woman surveying the property. "That must be Mrs. Taylor, Kyle's social worker. What do I do?"

Adrian came to stand beside her. Gently, he said, "Go and welcome her."

His simple reply made her realize how silly she was being. "Kyle was raised in an *Englisch* home. I'm worried that this *Englisch* woman won't think he belongs in an Amish home."

"You cannot discover the answers you seek by hiding here in the barn."

"Are you sure?"

"*Ja,* I'm pretty sure." He smiled and motioned her toward the door. "Go."

Gathering her courage, Faith walked out of the barn and toward the car, knowing this was the moment she had been dreading and praying for. She had had several letters from Mrs. Taylor, but she had no idea what to expect from the *Englisch* social worker.

The car door opened, and a tall, slender young woman got out. She wore a plum-colored suit and matching high-heeled shoes. Her hair was short and dark. It curled tightly against her skull. She held a briefcase in one hand.

Faith managed a smile. "*Velkumm.* Are you a Mrs. Taylor?"

"I'm afraid Mrs. Taylor no longer works for our agency. I'm Miss Watkins. Caroline Watkins. Are you Faith Miller?"

"Martin," Faith corrected her.

"My apologies." Caroline's gaze was fastened on Adrian standing by the barn. "Is that Mr. Martin?"

"No. That is my neighbor, Adrian Lapp. I am a widow. I thought you knew that."

"I'm sure it was in the file. I apologize if I sound unprepared. I've been swamped with work. Yours is my third home visit this week. Mrs. Taylor left on very short notice and I'm playing catch-up."

"Do come in the house." Faith gestured toward the front door.

Would her home pass inspection? Was it clean enough? Was it big enough? Would Faith pass as a prospective parent, or would this woman decide she didn't deserve her nephew? Worry gnawed at her insides. Exactly what would this home study entail?

Inside the house, Faith led the way to the living room. It was sparely furnished with a small sofa placed in front of a pair of tall windows. Two reading chairs flanked the couch. A small bookcase sat against the wall opposite the windows. Miss Watkins settled herself on the sofa while Faith perched on the edge of a chair facing her.

Miss Watkins must have seen the concern Faith was trying to conceal. "Please don't be nervous, Mrs. Martin. I'm here to make sure your home is a suitable, safe place for your nephew, not to pass judgment on your housekeeping or personal tastes."

"I am Kyle's only family. What could be more suitable than that?"

"I agree it is almost always best to place a child with a relative, but placing a child in a safe and loving home is our top priority, even if that means placing them with someone other than a blood relative."

The social worker searched through her papers.

"First, I need to see two forms of identification. I have to make sure I'm talking to the right person. Confidentiality laws and all that, you know. Your driver's license and a Social Security card will be fine."

"I do not have such documents."

Miss Watkins frowned. "You don't have a Social Security card?"

"I do not. The Amish do not believe in Social Security. It is the responsibility of everyone to care for the sick and elderly. We do not depend upon the government to do that for us. I do have my birth certificate and my marriage license, if that will do?"

Faith rose from the chair and crossed to the small bookcase in the corner. She opened her Bible and took out several pieces of paper and handed them to the social worker.

"Under the circumstances, I think these will be fine. Today, I'd like to gather some information about your background, family life, child care expectations and about your parenting philosophy. I know you must be frustrated at having to repeat some of this process since you began your adoption in Missouri, but now that you are in Ohio, you will have to abide by Ohio law."

"I understand my move came at a bad time, but it couldn't be helped."

"I will do what I can to expedite your home study. A few things won't have to be repeated. Your background check and criminal search records have been forwarded to us by the Missouri authorities."

"I only wish to have Kyle with me as soon as possible. He has been with strangers for two months."

Miss Watkins opened a folder. "Kyle King is in foster care in Texas, is that right?"

Faith nodded.

"And you've not been to visit him, is that correct?"

"I've spoken to him on the phone several times and written letters to him twice a week, every week, but I've been unable to travel to Texas." It wasn't much, but it was all she could do for now.

"I will admit I know very little about the Amish, so please forgive my ignorance. You are the first Amish client I've worked with. I understand you do not use electricity."

"We do not."

"And you have no phone and no car."

"There is a phone shack at the end of the lane that I and my Amish neighbors may use. It is permitted for work and for emergencies. I have a horse and buggy for ordinary travel, but I may hire a driver if I must travel a long distance."

"I'll make a note of that. After our interview, I'll make a brief safety inspection of your home. Typically, this first visit lasts from three to four hours."

"Four hours?" Faith thought of all the work that she had waiting for her.

"Yes. Is that a problem?"

"*Nee,* of course not."

"If I can't gather all I need today I will schedule a follow-up visit. I don't see a statement from your doctor. Did you receive the paperwork we sent you?"

"I haven't had a chance to schedule an appointment."

Miss Watkins frowned. "Ohio law is very clear on this. In order to adopt a child, you must be in good health."

"I am. My limp is the result of an accident, not an illness. I'll take care of it this week." A doctor's visit was another expense Faith didn't need. The money from her yarn sales wouldn't go far.

"All right. Let's get started. Are there any other adults or children living in this home?"

"Nee."

"Do you have adequate room to house a child?"

"Ja, this house has four bedrooms upstairs, although I don't yet have a bed for Kyle."

Miss Watkins jotted down some notes. "I will have to see all the accommodations prior to his arrival. Do you suffer from any physical or mental illnesses?"

"Only the limp you see."

"What is the reason for your disability?"

"I was injured when a pickup struck our buggy. My husband was killed."

"I'm sorry for your loss."

"It was God's will." Faith couldn't pretend there was sorrow in her heart, for there was none. Only relief and guilt for not loving Mose as a wife should.

"Do you have a history of alcohol, drug or substance abuse, even if it did not result in an arrest?"

"Nee."

"Do you have a history of child abuse, even if it was not reported?"

"Nee."

"Do you have a history of domestic violence, even if it did not result in an arrest or conviction?"

Faith's heart jumped to her throat. Would Mose reach out from the grave and snatch away her only chance to raise a child? She couldn't let that happen.

Never again would she place herself, or Kyle, in such a situation. She answered carefully for she didn't want to lie. "I have never abused anyone nor have I been accused of such behavior."

"Have you ever been rejected for adoption or foster care?"

Faith relaxed. "I have not."

For the next several hours, Faith answered all the questions put to her. Finally, Miss Watkins said, "Why don't we take a break and you can show me the house."

"Of course. I have only recently moved in. There is still much work to be done."

"I understand. Let's start with the kitchen."

Faith led the way. Miss Watkins made notes as she walked. To Faith, it seemed that she took note of every flaw, every uneven floorboard and even the stains on the wall behind the stove. The house might not be perfect, but it was a roof over her head.

In the kitchen, Miss Watkins went straight to the refrigerator and opened the door. The shelves were bare except for a few staples—butter, eggs and some bacon. She turned to Faith. "You don't have much in the way of food here."

"I have only myself to cook for. I don't need much."

"Will feeding a growing boy be difficult for you?"

"Not at all. Come. I will show you the cellar." Faith took a lamp from inside the cupboard and lit the wick. Opening a door at the back of kitchen, Faith descended the steps, cautioning Miss Watkins to use the handrail.

Down in the cool, damp cellar, Faith raised her lamp to show shelves full of canned fruits, vegetables and meats. It had taken her two solid days to clean out the cellar, repair the shelves and stock them. "I brought most of this with me from my previous home in Missouri. Some of my new neighbors have brought more as gifts."

"Impressive. Can we go back upstairs now?"

Clearly, Miss Watkins didn't care to remain in a small dark space. She frowned as she eyed the lamp Faith held. "I have some concern about the use of kerosene lamps around a small child."

"Amish children are all taught how to use lamps safely."

"Open flames are very dangerous. You will have to provide an alternate source of light."

"Would battery-powered lights be acceptable?"

"Absolutely."

"Then I shall purchase some." Faith smiled. More expenses.

After leaving the cellar, Faith gave the social worker a tour of the yard and outbuildings. Once again, Miss Watkins was scribbling furiously in her notebook. The alpaca herd came to the fence to observe the newcomer. Faith assured the social worker that they were not dangerous animals, but she gave Myrtle a wide berth. The rest of the herd remained well behaved, much to her relief.

Back in the house, Miss Watkins gathered together her papers. She closed her briefcase and handed Faith two additional pieces of paper. "I think that will do it for today. As far as paperwork goes, you will need to complete the health summary and you will need to have a fire safety inspection."

Was that a free service or was it something else she would have to pay for?

Miss Watkins held out her hand. "I will be back the same time next week. Hopefully, you will have everything completed by then."

Twisting her hands together, Faith asked, "What if I don't?"

"If there are deficiencies, it does not automatically

mean you can't adopt your nephew. It simply means that these are things we will have to work on."

As Faith watched the social worker drive away, she had no idea if she had passed inspection or not.

Why should they feel she deserved a child if God had not seen fit to answer her prayers for one? Simply because she was Kyle's aunt didn't mean she was the best person to raise him.

Glancing toward the orchard, she wondered if Adrian was still working out there or if he had gone home. An intense need to see him took hold of her.

Faith let herself through the gate behind the barn. Only Socks was grazing near the building. The rest of the herd had disappeared. Lifting her head, Socks ambled slowly in Faith's direction. When she reached Faith, she stopped and rubbed her head against Faith's side.

"What are you doing here all by yourself? Where is the rest of the herd?" Faith peered into the trees but couldn't see the animals. Giving Socks a quick pat, Faith headed deeper into the orchard.

She hadn't gone far when she spotted the rest of the group. They were clustered around a single tree and all gazing upward. A ladder stood propped against the trunk. She could just make out Adrian's legs halfway up the rungs.

She was startled when he called out, "How did it go?"

"I wish I knew."

A large, dead branch came crashing to the ground, sending the alpacas dashing in circles before they clustered again beside the ladder. Adrian descended from the tree. "How soon will you know if your nephew can live with you?"

"For all the hurry, hurry, hurry in *Englisch* lives,

their child placement process moves slowly. If all goes well, it may be two or three weeks."

"Where is he until then?"

"In a foster home."

"I'm sure they are taking good care of him."

"I pray so."

If the *Englisch* woman didn't find Faith acceptable, what would happen to Kyle? Was there someone else waiting and longing to adopt a child the way she was? Perhaps they deserved him more than she did.

She looked at Adrian. "Am I doing the right thing trying to bring an *Englisch* child here?"

"Why would you ask that?"

She crossed her arms and hugged herself as if she were cold. "Because in all the years I was married, God never saw fit to give me a child of my own."

Adrian heard the pain in Faith's voice. He saw the disappointment and loss in her eyes. He wanted to take her pain away, but he didn't know how. "Will you love this child?"

"I will."

"Then you are doing the right thing."

"If only I could be so sure. I must put my trust in God."

He said, *"And they that know thy name will put their trust in thee: for thou, LORD, hast not forsaken them that seek thee.* Psalm 9:10."

"You are so very right. He has not forsaken me."

Adrian wasn't sure why that particular Bible verse popped into his head. God had turned away from him. He had been forsaken. Faith, too, had suffered a great loss, and yet she still drew comfort and hope from God's word.

Why was her faith so strong when his was so weak?

Chapter Seven

On Sunday morning, Faith turned Copper off the highway and onto a farm lane two miles north of her home. At the edge of the road a homemade white sign with a black anvil painted on it said, "Horse Shoeing. Closed Wednesdays."

The church service was being held at the farm of Eli Imhoff, the local blacksmith, and the generous neighbor who, along with his sons, had painted the outside of her house.

Overhead, low gray clouds scuttled northward. The overcast sky was a welcome relief from the oppressive heat of the past few days, but the clouds were hanging on to any rain they held. Hopefully, any showers would remain at bay until after she was back home again.

At the other end of the long lane, Faith saw a two-story white house with a smaller *dawdy haus* built at a right angle from the main home. Both the grandfather house and the main house had pretty porches with white railings and wide steps. Three large birdhouses sat atop poles around the yard ringed with flower beds. Someday, her home would look like this.

Across an expanse of grass now crowded with buggies and groups of churchgoers stood a big red barn. In the corral, a pair of caramel-colored draft horses shared round hay bales with several dozen smaller horses. Copper whinnied a greeting. Several horses in the corral replied in kind.

A man came forward to take the reins from Faith. He tipped his black hat. "Good morning, *Frau.* I am Jonathan Dressler. I will take care of your horse." Although he looked Amish, he spoke in flawless English without a hint of the Pennsylvania Dutch accent she was accustomed to hearing.

"*Danki,* Jonathan." Faith stepped down from her vehicle and smoothed her skirt. Her stomach churned with nervous butterflies. More anxious than she cared to admit, she pulled a picnic hamper from beneath the front seat and stood rooted to the spot.

He pointed toward the farmhouse. "You may take your basket to the house. Karen Imhoff is in charge of the food today. It's nice to meet another newcomer to the community. Thanks to you, I'm no longer the new kid on the block."

"You are new here, too?"

"Yes, I guess I should say, *ja.*"

"You are *Englisch,* yet you dress plain."

"God has called me to live this simple life. Every day I give thanks that He led me to this place."

The smile on his handsome face was contagious. She asked, "Have you any advice to share with this newcomer?"

"The people of Hope Springs are wonderful, welcoming souls."

As they were speaking, another horse and buggy

came trotting into the yard. She recognized Adrian at the reins. With him were an older man and woman, two younger women in their early twenties, and a teenage boy.

Jonathan said, "I best get back to work, but I have to ask you one question. Did your alpaca really spit on the bishop's wife?"

Her shoulders slumped. "Has everyone heard of this?"

Jonathan chuckled. "It is not kind of me to say, but your alpaca sounds like a wonderful judge of character."

He laughed again as he unhitched Copper and led her to the corral.

Faith's heart sank to a new low. She would have to attend services several times in this church district before the congregation would be asked to accept her. Neither the bishop nor his wife was likely to want a new member who'd made Mrs. Zook a laughingstock.

Faith looked toward the house and saw the women from Adrian's buggy join a large group of women gathered on the porch. She recognized the bishop's wife standing among them. All eyes were turned in her direction.

She wanted to run home and hide.

"If I were you, I'd go in with my head up and smile as if nothing were wrong."

Faith glanced over her shoulder and saw Adrian unhooking his horse from the buggy. He wasn't looking at her, but she knew he was talking to her. There was no one else around.

He patted his horse's flank and spoke again, just as softly. "She will appear mean and petty if she snubs you when you are offering friendship, but if she senses fear, she won't have any trouble ignoring you. The other women will follow her lead."

"I should walk up to her and pretend my animal didn't spit in her face, is that what you suggest?"

"You have already apologized for that, haven't you?"

"More than once."

"Then it's over. Go, before they start to think you're *naerfich*."

She was nervous. But he was right, bless the man. His encouragement was exactly what she needed. Raising her chin, Faith limped forward and pasted a smile on her face.

As she approached the house, she nodded to Mrs. Zook. "Good morning. The Lord has blessed us with a fine morning, has He not? I look forward to hearing your husband's preaching for I hear God has graced him with a wonderful understanding of the Bible."

Mrs. Zook's smile wasn't overly warm, but at least she didn't cut Faith dead. She inclined her head slightly. "My husband speaks as God moves him. Joseph takes no credit for himself."

"That is as it should be. Where shall I put this?" Faith patted her basket, glad her voice wasn't shaking for her fingers were ice-cold.

A second woman spoke up. "Inside. Karen Imhoff will show you where she wants things."

Faith nodded her thanks, pulled open the front door and went inside with a huge sigh of relief. Behind her she heard the women's lowered voices begin to buzz. She knew they were discussing her. Unfortunately, she couldn't make out what they were saying.

Inside the kitchen, Faith was thrilled to see Nettie, Sarah and Katie at work arranging the food on the counters and long tables set up against the walls. Everything appeared ready for the meal the congregation would share after the service was finished.

A tall, slender woman came in from a back room with a box of glasses. She added them to the table where the plates were stacked. Her eyes lit with mischief when she spied Faith. She said, "Hello. I'm Karen Imhoff. You must be Faith Martin. I have been hearing so much about you."

Faith gave a quick glance around the room and saw Sarah and Katie trying to hide their grins. She looked back at Karen. "*Ja,* I am the one with the spitting alpaca."

Sarah and Katie dissolved into giggles. Nettie gave them both a stern look. The young women quickly pulled themselves together.

Karen said, "I hope you enjoy the service today. We are always glad to see new faces."

The front door opened and Jonathan stuck his head in. He said, "Everyone is here now."

Faith noticed the way his gaze rested on Karen. There was a softness in his eyes that bespoke great affection.

"*Danki,* Jonathan," Karen replied. "We will be there shortly." There was no mistaking the love that flowed between them.

What would it be like, Faith wondered, to love wholeheartedly and be loved in return?

Jonathan started to close the door but stopped as a little girl of about nine slipped beneath his arm and into the kitchen.

After he closed the door, Faith said, "Jonathan is a most unusual young man. I have never known an *Englisch* person to join our faith."

Smiling fondly, Katie folded her hands atop her bulging tummy. "You should have Karen tell you the whole story of how Jonathan came to be with us. It is the most romantic tale."

"I should tell it. I saw him first," the little girl declared. She was the spitting image of Karen and clearly not shy.

Karen laid a hand on the child's head. "You are forgetting your manners, Anna. This is Faith Martin. She is new to Hope Springs, and we must make her welcome. Faith, this is my sister, Anna."

Faith smiled at her. "I'm pleased to meet you, and I'm dying to hear the story."

Anna eagerly launched into her tale. "Just before Christmas, Karen was taking us to school. I looked out the buggy window and I saw a dead man in the ditch. Only, he wasn't dead. He was only hurt, but bad. God made him forget who he was, so we called him John. He stayed with us until God let him remember his name. And now he knows who he is and he wants to marry my sister."

Anna grinned broadly, Karen blushed rosy red and the rest of the women grinned.

Karen cleared her throat. "That about sums it up."

Nettie said, "It's almost time for the service to start. Girls, take Faith down to the barn. I'll be there shortly."

"I'll show you the way," Anna said as she bounced toward the door.

Outside, the solidly overcast sky gave way to intermittent sunshine. The women followed Anna to the far side of the barn where a sloping earthen ramp led to the barn's loft. The huge doors had been propped open to catch the cool morning breeze.

Inside, rows of wooden benches in the large hay-loft were filled with worshipers, men on one side of a center aisle, women on the other, all waiting for the church service to begin. Faith took a place beside Sarah, Karen and Katie. Anna wiggled her way in between Faith and Karen.

Glancing across the aisle to where the men sat, Faith caught Adrian's eye. He didn't smile, but he gave a slight nod to acknowledge her. He'd overheard her conversation with Mrs. Zook, and Faith had the feeling he approved. A moment later, Anna asked Faith a question, forcing her to look away from Adrian.

As everyone waited for the *Vorsinger* to begin leading the first hymn, Faith closed her eyes. This was a solemn time, a time to prepare her heart and soul to rejoice and give thanks to the living God. She listened intently, willing her soul to open to God's presence, preparing to hear His word.

She heard the rustle of fabric on wooden benches as people shifted on the hard seats. In the trees outside, birds sang cheerfully, as if praising the Lord with their own special voices. In the barn below, Faith heard the movement of horses and cattle in their stalls. The smell of alfalfa hay and barn dust filled the air. She drew a deep breath. Contentment filled her bones. This was where she wanted to be. This was where she had always belonged.

She remembered how nervous she'd been the morning she took her vows. At nineteen, she had been the youngest of the group preparing for baptism. In that final hour before the service, she had searched her heart, wondering if she was making the right decision. It was no easy thing to live Amish.

She knew she had made the right choice.

The song leader, a young man with a red beard, started the first hymn. More than a hundred voices took up the solemn, slow-paced cadence. There was no music, only the stirring sounds of many voices praising God. Two ministers, a deacon and the bishop took their places on benches facing the congregation.

When the first song ended, the congregation sat in silence waiting for the preaching to begin. For Faith, it was a joyful moment. This was her first service in her new district and it felt as if she had come home at last.

Adrian did his best to listen to the sermon being preached, but his eyes were drawn constantly to where Faith sat. At the moment, her eyes were closed. There was such a look of peace on her face that he envied her.

He had not known peace or comfort during services since his son was killed. As hard as he tried to find consolation in the words being spoken, all he felt was anger.

Anger at God for robbing him of those most precious to him.

If he had his way, he would have stopped coming to church, but to do so would only bring more heartache to his family. If he avoided services, he would soon find himself under the ban, shunned by those who loved him in the hopes that he would mend his ways.

His brothers and sisters, his mother and father, none of them understood the anger that filled his heart, so he kept it hidden. He went through the motions of his faith without any substance. His life, which had once been filled with daily prayers, was now filled with hollow silence. God knew Adrian Lapp had not forgiven Him.

Adrian glanced at Faith. Was she even better at pretending faith than he was, or had she discovered the secret of letting go of her anger and hurt?

Beside him Benjamin fidgeted. His brother was eager to see the preaching end so he could visit with the Stultz sisters. The pretty twins were nearly the same age as Adrian's little brother. They were always willing to share their sweet smiles and laughter with him. Benjamin would soon be of courting age.

Adrian no longer believed in asking God for favors, but he hoped Benjamin would be spared the kind of pain he had endured, if and when Ben chose a wife.

Three hours later, when the service came to an end, Benjamin practically leaped from his seat and rushed to join his friends outside. Adrian stayed behind to help convert the benches into tables for eating by stacking them together. As he worked, he visited with his friends and neighbors. He listened to his father catching up on who had a sick horse, how everyone's corn was doing and what they planned to sell or buy on market day.

As the groups moved out of the barn toward the house, Adrian kept an eye out for Faith. He wanted to see if she was fitting in with the women of the district. He'd seen how scared she was when she first arrived.

He'd offered his advice without thinking twice. It was strange how easily he read her face and demeanor. Stranger still was how often he found himself thinking about her. She was an unusual woman.

Since there wasn't enough room to feed everyone inside the house, the ordained and the eldest church members ate first at the tables set up for them inside. The rest of the congregation took turns getting their food and carrying it out to the barn.

When it was Adrian's turn, he saw Faith had joined

Nettie, her daughters and several other women and was working alongside them in the kitchen.

He relaxed when he saw her at ease, visiting with Sarah and Katie Sutter, holding Katie's baby on one hip as easily as any seasoned mother. It was good to see her happy and smiling.

He caught Nettie Sutter's eye. She smiled and nodded once. She was a good woman. She would do everything in her power to see that the women of the community welcomed Faith.

Adrian glanced away and caught Sarah studying him. She looked from him to Faith and then back again. Her grin widened. She beckoned him over. He immediately took his plate and went outside.

He finished his meal and was taking his plate back to the house when he saw Faith deep in conversation with Bishop Zook over on the front porch of the *dawdy haus*. Joseph motioned to Adrian. This time he had no choice but to obey.

The bishop smiled a broad welcome. "Adrian, I have been filling Faith in on our *Ordnung*. I suggested she refer to you if she has any doubts about changes to her home or business as you are closer than I."

Faith remained silent, but a rosy blush stained her cheeks.

"I will do what I can to help." He didn't need a new excuse to see Faith, but he accepted the responsibility. It was important that she be accepted in the community. To do that, she had to live within the rules of their church.

The bishop thumped Adrian on the back. "Bless you. I knew I could count on you. A few of the men are getting up a game of quoits. Will you join us?"

Similar to horseshoes but played with round metal rings, quoits was a game Adrian used to enjoy, but he rarely took part in such activities now. "I will go find Ben. He has the best aim in the family."

After passing the message to his brother, Adrian put Ben in charge of getting the family home. With his duty discharged, Adrian left early and walked the few miles back to his farm.

At the house, he took a sharp knife and cut two bunches of flowers from the garden. With a bouquet in each hand, he walked out to the small cemetery where Gideon and Lovina waited for him.

Kneeling between their graves, he placed his gift beneath each headstone. "I brought some daisies for you, Lovey. I remember how much you loved them. You always said they were the bright eyes of your flower beds. They've bloomed all summer for you."

He sat back on his heels. "We held church services at Eli Imhoff's place. That *Englisch* fellow is still attending. I didn't think Jonathan would stay but he has a plain way about him now. Our new neighbor was there, too."

Pausing, he considered what to say about Faith. "She smoothed things over with Esther Zook right nicely. Course, I gave her a hint on how to handle Esther. I hope that's okay. She's a smart one, that Faith is."

Suddenly, it didn't feel right to be talking to his wife about another woman. He rose and took his usual place on the cedar stump.

The silence pressed in on him. The wind tugged at his hat, and he settled it more firmly on his head.

"Gideon, you should see the crazy animals that live next door to us now. Alpacas. They're cute, but they spit on people and each other if they get annoyed. Faith has ten of them. The yarn she spins from their fleece is mighty soft. She gave me a pair of socks. The ones I'm wearing now, in fact."

He pulled up his pant leg and fingered the material. The warm softness reminded him of Faith's smile when he'd caught her humming as she worked her spinning wheel on her front porch.

Pushing thoughts of her out of his head, he said, "I'm glad I'm not the fella who has to shear those beasties come spring. I'll bet he gets spit on a lot."

Adrian chuckled as he imagined anyone trying to clip the wool from Myrtle's neck.

The wind carried his mirth away. There was no answering laughter here. No one to share the joke with. Only two gray headstones among many in a field of green grass. Sadness settled in his chest, making it hard to breathe.

Adrian rose to his feet, shoved his hands in his pockets and started for home. It wasn't until he reached his lane that he realized he hadn't said goodbye.

On Monday afternoon Faith walked to the end of her lane and crossed the highway to the community phone. A small gray building not much bigger than a closet sat back from the road near a cluster of trees. A solar panel extended out from the south side of the roof. She could see through the window that it was unoccupied. She opened the door and stepped inside.

The shack held a phone, a small stool and a ledge for writing materials along with an answering machine blinking with two messages. She listened to them in case the agency had left a message for her, but they hadn't. Adrian had a message that his mower part was in, and Samuel Stultz had a new grandbaby over in Sugarcreek. It was a girl.

A local phone directory hung from a small chain at the side of the ledge. Picking it up, she searched for and found the number for the medical clinic in Hope Springs. She pulled a pencil and a piece of paper from her pocket to make note of the number for later. As she laid her pencil down, it rolled off the ledge and fell under her stool.

In the cramped space she couldn't reach it. She blew out her breath in a huff of disgust, then awkwardly squatted down, bracing herself against the door. A second later the door opened and she tumbled out backward, landing in a heap at Adrian Lapp's feet.

"Faith, are you all right?" He immediately dropped to one knee beside her.

She looked up into his face filled with concern and could have died of embarrassment. "I'm fine, but my dignity is a little bruised."

He helped her to her feet. "I'm sorry. I didn't see you. What were you doing on the floor?"

His hands lingered on her arms. She could feel the warmth and strength of them through the thin fabric of her dress. He was so close. His masculine scent enveloped her, sending a wave of heat rushing to her face that had nothing to do with embarrassment or fear. She wasn't frightened of him. His touch was strong but gentle. She was frightened by how much she wanted to move closer, to step into the circle of his arms and rest there.

She took a step back. He slowly let her go, his hands slipping from her elbows to her wrists in a soft caress. She said, "I dropped my pencil."

"What?" He seemed as confused as she was by the tension that shimmered between them.

"I was trying to reach my pencil. I dropped it and it rolled under the chair." She brushed at the back of her dress. Her blood hummed from his nearness and the way his gaze lingered on her face. Suddenly, she saw an attractive man in the prime of his life. A single man.

She crossed her arms and looked down, hoping he wouldn't read this new and disturbing awareness in her eyes.

"No wonder I didn't see you." He stepped inside the building and retrieved her pencil.

He held it out and she took it gingerly, careful not to touch him. *"Danki."*

"I will let you finish your call."

"I'm only making a doctor's appointment. If you need the phone, you may use it now. I can wait."

His brow furrowed into sharp lines. "Are you sick?"

She was flattered by the concern etched on his face. *"Nee,* it is nothing like that. The adoption agency I'm using requires me to have a physical. I need to have a fire safety inspection of my home, too. Do you have any idea who I would call to see about that?"

"Michael Klein is our local fire chief. I'm one of the volunteer firemen. His number is in the book."

"Michael Klein. I will remember that. What would I do without you, Adrian? You have helped me at every turn."

"I have no doubt you would manage. Make your calls. I can wait."

He walked away to stand in the shade, giving her some privacy. She went back inside the phone booth, quickly placed her first call and was happy to find out the doctor's office could see her that afternoon.

The second call went smoothly, as well. The fire chief agreed to come by the following day and inspect her home. With her appointments made, she stepped outside. "I'm finished, Adrian."

He walked over, but instead of taking a seat inside the phone booth, he leaned against the doorjamb. "How is your adoption going?"

Faith struggled against the urge to linger here with Adrian and lost. She liked his company; she liked spending time with him.

"Things are going well, I think. The doctor can see me today and the fire chief can come tomorrow. The social worker did not run screaming from my house, although when we were in the cellar, I thought she might."

"You have not introduced her to Myrtle, have you?" There was a glint of humor in his eyes and in his voice.

Faith grinned. "*Nee,* I made sure Miss Watkins stayed away from her."

"That's *goot.* The bishop's wife and I are forgiving of such an insult, but an *Englisch* woman in her fancy suit might not be."

The clip-clop of a horse and buggy approaching made them look toward the highway. Samuel Stultz pulled to a stop. "Are you using the phone?"

Faith grinned for she already knew his good news. "You have a message, Samuel."

As he hurried to get down, Faith turned to Adrian. "I must be going. I will have to hurry if I am to find the clinic in time for my appointment. Poor old Copper isn't as fast as she once was."

"I need to take a harness into Rueben Beachy's shop

for repairs. I go right by the clinic if you want to ride with me."

"That is very kind of you, but I have no idea how long I will be."

They moved aside to let Samuel use the booth.

Adrian said, "I have several other errands to run. I need to pick up some bushel baskets and the new blades for my sickle mower should be in."

"They are. I heard it on the message machine." She leaned closer. "And Samuel has a new grandbaby."

Adrian chuckled, "I'm glad my blades have come in. It will be time to put up hay in another few days and I must be ready."

"Is the work in my orchard taking up too much of your time?"

"*Nee,* I'm glad of the extra work. I don't mind waiting for you at the doctor's office as long as you don't mind waiting there if you are done ahead of me."

A ride into town seated beside Adrian was more appealing than it should have been. Should she accept? What was the harm in it? There was no need for both their horses to make the trip. "I accept your offer, gladly, and I won't mind waiting."

"*Goot.* I will be back with my wagon in half an hour."

"I will be ready."

Samuel stuck his head out the door, a wide grin on his face. "I have a granddaughter."

Faith laughed. "I know. Congratulations."

When she looked back, Adrian had already started toward his farm. Faith bid Samuel good day and hurried as fast as she could to her house.

Once there, she quickly freshened up. She changed her worn and stained everyday dress and apron for her best outfit. After patting down a few stray hairs, she decided she looked well enough to go into town. The blue of her good dress brought out the color of her eyes. Would Adrian notice? The thought brought her up short. Now, she was being foolish.

Her practical nature quickly reasserted itself. It wasn't that she wanted to impress Adrian. She merely wanted to look presentable when she met the doctor. Having rationalized choosing her best dress, she gave one last look in the mirror, pinched some color into her cheeks, put on her bonnet and went out to wait for Adrian with excitement simmering in her blood.

Chapter Eight

Adrian called himself every kind of fool as he drove his green farm wagon up to Faith's gate. He was about to give his nosy neighbors and his family food for speculation by driving the widow Martin into town. Knowing smiles and pointed questions would be coming his way for days. What had he been thinking?

Cousin Sarah would be sure to hear about this. She would make certain his mother knew before the day was out. He began lining up explanations in his head so he would have them ready. His mother was certain to drop by his house before nightfall.

He tugged at his beard as the source of his coming discomfort limped down the walk and crossed behind the wagon to the passenger's side. He glanced down at her as she prepared to step up into the wagon. Something of what he'd been thinking must have shown on his face.

A look of concern furrowed her brow. "Is something wrong?"

There was no point in ruining her afternoon with his glum thoughts. He extended his hand to help her in. "*Nee*. I've much on my mind. That's all."

She laid her hand in his without hesitation. He realized it was the first time she hadn't flinched away from him. A sense of satisfaction settled in the center of his chest.

Her hand was small and delicate in his grasp. His fist completely engulfed it. She was light as a feather when he pulled her up. She might be a tiny thing, but what she lacked in size she more than made up for in determination. He admired her tenacity. She had done a lot with her run-down inheritance. She was making the place into a home.

He turned the wagon around in the yard and set his gelding to a steady trot when they reached the highway. The drone of the tires on the payment, the clatter of the horse's hooves and the jangle of the harness were the only sounds for the first few minutes of the ride.

Adrian suddenly found himself tongue-tied. He hadn't spent time alone with a woman since his single days. What should he talk about? Or should he keep his mouth shut?

He glanced at Faith sitting straight as a board on the seat beside him. The wide brim of her black bonnet hid her face from his view. What was she thinking? Did she regret accepting his offer? Was she worried that gossips might link their names?

She spoke at last. "What is your horse called?"

"Wilbur."

"He has a fine gait."

Wilbur was a safe enough topic. "He was a racehorse in his younger days, but he was injured. His *Englisch* owner didn't want to waste money caring for him. You met Jonathan Dressler, didn't you?"

"The *Englisch* fellow who has become Amish?"

"*Ja*. He works for a group that takes in abandoned

and injured horses. He nurses them back to health and retrains them for riding or buggy work."

"I'll remember that. My Copper is getting old and slowing down. I will need a new horse in a few years."

"Perhaps you can teach your alpacas to pull your buggy."

She giggled and shot a grin his way. "Can you see how many tourists would want my picture if I did such a thing?"

"Not many once they met Myrtle."

Faith laughed outright. His discomfort evaporated as warmth spread though his body. She had a way of making him forget his troubles. He said, "You should laugh more often."

Their eyes met, and she quickly looked away. "How soon will our peaches be ripe?"

"Another two or three weeks."

"Will you sell them from a roadside stand or take them into the market in town?"

"To market unless you want to run the stand?"

"I've been thinking about it. Do we get enough traffic on this road to make it worthwhile?"

Adrian relaxed and started to enjoy the ride as Faith asked about his plans for the orchard. A few pointed questions from him set her to talking about her alpacas and her plans for expanding her spinning business. It wasn't long before the town of Hope Springs came into view. As far as Adrian was concerned, the ride was over all too soon.

He left her at the door to the medical clinic and quickly set about completing his own errands so she wouldn't have to wait when she was done seeing the doctor. With a jolt, he realized he was eager for the trip home.

Faith entered the Hope Springs Clinic, a modern one-story blond brick building, with a sense of dread. She had spent more than enough time in hospitals and doctors' offices over the past two years. What if they found something new wrong with her? What if they thought she wasn't strong enough to take care of a child?

Inside the building, she checked in with the elderly receptionist and took a seat in the crowded waiting room. When her name was called, she followed a young woman in a white lab coat down a short hallway and took a seat on the exam room table.

The young woman introduced herself. "I'm Amber Bradley. I'm Dr. White's office nurse and a nurse-midwife. Can you tell me what kind of problems you've been having?"

"None." Faith withdrew her papers from her bag. "I am adopting a child, but first, I must have a physical."

Amber's smile widened as she took the paperwork. "Congratulations. The doctor will be with you in a few minutes. We will need to get any previous medical records you have. I'll bring you the forms to sign so we can get them faxed to this office."

"I'm very healthy. I did not see a doctor until I was in an accident two years ago." Faith opened her mouth for the thermometer Amber extended.

"That doesn't surprise me. Many Amish go their entire lives without seeing a doctor. We see a fair number here because of Dr. White's reasonable rates. I tell him he's just plain cheap." Amber chuckled as she recorded the temperature reading, then wrapped a blood pressure cuff around Faith's arm.

The outside door opened, and a tall, silver-haired

man walked in. "Good afternoon, Mrs. Martin. I'm Dr. Harold White. What can we do for you today?"

Faith again explained her situation. The doctor listened carefully, then took the forms from Amber. "This looks pretty straightforward. We'll get a chest X-ray, draw some blood and give you a complete physical while you are here today. My office will send you the results in a few days. Do we have your address?"

Faith recited it, and the doctor wrote it down. He said, "Isn't this the old Delker Orchard?"

"Ja."

Dr. White said, "That place has been empty for twenty years. I didn't know it was for sale."

"I inherited it when my husband passed away. He was the grandchild of the previous owner."

The doctor's eyebrows shot up. "He was that boy?"

Confused, Faith asked, "Did you know my husband?"

"I only met him once. I often wondered what happened to him. The whole thing was very hushed up at the time. Back then child abuse simply wasn't talked about."

Faith shook her head in denial. "You must be mistaken. He never spoke of such a thing."

"Was your husband's name Mose?"

"It was."

The doctor began counting to himself using his fingers, then said, "He would be forty-five years old if he were alive today."

She nodded. "He would."

"Did he have scars on both his wrists?"

"From where he was dragged by a runaway team of horses when he was small."

"I wish that were true. I'm not surprised he never spoke of it. Children who suffer such abuse often block it from their memory. His wrists were scarred from where he was tied up in his grandmother's basement. Apparently, he came to live with her when his parents both died of influenza. Old Mrs. Delker hated the Amish. Her only daughter ran away from home and wound up marrying an Amish fellow who left the faith for her."

"My husband said he was raised by his Amish grandparents after his parents passed away."

"Eventually, he was. I was called out to the farm when a utility worker reported he'd seen a boy chained in the cellar. The poor child was wearing only rags and he was thin as a rail. It was clear he'd been beaten and neglected. He hit and bit at anyone who came close to him."

Faith wrapped her arms around herself. "How terrible."

If only she had known. If only Mose had shared his pain instead of keeping it hidden all those years. Would their lives have been different? Surely they would have been.

Dr. White stared at the floor, as if watching that long-ago scene. "It was terrible. Eventually, the sheriff located his father's Amish parents and the boy was sent to live with them. Mrs. Delker spent some time in a mental hospital, but she came back within about six months. She was even more of a recluse afterward. She had a stroke and passed away ten years later."

Dr. White looked up, suddenly contrite. "I'm so sorry. I shouldn't go on like that. Sometimes we old people don't know when to stop reminiscing. The past can seem clearer than the present for us. This must be quite a shock for you."

"It explains a lot about my husband. He wasn't a happy man."

"I'm sorry to hear that. Let us talk of more cheerful things. You are adopting a child. That's wonderful. The sooner we get done here, the sooner that can happen. The first thing we need from you is a medical history." He became all business.

Faith answered what seemed like a hundred questions, had her X-ray taken and suffered through getting her blood drawn, but the whole time she kept seeing Mose's face. He had been a harsh man without peace in his life. She prayed he was at peace now.

When she left the doctor's office, she saw Adrian waiting for her. The sight of him lifted her spirits.

"Are you finished?" he asked.

"*Ja*. And you?" She climbed up onto the wagon seat.

"All done. Shall we head home?"

"Would you mind if we stopped at the fabric store? I need to see if I should bring in more yarn." She was in no hurry to return to the house that had seen such pain.

A fleeting look of reluctance flashed across Adrian's face. "*Ja*, we can stop at the fabric store."

"If it's too much trouble, I can wait," she offered, not wanting to upset him.

"It's no trouble at all," he drawled. Slapping the reins against Wilbur's rump, he set the black horse in motion.

When they reached Needles and Pins, Faith scrambled down from the bench seat. "I'll just be a minute."

A wry smile twisted his lips. "Take your time and say hello to Sarah for me. Tell her I'll be expecting *Mamm* this evening."

Faith wasn't quite sure what to make of his odd mood. He glanced toward the shop door as it opened and said, "Never mind. Here she comes now."

Faith turned around, expecting to see Sarah, but saw

instead a short, gray-haired woman coming out of the shop. She stopped abruptly when she caught sight of Adrian, then smiled broadly.

"Hello, my son. What are you doing here?"

"I had some errands to run. *Mamm,* have you met Faith Martin?"

"I have not." His mother subjected Faith to intense scrutiny.

Faith was glad she'd taken the time to change her dress and put on her best bonnet. "I'm pleased to meet you, Mrs. Lapp. Your son has been wonderfully helpful to me. He has been the best neighbor anyone could ask for."

"Please call me Linda. It does a mother's heart good to hear such things about her son. I saw you briefly at the last church service, but I failed to introduce myself. I've been remiss in not welcoming you. Please forgive me."

"There is nothing to forgive. Excuse me, I must check to see if Janet needs more yarn from me. I won't be long, Adrian."

"No hurry," he replied.

Linda's grin widened. There was a distinctive twinkle in her eyes. "Your papa and I must stop by for a visit one of these evenings, Adrian. We have some catching up to do."

He knew where she was going and sought to cut her off. "Don't read more into this than there is. I'm helping out a neighbor. That's all."

Her smile faded. "It's time you put your grief away and took a close look at your life, my son. Many wonders of God are missed by a man who will not open his eyes."

As his mother walked away, Adrian mulled her words. How did he put away his grief even if he wanted to? Did he want to?

His grief had become a high fence he used to hold others at bay. In spite of his efforts, and without meaning to, Faith Martin had made a hole in that fence. To close it back up meant pushing her out of his life. Was he willing to do that?

Even if he wanted to, he wasn't sure he could. There was something special about her, something more than her pretty face and expressive eyes. When he was with her…he felt alive for the first time in years.

True to her word, Faith was back in a few minutes. He glanced at her seated beside him as they rode homeward. She was unusually quiet. Her eyes held a faraway look, as if she were viewing something sad from her past.

Was she remembering trips she'd taken with her husband seated beside her? Had the doctor given her bad news? Did her leg hurt? Was she tired?

There were so many things he wanted to know about her, so many questions he wanted to ask, but he shied away from them because they might reveal the real question nagging at the back of his mind.

Did Faith enjoy being in his company as much as he enjoyed being with her?

The afternoon sun beat down on them as they traveled along. Faith untied her dark bonnet and laid it on the seat between them. He asked, "Are you warm?"

"A little."

Stupid question. Of course she was or she wouldn't have taken off her bonnet. Why did he revert to acting like a tongue-tied teenager around this woman?

They made the rest of the journey to her home in silence. When he pulled to a stop in front of her gate, she didn't get down but sat staring at the house like she'd never seen it before. She asked, "Did you know the woman who lived here before I came?"

"Vaguely."

"Was she evil?"

What a strange question. "I don't think so. She was old, and *ab im kopp*."

"Off in the head? Crazy?"

"Ja."

"She must have been," Faith whispered.

He covered her hand with his. "Is something wrong?"

She didn't look at him. Her eyes remained fixed on the house. He checked out the building but didn't see anything amiss. What was going on?

Gazing back at Faith, he studied her face intently. It was as if she couldn't see or hear him. He squeezed her fingers. "Faith, what's the matter?"

Her gaze slid to their hands and then to his face. She pulled away sharply and climbed down from the wagon, mumbling, "Goodbye."

Stunned by her abrupt departure, Adrian stared after her. Had he done something wrong? Had he upset her with something he said? Should he follow her and ask or leave her be?

The safe thing to do was to leave her be. He was becoming far too caught up in Faith Martin's life. He'd been neglecting his own work to help her, something he never did. This had to stop.

He turned the wagon and started for home. He'd only gone a hundred yards when he noticed her bonnet on the seat beside him.

Stopping the horse, he picked up the bonnet and held it in his hands. The dark fabric was warm from the sun. He lifted it to his face and breathed in. It held her scent.

He looked over his shoulder toward her house. Perhaps he was too caught up in her life, but he was ready to admit he was deeply drawn to Faith. He saw no way to free himself unless she turned him away.

Looping the reins over the brake handle, he jumped down from the wagon and strode toward her gate not knowing if he was simply returning her belonging or starting down a whole new path in his life.

When he reached the porch, he saw the front door stood open. He climbed the steps and called her name. She didn't answer. Pausing in the doorway, he started to call out again when a sound stopped him. Someone was crying.

"Faith?" He took a step inside. The muffled sounds of sobbing were coming from a doorway at the back of the kitchen. Hesitantly, he walked that way.

The second he realized the door led to the cellar, he rushed forward. Had she fallen? Was she injured? "Faith, is that you? Are you all right?"

It took a second for his eyes to adjust to the darkness below him. When they did, he could just make out her form at the bottom of the stairs. She sat huddled in a ball on the bottom riser with her arms around her knees. Her shoulders shook with sobs.

He descended quickly, stepping past her to crouch in front of her. He laid his hand gently on her shoulder. "Faith, did you fall? Are you hurt?"

She lifted her head and shook it in denial as she wiped the tears from her cheeks.

His heart began beating again with rapid erratic thuds. "You scared the life out of me. What's wrong?"

Words began pouring out of her. "If only I had

known, I would have been a better wife. How could he keep such a thing locked away from me?"

"Faith, I don't understand."

"I married Mose because my parents were gone, my brother had left the faith and I had no one. I didn't love him as a wife should. I tried, but I couldn't, and I'm so ashamed." She buried her face in her hands.

This was way out of his depths. Faith needed another woman to talk to. Someone like his mother or Nettie, but he couldn't leave her weeping in the cellar.

No, that wasn't true. He could leave, but he didn't want to.

Adrian settled himself on the narrow step beside her. His hip brushed against hers. Her shoulder, where it touched his, spread warmth all down his arm. He wanted nothing more than to slip his arm around her and comfort her, but he knew it wouldn't be right. Such closeness between a man and a woman was for husbands and wives.

He had no idea what to say. He simply started talking. "I loved my wife dearly, but I can't remember her face. I try so hard to see her, but she isn't clear anymore. I'm ashamed of that. How can I forget the one I loved more than my own life?"

Faith sniffed and slanted a look his way. "You should not feel ashamed for that."

"Nor should you feel shame. We are only human."

Nodding, she looked away from him, staring into the dark corner of the room. "My husband was a cruel man. I think he tried not to be, but he couldn't help himself. I used to think it was my fault. I thought I couldn't make him happy because I didn't love him enough."

Adrian's breath froze in his chest. "He was cruel to you?"

She looked down at her hands and gave a tiny nod.

Was she saying what he thought she was saying? "Faith, did your husband beat you?"

She nodded again, as if words were beyond her.

His stomach contracted with disgust. No wonder she flinched from his touch. What kind of man could abuse someone as sweet and kind as Faith?

"No man has the right to be cruel to another in such a fashion. It was not your fault."

Scrubbing her face with her hands, she said, "I know."

She drew a deep breath and looked at Adrian. "My husband's grandmother lived here. Her daughter ran away with an Amish lad. When they died, Mose came back to stay with her."

"Are you sure? I don't remember a boy living here."

"Mose was twelve years older than I. You wouldn't have been old enough to know him, but, in truth, no one knew he was here. His grandmother kept him locked away in this cellar until the sheriff learned of it and took him away. Dr. White told me the whole sad story today."

"That's why you were so quiet on the way home."

"I kept thinking that I was the one person who should have loved him and I didn't. If I had, he might have shared this pain with me and been healed."

"You take too much onto yourself. Only God can know the hearts and minds of men. You would have helped your husband if you could. You have a kind heart, Faith Martin."

She shook her head in denial. "You are the one with the kind heart."

He gently cupped her face and turned it toward him.

With the pad of his thumb, he brushed the tears from her cheeks. Her luminous, tear-filled eyes widened, and her lips parted.

She was so close, so warm, so vibrant, and yet so vulnerable. He could kiss her—wanted to kiss her. He wanted to taste the sweetness of her soft lips, but something held him back.

Faith needed a friend now, not another complication. If he gave in to his desire it would change everything between them. She had given him a rare gift. Her trust. He didn't want to do anything to jeopardize that.

Faith closed her eyes and leaned into Adrian's hand, drawing strength from his gentle touch. If only she could hold on to this moment forever. She'd never felt so safe.

Why did this man make her wish for things that could never be? Long ago she'd given up the notion of having a happy marriage and children of her own. That wasn't God's plan for her. She accepted that.

And now this man had come into her life. A kind, sweet man who made her wish she still believed in a marriage with love between a husband and a wife. She cared for Adrian. Deeply.

As much as she wanted to hold on to this moment, she couldn't. She couldn't allow her growing feelings for Adrian to distract her. She had to think about Kyle. She had to focus on his adoption and on providing him with a safe, secure home.

She pulled away from Adrian. He withdrew his hand. The coolness of the cellar air made her shiver.

Pity filled his voice as he said, "Come upstairs, Faith. You cannot change what happened here. It is all in God's hands now."

Pity for her or for her husband?

She'd shared her darkest secret with Adrian. Did he think less of her for suffering in silence all those many years? Maybe she didn't want to know.

She struggled to her feet. "I didn't mean to burden you with my woes."

"They are no burden, Faith. Sharing your troubles makes them lighter."

She realized he was right. Her unhappy past didn't loom over her the way it once had. Her sense of relief left her light-headed. She started up the stairs. "You have work to do. You should go home."

"There's nothing that can't wait. Are you sure you're okay?"

"*Ja,* a stout cup of tea will fix me right up." She entered the kitchen and crossed to the sink. Her hands trembled as she reached for the teakettle. The room began spinning around her.

Adrian was beside her in an instant. His hand closed over hers as he gently took the kettle from her. "Let me do this. You sit down."

He took her by the elbow and led her to the table. Pulling out a chair, he held it while she sat, then he returned to the sink and began to fill the kettle.

She drew several deep breaths. "Adrian, you don't have to take care of me."

"If I don't, who will?" He carried the kettle to the stove. He turned on the burners and set the kettle over the flames, then started opening cabinets. "Where do you keep your tea?"

"In the green tin on the counter beside the refrigerator."

He found it and soon had a mug ready for the hot

water. As he waited for the kettle to boil, he took a seat across the table from her.

She managed a small smile. "God is *goot* to give me a friend such as you. Are you so thoughtful of all your neighbors?"

"Only the ones with animals that spit on me."

She chuckled. "Poor man. What an impression we must have made on you. It's a wonder you ever came back."

"I reckon I came back because I didn't think you could make a go of this place. You proved me wrong."

Lacing her fingers together in front of her on the table, she said, "I've managed to hang on for a few weeks. That doesn't mean I can hang on forever. It doesn't mean the *Englisch* will think this is a good home for my nephew."

"What will happen if they don't let you adopt him?"

Faith closed her eyes. "I can't think such a thing. They *must* let him stay with me. I don't think I could bear it if they don't."

Adrian laid his hand over her clenched fingers. She opened her eyes to find him gazing at her with compassion and something else in his eyes. Longing.

Her heart began beating faster. He started to speak, but the shrill whistle of the kettle cut him off.

He pulled his hand away and rose to fix her tea. Whatever he had been about to say remained unsaid. After bringing her mug to the table, he muttered a goodbye and left abruptly. As the screen door banged shut behind him, Faith was left to wonder if she had imagined the closeness they had shared so briefly.

Chapter Nine

Two days after taking Faith into town, Adrian was cutting hay in the meadow when a car turned in his lane. It stopped on the road not far from him, and an *Englisch* lady got out. He drew his team to a halt. She approached but kept a wary eye on his horses. "Are you Mr. Adrian Lapp?"

"I am." He waited for her to state her business.

"I'm Caroline Watkins. I'm the social worker in charge of your neighbor's adoption application. I've just come from my second visit here, and Mrs. Martin has given me permission to speak with some of her neighbors. May I have a few minutes of your time?"

He wiped the sweat from his brow with his shirtsleeve and adjusted his hat. "A few. I must get my hay cut."

"I won't take long, I promise." She opened a leather folder and began to write in it.

Meg, the horse closest to her, stomped at a fly and shook her head. Miss Watkins stumbled back a step and looked ready to run to the safety of her car. Time was a wasting. Adrian said, "What questions have you?"

She gave an embarrassed smile but didn't come closer. "How long have you known Faith Martin?"

"Three weeks, I reckon."

"Is that all?"

"I met her the day after she arrived here."

Miss Watkins kept writing. "Are you aware of any reason why Mrs. Martin should not adopt a child?"

"Nee."

"Do you believe she can provide for a child?"

"I do, but it makes no difference if she can or not."

Miss Watkins's brows drew together in a frown. "Of course it makes a difference."

"An Amish parent does not need to worry about what will happen to his or her family if something tragic befalls them. All our widows and children are well cared for."

"By whom?"

It was clear this outsider didn't understand Amish ways. "Our church members will see that Faith and her child have food, clothing and a roof over their heads if ever they need such help."

"That's very admirable."

"It is the way God commands us to live."

"Have you seen Mrs. Martin interacting with children?"

He thought back to last Sunday. *"Ja."*

"Tell me about it."

"I saw her holding Katie Sutter's daughter, Rachel. She had the babe settled on her hip. It looked as if she had done it many times. I also saw her with Annie Imhoff. She is nine, I think. Faith gave her attention and directed her to help with the work as was right."

"What are your feelings about Faith's adoption plan?"

"It is a *goot* thing for her to take in her brother's child, or any child."

"How often do you see Mrs. Martin?"

"I've seen her almost daily since she arrived."

"And why is that?"

The question shocked him. Why had he found excuse after excuse to trek across the field to see her so often?

Wasn't it because he was happier when he was near her? Wasn't it because her smile drove away his loneliness?

Miss Watkins waited for his reply. He said, "Because she needs help and it is the neighborly thing to do."

"Describe her personal qualities and limitations."

At last an easy question. "She is hardworking. She is devout. Modest. She is kind to her animals."

Miss Watkins stopped writing and looked up. "And what about her limitations?"

A not-so-easy question. What could he say that wouldn't undermine her chances of adopting her nephew and yet was the truth? "She sometimes takes on more than she can handle."

"Do you see her physical handicap as a limitation?"

"You and I might see it as such, but she does not," he stated firmly.

"Can you describe her potential ability to parent?"

"She will make a fine mother." Of that he had no doubt.

Miss Watkins folded her notebook tight against her chest. "Will a child of a different faith be accepted in your community?"

He shouldn't be annoyed by her ignorance, but he was. "God loves all His children. How could we do any less? Faith's nephew will be raised to know and serve God, as all our children are. To become Amish is a choice, not a requirement. When he is old enough, he will make that decision for himself. I must get back to work now."

"Thank you for your time."

He clicked his tongue. "Get up, Meg. Go along, Mick."

The team began moving and set the sickle in motion. The clatter of the razor sharp blades drowned out the sound of Miss Watkins's car as she drove away.

It wasn't right that an outsider was the one to decide if Faith could adopt her nephew.

For the first time in many years, Adrian opened his heart and prayed. He prayed for God to smile on Faith and the child who needed her.

In the middle of the week, Faith purchased a used woodstove at a farm sale and had it installed in her home. She bid a sad goodbye to the propane stove but happily pocketed the money from its sale. Her first attempt to use her new stove resulted in a charred meal, but by the third day she had the hang of it again.

The fire chief's favorable inspection report arrived in the mail a week later, the same day her medical report came. Dr. White had found her in sound health. She mailed the reports along with mounds of paperwork to the adoption agency and waited for a reply.

The following week she opened her mail to find the news she had been waiting for.

Kyle was coming to stay with her...on a trial basis. Finally!

Faith hugged the letter to her chest and twirled in a circle, nearly falling in the process.

When she was calm enough, she read the details

again. There would be more follow-up visits by the agency after Kyle arrived, but if all went well, the adoption hearing was scheduled for the last Monday in September.

There could still be stumbling blocks, but Faith didn't care. Kyle was on his way. She was finally going to meet her brother's child.

As she waited impatiently on the porch the day he was to arrive, she worked at carding her fleece. The process of combing sections of hair over and over again between two brushes was a mindless task she could do as she watched the driveway. Each passing minute felt like an hour.

When Miss Watkins's car finally appeared, Faith dropped her work into a basket and walked toward her gate, her hands shaking with excitement. She had waited so long for this moment.

Caroline stopped her car and got out. Without a word, she opened the back door of the automobile. Faith smiled happily at the boy who emerged. With his flaming red hair and freckles, young Kyle was the spitting image of his father at the same age.

The anxiety Faith had been living with for weeks lifted away and vanished into the air like smoke. It took but a moment for love to form in her heart. This was her brother's son, and she would love him as she had his father. As she would love her own child.

"Welcome, Kyle. I am your *Aenti* Faith, and I am very pleased to meet you."

He looked ready to bolt back into the car. His green eyes held sadness and fear. The tragedy had left its mark on him. Faith could have wept for all he had endured. It would be up to her and God to see that Kyle's life was safe and happy from now on out.

Miss Watkins said, "Today is a very special day. It's Kyle's birthday. I didn't know if you knew that or not."

Faith grinned at Kyle. "I didn't know. Happy birthday, dearest. My goodness, you are six. We will have to get you enrolled in school right away if you are to start this fall."

She took a step closer and bent to his level. "I have a surprise for you. Someone else has arrived just this morning and I think he would like to meet you."

Kyle's gaze moved from her face to the house behind her. "Who is it?"

Faith straightened and crossed her arms. "Well, I don't know what to call him. He's down in the barn. Would you like to meet him?"

Kyle eyed the barn with uncertainty. "I guess."

"*Goot.* Come along. Miss Watkins, you are welcome to come, too." Faith nodded in that direction.

The social worker looked from the barn down to her high-heeled shoes. "I believe I'll wait in the house."

Faith extended her hand to Kyle but he didn't take it. She tried not to feel rejected. She knew she needed to give him time to warm up to her. She started toward the barn and glanced over her shoulder. Kyle followed.

Happiness warmed her heart. It had been a long time since she'd dared believe she could be this happy.

At the barn door, she waited for him to catch up. "Have you ever been to a farm before?"

He hooked his thumbs in the waistband of his jeans. "We stayed on a ranch once. The rancher was a friend of my mom's. They had a whole lotta cows and cowboys, too."

Faith smiled at his Southern drawl. He had lived his whole life in Texas and it showed.

She opened the door. "I don't have a cow yet, but we will have to get one soon so you can have fresh milk to drink. There are lots of things you will learn about living on a farm, but one of the most important things is to respect the animals."

A loud whinny came from inside. Kyle's eyes grew round. "You've got a horse?"

She grinned at the excitement in his voice. "It is your horse now, too."

"Can I see him?" His wariness gave way to tempered eagerness.

"It's a she. Our mare's name is Copper. You can see her in a minute. A horse is a very strong animal and can hurt you if you aren't careful. I want you to listen carefully to these two rules. Are you listening?"

He nodded.

"Never run behind a horse. Never. Always speak to them softly so that they know where you are. Can your repeat these rules for me?"

"I never run behind one and I speak softly so they know I'm there."

"That's right. Okay, come and meet Copper," Faith led the way down the narrow center aisle to the first stall on the right. Copper hung her head over the boards to investigate the newcomer.

Kyle took a step closer to Faith. "She's really big."

"Wait until you see my neighbor's draft horses. They are really, really big. They make poor Copper look like a pony beside them."

Kyle started to hold out his hand but snatched it back when Copper nibbled at it. "Does she bite?"

"She is looking for a treat. I just happen to have something she loves in my pocket. I will show you how to feed her."

Faith withdrew a kerchief from her pocket and opened it to reveal several apple slices. Taking one, she laid it in the center of Kyle's palm. "Keep your hand flat. You don't want her to think your fingers are the treats."

He bravely held up the slice. Copper daintily nibbled it up. Kyle wiped his hand on his jeans. "Her lips are soft but her chin whiskers tickle. Can I give her another one?"

"Of course."

He fed her two more apple bits and then grew brave enough to pet her nose. "Can you teach me how to ride her?"

"I can, but Copper is a buggy horse."

"Like the ones I saw on the highway coming here?"

"*Ja,* just like those. Come, I have some more animals for you to meet." She smiled at Kyle and wondered what Adrian would think of her *Englisch* nephew.

Leading the way to the back of the barn, Faith stopped beside the last stall. "This is who I want you to meet."

She pointed through the board to the farthest corner. Myrtle lay in the thick bed of hay Adrian had spread out for her. At her side, a coal-black cria lay beside her. He raised his long neck that still wobbled slightly and batted his thick eyelashes in their direction.

"Is that a camel?" Kyle climbed up the boards to get a better view. Faith was pleased to see his curiosity pushing aside his unease.

"It's an alpaca. Her name is Myrtle and that is her

new son. He doesn't have a name yet. He was just born this morning."

"Sweet. Can I pet him?"

"As long as his mother doesn't object. Come, I will introduce you so that she knows you are a friend."

Faith opened the gate and stepped inside the pen. Her feet sank into the soft hay, making her stumble. Myrtle shot to her feet in alarm. The cria struggled to its feet and ducked under his mother's body to hide on the other side of her legs.

"What's the matter with your leg?" Kyle had noticed her brace.

"I hurt it a long time ago and it didn't heal well so now I have to wear this brace."

"Does it hurt?"

"Sometimes, but not today."

Grasping the gate to steady herself, Faith spoke soothingly to Myrtle in Pennsylvania Dutch. When the new mother was calm, Faith crossed the pen carefully with Kyle at her side. Myrtle allowed them both to admire her baby, but the baby remained hidden behind his mother.

Kyle squatted down in the bedding and held out his hand. "Come here, little fella. I won't hurt you."

"Perhaps he wants a name first. What do you think we should call him? He's black as night. Shall we call him Midnight?"

"No, that's a girly name."

Feeling put in her girly place, Faith held back a chuckle. "All right, what would you like to call him?"

"I want to call him Shadow."

She considered it. "Shadow. I think that's a very good name for him."

By this time the cria had grown accustomed to their presence and ventured out from behind his mother. Kyle extended his hand. "Come here, Shadow."

Shadow approached slowly, wobbling as he walked. Barely bigger than a tomcat with impossibly long legs, he was still trying to learn to use them.

It was clear he was as curious about the boy as the boy was about him. Kyle inched forward and touched the baby alpaca's head. Shadow frisked away behind his mother but didn't stay there. He returned after a moment to investigate further.

Faith said, "Kyle, I think he likes you."

"I think so, too."

"Since you have chosen his name, would you like to be his owner?"

"Can I?" Kyle looked up with uncertainty in his eyes.

"There are many things you will have to learn in order to take good care of him. It will be hard work. Are you willing to do that?"

"Sure."

"I don't mean for one day. I mean every day."

"If you show me what to do."

Myrtle began stamping one foot and making huffing sounds. Faith said, "His mother says he has had enough playtime. We should let him rest."

"He's really neat. Thanks, Aunt Faith."

She held open the gate to let him out of the stall. "You're welcome, Kyle. Let's go back to the house. I'm sure Miss Watkins is wondering where we are."

When they reached the house, Kyle went in ahead of her. Miss Watkins sat at the kitchen table fanning herself with a sheet of paper. Faith said, "Kyle, why don't you go explore the house."

"Okay." He left the room.

Miss Watkins slid several sheets of paper toward Faith. "We have only two more documents to sign, Mrs. Martin. It won't take long. Now, you understand this is a temporary guardianship until the court hearing next month."

"*Ja,* I understand."

"Good. I'll be back to visit Kyle several times before the hearing and see how things are going for the two of you. Expect me at noon the day after tomorrow. These transitions don't always go smoothly, so be prepared for that."

"I will."

After Faith signed the papers waiting for her, she walked with Miss Watkins to the door. "Thank you for all your help."

"I'm just doing my job. The judge will consider my recommendations when making a decision about the adoption."

"Of course." Faith wanted to hug the woman. It was finally sinking in. Kyle was here. At long last, God had given her a child.

"Aunt Faith?"

She and Miss Watkins turned around. Faith asked, "What is it, Kyle?"

"Where's your TV?"

At the end of their first day together, Faith helped Kyle get ready for bed. The scared, lost look she'd seen on his face when he'd first arrived had returned.

Setting his suitcase on a chair beside the bed, she began putting his clothes into the lowest drawers of the dresser against the wall where small hands could reach them easily.

Her hand encountered something hard tucked in between his pajamas and T-shirts. When she pulled it out, she saw it was a photograph of her brother and his wife.

Faith let her hand drift over the glass as she studied her brother's face. He had changed a great deal in the twelve years that he'd been gone. A man looked back at her, not the boy she remembered. The woman with him had dark brown hair and green eyes, a stunning combination.

"That's my mom and dad." Kyle reached for the picture.

"You look just like him." She handed the forbidden image to the boy.

He kissed the picture and looked around the room. "I think I'll want this by the bed so I can see it when I open my eyes."

She didn't have the heart to tell him the photograph would have to be put away. He had lost too much already. She wouldn't take away this reminder of his parents. Not yet.

She patted his head. "On your bedside table will be fine for now."

Turning away, she opened his windows to dispel the room's stuffiness and to hide the tears that stung her eyes. When she had a grip on her raw emotions, she turned around. He was already under the covers.

"You will be too hot under all of this." She drew back the quilt and folded it to the foot of the bed, leaving him with just a sheet.

He looked around, then sat up in bed. "I need a fan to sleep with."

"I don't have one. The breeze from the windows will keep you cool."

He pointed at the lantern she had placed on the dresser. "Can I keep the light on?"

"If you leave it on all night the battery will go dead."

"Please? I don't like the dark."

"I reckon it'll be okay. I have more batteries."

Relief flickered in his eyes. He scooted down in bed and pulled the sheet up to his chin. His red hair and freckles stood out in stark relief against the white bed-clothes. Once again she was reminded of his father.

She asked, "Do you want to say your prayers before you go to sleep?"

He pressed his lips together and shook his head. "I don't know any."

Surprised, she asked, "You don't? Did not your mother and father teach you your prayers?"

"I know one but I don't like it anymore."

"I'll tell you what. I will say my prayers and you can listen and add anything you want to say. How's that?"

He didn't consent, but he didn't object so Faith dropped awkwardly to her knees. Pain shot through her leg, but she ignored it. She folded her hands and bowed her head.

"Dear Father in heaven, Kyle and I give you thanks for the blessings You have shown us today. I'm so happy that he is here with me. Thank You for bringing him safely to my home."

"You could say thanks for giving me Shadow," Kyle whispered.

She nodded and closed her eyes. "Kyle and I both want to thank You for the gift of little Shadow. He brings us great joy with his playful ways."

She peeked at her nephew. "Anything else?"

He shook his head. Closing her eyes again, she said, "Bless us and help us to do Your will, Lord. Help us to live as You would have us live, humbly and simply, ever mindful of Your grace as we go about our daily tasks. Forgive us our sins as we forgive those who have sinned against us. Amen."

"Are you done?" he asked.

She smiled softly at him. "I'm done."

"Where are you going to sleep?" Worry crept back into his voice as she struggled to her feet.

Tucking the sheet around him, she said, "I will be right across the hall. If you need anything, just call out. Okay?"

"I guess. Can you leave the door open?"

"Certainly. Try to get some sleep."

"Am I going to stay here a long time?"

"I hope so, darling."

"Who decides if I stay or go to a another house? Do you?"

"It will be up to Miss Watkins and a judge to decide. If God wishes it, you will stay with me a long, long time." She bent down, kissed his brow and went to her own room.

Hours later she came awake with a jolt. Someone was screaming.

"Mommy! Mommy!"

Kyle! She shot out of bed, stumbling without her brace toward his room.

Chapter Ten

The door to Kyle's room stood open, but he wasn't in the bed. Frantic, Faith rushed in and searched the room. The lantern's battery was nearly depleted. It gave only a feeble, flickering light, but it was enough to let her see him huddled in the corner by the closet.

Some instinct made her approach him slowly. "Kyle, dearest, what's wrong?"

His eyes were open, but she knew he wasn't seeing her. He turned his head from side to side, sobbing. "Mommy? Mommy?"

Faith lowered herself to the floor. "Kyle, it's *Aenti* Faith. Can you hear me? Everything is all right. You've had a nightmare, that's all."

He sat with his arms around his knees. His little body trembled violently.

Faith moved closer. "It's all right, baby. It's all right. I'm here."

Suddenly, his eyes focused on her. He launched himself into her arms. Faith held him close, rocking him and stroking his hair as she murmured words of comfort.

He said, "I don't like it here. I want to go home."

"You are home, sweetheart. This is your new home, now."

He didn't answer, but slowly, his sobs died away. After a time, he fell asleep.

Faith sat holding him for a long time. Her heart bled for the pain he had endured in his young life. She could only pray that time and her love would heal his wounded soul.

When she was sure he was fast asleep, she struggled to her feet and carried him to his bed. After tucking him in, she lay down beside him in case he woke again and waited for the morning to come.

Miss Watkins would be back to check on him at noon tomorrow. If she learned how unhappy he was, would she take him away?

Late-morning sunshine glinted through the orchard canopy dappling the ground with dancing patterns of light and shadow as Adrian set to work harvesting the first of Faith's fruit. He hadn't been at it long when the hair at the back of his neck started to prickle.

Someone was watching him.

He lowered his fruit-picking pole to the ground. One of the alpacas, perhaps?

A quick check around showed he had Faith's orchard to himself. Shrugging off the feeling, he raised a long pole with a wire basket and a branch snipper on the end up into the branches of Faith's trees. As he worked, he transferred the peaches he'd plucked into a bushel basket at his feet. When he was finished gathering the fruit from one tree, he moved on to another. The feeling that he was being watched didn't leave.

As he emptied the pole basket into a larger one, a shower of leaves made him look up into the tree above him. The sight that greeted his eyes sent a slash of pain through his heart.

A red-haired, freckled-faced *kind* peered down through the leaves of a peach tree. The boy looked so much like his son that for a second he thought he was dreaming.

"Gideon?" He barely breathed the name.

The face disappeared back into the foliage. A small, disembodied voice asked, "Are you going to make me go away?"

The voice didn't belong to Gideon. This wasn't his son come back from the grave. Who was it? Adrian said, "Come down from there."

A few seconds later a pair of sneakers appeared. A boy lowered himself until he hung suspended from a branch with his shoes about three feet off the ground.

The kid shot Adrian a scowl. "Can I get a little help here?"

Adrian's racing heart slowed. Now that he had a better view of the boy, he could see the red hair and freckles were the only things that were similar to his son. This was an *Englisch* boy. He was several years older than Gideon had been. Stepping forward, Adrian grasped the boy's waist and lowered him to the ground.

"Thanks." The kid dusted his hands together, then cocked his head to the side as he studied Adrian. "Well?"

"Well what?"

"Are you going to take me away?"

"Nee."

"Are you going to be my new dad if the judge makes Aunt Faith my new mom?"

Realization dawned on Adrian. The boy was Faith's

nephew. He breathed a silent prayer of thanks that God had seen fit to bring her the child she longed for.

"I will not be your father. I'm a neighbor from down the road. I'm helping your *aenti* harvest her peaches."

"Oh. That's okay then. I didn't want a new dad. Aunt Faith is nice and all, but I want my real dad and mom to come back."

"They cannot come back from heaven."

Looking down, the boy kicked a fallen peach and sent it rolling through the grass. "Yeah, I know."

Adrian knew exactly what the boy was feeling. He said, "My name is Adrian Lapp. What is yours?"

"Howdy, Mr. Lapp. I'm Kyle King," the boy drawled.

"If you have nothing better to do, Kyle King, you can help me finish picking this fruit."

He didn't look enthused. "I don't know how. Do you have TV at your house?"

"*Nee,* it is *veldlich* and is *verboten.*"

"Huh?"

"It is a worldly thing and forbidden to us."

"How come you talk so funny?"

"Because I am Amish. How come you talk so funny?"

Kyle's solemn face cracked a tiny smile. "Because I'm a Texan."

"Ah. Do they have peaches in Texas?"

"I guess."

"But you have never picked peaches in Texas."

"Nope. We lived in Houston. Mom got our peaches from the grocery store."

"Houston, is that a big town?"

Kyle raised one eyebrow. "Are you kidding me?"

"*Nee,* I am not."

"What does *nee* mean?"

"It is Pennsylvania Dutch and it means no."

"Then why don't you just say no?"

"Because I am Amish and that is the language we speak."

"Oh. My aunt Faith is Amish, too. That's why she wears those funny dresses and that thing on her head."

"It is called a prayer *kapp*. It signifies her devotion to God."

"I'm not going to wear one 'cause I don't like God. He's mean."

"You must not say such a thing."

"It's true. My foster mom said God wanted my mom and dad with Him in heaven more than He wanted them to be here. That proves He isn't nice."

"I think she meant God *needed* them in heaven more than He needed them here."

Those were the same words Adrian's family and friends had used to try and comfort him, to help explain the inexplicable reasons why first his wife and then his son had been taken away. Like Kyle, Adrian found no comfort in the words.

The boy picked up a peach and threw it against a nearby tree, splattering the soft fruit against the rough bark. "I needed them more."

Faced with the impotent fury of this child, Adrian put aside his own feelings of bitterness and sought a way to help the boy. "You have a good arm, Kyle. Do you like baseball?"

"Sure. My dad was the coach of my team. He taught me everything about baseball. He was going to get me a new mitt when he picked me up after school, but he never came back. Why did God have to take him away?"

Adrian plucked a wormy peach from an overhead branch and threw it. It smashed into bits against the same tree. "We cannot know God's reasons. We can only pray that one day we will see our loved ones again."

"Did your parents die, too?"

"No. God took my wife and my son to heaven."

Kyle chucked two peaches toward the hapless tree. Only one hit the target. He squinted up at Adrian. "So, do you hate God, too?"

Faith faced Miss Watkins across the kitchen table. This was the social worker's first visit to see how Kyle was adjusting to life on the farm. Faith had never been more nervous in her life. She wished Adrian were here. She could use his solid presence beside her to bolster her courage.

Caroline checked the contents of the refrigerator, made a few notes in her folder and asked, "How's it going?"

"As well as can be expected." Faith kept her hands still, trying not to fidget.

"Can you elaborate a little more?"

Faith wasn't sure what the woman wanted to know. "Kyle didn't have much of an appetite yesterday, but he ate a good breakfast this morning. He adores the alpacas, especially the baby. He misses his friends and his foster parents. We went to the phone booth yesterday evening and called his buddies, Tyrell and Dylan."

Should she mention Kyle woke in the night and was crying, or would that count against her?

"Did talking to the boys upset Kyle?"

"Maybe a little. It has to be hard being pulled from all he knew."

"Where is he now?"

"Upstairs in his room. Shall I get him?"

"We can go up together. I'd like to see his room now that he's settled."

Faith led the way up the narrow fight of stairs to the bedroom opposite hers. She opened the door to Kyle's room expecting to see him reading or coloring at his desk. He wasn't in the room. His bedroom window stood wide-open with the screen pushed out.

She rushed to the window. The porch roof beyond was empty. The limbs of the old oak beside the house overhung the porch offering an adventurous boy a way down to the ground.

"He's gone." Faith heard the panic in her voice as she turned to the social worker.

Miss Watkins said, "Maybe he came downstairs and we didn't notice."

It took only a few minutes to search the house and see he wasn't in it. Where could he be? Faith opened the front door and stepped onto the porch with Miss Watkins right behind her. Faith scanned the yard. At least Kyle wasn't lying unconscious on the ground beneath the tree.

"He's likely out in the barn with Shadow." She tried calling his name but got no answer.

Crossing to the barn, Faith pulled open the door and called him again. Still no answer.

Inside, she found Myrtle and Shadow lying together undisturbed. Copper dozed in her stall. Kyle wasn't in here. Faith's worry took flight like the pigeons fluttering in the rafters. Where could he be?

Caroline asked, "Did he talk about running away?"

"He hasn't run away. I'm sure he's playing nearby."

Why would he run away? Was she such a terrible parent that he couldn't bear to live with her?

Faith opened the back door of the barn and went out into the alpaca's pen. They were milling about near the gate to the orchard and looking in that direction. The gate was closed. Faith knew she had left it open that morning so they could go out to graze.

She cupped her hand around her mouth and shouted for Kyle.

"He's with me!"

The booming voice from the orchard belonged to Adrian. Faith relaxed. Kyle was safe if he was with Adrian.

When the pair emerged from the trees, Faith crossed her arms and scowled at her nephew. "Did you climb out your bedroom window?"

"Yes."

"Why would you do such a thing? You could have fallen and been badly hurt."

He glanced from her to Miss Watkins. "I'm sorry. I won't do it again."

Miss Watkins dropped to his level. "Kyle, why did you sneak out of the house?"

He shrugged. "I don't know."

She laid a hand on his shoulder. "I understand that this is very difficult for you. If you aren't happy here, it's all right to tell me."

Faith held her breath. Would this woman take Kyle away from her so soon? They had barely gotten to know each other.

"It's okay. Sometimes it's boring, but it's okay." His voice wobbled.

Adrian said, "Idle hands are the devil's workshop. The boy needs work to occupy his mind. He can help me pick peaches if he is bored."

A quick frown crossed Caroline's face, but she didn't say anything to Adrian as she rose. Instead, she patted Kyle's head. "I'll be back in a week to check on you. All right? You have your aunt call me if you need anything. Will you be okay until then?"

"I guess." He shoved his hands in the waistband of his jeans.

As Miss Watkins headed for her car, Faith turned to Kyle. "You may help Adrian gather fruit until lunchtime. I'll call you when it's ready."

Kyle ventured a small request. "Can we have burgers and French fries?"

As a reward for climbing out your window and scaring me half to death?

Faith put aside her fright and forgave the boy for his behavior. "I think I can manage that, but it won't be like the fast food you get from town. Adrian, would you care to join us?"

Would he accept? She didn't want to appear too eager for his company, but she had missed him the past several days.

"I reckon I can. My hay is cut and drying in the fields. I have no need to rush home."

"*Goot.* Kyle, you must do as Adrian says."

"I will." The boy's smile returned.

Adrian said, "There are some wooden boxes inside the barn door. Bring them out to the tree where we were working."

"You got it." Kyle took off at a jog.

Faith said, "It's kind of you to let him help."

"You look tired. Is everything all right?"

"Kyle has nightmares. I haven't been sleeping well, either."

"He's had it tough, poor tyke."

"When we unpacked his things, I saw he had a picture of his mother and father. He wanted it on his bedside table. I let him keep it." She chewed the corner of her lip. Would he think she had done the wrong thing by going against their Amish teachings? Photographs were considered graven images and thus banned from Amish homes.

"The boy is not Amish. He does not know our ways. Give him time to learn about the things we believe."

She nodded, pleased that Adrian's advice mirrored her own feelings.

He leaned close. "But don't tell the bishop's wife. You already have one strike in her book."

Faith held back a giggle as Kyle came through the barn, his arms filled with a tall stack of boxes. "Are these the ones you need?"

Adrian said, "*Ja,* those are the ones. Your *aenti* and I will earn a pretty penny if we can fill and sell this many boxes of peaches."

Kyle looked between them. "You should charge more than a penny."

Adrian laughed. "Your nephew has a head for business, Faith. Should we follow his advice?"

Pretending to consider it, she finally said, "I agree. I say we ask for a nickel."

Adrian ran his fingers down his chin whiskers. "Let's think big. We should ask for a dime."

Kyle scrunched up his face. "Are you making fun of me?"

Faith ruffled his hair. "Perhaps a little."

Kyle rolled his eyes. "Whatever."

Adrian said, "Come along. Our work is waiting."

Faith watched them walk away together with mixed emotions. Kyle would need the influence of a man in his life, someone to teach him how to earn a living and work the land. Was she wrong to hope that Adrian could fulfill that role? It was a lot to ask of a neighbor. Those were things a father should teach a son.

Adrian would make a great father. He was kind and patient. She'd never heard him utter an angry word. While she never intended to marry again, if she did, someone like Adrian would be the kind of husband she'd look for. Someone exactly like Adrian.

The idea of being his wife made her blush. She quickly dismissed it as a fantasy that could never come true. Adrian wouldn't marry again any more than she would. The love he held in his heart for his first wife didn't leave room for another.

Wishing things could be different was foolish. Daydreams about Adrian were a sure path to heartache. She knew that.

So why couldn't she put her foolish yearning away?

Chapter Eleven

Several days later, Faith rose at five o'clock. She dressed, brushed and rolled her hair, fastened on her *kapp* and went down to start a fire in the kitchen stove. Stacking kindling and newspaper inside the firebox, she put a match to it. When she was sure the fire was going, she closed the firebox door.

While the stove heated, she straightened up in the living room. Adrian would be over soon to start work in the orchard. She didn't want him to see her home in a state of disarray.

Grabbing her broom, she began sweeping the floors. Soon she would have to have the offending pink-and-white linoleum replaced. The bishop had generously given her eight months to convert the old *Englisch* house into an Amish home. A home for her and Kyle, where the ghosts of the past could be put to rest and their new lives could flourish. It wouldn't be easy, but it would be worth all her hard work.

She finished her floors, washed up and began making breakfast. At half-past five o'clock, Faith called to

Kyle from the bottom of the stairs. "Kyle, time to get up. Breakfast is ready."

She had to call one more time before he appeared in the kitchen, his hair tousled and his eyes puffy with sleep. "What time is it?"

"Almost six o'clock, sleepyhead. We have a lot of work waiting for us."

"We do?" He sat at the table and yawned.

She loaded both their plates with pancakes and scrambled eggs and carried them to the table. "Adrian will be here soon to start picking peaches. You don't want to keep him waiting, do you?"

"No. Is Miss Watkins coming today?" Kyle folded his arms on the table and laid his head down.

"Not that I know of."

"Good."

Outside, a loud whinny came from the barn. Faith said, "Sounds like Copper is wanting her breakfast, too."

Kyle raised his head to squint at Faith. "Can I feed her?"

"*Ja,* but first eat before your eggs get cold." Faith sat beside him, bowed her head to say a quick silent prayer and then began eating.

"Can I feed Shadow, too?" Kyle forked in a mouthful of eggs.

"His mother will give Shadow all he needs for a few months yet, but we need to feed her."

"Okay. Then can I play on the swing Adrian made me yesterday?"

Adrian had turned a length of rope and a broad plank into a swing that now hung from the oak tree beside the porch. Faith said, "After all your chores are done."

"What chores?"

"We must feed the horse and turn her out to graze. We must feed and water the chickens and gather their eggs."

"Then can I play?"

"Not until we feed the alpacas, clean up their pen, pick the debris out of their coats and let them out to graze."

"How long will that take?"

"It takes as long as it takes, Kyle."

It might sound like a lot of work to him now, but wait until next spring when there would be a garden to hoe and weeds to be pulled every day and all before he went to school. Faith smiled. Amish children did not have time to be bored.

Kyle finished his breakfast and waited impatiently for Faith to wash the dishes. When they were done, he dashed ahead of her to the barn. "Remember the rules," she called out.

He immediately slowed down. "Don't run behind a horse and always speak softly to let them know where you are."

"Very *goot*."

She passed Adrian's farm wagon sitting in the shade. The bed of the wagon was half full of boxes of peaches. The scent of the ripe fruit filled the still morning air. Today they would load the rest of the wagon and head into the farmer's market in Hope Springs where Faith hoped her fruit would fetch a good price.

She opened the barn door, and Kyle ducked under her arm to get inside ahead of her. He made a beeline for Shadow's stall. His little buddy rushed away to hide beneath his mother.

Faith showed Kyle how to measure and pour the feed into the troughs for the alpaca. While Myrtle was busy with her breakfast, Shadow ventured close to Kyle and allowed the boy to pet him.

Kyle's bright grin gladdened Faith's heart. She took a small rake and a shovel from their place on the wall and handed them to the boy.

He said, "What's this for?"

"To *redd-up* the stall. To clean it." She indicated the manure piles.

He wrinkled his nose. "Yuck!"

She folded her arms and scowled at him. "Shadow is your responsibility. You said you would take care of him. Do you want him to sleep on a messy floor?"

"No."

She held out the tools. He approached with lagging steps and took them from her. Faith had trouble holding back her laughter as he carefully raked the manure onto the flat shovel. He looked at her. "Now what?"

"I will fetch the wheelbarrow. When we have done everyone's stall we will empty it onto the pile behind the barn."

"We're keeping it? Why?"

"Because it will make very *goot* fertilizer for the orchards and gardens next spring."

It took most of an hour to feed all the animals and clean the stalls. To Faith's delight, Kyle didn't complain or shirk from the work. They let Myrtle and Shadow out into the pen. Shadow raced about in delight at finding himself outside.

Faith and Kyle were crossing back to the house when she saw Adrian striding toward them across the field. He was pulling a small wagon behind him.

He raised a hand and waved. Her heart flipped over with unexpected joy at the sight of him.

Kyle took off toward him. "Hi, Adrian. I cleaned out the barn and fed all the animals and Shadow let me pet him."

Adrian grinned at Kyle. "Then you have done a man's work already this morning. You must be tired."

"No. Well, maybe a little."

"You deserve a rest." Adrian picked the boy up and balanced him on his shoulder. Kyle's squeal of fear quickly turned into giggles of delight.

Faith waited until the two of them caught up with her before falling into step beside them. Adrian immediately shortened his stride to match hers. Something Mose had never done.

She needed to stop comparing the two men in her mind. There was no comparison.

"Aunt Faith says we are going to town later. Are we?"

"We are. It is Market Day. Almost everyone goes to town on Market Day."

"Cool beans. Can you teach me to drive the horse?"

By this time they had reached the porch. Adrian swung Kyle down and deposited him on the steps. "Someday, but not today. We must take my team and they are too big for you to handle."

"I'm strong." Kyle flexed one arm and pushed up his sleeve to show his muscles.

Adrian whistled his appreciation. "We must put those muscles to work in the peach orchard. Are you ready?"

Kyle fisted his hands on his hips. "*Ja.* I'm ready."

Faith pressed her hand to her lips to hide her smile. "Spoken like a true Amishman."

Adrian folded his arms over his chest. "Grab a couple of boxes from the big wagon and put them in this one. We won't have to carry our peaches so far this way. Can you pull this out to the tree where we stopped working yesterday?"

"Sure." The boy took off at a run, the little wagon bouncing behind him.

Faith spoke softly to Adrian. "He has taken quite a liking to you. God was wise to bring you into his life."

"He is a fine boy. He reminds me of my son."

Faith laid a hand on Adrian's arm. "This must be very difficult for you."

Adrian waited for the pain of his son's loss to strike his heart, but it didn't. Instead, he recalled the way Gideon had always wanted to help, sometimes to the point of being in the way. Kyle had the same burning desire to prove his worth.

Adrian glanced at Faith's small hand on his arm. Her touch was warm and comforting. Was she right? Did God have a purpose for bringing him into Kyle's life?

For the past several years Adrian had thought only of what he had lost. He'd never once considered that God might use him as a gift to others.

He gazed into Faith's sympathetic eyes. "Kyle reminds me of Gideon, but he is not Gideon. I see in Kyle a boy with joys and pain, hopes and fears that are all his own. I'd like to think that they would have been friends. I know Lovina would have liked having you for a neighbor."

"I wish I could have known her."

"Me, too."

Adrian moved away from the comfort Faith offered. "We'd better get busy or we'll miss the start of the market."

"You're right. I need the best possible price for my fruit. My yarn is selling fairly well, but not well enough." They began walking toward the orchard.

"I've been thinking about that. Have you any items you'd like to sell at the market?"

"You mean things made from my yarn? I have several baby blankets and two dozen socks ready. Should I take them?"

"Many tourists come for the quilt auction that will be held this afternoon. They might buy your work."

She shook her head. "My plain socks hardly compare to the beautiful quilts they come to buy."

They reached the gate leading into the orchard. Kyle joined them carrying more boxes than he could safely manage. Shadow was prancing and bouncing beside him.

Adrian opened the gate for him. As usual, the curious alpacas came galloping up to investigate this new activity.

Kyle petted his little buddy. "I wish Shadow could come to town with us. I bet he'd like it."

Faith chuckled. "The tourists would stare at an alpaca riding in an Amish buggy, that's for sure."

Adrian stopped in his tracks. "They would, wouldn't they?"

Faith and Kyle walked on until they noticed he wasn't following. Faith stopped and looked back. "What's the matter?"

"Kyle and Shadow have given me an idea."

"We have?" Kyle looked perplexed.

"A very good idea. Faith, can you bring your spinning wheel to market and spin yarn while others are watching you?"

"*Ja.* What are you getting at?"

"Could we take Shadow to town with us?"

She shook her head. "He's only a few days old. It wouldn't be good for him to be separated from his mother for any length of time."

Adrian pondered the problems involved in his scheme. "And Myrtle is known for her spitting skills. That wouldn't work."

Faith's eyes lit up. "You want to take one of the alpacas to market with us as an advertisement for my yarns."

"You said it yourself. People would stop and stare. They might also stop and buy. Which of your animals has the best temperament?"

"Socks," she said without hesitation. "She loves attention and she loves people."

He nodded. Socks was the least likely to spit on an unsuspecting customer. "Would she follow behind the wagon into town?"

Faith's face showed her growing excitement. "I don't see why not. She's halter trained."

He held up his hand. "What's wrong with this plan?"

Faith shrugged. "Nothing that I can see."

Adrian nodded slowly. "Kyle and I will get started on the peaches. You get together the things you'd like to sell."

He turned and scratched Socks between the ears. "Looks like you're going to town, girl. What do you think about that?"

Kyle ran ahead with the wagon into the orchard with Shadow hot on his heels.

Faith once again wore her best bonnet and Sunday dress as she sat on the high seat of Adrian's wagon.

Kyle sat between them as excited as any six-year-old child on his way to a special treat. The boy had been awed into silence by the size of Adrian's draft horses but soon recovered his chatty nature.

As they approached Hope Springs, they met dozens of other Amish families all heading in the same direction. The influx of lumbering produce-laden wagons and buggies forced the traffic in town to drop to a crawl. The slow pace allowed many drivers and their passengers to gawk at Socks as she ambled along behind Adrian's wagon.

The alpaca didn't seem at all upset by the commotion going on around her. With her head held high, she surveyed the activity with wide, curious eyes.

Adrian turned off Main onto Lake Street. "The regular weekly markets are held every Friday afternoon in a large grassy area next to the lumberyard up ahead."

"Is it all produce?"

"You will find a wide range of fruits and vegetables sold here including certified organic produce. There will also be homemade baked goods, homemade jams, local honey, meat, eggs and cheeses. You can even find fresh-cut flowers as well as fresh and dried herbs and spices."

Faith could already see the striped canopies of numerous tents being set up. "I'm surprised at the size, given the fact that Hope Springs isn't that big of a town."

"This isn't a regular market day. This is our Summer Festival. It's held every year on the last day of August. The big draw this year is the Quilts of Hope charity quilt auction. My mother mentioned that they have over fifty quilts to sell."

Adrian maneuvered his wagon to a tent marked for

fresh produce and fruit. With Faith's and Kyle's help, he began unloading the wagon and stacking their boxes of peaches in neat rows inside the tent. The work would have gone faster if not for the crowd of children and adults who quickly gathered around Socks. Faith answered numerous questions about her animal while helping Adrian and keeping an eye on Kyle.

When they had the wagon unloaded, Adrian parked the wagon near a row of buggies and unhitched his team. He slipped off their bridles and put halters on the pair but left them in their harnesses. He turned to Faith. "Where would you like to set up your spinning wheel?"

"I wish I had a tent." The afternoon sun beating down on her head promised to make her demonstration hot work unless she could find some shade.

"*Ja,* we need to get one for you."

Faith liked the way he said "we," as if they would be doing this together again.

Kyle pulled at her sleeve. "Can I go look around?"

On one hand, she was as eager to explore all the tents and displays as Kyle was, but on the other hand, she didn't want Adrian to be stuck looking after Socks. The alpaca was her responsibility.

She put aside her childish desires and said, "Perhaps Adrian can show you around."

Kyle turned his pleading eyes toward Adrian. "Can you? Please?"

"I must stay with the wagon," he replied.

Faith wasn't about to let him miss out on a fun afternoon. "Socks belongs to me. I will stay with her. Please take Kyle and show him the sights."

A young man made his way though the crowd and

straight to Socks. "So this is an alpaca! They are cute. Is this the one that spit on you and the bishop's wife?"

The resemblance between the two men was unmistakable. Faith wasn't surprised when Adrian said, "Faith, this is my *bruder* Ben."

Ben's grin lit up his face. He touched the brim of his straw hat. "I'm pleased to meet you, Faith Martin."

She bowed slightly. "I'm pleased to meet you, as well. Myrtle was the ill-mannered one. This is Socks. She likes people."

"May I pet her?" Ben asked.

Faith nodded. Ben reached out hesitantly and stroked his hand along Socks's jaw. She showed her appreciation by stepping close and wrapping her long neck around him in a hug.

From behind her, Faith heard a pair of girls' voices cooing in unison. "Isn't that sweet?"

The girls, identical twins, joined Ben in petting Socks. Adrian spoke to his brother. "Ben, would you mind watching Socks while Faith and I show Kyle around?"

Ben winked at Adrian. "Not a bit."

"Danki." Adrian looked to Faith and tipped his head toward the nearest tent. "Shall we?"

She nodded and reached for Kyle's hand. As she grasped it, he let out a hiss of pain. Startled, she let go. "Did I hurt you?"

He put his hands behind his back and shook his head. Adrian squatted to his level and said sternly, "Let me see."

Reluctantly, Kyle extended his hands. There were large blisters on both palms.

Faith sucked in a sharp breath knowing how painful they had to be. "Kyle, why didn't you tell me you'd hurt yourself?"

"I was afraid you would make me stay home."

She thought of all the raking and wheelbarrow pushing he'd done as well as the heavy boxes full of peaches he'd pulled through the orchard in the little wagon. Never once had he complained.

"Darling, you mustn't be afraid to tell me when something hurts. We need to find somewhere to wash these and put some bandages on them."

Ben said, "There's a first-aid tent near the front of the lumberyard."

Faith flashed him a grateful smile. "*Danki.* Come along, Kyle. We'll get you fixed up in no time."

She and Adrian guided him through the crowds to the tent run by the local firefighters. A kindly fireman rinsed Kyle's hands, applied an antiseptic cream and a large Band-Aid to each palm. When he was done, he gave Kyle a lollipop. "For being so brave."

Faith thanked him. He said, "No problem. If you go out behind this tent you'll see we are providing free pony rides to all the children attending the market today. Our police and fire departments are giving out snow cones and popcorn, too."

Kyle looked hopefully at Faith. "Can I ride a pony?"

He certainly deserved some fun after all the work he'd done. "You may."

They found the ride without difficulty. Kyle waited patiently until it was his turn. Adrian lifted him aboard a small white horse and stepped back beside Faith as he and several other Amish children went round and round on the plodding ponies.

Standing beside Adrian and watching Kyle enjoying himself, Faith had a glimpse of what her life might have been like if she had married the right man and been blessed with children of her own.

While she might never be a wife again, she now had a chance to raise a son. The thought was bittersweet.

After the ride came to an end, they walked on together exploring the various tents and booths until they came to the largest tent. Two sides of the tent had been rolled up to take advantage of the gusty breeze. Inside, dozens of beautifully crafted quilts hung from wooden frames meant to display them to full advantage. The room was already crowded with *Englisch* men and women examining the quilts closely.

Faith was admiring a wedding ring quilt pattern done in cream, pinks and blues when she spotted Nettie Sutter, Adrian's mother and several other women conferring at a table near the back of the tent.

"Adrian, there's your mother."

"Where?"

She pointed. He quickly turned the other way and took her arm. "Let's go. I don't need any quilts."

Chapter Twelve

Adrian hoped to avoid his mother's too-sharp eyes but he should have known better. She had already seen them and was headed in their direction with Rebecca Beachy holding on to her arm. His mother's cheeks were rosy red from exertion. Wisps of her gray hair had escaped from beneath her *kapp*.

"Adrian, you are just what we need—a strong son to help me set up these tables. Hello, Faith." His mother's eyes darted between the two of them with intense speculation. No doubt she had already jumped to the wrong conclusion about his business association with Faith.

He said, "We've brought peaches to sell."

She winked at him. "What a clever excuse to bring Faith to our market. Faith, I'd like you to meet Rebecca Beachy. She and her aunt are neighbors of mine. Although Rebecca is blind, she stitches beautiful quilts."

Rebecca held out her hand. "My talent comes from God, it is not of my own making."

Faith stepped forward and took Rebecca's hand. "I'm pleased to meet you."

Rebecca tipped her head to the side. "And who else do you have with you?"

Adrian saw Kyle peeking from behind Faith's skirt.

Faith urged the boy forward. "This is my *Englisch* nephew, Kyle."

Kyle frowned up at her. "I'm not English, I'm from Texas."

Adrian's mother chuckled. "It's nice to meet you, Kyle from Texas."

"Have you had a pony ride yet?" Rebecca asked.

He nodded. "Aunt Faith says I can have a snow cone, too."

Rebecca grinned. "*Ach,* I love them. You must try the pineapple ones. They're the best."

"Adrian, can you spare a few minutes to help us?" his mother asked.

He looked over the number of visitors filing through the tent. This would be the best place for Faith to set up her wheel. "If I may ask a favor in return?"

Mamm nodded. "Of course."

"May Faith use one of your tables to sell her yarn?"

His mother grinned at Faith. "I don't see why not. The more, the merrier. Show Adrian where you want to set up."

Within a few minutes he'd set up the tables his mother needed and placed one for Faith near the open side so that Socks could be tethered out on the grass. His mother promised to keep an eye on Kyle while he and Faith returned to the wagon to collect Faith's spinning wheel and the yarns she had boxed up to sell.

They found the wagon surrounded by a dozen young Amish girls admiring Socks. Ben, seated casually on the tailgate of the wagon, was clearly enjoying the attention.

Faith and Adrian shared an amused glance before Adrian stepped inside the circle of young women. "*Danki,* Ben, I'll take over now."

Standing up, Ben said, "I don't mind watching Faith's pet a little longer."

"If you want to be useful, little *bruder,* you can carry Faith's spinning wheel to the tent where the quilts are being auctioned."

"I can handle that if one of you girls can show me the way." Ben's charming smile gathered him several volunteers.

After Ben left, Adrian stacked together Faith's wares and carried the boxes while she led Socks through the maze of vendor stalls back to the quilt tent.

Adrian staked Socks's lead rope just outside the tent. The alpaca promptly lay down in the thick green grass.

Kyle was waiting for them with a snow cone in his hand. Adrian's mother sat beside him enjoying one, too.

Kyle held his out. "These are really good. You should get one, Aunt Faith."

Faith said, "I hope you thanked Mrs. Lapp."

"I did." He slurped at juice dripping over the paper holder.

Adrian's mother rose and came to stand beside Faith. "He's been well behaved. Is this one of your alpacas? They are cute."

She leaned closer, and Adrian heard her ask, "Is this the one that spit on the bishop's wife?"

Faith blushed a becoming shade of pink. "No."

He took pity on her and tried to distract his mother. "*Mamm,* do you need anything else?"

"Not that I can think of," she replied.

"Faith, can I do anything else for you?" he asked. He needed to get back to the produce and see that it sold for a decent price, but he didn't want to leave her side. He was happy when he was near her.

She smiled sweetly at him. "I will be fine, *danki.*"

He turned to Kyle. "You must keep an eye on Socks while your *aenti* is busy and don't wander off without telling her."

"Okay." Kyle took his snow cone and went out to sit in the grass beside Socks. A number of people had already gathered to stare at the unusual creature. When they saw Kyle sit beside her, they pressed in for a closer look.

Faith, having arranged her yarns by color in small baskets on the table, sat down at the spinning wheel and began pumping the pedals that made it turn. Adrian stood back and watched to see how she would handle being on display along with her work. He didn't have long to wait.

A middle-aged *Englisch* woman with her husband stopped to watch Faith spin. She asked, "Is this all handmade yarn?"

"*Ja,* from my own alpacas." She seemed so nervous. Adrian wondered if he'd made a mistake in suggesting the venture.

The man asked, "What type of dye do you use?"

Faith glanced to Adrian. He gave her a thumbs-up sign.

She turned back to the prospective buyers. "Alpacas come naturally in twenty color variations. I have white, fawn, brown, gray and black, with many shades in between. The fleece dyes beautifully if you'd like colors other than these natural shades."

Nettie Sutter stepped up to the table. "I've heard it's better than wool."

"Alpaca has a softness unlike any other natural fiber. Most people find it doesn't itch like sheep's wool. It is also very lightweight and yet is warmer than wool. I have a receiving blanket made from white alpaca that you might be interested in for Katie's baby when it arrives." She indicated a box at the end of her table.

Adrian could see that the more Faith talked about her alpacas and her spinning, the more relaxed she became.

Nettie withdrew the blanket and gushed, "This is wonderfully soft. Feel it." She held the blanket out to the *Englisch* woman. She exclaimed over the quality, too. In a matter of minutes Faith made her first sale. Adrian turned to leave and found his mother at his side.

She said, "I like your new neighbor."

He scowled at her. "That's all Faith is. A neighbor. Nothing more."

A smug look settled over his mother's features. "Isn't that what I said?"

"What you say and what you mean are often two different things."

She patted his arm as if he were a child. "Now you sound like your father. Go and take care of your peaches. Don't worry. I will keep a close eye on your neighbor and her child. I think it's about time I got to know them better."

Chapter Thirteen

On Sunday morning Faith entered the home of Adam Troyer, the handyman in Hope Springs. His house had been chosen for the preaching service. Kyle was at her side.

She glanced down at him. It would be a long morning for a boy who wouldn't be able to understand the Pennsylvania Dutch preaching or the readings from the German Bible. How would he handle it? In the five days that he'd been with her he seemed to be adjusting well, but this might be stressful for him.

Sitting on a bench on the women's side of the aisle, she looked Kyle in the eyes. "You must sit on that side with the men today."

"But I want to stay with you."

"You are too old to sit with the women. I'll be right here. You must be quiet and respectful as we talked about last night. Amish children do not make a fuss, even when they are bored or tired."

"But I don't want to sit by myself," he whined.

"The boy can sit with me."

Faith glanced up to see Adrian standing beside them.

She couldn't control the rush of happiness that swept though her. Even Kyle's face brightened.

He said, "Hi, Adrian. I didn't know you were going to be here."

Faith nodded her appreciation for Adrian's offer to sit with Kyle. "*Danki,* Adrian."

His gaze settled on her face. Heat filled her face, and she knew she was blushing. She looked away determined to control the intense longing that took over whenever he was near.

No matter how often she told herself a match between them was impossible, her desire to spend time with Adrian grew stronger, not weaker.

Adrian placed his hand on Kyle's shoulder. "Come along. We must find our place."

He led the boy away and found a seat near the back of the room in case he had to take the boy outside. He wasn't sure how Kyle would act during the long, solemn service.

Amish children were taught from infancy to keep quiet during Sunday preaching. Amish mothers usually brought a bag of ready-to-eat cereal or snacks to help occupy the *kinder* who became restless. Adrian wished he'd thought of bringing something for Kyle.

Throughout the service, Adrian remained acutely aware of Faith across the room from him. There was a look of serenity on her face as she listened to the Word of God.

Her sweet voice blended well with the congregation when the hymns began. She sang almost as well as his cousin Sarah. Both women had received the gift of song from the Lord.

Adrian was no songbird. His wife used to joke that

he couldn't carry a tune in a wooden bucket if his life depended on it. He joined the congregation for each and every hymn, but he kept his voice soft and low enough not to trouble his neighbors' ears.

To Adrian's relief, Kyle remained well behaved. During the second hymn, he stood on the bench to better view the hymnbook Adrian held. The pages contained only the words of each hymn in German. The melody itself had been passed down from generation to generation in an unchanging oral tradition that reached back hundreds of years.

During the second hour of preaching, Adrian noticed Kyle's head nodding as he struggled to stay awake. He wasn't the only one. Several of the elderly members and a few of the youngsters were having trouble, too. Adrian slipped his arm around Kyle's shoulders and pulled him against his side. Kyle soon dozed off.

From across the aisle, Faith caught Adrian's eye. Her soft smile encompassed both he and the boy. It was the kind of smile that made a man feel special. Made him want to earn more of them.

At the end of the service, Bishop Zook rose and faced the congregation. He read off the names of the young people who wished to be baptized into the faith two weeks from today. Adrian recognized all the names. He knew them and their families. He had watched them grow up. All of them were making the commitment after having experienced something of the outside world during their *rumspringa*. Like himself, most of them were ready to marry and start families of their own.

None of them had any idea of the heartaches that might await them.

Bishop Zook said, "And now I have one more matter to place before you. Our sister, Faith Martin, has come among us seeking to practice the faith of her fathers with piety and humility. She has asked to become a member of our congregation. As you know, this decision is not up to me alone. Therefore, I ask this question of all. Is there anyone who knows a just reason why this sister should not become one of us?"

Silence filled the meeting room. Adrian glanced at Faith. Her eyes were downcast as she awaited the verdict. The bishop's wife shifted in her seat but didn't stand up. No one spoke.

After a few moments, the bishop smiled broadly and said, "Come forward, Sister Faith. In the name of the Lord and the Church, I extend to you the hand of fellowship. Be ye a faithful member of our church."

Adrian relaxed. No one had spoken against her. Faith stood and walked to stand before the bishop. He took her hand, but because she was a woman, he then gave her hand to his wife who greeted her with a Holy Kiss upon her cheek.

Faith was now a member of their community and subject to all the rules of their faith. Adrian glanced at the boy sleeping against his side. She would have to raise Kyle in the ways of the faithful. It was a good life, and he was happy for the boy.

When the services came to an end a few minutes later, Adrian woke Kyle, and the two of them followed the other men outside. Kyle yawned and squinted up at Adrian. "I'm hungry."

"We'll eat soon."

Faith approached them. Happiness radiated from her face. She said, "Kyle, you were very well behaved today."

"I fell asleep," he admitted.

Her happy smile made her even prettier this morning. Adrian said, "Congratulations."

"*Danki.* Kyle, why don't you come with me now and let Adrian visit with his friends."

Other members of the church crowded around to offer their congratulations and welcome. Adrian stepped aside. It was her special day, and he was glad for her.

Because it was such a beautiful day, the meal was set up outdoors. The younger people soon had a volleyball net set up between two trees on the lawn. A dozen of the boys and girls quickly began a game. The cheering and laughter from both participants and onlookers filled the late-summer afternoon with joyous sounds. Faith sat on a blanket in the grass with Kyle beside her. They were cheering for the girls.

"She has the makings of a good mother, don't you think?"

Adrian looked over his shoulder to find his cousin Sarah observing him with interest. She'd always had an uncanny knack for knowing what he was thinking. He didn't pretend ignorance.

"She is good with the boy."

Sarah settled herself on the tailgate of the wagon beside him. "Faith tells me that you have been good for the boy, too."

"He reminds me of Gideon."

Sarah cocked her head to the side as she studied the boy. "A little maybe because of his red hair, but Kyle's hair is darker and curlier. Is she going to send him to our Amish school or to an *Englisch* one?"

"I don't know."

"You haven't asked her?"

"It's none of my business." He looked down to pretend he didn't care one way or the other.

"That's odd."

"What is?" he muttered.

"It's just that the two of you seem so close."

He slanted a glance her way. "What's that supposed to mean?"

"The two of you seem close, that's all. You've been working at her farm since the day she moved in. People notice."

"People should mind their own business."

"You know that's not going to happen. You're single. She's single. She's a member of our church district now. There's nothing wrong with courting her."

He drew back in shock. "Is that what you think I'm doing?"

"Me? No, of course not. I know you better than that."

Mollified, he said, "I should hope so."

"You're being kind, that's all."

"Exactly."

"What your mother or others think is beyond my control."

"Mother thinks I'm courting Faith? I will straighten her thinking out on the way home, today."

"Before you do that, let me ask you something. Has your mother invited any single women to your family dinners recently?"

He thought back over the past month and realized she hadn't. "No."

"See."

"See what?" He couldn't follow her reasoning.

"Kindness brings its own reward."

"Speak plain, Sarah. What are you hinting at?"

She patted his arm. "All I'm saying is that while you are being kind to your neighbor, your mother has stopped searching high and low for someone to catch your interest."

"That's not my reason for helping Faith."

"I'm not suggesting it is. You have a kind heart, and Faith needs all the help she can get until she has her yarn business up and running well."

"That's right."

"It would be okay if you did decide to court her."

He looked into Sarah's eyes. "I don't know if I can take that chance again."

She laid a hand on his arm. "You can, otherwise you will miss out on something special. Lovina wouldn't want you to waste your life grieving for her. You know that. She is happy with God in heaven. She wants you to be happy, too."

"What if something happens to Faith or to Kyle? How could I live through such a loss again?"

"Adrian, you can do one of two things. You can blame God for your misery or you can turn to Him and draw strength from His love. He is always there for us."

"You make it sound so easy. It isn't."

"Answer me this. Were you better off before you met Faith?"

"Nee."

"If you were given one and only one chance to kiss her, would you take it?"

He would take it in a heartbeat. *"Ja."*

"Then why are you turning down the chance to love her for a lifetime?"

He had no answer for Sarah, but she didn't seem to

expect one. With a pat on his arm, she left to join Faith and Kyle on their quilt.

As was his custom, Adrian left the gathering early, went home and cut flowers from his garden. On his way to the cemetery, he pondered his feelings for Faith, what they meant and what he was willing to do about them. Did he have a chance to love her for a lifetime? Was that really within his grasp? The thought excited and frightened him. What if he loved and lost her, too?

At his wife's graveside, he laid the new flowers over the dried husks of the old ones. He stared at her headstone, but he was at a loss for something to say.

Turning away, he took his usual seat and leaned forward with his elbows braced on his thighs. Suddenly, the words came pouring out. "I never meant it to happen, Lovey. I wasn't looking for someone to care about. In my whole life I never wanted to share my hopes and dreams with anyone but you."

Until now. Until Faith. He raised his face to the sky. "Is this wrong? How can it be wrong to care about such a good woman? Faith is a good woman, a strong woman, but she needs someone to take care of her and her boy."

And I need someone to care about me.

Wasn't that the truth he'd been hiding from?

Adrian closed his eyes. "I've been dead inside for a long time. Waking up is painful, Lovey. I'm not sure I can do it."

Chapter Fourteen

Faith sat at her kitchen table with her checkbook in front of her on Thursday morning. She'd been able to pay her outstanding bills with the money she'd made at the market and she still had money left over. Her small bank account was growing at last.

In her wildest dreams she hadn't imagined doing this well so quickly. She'd sold all the yarn she'd taken with her to the market and had taken orders for several dozen additional skeins plus eight of her white baby blankets. She would have to redouble her spinning and knitting efforts to keep up.

Adrian's mother had invited Faith to join their co-op group and display her handmade wares each week on market day. With the cool days of fall not far away, yarn for warm socks, sweaters and mittens were sure to be in high demand.

Kyle came running into the room. He stopped beside Faith to grab a leftover breakfast biscuit from a plate in the center of the table. "My room is clean."

"*Danki,* Kyle."

"Is Adrian coming over today?"

She missed Adrian's presence as much as Kyle did. Maybe more. She'd gotten used to having him around. Some foolish part of her heart continued to hope that he'd come over with a new excuse to spend time with them, but it hadn't happened.

"I doubt it, dear. His work in the orchard is done. You will see him at the next preaching service."

"But that's another whole week away." Pieces of biscuit sprayed from his lips.

"Don't talk with your mouth full."

He swallowed. "I don't want to wait until church. Can't we go visit Adrian today?"

"No. Miss Watkins is coming today."

Faith hoped his sudden pout wasn't going to lead to a temper tantrum. "Why is *she* coming?" he demanded.

"It's her job to find out if you are happy here. Are you happy?"

Confusion clouded his eyes. "Can I go play with Shadow?"

A pang of disappointment stabbed her. Why couldn't he answer a simple question? "You may, but try not to get dirty."

He darted outside, letting the screen door bang shut behind him.

Was he unhappy living with her? He seemed to be adjusting well to this new way of life. She had been worried those first few nights, but he'd not had a nightmare for the past week.

Faith closed her eyes and took a deep breath. Her new life in Hope Springs was turning into a dream come true. Kyle was with her. The church community had welcomed her with open arms. Her business was off to a great start, and her share of the peach money had been an added bonus.

"Through you, Lord, all things are possible. I humbly give thanks for Your blessings."

Little more than a month ago she had arrived in Hope Springs with barely enough to support herself. Now, she had enough to support Kyle, too. An important step toward his permanent adoption. Would his social worker think it was enough? The Amish were frugal people. Faith didn't need a large sum of money to live comfortably. Could Caroline Watkins be made to understand that?

An hour later, the sound of a car pulling into the yard alerted Faith to Miss Watkins's arrival. Faith opened the door and waited as Caroline came up the steps. "Good morning, Miss Watkins. Do come in. How are you?"

Caroline said, "I'm fine. This shouldn't take long today. I'll make a quick tour of the house and then I'd like to talk to you and Kyle separately. Is that all right?"

"Certainly." Faith took a seat at the kitchen table and waited. She tried to ignore the nervous dread that started gnawing at the inside of her stomach. She knew there was nothing to fear, but she was afraid anyway. This woman had the power to remove Kyle from her home.

Ten agonizing minutes later, Caroline came back into the kitchen with smile on her lips. "Everything seems in order, Mrs. Martin. How are you getting along with Kyle?"

Faith let out the breath she'd been holding. "It's going well. He works hard and plays hard. We went to the Summer Festival in Hope Springs last week, and I think he really enjoyed himself."

"That's great to hear. Where is Kyle?"

"He's down in the barn playing with Shadow, the baby

alpaca. The two of them have become fast friends. Shadow is living up to his name for he follows Kyle around whenever the boy is near. Would you like me to go get him?"

"I'd rather talk to him alone." Caroline went out the door.

Faith began her preparations for making bread. Keeping busy was better than pacing the floor and wondering what was going on between Kyle and Miss Watkins. What if Kyle told her he didn't like it here? What if he complained that he had too much work to do? A dozen unhappy scenarios ran through Faith's mind. Her stomach rolled into a tight knot.

A few minutes later, Miss Watkins returned to the house. Faith dusted the flour off her hands, set her bread dough aside and turned around. "Are you finished already?"

Her worry knot doubled in size when she saw the green speckles on Miss Watkins's clothes. Myrtle had been at it again.

"I'm so sorry. I should have warned you about Myrtle." Faith wet a kitchen towel and handed it to Caroline.

Caroline wiped her face and brushed at her blouse. "Their spitting is a disgusting habit. I couldn't find Kyle. Where else might he be?"

"He said he was going to the barn."

"He isn't in the barn. I called but he didn't answer. He wasn't with the baby alpaca." She scrubbed at her shoulder.

"Perhaps he's in the orchard."

"Does he disappear like this often?"

"No, of course not." Faith rushed outside and began frantically calling for Kyle. She and the social worker made their way from one side of the orchard to the other without any sign of the boy.

When they arrived back at the house and saw Kyle

hadn't returned, Faith said, "We should go to the neighbor's farm and see if he is there."

"Has he done that before?"

"No."

Miss Watkins pulled her cell phone from the pocket of her slacks. "Can you call them and see if he's there?"

"My neighbors are Amish. They have no phones."

Miss Watkins bit her lip, then opened her phone. "We are wasting valuable time. I'm going to notify the sheriff that we have a missing child."

Adrian lay on his back beneath his grain binder and loosened the last bolt holding the sickle blades in place. It came loose easily, and he lowered the bar to the ground. His cornfields would be ready to cut soon, and he needed to make sure his equipment was in good working order. Sharpening the sickle blades was his first priority.

"What ya doing?"

Adrian twisted his head around to see Kyle squatting beneath the equipment with him. "I'm getting my machinery ready to harvest corn. What are you doing?"

"I came to help you."

"You have, have you? Where is your *aenti* Faith?" Adrian wormed his way out from beneath his equipment with the long row of blades in hand. He looked eagerly toward the house, but he didn't see Faith anywhere.

He had stayed away from her the past few days because he knew if they came face-to-face, he wouldn't be able to hide his longing or his fears. He hadn't been ready for that. Was he ready now?

Kyle said, "She's at home with that mean social worker."

Faith wasn't here. Adrian tried not to let his disappointment show. He focused on Kyle. "You must not speak badly of others, Kyle. You must forgive them for the wrongs they do."

"Why?"

"Because that is what God commands us to do. Why do you say your social worker is mean?"

"'Cause social workers take kids away from their moms." Kyle glanced over his shoulder as if expecting to see one swooping down on him like a hawk.

"Where did you hear this?"

"Dylan and Tyrell told me."

The names weren't familiar. Adrian asked, "Who are they?"

"My friends in Texas. They were in foster care with me because a social worker took them away from their mom. They told me not to like Becky too much cause a social worker would come and take me away to a new place, and one did. Dylan and Tyrell had been in three foster homes so they knew it would happen and it did."

"Becky was your foster mother?"

Kyle nodded. "I liked her a lot."

Adrian sat on the steel tongue of his grain binder. "I'm sorry you were taken from someone you cared about, but I know that Faith loves you and she wants you to stay with her for a long time."

Kyle turned away from Adrian and patted the side of the machine. "What does this thing do?"

"This is a grain binder. It cuts cane or corn into bundles of livestock feed."

"How?"

Adrian understood Kyle's reluctance to talk about matters that troubled him. Wasn't he the same way?

Didn't he avoid talking about his family because it brought the pain back sharp as ever?

He said, "The machine is powered by this gasoline engine. My team pulls it through the field while I stand up here to guide them." He indicated a small platform at the front.

"Up here?" Kyle climbed the three metal ladder rungs and stood behind the slim railing that allowed the driver to lean against it and kept him from falling while he drove his team.

The boy grinned when he realized he was now taller than Adrian. He stretched his hands out pretending to hold the reins of a frisky team. "What do I do next?"

Adrian walked around to the side of the machine. "You guide your team along the corn rows. This sickle bar cuts the thick stalks about a foot off the ground. The reel lays them evenly onto this wide canvas belt. The belt feeds the stalks into a mechanism that gathers them together into a bundle, then wraps it with twine and knots it."

"Then what?"

"You must decide. See that lever in front of you?"

"Yup." Kyle reached beneath the safety rail to grasp a metal handle.

"Pull it back and the bundle is kicked out the side of the machine where it will lay in the field until I come back and stack them into tepee-style shocks."

"Why make a tepee out of them?"

These were things Adrian would have explained to his son if Gideon has lived. It was part of being a father, teaching the children how to farm and wrest a living from the land.

Kyle wouldn't have anyone to teach him unless Faith chose to remarry.

Would she remarry for the boy's sake? The thought didn't sit well with Adrian. What if the man she chose was unkind to her or to Kyle the way her first husband had been? He knew a few Amish husbands who believed they should rule their families with an iron fist.

"Why build tepees with them?" Kyle asked again.

"Because they shed water if you put the bundles together in an upright position. As they dry and shrink, it allows more air to flow around the inside of the bundles and they dry better. I put about twenty bundles into each shock."

"What if I push this lever forward?"

"Then the machine dumps the bundles onto a trailer that is pulled behind me, and my brother stacks them together so we can haul them to the barn."

"I wish I had a brother. That would be cool."

"It is sometimes, but sometimes they can be a pain in the neck."

Kyle climbed down from his post. "Can I see Meg and Mick?"

The boy had taken a liking to Adrian's team and had begged to ride one on the way home from market. Adrian hadn't allowed it then as they were on the highway, but he saw no harm in it now.

"*Ja,* they are in the barn."

"Can I ride one of them? They are like ten times bigger than the ponies at the fair."

Adrian thought of all the work he had to finish. Put side by side with Kyle's eager face, Adrian found only one conclusion. The work could wait.

In the barn, Adrian opened the door to Meg's stall and led her out to the small paddock. He hoisted Kyle to her broad back. She was so wide that the boy's feet stuck out straight instead of being able to grip her sides.

Adrian said, "Wrap your hand in her mane."

"Won't that hurt her?"

"*Nee,* it will not, but it might keep you from falling off."

Grasping the halter, Adrian led the mare around the paddock. She walked slowly and carefully, as if aware of the precious cargo she carried.

Kyle grinned from ear to ear. "I can see all the way to Texas from up here."

"How's the weather down that way?"

Shading his eyes with one hand, Kyle said, "Sunny and hot."

After the third time around the corral, Adrian stopped Meg and held his hands up to Kyle. "Come along. I have much work to do. I must sharpen my sickle and get my binder back together and Meg wants to have a good roll in the dust."

"Okay." Kyle reluctantly left his high perch. They walked back into the barn, leaving Meg in the pen where she promptly lay down, rolled onto her back and frolicked in the dust she raised.

As they passed her stall, Kyle looked at Adrian. "Do you want me to *redd-up* her stall?"

Tickled by Kyle's use of an Amish term, Adrian knew the boy would soon fit into their Amish ways and leave his *Englisch* past behind. He stared into Kyle's eyes and saw he was dying to please.

Adrian stroked his beard. "Reckon I could use a good stable hand now and again."

Puffing out his chest, Kyle asked, "Where's your wheelbarrow and your shovel?"

"I will get them for you."

When he returned with the requested tools and gave them to Kyle, Adrian leaned on the stall gate to watch the boy work. It took him a while, but he managed to rake up the mess and push the wheelbarrow back to Adrian.

Sighing heavily, Kyle said, "Alpacas are much easier to clean up after."

"They are not as big as Meg."

"No wonder Aunt Faith raises them instead of horses."

Adrian chuckled. "No wonder."

Kyle pulled at the Band-Aid on his palm. "It came loose."

Adrian bent down to see. He removed the bandages and looked at the angry red sores. "You should have told me they were hurting you."

"They don't hurt." Kyle put his hands behind his back.

"Lying is a sin, Kyle. I know you want to please and prove that you are a good helper, but Faith will have my hide if these get infected. Come up to the house and let's get them clean."

In the kitchen, Adrian gently washed Kyle's hands and patted them dry. He applied an antiseptic cream to them and wrapped a length of gauze around each palm. "Is that better?"

Kyle flexed his fingers. *"Ja."*

"I think I may have a pair of gloves you can wear over them." He rose and led the way to Gideon's room. Opening the door, he experienced the same catch in his chest that always hit him when he stepped over this threshold. The room looked the same as the day his son had left it.

On the blue-and-green quilt that covered the bed lay a baseball glove and a carved wooden horse. Gifts meant for a birthday that had never arrived. Crossing the room, Adrian pulled open a dresser drawer and retrieved a small pair of knit gloves.

"Try these on." He turned to hand them to Kyle and froze. Kyle was on his knees by the bed galloping the toy horse across the quilt.

He grinned up at Adrian. "This looks like Meg."

Adrian held back the shout that formed in his throat. *Leave that alone. It belongs to my son.*

He knew Kyle wouldn't understand. The boy meant no harm. He was simply doing what boys did—playing with a toy as it was meant to be played with.

Is this part of Your plan, Lord? Am I to see that I'm being greedy and selfish by hanging on to these things? Gideon would share his toys with this boy, I know he would. He had a kind heart like his mother.

Adrian forced a smile to his stiff lips. "I made it to look like Meg. I was going to make another one that looked like Mick."

"You made it? Cool beans." Kyle stared at the toy in awe.

"Would you like to have it?"

"Can I?" His eyes grew round.

"It is yours if you want it."

Kyle grinned. "Thanks. I mean, *danki*."

"You're welcome. Now try these on." Adrian held out the gloves. They proved to be too small.

Knowing a pair of his would be much too large, Adrian said, "Try not to get dirty."

"That's what Aunt Faith tells me."

"Does it work?"

"Not so much."

Adrian smiled as he ruffled Kyle's hair and went

outside to finish his work. He sharpened his blades while Kyle galloped little Meg across the workbench and jumped her over hammers and assorted tools. It felt good to have a child with him again.

He still missed his son, still wished it was Gideon with him, but he was able to enjoy Kyle's company and appreciate the boy for who he was.

Adrian was reattaching his sickle blades when the sound of a car coming up his lane drew his attention. He rose to his feet and saw the sheriff's white SUV roll to a stop in front of his house.

Adrian looked at Kyle seated on the ground beside him. "Does your aunt know you are here?"

The boy shrugged.

Adrian shook his head at his own thoughtlessness. "That is a question I should have asked an hour ago."

He held his hand out to Kyle. "Come. You have some explaining to do."

Reluctantly, Kyle rose and walked with Adrian toward the sheriff's vehicle. The passenger's door opened, and Faith rushed toward them, a look of intense relief on her face. In her hurry she stumbled and would have fallen if Adrian hadn't lunged forward to catch her.

He held her tight against his chest and breathed in the fresh scent of her hair. She fit perfectly against him. It felt so right to hold her this way. She looked up at him with wide, startled eyes. Eyes filled not with fear, but with the same breathless excitement she had awakened in him.

In that instant he knew she felt as he did. The next move was up to him. Did he dare risk his heart again?

Chapter Fifteen

Faith rested in the safety of Adrian's embrace, relishing the strength and gentleness with which he held her. Gazing up into his face, she saw his eyes darken.

Did he feel it too, this current between them that defied her logical, sensible mind?

How had it happened? How had she fallen in love with him?

He said softly, "Kyle is okay."

"I knew he would be if he was with you," she whispered. She and Kyle would always be safe if Adrian was with them. If only it could be this way forever. It couldn't. She knew that.

Adrian was still in love with his wife. She couldn't compete with a ghost.

Besides, she had to concentrate on Kyle. Finalizing his adoption had to be her top priority. Adding Adrian to the picture would only complicate and delay things.

Reluctantly, she left the comfort of Adrian's embrace and sank awkwardly to the ground beside Kyle. She gathered him close in a tight hug. "I was so worried when I couldn't find you."

He wrapped his arms around her neck and hugged her back. Suddenly, he let go and stepped away. Faith saw he was looking at the sheriff and Miss Watkins as they approached.

Faith cupped his chin and turned his face toward her. "It's all right. You aren't in trouble."

The sheriff pushed his hat back with one finger. "Looks like the lost sheep has been found."

Miss Watkins clasped her hands together. "I am so sorry that we wasted your time, Sheriff Bradley."

"Don't be. I like a happy ending. I just wish all my calls were so easy."

Miss Watkins focused her attention on Kyle. "You frightened us very badly, Kyle. Why did you run away from home?"

"I didn't."

Faith accepted Adrian's hand as he helped her to her feet. She said, "Kyle, you must let me know when you are going to visit a friend or a neighbor."

"Okay."

Miss Watkins stepped forward with a sharp frown on her face. "What's wrong with your hands, Kyle?"

"I got some blisters. Adrian fixed me up. He gave me this horse." He held up the toy.

Glancing between the adults, Miss Watkins leaned down to Kyle's level. "How did you get blisters? Did you touch something hot?"

"No." He shrank away from her and toward Faith.

Faith said, "He got them cleaning out a stall and helping us with the peach crop."

Adrian spoke up. "He rubbed his bandages off cleaning one of my stalls. I washed his sores and redressed them. He'll be okay in a few days."

Holding out her hand, Miss Watkins asked, "May I see your blisters?"

Kyle buried his face in Faith's skirt and put his hands behind his back.

Turning his face up to hers, Faith smiled encouragingly at him. "Is it okay if I unwrap them?"

He held out his hands. Faith unwound the dressing from his right hand. Miss Watkins took a closer look, then said, "Okay. Kyle, why don't you go to the car with Sheriff Bradley. I bet he'll show you how the radio works."

The sheriff nodded toward his SUV. "Come on, Kyle. Would you like to turn on the flashing lights?"

Kyle glanced from Faith to Adrian. "Is it *verboten*?"

Faith exchanged an amused look with Adrian, then said, "It's not forbidden. It is okay for Amish boys to do such a thing."

Kyle followed the sheriff, but the worried expression lingered on his face.

Miss Watkins folded her arms. "I will be the first to admit that I'm not familiar with Amish ways, but to work a child of six until both his hands are covered in blisters is not acceptable."

Faith cringed before the social worker's anger. Fear stole her voice. Beside her, Adrian said, "The boy worked hard to prove that he belongs among us. We did not make him do this."

Caroline shook her head. "Be that as it may, I'm not convinced this is the best arrangement for Kyle."

"Please, don't take him away from me." Faith wanted to race to the car, grab her child and hold on to him so tightly that no one could take him from her. Adrian's hand settled on her shoulder holding her in place.

Caroline sighed heavily. "I don't want to take him away, Mrs. Martin, but I have to know that he's in a safe environment. I would be neglecting my job and Kyle's welfare if I placed him in a questionable home."

"I'll do anything you ask. Please, don't take him away," Faith pleaded.

"Ultimately that decision is up to a judge. I'm here to help make the adoption possible. I want you to rethink how much work a child of six should be doing. I'll be back to visit again next Friday. Before then, you will need to make a list of Kyle's chores. We can go over them together and see if we can agree on what's appropriate for his age."

"I can do that," Faith quickly assured her.

"Keep in mind that he's going to be in school. There will be even less time for him to do chores." She walked back to the sheriff's vehicle leaving Faith and Adrian alone.

Faith started to follow her, but Adrian caught her arm. "Faith, we need to talk."

"I can't. Not now."

His shoulders slumped in defeat. "All right. Go home and take care of your child."

She squeezed his hand. "Thank you, Adrian."

"For what?"

"For understanding." Faith left him and took a seat inside the sheriff's vehicle.

"Are you ready for your first day of school?"

Bright and early Monday morning Faith climbed into the buggy beside Kyle.

He hooked his thumbs through his new suspenders giving them a sour look. "Do I have to wear these? I look like a dork."

"You must dress plain now. All the boys will be wearing them."

"Are you sure?" He let them snap back against his chest.

"*Ja,* I'm sure. Do you like your hat?"

He raised his flat-topped straw hat with both hands and looked up at it. "It's okay. It's like the one Adrian wears."

"He wears suspenders, too."

"Yeah, he does, doesn't he?" That mollified him.

"Are you excited about school?"

He sat back and folded his arms over his chest. "No. Everyone's gonna think I'm stupid 'cause I can't speak Pennsylvania Dutch."

She folded her hands in her lap. "Kyle, you are learning our language just as the Amish children at school will be learning English. If you help them, they will help you and nobody will be stupid."

"Maybe." He didn't sound convinced.

Faith cupped his chin and raised his face so she could see his eyes. "I know this is hard for you, but school is not all bad. You will learn many good things. Do you like to play baseball?"

"Yes."

"Amish children also like baseball. When I was in school, we played it almost every day. Not in winter, of course. In the winter, we went sledding during recess."

"Really?" He looked at her with interest.

"Really."

"That sounds kinda cool."

She grinned. "It wasn't cool. It was downright cold." She poked his side making him giggle.

"Can I drive the buggy?" he asked.

"You may, but just to the end of the lane." Faith had no fear that Copper would bolt. The mare was well trained and placid. In fact, it was hard to get her into high gear anymore.

"Hold the reins like this." Faith demonstrated. Kyle was quick to copy her and soon had Copper moving down the lane. Faith sat ready to take the lines at the first sign of trouble. Thankfully, they reached the highway without incident.

"How'd I do?" he asked as he handed the reins back.

"Very well. You're a natural." She headed Copper down the road toward the schoolhouse a mile and a half away. After today Kyle would be walking, but she wanted to make sure he could find his way. Besides, the first day of school was special for any child, and she wanted to be a part of it.

When the building came into view, she said, "We're almost there."

Kyle slumped in his seat again. "Do I have to go? I feel sick."

She understood the anxiety he was feeling, but she knew he would soon make new friends. Faith had met earlier with his teacher, Leah Belier. A young Amish woman in her early twenties, Leah seemed devoted to students and to helping them learn. She had promised she would do her best to help Kyle adjust to his new surroundings.

Faith stopped the buggy on the sloping lawn of the one-room schoolhouse. Several other buggies were tied up alongside the building. Children were already at play on the swing set and the long wooden teeter-totter.

Faith sensed Kyle's interest, but he moved closer to

her. Before she could convince him to get down, Leah came out of the schoolhouse door and waved to Faith.

Faith returned her greeting. Kyle buried his face in Faith's lap. "Can we go home, please?"

Leah was quick to assess the situation and approached the buggy. "You must be Kyle King. I'm so glad to meet you. I was hoping you could help me this morning."

Kyle eyed her with suspicion. "How?"

"I need a strong young boy to ring the bell for me."

Looking past her, Kyle assessed the situation. "I guess I could do that."

"Wonderful. Faith, would you like to sit in on class today?"

"I would."

After securing Copper to the hitching rail, Faith walked with Kyle to the school building where Leah waited for them. The teacher pointed to the bell rope hanging inside the doorway. "Give it a yank, Kyle. It's time to start our classes."

Gritting his teeth, Kyle pulled with all his might. The bell clanged loudly.

Leah clapped her hands. "Very good, Kyle. You're every bit as strong as you look. Now, I need someone to put pencils and papers on all the desks. Can you help with that?"

"Sure."

"*Danki.* That means thank you."

"I know."

"The papers and pencils are on the table behind my chair. The desk directly in front of mine belongs to you."

The other children began entering by twos and threes. Leah welcomed them all by their first names, asking after family members and previous students. It was clear she enjoyed her job.

Faith took a seat at the back of the room where several young mothers sat visiting with each other.

She stayed for the first hour of class, just long enough to make sure Kyle was going to be okay. Leah kept all the students well in hand as she switched back and forth between English and Pennsylvania Dutch to make sure everyone understood her instructions.

After leaving the school, Faith drove home and set to work spinning another batch of yarns. Once they were done, she would take them into town after she picked up Kyle. She had a special treat in store for him.

By early afternoon, she had several dozen skeins ready to be dropped off at Needles and Pins. She hitched up Copper again and arrived at the schoolhouse just as the main door opened and a rush of children poured out.

Kyle, grinning from ear to ear, skidded to a halt beside her and held up a piece of paper. "I drew a picture of Shadow. Did you know we're the only people in Hope Springs who have alpacas?"

She grinned at his enthusiasm. "I suspected as much."

"Anna Imhoff and her brothers want to come over and see Shadow. Can they?"

"Perhaps tomorrow. Today, we must go into town and celebrate."

"Celebrate what?"

"Your first day at school. It's a big deal and it calls for a celebration."

"What kind of celebration?"

"I'm treating you to supper at the Shoofly Pie Café."

"Can we get pizza?"

"That sounds perfect."

"*Goot.* That means good in Pennsylvania Dutch. I learned it and some more words, too."

"I'm pleased to hear your day wasn't wasted. Did you make some new friends?"

"Anna Imhoff wants to be my friend, but she's a girl."

"Girls can be friends, too."

"Her brother, Noah, started teasing me 'cause I can't talk Amish. Anna got mad and scolded him."

"Then she sounds like a very good friend to have. Did everyone play baseball at recess?"

His mood went from happy to dejected. "Yeah, but no one picked me for their team."

"You are little yet. I'm sure you'll play many games when you're older."

"Maybe if I got a glove."

Leah approached the buggy. "He did well, Faith. He needs to work on his sums and his reading, but overall he's a bright, friendly boy."

"Wonderful." It was a relief to know that Kyle was fitting in. She had worried that the language barrier would make school unhappy for him.

Leah left to speak to other parents, and Faith turned Copper toward town. Once they reached Hope Springs, Faith dropped off her yarns at the fabric store and drove on to the Shoofly Pie Café.

She and Kyle entered the homey café and were instantly surrounded with the smell of baking bread, cinnamon and frying chicken. A young Amish girl came forward. "*Velkumm* to the Shoofly Pie café. My name is Melody. Would you like a table or a booth?"

"A booth," Kyle answered before Faith could say anything.

The waitress led them to one of the high-backed seats that lined the walls of the room. Faith slid into the nearest bench. Kyle scooted in opposite her and propped his elbows on the red Formica tabletop.

Suddenly, Kyle's eyes lit up. "It's Adrian."

The boy waved. Faith turned to see her neighbor entering the door. He raised a hand and waved back. He was carrying a small package wrapped in plain brown paper and tied with string.

He stopped beside their booth. Faith wished her heart would stop trying to gallop out of her chest each time he was near.

Kyle spoke up eagerly. "I went to school today."

Adrian grinned at him. "So I heard. How was it?"

"Pretty fun. I learned to count to ten in Amish and how to say please and thank you."

"Those are all good things to know." Adrian focused his gaze on Faith. "How have you been?"

Missing you madly. "Fine, and you?"

"Busy. I'll start cutting corn tomorrow if this nice weather holds."

She couldn't care less about the mundane details of his life. Just seeing his face brightened her day.

He asked, "May I join you?"

Surprised and delighted, she said, "Certainly."

Kyle scooted over to let him sit down. Adrian said, "I brought you a present, Kyle." He slid the package toward the boy.

"Why? It's not my birthday." Kyle tore open the wrapping to reveal a baseball mitt. It was too big for his hand, but he didn't seem to mind. "Cool. I've been wanting one like this forever."

Adrian smiled at him. "Happy first day of school."

Faith couldn't put her finger on it, but there was something different about Adrian today. He was more lighthearted, happier than she had seen him. She liked the change. She liked it a lot.

He met her gaze. "Every boy needs a good baseball glove."

She said, "You didn't need to spend money on Kyle. I could have gotten him one."

"It's an old glove I had lying around. I thought Kyle might put it to good use."

"I sure will. Now they won't pick me last." Kyle smacked his fist in the pocket.

Faith's heart warmed to see Kyle so excited and happy. She started to convey her thanks, but Adrian stopped her with a shake of his head. "It's nothing."

The look in his eyes said differently. Then it hit her. She reached across the table to lay her hand on Adrian's arm. "It was Gideon's glove, wasn't it?"

"It was, but now it is Kyle's." His glance settled on her nephew. It was easy to read the deep affection he had for the boy.

It was only when Adrian looked into her eyes that she became unsure of his feelings. He said, "I know Kyle's adoption is your main priority right now, but when that's over, I'd like to talk about the future."

Faith pulled her hand away. The future? What was he suggesting? Did he have more plans for the farm, or was he suggesting they could have a future together? Her heart raced as her breathing quickened. "The hearing is the last day of this month."

He winced. "That is a long time to wait."

"Then perhaps you should come over this evening

if it's important." She bit the inside of her lip as she waited for his reply.

"It is important to me and I hope to you. *Ja,* I will come by later."

"I'm having pizza," Kyle announced.

Adrian tweaked the boy's nose. "Sounds good to me. I like pepperoni and extra cheese."

"Me, too." Kyle looked at Faith. "What kind do you like, Aunt Faith?"

"I'll have whatever the two of you are having."

Food was the furthest thing from her mind at the moment. What was on Adrian's mind that couldn't wait? Did she dare hope he returned her feelings of affection, or was she tricking herself into imagining what wasn't there?

"You're late getting back from town," Ben said, as he finished greasing the wheels of the grain binder and wiped his blackened fingers on a piece of cloth lying on top of the machine.

"I had supper at the café. Are you done already?" Adrian checked his brother's work and found it satisfactory.

"*Ja.* When will you start cutting?"

"I took a walk through the corn this morning. I think it will be ready by the end of the week, if it doesn't rain."

"*Dat* wants to start on our fields early tomorrow. We should be done in four or five days. When we're finished, I can come and give you a hand."

"I always appreciate your help with the farmwork." Could he trust Ben with an even more important task?

Adrian hooked his thumbs in his suspenders. He wasn't ready to reveal his intentions toward Faith to his family just yet. He wanted to know her feelings first.

She had been adamant that she would not remarry. If those were her true feelings, he would respect them and never bring up the subject again.

He needed to speak to her alone, but he couldn't do that with Kyle listening in. Knowing the boy's penchant for turning up in the wrong place at the wrong time, Adrian didn't want to risk it.

The smart thing to do would have been to wait until the adoption was over or at least until the boy was in school tomorrow, but Adrian didn't want to wait another day to know if Faith cared for him as he'd grown to care for her.

Oh, he'd had every intention of waiting until the time was right…then she'd smiled at him in the café and laid her hand on his arm to comfort him. The understanding in her eyes had done something wonderful to his heart.

His carefully laid plans had flown out of his head, and he'd told her he would be over tonight.

Tonight! This was what he got for his impatience. He had to rely on his baby brother to help him secure time alone with Faith.

"Ben, I'm wondering if you could give me a hand with something this evening?"

"Sure. What do you need?"

Drawing a deep breath, Adrian forged ahead before he could change his mind. "I need someone to stay with Faith Martin's boy for an hour or so."

There was a long moment of silence, then Ben crossed his arms. "Why?"

"Because…because I need to speak to Faith, alone."

Ben grinned from ear to ear. "You're going courting."

Adrian closed his eyes. This had been another bad

idea. What was wrong with him today? "I never said that."

"You don't have to say anything. It's written all over your face. The whole family has been wondering when you'd finally wise up. Wait until I tell *Mamm* she was right about you two."

"Please, don't. Not until I know how Faith feels."

Ben stepped forward and laid a hand on Adrian's shoulder. "She'd be a fool to turn you down and I don't think Faith Martin is anyone's fool."

"I pray you are right."

"Let me wash off this grease and then we can go. I won't keep you waiting to see your lady love." Ben walked away, chuckling to himself.

Adrian blew out a deep sigh of frustration. This was to be his punishment for involving his baby brother. Ben was never going to let him live this down, and he was never going to keep it a secret.

Twenty minutes later, the two men were driving toward Faith's house with Ben at the reins. Adrian's stomach churned with butterflies now that he was actually on his way. He rubbed his sweaty palms on his pant legs and tried to figure out what he was going to say.

Ben slipped his arm around Adrian's shoulder and gave him a brotherly hug. "Relax. She isn't going to bite your head off and I doubt she spits like an alpaca. You should drive her over toward the Stultz place and take the left fork just past their barn. The road winds up in a pretty little meadow beside Croft Creek."

"Where the old stone bridge has fallen down?"

Ben shot him a surprised look. "You know the place?"

"You don't think you're the first fellow to take a girl

out there for a picnic, do you? *Dat* took *Mamm* there when he was courting her."

"No kidding? Our folks?" Ben looked as if he'd bitten a lemon.

It was Adrian's turn to laugh. "Love finds all sorts of people, little *bruder*. Every papa and granddad you see was once a young man with stealing a kiss on his mind."

"I reckon you're right." Ben pulled the horse to a stop in front of Faith's gate.

She and Kyle were both outside. Faith sat at her spinning wheel on the porch. Kyle was playing on the swing Adrian had built for him. The moment Kyle caught sight of them, he jumped out of the swing and ran toward them.

"Howdy, Adrian. Howdy, Ben. What are you doing here?" He slowed to a walk when he drew near the horse.

Ben hopped out of the buggy. "I've come to see your alpaca herd up close."

"I'll show them to you. We've got a new cria. His name is Shadow and he belongs to me. Adrian gave me a baseball glove. Want to see it?"

"Sure. Maybe we can play some catch after we're done seeing your critters."

"Cool beans."

Ben gave Adrian a wave and walked toward the barn with the boy dancing beside him.

Adrian sat in the buggy as Faith came down the steps toward him. She looked so pretty this evening in a dark purple dress with an apron of the same color over it. His butterflies returned in full force. He nodded toward her. "Evening, Faith."

She paused behind her gate. "Hello again."

"It's a right nice evening, isn't it?" He tried not to fidget.

"Very nice."

"I was wondering if you might like to take a buggy ride?"

She glanced toward the barn. "I'm sure Kyle would enjoy that."

"Ben is going to stay here with Kyle until we get back."

"Oh." Her eyes widened.

Adrian held out his hand. "It will be just the two of us."

Faith hesitated. She wanted to go with him, but what was she getting herself into? This wasn't going to be a farming discussion. She had sense enough to know that. Could he really want to be alone with her because he was ready to open his heart to another woman? To her?

Was she ready for another relationship?

There was only one way to find out. She pushed open the gate and took his hand to climb in his buggy.

When she was settled beside him, he clicked his tongue and slapped the reins to set Wilbur in motion.

At the highway, he turned south toward his farm but passed by his lane without stopping. She asked, "Where are we going?"

"Some place we can talk without being interrupted."

He turned off at the first dirt road to the Stultz place and then took the left fork just past their big white barn. The little-used road wound around the side of a hill and came out into a small meadow. A white-tailed doe grazing near the trees along the creek threw up her head and then bounded away in alarm.

Adrian drew his horse to a stop. "Will it bother you to walk a little way?"

"I'll be fine."

"It isn't far." He got out and helped her down. As his strong hands grasped her waist, she realized she didn't fear his touch. It didn't matter how strong Adrian was. He was always gentle.

Together, they walked side by side into the forest and down a faint path. She could hear the sound of the water splashing over rocks. The smell of damp earth and leaves mingled with the scent of pine needles crushed underfoot. A few yards later, they came to the remnants of an old stone bridge, an arch broken in the middle and covered by leafy vines. Just below it, a wide flat slab of stone jutted out over the creek. A single boulder made a perfect seat in the center of it.

"How pretty it is in here." Faith sat on the moss-covered stone. The coolness of the forest and the rushing water brought a welcome relief from the summer heat and the heat in her cheeks.

Adrian took a seat beside her. "This was one of my wife's favorite places."

There it was, the reminder that he still loved his wife. Faith's heart sank. She looked down at her hands clasped together in her lap. How foolish she'd been to think there could be something between them. "I can see why she liked it."

Adrian said, "I'm sorry. I didn't bring you here to talk about Lovina."

"I understand if you feel the need to talk about her. You must miss her very much." If nothing else, Faith could lend a sympathetic ear. If that eased his pain even a little, then she would be glad.

"I did miss her deeply for a very long time, but lately I haven't been thinking about her as much."

"Why is that?"

"Because I've been thinking about you."

Faith raised her face to look at him. "Me?"

"You have no idea what kind of effect you have on me, do you? You and your creatures upset my solitude, played havoc with my work, forced me to take a look at the way I…wasn't living. Until you came, I was only biding my time until I died, and I didn't even know it."

"I'm sorry." She didn't understand what he was trying to say.

He smiled at her. "Don't be sorry. Don't ever be sorry, Faith Martin."

He reached out and cupped her face in his hands. "You and Kyle have brought joy to me when I never expected to have it again. I will never be able to thank God enough for bringing you here."

Before she could say anything, he bent his head and kissed her.

Startled, Faith pulled away. Adrian's hands still cupped her face. He stared into her eyes, waiting.

Waiting for her to say yes or no.

Oh, she wanted to say yes. She closed her eyes and leaned into his touch. Softly, his mouth covered hers again.

The sound of the rushing water faded away as Faith tentatively explored the texture of his lips against hers. Firm but gentle, warm and tender, his touch stirred her soul and sent the blood rushing through her veins. She had never been kissed like this. She didn't know it was possible for her heart to expand with such love and not burst.

When Adrian drew away, she kept her eyes closed, afraid she would see disappointment or regret on his face.

"Faith, look at me," he said softly.

"Nee."

"Why not?"

Old insecurities came rushing back to choke down her happiness. "You will say you're sorry. That this was a mistake."

"It was not a mistake. I will kiss you again if you need me to prove it."

Her eyes popped open. She couldn't believe this was happening.

He sat back. "I'm rushing you. That wasn't what I had in mind when I brought you here."

"Why did you bring me here?"

"To tell you that I care about you and about Kyle. To discover if you care about me. I know this is too soon, we've only known each other a short time. I know you have much on your mind and you are worried about Kyle's adoption, I know you have said you'd never marry again, but—is there a chance you could look with favor on me and allow me to court you?"

"Adrian, I don't know what to say."

"If you'd but nod, I'd take that as a *goot* sign."

She smiled at his teasing, even though she saw the seriousness in his eyes. How was it possible to feel so happy?

"Ja, Adrian Lapp, you may court me, but I warn you, I'm no prize."

"I will be the judge of that."

The word "judge" brought her back to earth with a thump. Would the adoption proceeding be put on hold if Miss Watkins or the agency learned of this? Would Adrian be subjected to the same scrutiny she had endured? It could take months. Now that the hearing was finally drawing near, she couldn't face another delay.

"Adrian, this must remain just between us until after Kyle's adoption is final."

"Why? Surely it could not hurt your case for the *Englisch* to know I stand ready to serve as Kyle's father."

She grasped his arm. "Perhaps not, but I can't take that chance. We must be friends until then and nothing more."

He covered her hand with his large warm one. "I will always be your friend. Do not look so worried, Faith. It is all in God's hands."

He was right. She relaxed and nodded. "I have faith in His grace. It will be fine."

Faith tried to retain her positive attitude as the week slowly rolled by. Miss Watkins's coming visit would be the last one before the official adoption hearing. Her recommendations would weigh heavily with the judge.

After supper on Thursday evening, Faith cleared the table and then sat down beside Kyle. He was coloring a page for his homework assignment. She said, "I have something important to talk about."

"What is it?" He exchanged a red crayon for a green one and began to work on the grass in his picture.

"Miss Watkins is coming tomorrow."

His small browed furrowed. "Why does she keep coming back?"

"Because she wants to make sure you have a safe place to live."

"I want to live here."

She planted a kiss on his brow. "I want you to live here, too. I love you."

He kept his mouth closed. He wasn't ready to say those words to her. Would he ever be? She went on as if nothing were wrong. "I want you to promise me that you'll stay close to the house tomorrow while Miss Watkins is here."

"Why?"

"We don't want her to think you don't like it here. That you'd rather live someplace else, do we?"

Confusion deepened his scowl. "I don't like it here a whole bunch."

Faith drew back in surprise. "You don't? I thought you were happy here. Is it school? Do you dislike your teacher, or is someone bullying you there?"

"School is okay. I don't want to talk about it." He gathered his paper and crayons and ran out of the room.

Faith stared after him in shock. Was she doing the wrong thing trying to raise him as Amish? Would he be happier in a home with *Englisch* parents? What should she do?

If only Adrian were here. She looked out the window toward his farm. What advice would he give? She hadn't seen him since he'd asked permission to court her. She wanted to believe it was God's plan for them to have a future together, but she was afraid to hope for such happiness.

It seemed as if she'd spent her entire life being afraid.

That night she went to bed but sleep proved elusive. She tossed and turned beneath the covers and prayed that she was doing the right thing.

When the morning finally came, she made breakfast and went out to do the chores. When she called Kyle down, her heart ached for him. His eyes were puffy, and he looked as if he hadn't slept any better than she had.

"Kyle, we should talk about what's bothering you."

"Nothing's bothering me. Can I have jelly on my toast?"

She set a jar of peach preserves on the table and waited until he helped himself. "Kyle, do you want to live somewhere else?"

He put down his toast without tasting it. "No."

"If you do, that's okay."

"Where else could I go?"

"I'm not sure, but there are a lot of people who would love to have a little boy like you."

"No, I can't go anywhere else. I have to stay and take care of Shadow. Shadow needs me. I'm his friend."

"All right. It's time to get ready for school. You'd better hurry. You don't want to be late."

She walked Kyle to the end of the lane and waited with him until the Imhoff children arrived. Faith bit her lip as she watched them walk down the road toward the school swinging their lunch coolers alongside.

When they were out of sight, she glanced toward Adrian's farm. She wanted to talk to him, to share her burden and her fears. Biting her thumbnail, she waged an internal war. Tell him or don't tell him? Before she could decide, she caught a glimpse of him driving his grain binder into the cornfield.

He had more than enough work to do. She didn't need to add to his troubles.

She opened her heart and began to pray. "Dear Lord, please let the social worker's visit go well. Let Kyle come to love me as I love him and to be content here among Your people. Give me the strength and wisdom to guide him throughout his life."

A car whizzed by, bringing her attention back to the present. She turned and walked toward the house. There was plenty of spinning to keep her busy until Kyle came home again. Praying while she was spinning was easy, too, and she had a lot of praying to do.

It was a few minutes before four o'clock when Miss Watkins arrived for her last visit. Faith put her spinning away and went out to greet her. After exchanging pleasantries, Miss Watkins got down to business. "Have you had a chance to make out a chore list for Kyle?"

"I have." Faith produced the paper hoping she had done as Miss Watkins wanted.

After reading it, the social worker looked at Faith. "Is he to clean stalls every day?"

"It is a chore most Amish children take care of at his age without a problem. I've limited it to just Myrtle's stall. Shadow is his animal, and he must take care of her."

"All right. That's a valid point." She reviewed the rest of Faith's paper and said, "It seems like a lot of work for one boy."

"There is much work to be done around here and I can't do it all."

Caroline glanced at her watch. "I thought you said he normally gets home from school at four o'clock. It's four fifteen."

Faith rose to look out the window. The lane was empty. "He should be here any minute."

"I'm concerned that he doesn't have enough supervision on his way to and from school."

"Amish children walk to school. He doesn't walk alone. The Imhoff children walk with him."

The two women sat together in silence until another fifteen minutes had passed. Faith rose to her feet again as worry gnawed at her insides. She opened the door and walked out onto the porch. Had Kyle gone to Adrian's instead of coming home?

A splotch of red by the barn caught her eye. Kyle's lunch pail sat beside the barn door. She turned to Miss Watkins. "He's here. That's his lunch cooler by the barn door. He must have gone to do his chores first."

Faith walked down the steps and crossed the yard with Miss Watkins right behind her. As soon as Faith opened the door, she knew something was wrong. Myrtle was calling frantically for her baby as she rushed from one side of the stall to the other. Shadow was gone.

"Oh, Kyle. What have you done now?"

Miss Watkins came up behind Faith. "What's wrong?"

"Kyle has taken Shadow. I need to find Adrian."

Faith rushed out the back door of the barn and through the orchard to the cornfield where Adrian was working. His horses plodded along with their heads down as they pulled the large grain binder. The noise of the gasoline engine running the belt almost drowned out the clatter of the mower head as it sheered off cornstalks as thick as her wrist with ease.

He was headed toward her, but he didn't see her. His attention was focused on the binder as it dumped out bundles of cornstalks and on keeping his horses traveling in a straight line. Faith hurried toward him knowing he would help her find Kyle.

She stumbled several times as she crossed the rough

ground. Where could Kyle have gone? Why had he run away again?

She was within fifty yards of Adrian when movement in the cornfield caught her eye. She crouched down to see better between the stalks. Was that Kyle hiding in the corn?

A scream erupted from Faith as she realized the danger Kyle was in. Adrian didn't see him. The deadly blades of the binder would cut through a boy as easily as it did the tough corn.

She began to run, screaming at the top of her lungs to get Adrian's attention. Screaming at Kyle to get out of the way. She had to reach him. She tried to run faster, but her weak leg gave out and she fell.

Lying in the dirt, she screamed Kyle's name as tears blurred her vision.

Please, God, let them hear me. Please save my child!

Chapter Sixteen

Adrian wiped the sweat from his brow and braced his tired body against the rail at the front of his binder. His head pounded from the constant roar of the gas engine and the exhaust fumes that drifted toward him. As much work as he'd gotten done today, he knew the hard part was still ahead of him. Gathering the bundles of corn and stacking them together was a backbreaking chore.

He kept his eyes glued to the binder reel. For some reason, it occasionally threw out a bundle that wasn't tied. He felt the tension in his reins change, and he looked toward his team. It was then he saw Faith running toward him across the stubble field.

She was shouting and waving her arms, then she fell. He didn't know what was wrong, but he knew he had to reach her quickly. He slapped the reins against his horses' rumps and urged them to a faster pace. The bundles of corn fell off the conveyor belt and broke open on the ground.

Faith waved him back. He could hear her shouts now, but he couldn't make out what she was saying. Miss Watkins was running toward him, too.

Suddenly, a black blob darted out of the cornfield directly in front of his horses. They shied, and he pulled them back into line when he realized it was Shadow. In the next instant he heard Faith yelling Kyle's name, and he saw the boy step out directly in front of him.

"God, give me strength!" Adrian hauled back on the lines to stop his horses, kicked the shutoff switch on the engine to kill it and threw the lever that stopped the mower blades. The horses reared back at his rough handling. The noise of the machine died away to silence.

He kept his eyes shut as the vision of Gideon running in front of that car played out to its horrible end.

"Not again, God. Don't let me see him die. Please, don't let me see him die."

He heard Faith's voice first. She was sobbing. He opened his eyes and blinked to focus. Kyle stood barely six inches away from the blades.

Adrian tried but couldn't catch his breath. He collapsed onto the platform with his head spinning. By this time Faith had reached Kyle. She had him in her arms, holding him close. Shadow, frightened and lost, called pitifully for his mother.

Faith carried Kyle toward Adrian. She called out, "He's fine. Praise God, he's fine."

He waved her away. He didn't have the strength to stand. "Take him home."

God had given him a chance to redeem himself. He hadn't been able to save Gideon, but Kyle was alive. "Thank you, God."

Adrian gained his feet and turned his team toward home. He couldn't work any more today. Being afraid was part of being human, but shutting himself off from others hadn't lessened the pain of his son's loss. Like a knife left in a drawer unused, the edge stayed sharp. He vividly recalled every second of that terrible day.

Living meant using all his emotions. Living his faith meant trusting God to strengthen him in times of sorrow and of joy. He loved Faith and he loved Kyle, but was he strong enough to live each day knowing he could lose either one of them as he'd almost done today?

He wasn't sure.

Faith knocked at Adrian's door a few minutes before seven o'clock that night. She wiped away her tears as she waited for him to answer. She didn't know where to turn, so she had turned to the one constant in her life.

The door opened and Adrian stood before her, his face gray, his eyes sunken. He looked as if he'd aged ten years in one day. She probably looked worse.

His voice sounded raw when he asked, "How is he?"

She thought all her tears were done, but apparently she had more. They began to flow again. "They took him away, Adrian. The social worker thinks I can't provide a safe home for him and that his running away is proof that he's unhappy living Amish."

"Faith, I'm so sorry." He stepped out of the shadows and drew her into his arms.

"I don't know what to do," she wailed. Clinging to Adrian was like holding on to a rock in the middle of a raging river. She'd never needed anyone more than she needed him at this moment.

He led her into his kitchen and deposited her on a worn wooden chair. "Would you like some coffee?"

She missed his touch the moment he pulled away. "*Ja*. I'm sorry to come running to you with this, but I didn't know where else to go. I haven't even thanked you. Your quick reactions saved Kyle's life."

"We must thank God for little Shadow. I knew as soon as I saw him that Kyle couldn't be far away."

Adrian sat beside Faith and took her hand in his. "When I saw Kyle in danger I saw my son dying again, and I couldn't deal with that. I came home and lay on Gideon's bed. As my fright faded, I felt he was there with me. He was not. He's in a wonderful place where I can't go yet. I must remain here until God calls me. I realized my fear was part of being alive. You and Kyle have brought me back to life."

Tears choked her. Clearing her throat, Faith said, "I can't lose him, Adrian. I can't."

What she was about to say would put an end to anything between them. "If I move to town and live in an *Englisch* house with electricity and a telephone and enroll Kyle in the public school, they might let me keep him. To do that, I need money. You once told me if I couldn't manage the farm alone that you would buy it. Well, I want to sell it to you now."

The sadness in his eyes deepened. She couldn't bear to cause him pain, but if she had to choose between their happiness and Kyle, then it would be Kyle.

"Faith, do you know what you are saying? To do such things would go against the *ordnung*. It would put you outside of our faith. You would be shunned by everyone in the church. Your friends, my family. Can you really want this?"

She didn't, but what choice did she have? She was so confused and scared. "I don't know. I only know that I don't want to lose Kyle. Will you buy my farm?"

He sat back in his chair. "*Nee.* I will not. Do not turn your back on your faith at a time like this, I beg you. I did, and it was wrong. Grasp on to it, and it will become your strength. It took me long years to discover that, but I know it is true."

"You will not help me?"

"Not like this. Ask me anything, but I can not help you turn your back on God."

"You know what it is to lose a child." She couldn't believe what she was hearing. She'd been so sure she could depend on him.

"I know what it is to lose a child and I know what it is to find God."

The kettle on the stove began whistling. Faith rose to her feet. "I'm afraid I can't stay for coffee, after all. Good night, Adrian."

She had to get out of his house before she started weeping again. Tears would not fix this.

Adrian took the kettle off the stove and leaned against the counter with his mind whirling. Today, he'd finally come to realize God had already given him the strength he needed to face life's frailties and uncertainty. He'd come to believe that a single day loving Faith and Kyle was better than a lifetime of hiding from more pain.

Now, he was losing them both. Not by death, but by her choice.

He understood why, but that didn't ease his sense of betrayal or loss. Faith had made a vow before God and men to remain true to the Amish religion their ancestors had died to preserve and to live separate from the world. God commanded them that it must be so in 2 Corinthians 6:14

"Be not yoked with unbelievers. For what do righteousness and wickedness have in common? Or what fellowship can light have with darkness?"

This was a mistake Adrian could not let Faith make. He took up his hat and headed for the door. He needed wiser counsel and he prayed Bishop Zook would be able to give it.

"Good luck in there today." Samson Carter, a white-haired man with a neatly trimmed white beard turned around in the front seat of his van to smile encouragingly at Faith.

"*Danki,* sir." She gathered courage before stepping outside.

He said, "I'll wait for you here."

"I have no idea how long this will take."

"Not to worry. I brought a book to read."

Mr. Carter ran a van service in Hope Springs. The retired railroad worker earned extra income by driving his Amish neighbors when they needed to travel farther than their buggies could comfortably carry them.

Faith got out of the vehicle in front of the county courthouse in Millersburg. She had just enough money left to pay Samson when he took her home.

Her farm was on the market, but until it sold she wouldn't have the money to rent a place in town. The extra money in her bank account had gone to pay the lawyer that was meeting her here today.

She glanced up at the courthouse. Three stories tall and built of time-mellowed stone, the building was capped with an elaborate clock tower that rose another story higher. A long flight of steps led up to the main doors on the second story. Narrow arched windows looked out over the well-manicured grounds and a monument to Civil War veterans.

As Faith stared at the building, her anxiety mounted. Behind which window would Kyle's fate be decided?

She remembered Adrian's words about holding on to her faith. Could she do it if it meant losing Kyle?

She closed her eyes. "May Your will be done here today, Lord. Grant me the strength to face the outcome, whatever it may be. Pour Your wisdom into the heart and mind of the judge that he may rule wisely."

Did God listen to the prayers of someone about to turn her back on her faith? When it came time to tell the judge she would leave the Amish world in order to adopt Kyle, could she break her most sacred vow? She closed her eyes and saw Adrian pleading with her not to make that choice.

Why had God put this test before her? Hadn't she suffered enough?

It took her a few minutes to climb the steps. Once inside, a friendly security guard directed her to the correct courtroom.

Mr. Reid, her attorney, waited for her in a chair outside the courtroom door.

He rose to his feet. His smile was polite. "Are you ready for this?"

Was she? Did she have the courage to speak up for herself and for Kyle? A second later, she remembered Adrian's advice at her very first church meeting.

"If I were you, I'd go in with my head up and smile as if nothing were wrong."

It had been good advice that day. She would follow it again. Putting her shoulders back, she pasted a smile on her face and nodded. "It is in God's hands."

"Indeed it is. I will do most of the talking. You may answer any questions the judge directs at you. Have him repeat it if you don't understand."

"Will Kyle be here?"

"He won't be in the courtroom, but it's my understanding that he will be nearby."

"Will I be able to see him if the judge rules against me?"

"Let's cross that bridge if we come to it. Are you ready to go in?"

Fear closed her throat. All she could do was nod.

Mr. Reid held the door open. The room beyond was paneled from floor to ceiling in rich dark wood. At the front, the judge's bench stood on a raised platform. A large round seal was centered on the wall behind it. Flanking the seal were two flags, the United States flag and the Ohio State flag.

It wasn't until she took a step inside the room that she realized she wasn't alone. The few dark wooden benches were filled with Amish elders. Around the outside of the room, three deep, stood more Amish men and women waiting quietly, some with small children at their sides or in their arms.

Many of the faces she knew from her own church district, but there were many people who were unknown to her. Faith stood rooted to the spot. What were they all doing here? As she gazed about, one man stepped forward from the group and walked toward her.

Adrian.

Her heart turned over in her chest. Tears blurred her vision. When he said he wouldn't help she had been crushed. Why was he here now? Had these people come to denounce her?

She stiffened her spine. "Adrian, what are you doing here? Who are all these people?"

"These are your friends and your neighbors and the people you will do business with in the years to come.

We are here to speak for you and for our way of life. The Amish way is a *goot* way for Kyle to grow up. He may have been *Englisch* when he came among us, but he is Amish in his heart and so are you. The judge must understand this. You do not have to face this alone, Faith. We stand with you."

In that moment, Faith could not have loved him more. He had done this for her, gathered together people to speak on her behalf. *"Danki."*

"You are welcome, *liebschen.*"

The heat of a blush crept up her neck. "How can you call me dearest when you know I was ready to turn my back on our faith?"

He took her hand. "Because I must speak what is in my heart. Listen to God, Faith, and then speak what your heart says is right."

Mr. Reid spoke in Faith's ear. "We should take our places. It's almost time to begin."

Letting go of Adrian's hand was one of the hardest things she'd ever done in her life. He gave her fingers one last squeeze and then went back to his place beside Elam Sutter and Eli Imhoff.

Her attorney led her to a small table just behind the railing that separated the judge's bench from the rest of the courtroom. Caroline Watkins sat at an identical table on the opposite side of the aisle. She nodded politely to Mr. Reid but didn't speak as she opened her briefcase and pulled out several files.

Faith sank gratefully onto the chair Mr. Reid held out for her but had no time to gather her thoughts. The bailiff at the side of the bench called out, "All rise for the Honorable Judge Randolph Harbin presiding."

A small man with silver hair entered from the door

behind the bench. He wore a dark suit and a bright green striped tie.

He paused for a second to survey the packed room in surprise before stepping up and taking a seat behind the bench. He beckoned to the bailiff, and the two men shared a brief whispered conversation.

When the judge was ready, he spoke to the entire room. "This is a hearing on the petition of Faith Martin to adopt the minor child, Kyle King. Is Mrs. Martin here?"

Her attorney rose to his feet. "She is, Your Honor."

"Very good. Miss Watkins, I understand you represent the child for the State of Ohio."

She rose also. "I do, Your Honor."

"Good, then let us proceed." The judge leaned back in his chair and clasped his hands together. "Mrs. Martin, it is my understanding that you wish to adopt Kyle King and that you are his only living relative. Tell me a little bit about your circumstances and your wish to adopt Kyle."

Faith's pulse hammered like a drum in her ears. She expected it to leap from her chest at any second. She glanced over her shoulder and saw Adrian standing with his arms crossed over his chest, just the way he had been standing the first time she'd seen him outside her door. He nodded once and lifted his thumb. He believed she could do this. She believed because he did.

She rose to her feet and faced the judge. "Your Honor, I am Kyle's aunt. His father was my only brother. I can't tell you how much Kyle reminds me of him. Every day he says something or does something, and I see my brother all over again. I loved my brother and I love his child. I love Kyle's smile and his sense of humor.

I love the feel of his hand in mine when we cross the street together. I know he loves me, too. I would do anything for him."

"I see that you are Amish, as are the many people you have brought to support you."

Faith heard a voice say, "If I may speak, Your Honor?"

She turned to see Bishop Zook rise from a seat behind her.

The judge arched an eyebrow. "And you are?"

"I am Bishop Joseph Zook. Mrs. Martin did not ask us to come today. We heard that this good woman might lose custody of her nephew because she holds to our ways. We wish only the chance to say that our ways are not simple and backward as some may think."

"I am very familiar with the Amish and their ways. My grandfather was Amish but left the church. Had he not, chances are I would be a farmer or furniture maker and not a judge. You'll have your chance to speak after I've heard from everyone else. Thank you."

The bishop resumed his seat. Judge Harbin said, "Miss Watkins, you've investigated this case. I have read your report, but would you summarize your findings for the court, please?"

She looked at Faith sadly. "No matter how much I wish I could say having Kyle stay with his aunt would be in his best interest, I simply can't do it. Kyle's father left the Amish faith and chose to raise his son in the modern world. He had money put aside for his son's college education. If Kyle were to grow up with his aunt, he would only receive an eighth grade education."

The judge turned his pen end over end. "The ability of a parent to provide higher education is not a prerequisite for adoption. Are you sure you're not letting your personal feelings on the subject influence you?"

"I don't believe I am, Your Honor. My job is to do what's best for him. Kyle has had significant difficulty adjusting to an Amish home. They live without electricity, something he's never done before. He has run away at least three times that I know of. The last time put him in great danger. I feel an Amish farm environment is simply too dangerous for this young boy who has grown up without any experience around machinery and animals. Now, if Mrs. Martin would agree to move into town and enroll Kyle in the public school, I think he would be much happier. I also think it would make his adjustment to living with his aunt much easier. I would agree to a new trial period of six months if this were the case."

"I see. Mrs. Martin, would you be agreeable to such a move?"

These were the words Faith dreaded hearing. She could keep Kyle if she gave up her faith, or she could stay true to her faith and perhaps lose the child she loved.

Please, God, let this be the right decision.

She shook her head. "*Nee,* I would not. She wishes me to raise Kyle in an *Englisch* home with electricity so that he might have television and video games to play with. Yes, he is used to such things, but they do not make a home. A home is a place where a child is loved and raised to know and love God."

She studied the judge's face, but she could not tell what he was thinking. He began reading the documents before him, turning each page slowly. After a few minutes, he looked toward Bishop Zook. "Bishop, what is it that you would like to say to this court today?"

The bishop rose to his feet again. "I would ask that Adrian Lapp speak for us today."

Adrian came forward and stood beside the bishop. "I have come to know both Faith Martin and her nephew, Kyle. It is true that Kyle has had a hard time adjusting, but it is not because he can't watch television. It's because he is afraid to love his aunt. He's afraid God will take her away as He did his parents."

Miss Watkins spoke up. "Your Honor, this man is not a child psychologist."

"But I am a man who knows about loss and about the fear of losing someone if I allowed myself to love again. I lost my wife and then my son when he was only four years old. But I lost more than my family. I lost my faith. I no longer trusted God. I was afraid to love again just as Kyle is afraid. But God brought Kyle into my life to show me how wrong I've been."

Adrian turned to Faith. "I see now that loving someone is never wrong, be it for a little while or for a lifetime."

She bit her lip to keep from crying.

He faced Miss Watkins. "By taking Kyle away from Faith, you are proving him right. Don't take away the person he is afraid to love. Let him come to know God's goodness and mercy. Let him find the strength to love again."

The judge laid his papers aside and rubbed his chin. "You speak very eloquently, Mr. Lapp. I appreciate your insight. Miss Watkins, would you have the boy brought to my chambers?"

She objected. "Your Honor, the child is barely six

years old. He's far too young to know what is in his best interest."

"That's true, but that's not what I'm going to ask him about. Mrs. Martin, will you and your attorney join me in my chambers? Mr. Lapp, I'd like you there, as well."

"Yes, Your Honor." Mr. Reid gathered his papers together and closed his briefcase.

The bailiff called out, "All rise."

When the judge left the room, Faith turned to look at her attorney. "Is this a good thing?"

"I'm not sure, but let's not keep him waiting." Mr. Reid held out his hand, indicating Faith should precede him.

Chapter Seventeen

Together, Faith, Adrian and her attorney entered a spacious office situated just beyond the courtroom. The same dark paneling lined the walls except where floor-to-ceiling bookcases jutted out. They held hundreds of thick books bound in dark red, green and gray.

"I'll have you three sit over there." Judge Harbin indicated a group of brown leather chairs near the windows. He then proceeded to make himself comfortable on a matching leather sofa in the middle of the room. Before it sat a low coffee table. It held an elaborate chess set with figures carved from dark and light woods.

The door to the outside hallway opened, and Miss Watkins came in holding Kyle by the hand. Faith's heart contracted with joy at the sight of Kyle's face. She longed to race across the room and snatch him up in a fierce hug. She made herself sit still. When Kyle saw her, he tore away from Miss Watkins and launched himself into Faith's arms.

Tears blurred her vision. She whispered, "I have missed you terribly."

His voice shook as he said, "I'm sorry I ran away. I won't do it again."

Adrian laid a hand on Kyle's shoulder. "You are forgiven."

Faith stroked his hair. "I'm just happy you are safe."

Miss Watkins took the child by the hand and said, "Kyle, I have someone you need to meet. This is Judge Harbin and he has a few questions for you."

Faith and Kyle reluctantly released each other. She said, "Go and talk to the judge. I'll be right here."

"Promise?" There was such pleading in his eyes that it broke Faith's heart.

"I promise," she managed to whisper past the lump in her throat."

Kyle allowed Miss Watkins to lead him away. Adrian took Faith's hand and held it between his strong, warm fingers.

The judge patted the cushion beside him. "Have a seat, young man."

Kyle glanced at Faith. She nodded to tell him it was okay. The boy climbed on the sofa and propped his hands on his thighs. Miss Watkins took a seat near Faith.

The judge leaned toward Kyle. "My name is Randolph Harbin. These people have to call me Your Honor, but you can call me Randy. Kyle, do you know what a judge is?"

He pondered a second or two, then said, "A guy who sends people to jail?"

"Some judges do send people to jail, but I'm not that kind of judge. I'm the kind of judge who decides what's best for kids like you. Do you know how to play chess?"

Kyle shook his head.

"I guess you're a little young for that. How about checkers?"

The boy's eyes lit up as he nodded quickly and pointed toward the windows. "Adrian has been teaching me."

The judge swept the chess pieces from the board and set it between him and Kyle. From a drawer beneath the coffee table, he pulled out a stack of red and white disks and offered them both to the boy. "Tell me how you know Adrian."

After choosing the red pieces, Kyle began placing them on the board. "He's our neighbor. He's helping me become Amish so the boys at school will stop teasing me."

Judge Harbin slowly laid out his pieces. "Do they tease you a lot?"

"Not as much as they first did. Anna Imhoff gets mad at them if they do."

"And who is Anna?"

"She's my friend. She doesn't make fun of me because I can't speak Pennsylvania Dutch. She says her friend, Jonathan, can't speak it either and he's a grown-up. She's giving us both lessons. I can say a few things. Do you want to hear?"

"Sure."

"*Mamm* means mother. *Dat* means dad. *Grossmammi* is grandmother. *Velkumm* is welcome."

"I'm impressed with what you've learned so far. Has your aunt been helping you?"

"Lots."

"I imagine she's a very good cook. What kind of things do you like to eat?"

"Have you ever had shoofly pie? It's the best. Aunt Faith makes it for me twice a week."

"I like mine with a tall glass of milk."

"Me, too!" Faith smiled at the amazement in Kyle's voice. She squeezed Adrian's hand.

"Do you have a pet at your aunt's house?" the judge asked.

Kyle grinned and folded his arms over his chest. "Yes, but it's not a cat and it's not a dog. I bet you can't guess what it is."

"Is it a horse or a baby calf?"

"Nope. It's a baby alpaca. I bet you never would have guessed that."

"Never in a million years."

"A baby alpaca is called a cria. Mine is black. Aunt Faith let me name him Shadow. When we sell his fleece, I get to keep *all* the money."

"You sound as if you really love your aunt."

Kyle's shoulders slumped. He glanced from the judge to Faith, then down at his feet. In a tiny voice he said, "Not too much."

Faith pressed her fingers to her lips. Her heart ached for Kyle.

The judge moved a checker. "How much would be too much?"

"I don't know." His voice got smaller.

"You don't know or you don't want to tell me?"

"I don't want to tell you."

"Why not?"

"'Cause I don't want God to hear."

"You don't want God to hear that you love your aunt?"

Kyle held a finger to his lips. "Shh! If God thinks I love her, something bad will happen."

"What makes you say that?"

"Because I told Mommy and Daddy I loved them when they left me at school and then God took them away. God wanted them in heaven instead of with me. He's very mean."

"I'm sure it must seem that way to you, but He isn't."

"He's not?"

"No. In this job, I talk to God all the time."

"You do?"

"Absolutely. I need His help to make good decisions. Sometimes those decisions are very hard, but I believe His will guides me."

"Would you ask him to bring my parents back? I really miss them."

Faith squeezed Adrian's hand. Poor Kyle. He had suffered so much. She only wanted to hold him and make the hurt go away.

The judge shook his head. "I know you miss them, but they can't come back. They are watching over you. Right this very minute. God is watching over you, too."

"That's what Aunt Faith says."

"Kyle, God has His own way of arranging our lives. Things happen that we don't like, that frighten us and make us sad, but He loves us, just as your parents loved you. Now, since I talk to God all the time, is there anything you'd like me to tell Him?"

Kyle glanced toward Faith. She read the indecision and the longing in his eyes. He turned back to the judge. "Tell God I want to stay with Aunt Faith and not to take her away to heaven."

Judge Harbin patted Kyle's head, then said, "Miss

Watkins, would you take Kyle out to the courtroom and wait for me there? Counselor, you and Mrs. Martin may return to the courtroom, too."

"Yes, Your Honor."

"What does this mean?" Faith glanced at her attorney, but he simply shrugged.

Adrian helped her to her feet. "Be brave. It is in God's hands."

When everyone was assembled in the courtroom again, Judge Harbin motioned to Kyle. "Come up here, young man."

Hesitantly, Kyle walked up and stood beside the bench. Judge Harbin picked up his gavel. "Kyle, do you know what this is?"

"A hammer."

"It's called a gavel. It's a very powerful tool. If I say, 'order in the court' and bang this gavel, everyone has to be silent."

"Cool."

"It is way cool. Today, I'm going to let you use my gavel because this is a very special day. It's a day you will always remember. Today, we are going to change your name to Kyle King Martin. Do you know why?"

"Because you are going to let my aunt adopt me?"

"That's right. And when I say it, I want you to bang that gavel so that everyone knows it's official. Are you ready?"

Kyle nodded and took the gavel in his hand. Judge Harbin looked out over the courtroom. "I do hereby grant the petition of Faith Martin to adopt the minor child, Kyle King."

Grinning from ear to ear, Kyle smacked the gavel

down as hard as he could. The courtroom immediately erupted into cheers.

Late in the afternoon, Faith and Kyle got out of the van in front of her house. Samson carried Kyle's bag to the porch, congratulated Faith again and drove off. On the front steps of her home, holding Kyle's hand in hers, she raised her face to the sun and closed her eyes. Kyle was staying! Praise God for His goodness.

Kyle was hers.

The phrase echoed inside her mind in an endless refrain. She could scarcely believe it. Her prayers had been answered. She had regained her child and her faith all in one day.

When she opened her eyes, they were drawn across the fields to Adrian's farm. Much of the happiness in her heart was due to him. If Adrian had not gathered the church members together and spoken for Kyle, the day might have had a very different outcome. Love for Adrian warmed her soul.

Her thoughts were interrupted when another car came up the drive. To her surprise, she saw it was Miss Watkins. What was she doing here?

When Kyle saw the social worker get out of her car, he threw himself against Faith, wrapping his arms around her legs. "I get to stay, right? The judge said so."

Faith quickly sought to reassure him. "You will stay forever and ever."

He looked into her eyes. "Are you sure?"

"I am."

Looking to Miss Watkins and then back to Faith, he whispered, "You promise?"

She picked him up and kissed his cheek. "I promise."

Miss Watkins came forward. "I give you my word

that you can live here for as long as you want, Kyle. Just promise me you won't run away again."

"I won't. Not ever. Aunt Faith, can I go tell Shadow I'm staying?"

Faith lowered him to the ground. "Go tell all the animals."

He raced away to the barn. Faith pressed her hand to her lips to hold on to the joy that filled her to overflowing. To think she'd once wondered if she could love her brother's child as much as her own.

Miss Watkins cleared her throat. "I hope you realize that I only wanted what was best for Kyle."

"I know that."

"Would you mind if I stop in to see him from time to time? He's a remarkable young man." Tears sparkled in the depths of her eyes.

Faith grasped her hand. "You will always be welcome in our home."

"Thank you." Caroline returned to her car and drove away. When the dust settled, Faith saw Adrian walking across the field toward her.

How could one heart hold all the love she felt without bursting? It truly was one of God's miracles.

On the day they'd first met, she had wondered what it would be like to have a husband so strong and sure of his place in life. Would she have the chance to find out or had she ruined her chance at happiness by her willingness to put aside her religion?

She prayed he could forgive her.

She waited until Adrian reached her side. He took off his hat. "Faith Martin, I have something I wish to speak to you about."

He sounded so nervous. Had he to come to tell her

he wanted to call off their courting? His reaction at the courthouse had given her hope that he still cared for her. She said, "I'm listening.

"You have too much work to do to get this place ready before winter. You don't even have hay put up for your animals yet and your barn needs repairs."

"That is true." A lecture on her property wasn't what she had been expecting when she'd seen him coming.

"It will take the entire fall to get things ready."

"You're right. It will."

"I have hay and I have paint."

She crossed her arms. "Is there a point to this?"

He turned his hat around and around in his hands. "Your boy needs a man to help guide him on the path of the righteous."

"I agree. Bishop Zook has offered to help in just such a fashion."

"That is *goot*. You are not alone, Faith. There are people who will willingly help you carry your burdens."

"You mean like pruning my trees and shearing my alpacas?"

"*Ja,* those things, too."

It wasn't exactly the declaration of love she longed to hear. Maybe he had changed his mind. Did he see her as fickle and weak? Mose always said she was weak. Had he been right?

"Adrian!" Kyle's excited shout made them look toward the barn. The boy came running toward them at full speed. Adrian dropped to one knee as the boy raced into his arms.

Wrapping his arms around Adrian's neck, Kyle said, "I get to stay here forever and ever."

"That's something I was hoping to talk to you about."

Kyle drew back to look him in the face. "What do you mean?"

Adrian glanced up at Faith. "I reckon I should ask both of you since you're a pair now."

"Ask us what?" Kyle demanded.

Adrian rose to his feet still holding Kyle. "I never thought I would love anyone the way I loved my son and my wife. But, Faith, I love Kyle as much as I loved my own son, and I love you as much as any man can love a woman."

Faith heart began pounding in her chest as it swelled with happiness. She couldn't speak.

Kyle said, "Are you gonna get mushy with my Aunt Faith? Ben said you were gonna."

Adrian grew serious as he gazed into Faith's eyes. "I must have a chat with my brother, but in this case he was right. Faith, will you marry me and live as my wife for all the days God gives to us?"

She choked back her tears of joy. "I will."

She took a step closer and cupped his face with her hands. "I didn't believe love like this was possible, but now I know it is. We are truly blessed."

Adrian lowered Kyle to the ground and took Faith in his arms. His kiss was everything and more than she'd dreamed it would be. After a long breathless moment, he drew back and tucked her head beneath his chin. "Thank you for saying yes. Thank you for showing me my way back to God."

Kyle wrinkled his nose. "Does this mean we're going to live at your place?"

Adrian smiled at him. "If that's all right with you?"

"I reckon it is. Guess I'd better go tell Shadow we're moving, after all." He took off and jogged toward the barn.

Adrian's eyes softened as he watched Kyle. "I can't believe I was so afraid of love and hid from it all this time."

"I was afraid, too, but you have shown me that a man can be kind even when he is upset. I learned to trust you, Adrian. That is something I was sure I would never do again. You've given me the one thing I need that no one else can give me."

"What is that?"

"Your love."

He smiled and pulled her close. "*Ja,* my heart holds all the love you will ever need."

She gazed into his eyes, happier than she could ever remember being.

He said, "I don't want to wait to marry you. I hope you weren't planning on a long courtship."

Unable to resist teasing him, she said, "I don't think we should rush into anything. It takes a long time to get to know a person well."

He nodded. "You're right. We should give ourselves two years."

"At least." She tried to keep a solemn face but failed. There was no way she could wait that long.

Pulling her close again, he whispered, "I'll be lucky to last a week. How soon can we get hitched?"

"With all the preparations I need to make…six months." When he was holding her close it sounded much too long to wait.

"My mother will help, and if I know her, she'll cut that time in half."

"If she can help arrange a wedding in three months, she is a worker with great talents."

"Then both of you should get along fine for you are one, too, my love."

When his lips closed over hers once more, Faith knew she'd found more than a home in Hope Springs. She'd found courage, a family and a love unlike anything she'd dreamed was possible.

* * * * *

LOVE INSPIRED

Stories to uplift and inspire

Fall in love with Love Inspired—
inspirational and uplifting stories of faith
and hope. Find strength and comfort in
the bonds of friendship and community.
Revel in the warmth of possibility and the
promise of new beginnings.

Sign up for the Love Inspired newsletter
at **LoveInspired.com** to be the first
to find out about upcoming titles,
special promotions and exclusive content.

CONNECT WITH US AT:

Facebook.com/LoveInspiredBooks

Twitter.com/LoveInspiredBks

Had he really come to the woods before going to the ranch house? She had a feeling she was right and that he had. She wondered why—another habit of journalists. She needed to know everything, especially motives.

Yates's gaze seemed glued to her face, and she fought off a blush that would let him know he still affected her on some unwanted, visceral level. People say you always remember your first love. Yates had been her first and only.

She'd spent the better part of a year waiting to hear from him and another year getting over him.

Now here he was in the flesh, stirring up old memories. At least for her.

The annoying blush deepened. Laurel turned her attention toward the children and the dog. With a smiling

Justice in the center, they formed a circle of petting hands and eager chatter.

"Those aren't all your kids, are they?"

A small pain pinched inside her chest. "Sunday school class." To turn the focus away from her, she asked, "Was he really a military dog? Like a bomb or drug sniffer?"

"Explosives."

"Did something happen to him? Why'd he retire?"

Yates's face, already closed, tightened. "Stuff happens. Soldiers retire. Look, I should go. Enjoy your picnic."

With a snappy military about-face, he started to walk away.

"Yates, wait."

He paused, gazing back over his shoulder.

"After you get settled, come by the *Times* office. I'd love to interview you and the dog for the paper." She put her fingers up in air quotes. "'Hometown Hero Returns' would make a great feature."

"No interview. We're civilians now. Nothing heroic about that." Turning away, he gave a soft whistle. "Justice, come."

Before she could say more, Yates and his dog disappeared into the foliage.

Don't miss
The Cowboy's Journey Home *by Linda Goodnight,*
available August 2022
wherever Love Inspired books and ebooks are sold.

LoveInspired.com

IF YOU ENJOYED THIS BOOK, DON'T MISS NEW EXTENDED-LENGTH NOVELS FROM LOVE INSPIRED!

In addition to the Love Inspired books you know and love, we're excited to introduce even more uplifting stories in a longer format, with more inspiring fresh starts and page-turning thrills!

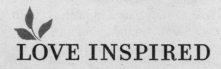

LOVE INSPIRED

Stories to uplift and inspire.

Fall in love with Love Inspired—inspirational and uplifting stories of faith and hope. Find strength and comfort in the bonds of friendship and community. Revel in the warmth of possibility, and the promise of new beginnings.

LOOK FOR THESE LOVE INSPIRED TITLES ONLINE AND IN THE BOOK DEPARTMENT OF YOUR FAVORITE RETAILER!